#POSER

The Hashtag Series #5

by Cambria Hebert

Published by: Cambria Hebert Books, LLC

http://www.cambriahebert.com

Interior design and typesetting by Sharon Kay of Amber Leaf Publishing
Cover design by MAE I DESIGN
Edited by Cassie McCown of Gathering Leaves Editing

ISBN: 978-1-938857-76-8

#POSER

THE BROMANCE (AKA PROLOGUE)

BRAEDEN

I suck at good-byes.

Yeah, sure, technically this wasn't good-bye. Still felt like it. Still sucked.

It was more of a *see ya later.*

But how do you say see ya later when it's more like see ya in a couple months? Especially when you've seen that person practically every single day since you were in first grade?

I'd never say it out loud at the risk of someone taking away my man card, but Rome and me had a bond.

We weren't just friends. We were brothers from another mother.

And the part I would never speak out loud? Bromance. We had a bromance, okay?

I knew this day was coming. Everyone knew it was coming from the second the ink dried on his contract with the Maryland Knights.

Hell, I knew this was coming from the first moment I saw him throw a football.

Knowing something didn't make it any easier.

So many changes lately. Most of them I was doing good with; some weighed on me more than others. Like *a lot* more. But I never really thought Romeo leaving for training would feel like such a rift in my life.

But here I was.

Feeling all sentimental and shit.

It was embarrassing.

When this conversation was over, I was gonna have to go do something manly like build something with my bare hands.

Or maybe I'd just eat some sprinkles.

I pulled up next to the Hellcat and parked. I knew he'd be here. If I were in his position, this is where I'd be too.

I walked through the tunnels, past the locker rooms, and into the stands. The field stretched out before me like the ocean at the beach. The field was immaculate, vibrant green, cut meticulously and slightly damp from the sprinkler system.

Even in the off-season, Alpha U knew where its priorities lay. This football field represented so much more than a sport.

To me, it was family. It was life. It was an escape.

Rome was standing at the railing, looking out across the field we'd played on more times than I could count.

I couldn't believe it was over. We'd played our last game together and didn't even known it at the time. I was glad, though. I wanted that last game to be exactly as it had been. Nothing but the sport and the fun. Nothing but watching each other's backs and keeping our heads in the game.

It made for good memories.

I stopped beside him at the railing, silent.

We stood there for a while. I knew his thoughts mirrored my own.

"I'll never quit you, B," Romeo said eventually, a hint of sarcasm in his tone.

It wasn't the first time he said that to me. I swung my head to scoff at him, but the sound never made it out. His words might be a joke, but their meaning wasn't. There was no smirk on his face, no laughter in his eyes.

He meant it.

"I'll never quit you either, Rome."

He lifted his fist from the rail and held it between us.

We pounded it out.

Pounding it out made everything official.

"Seems like I worked my whole life for this. I waited and thought it might never come," he said, still gazing out across the field. "But damn, it came fast."

"You having second thoughts?" I glanced at him out of the corner of my eye.

He shook his head. "It's just hard to walk away, you know?"

I did know. For a guy who planned to live his whole life in the moment and just for fun, things got complicated. Things got real. It was hard to live in the moment all the time when you sometimes worried there might not be another one.

Or that past moments would come back to destroy what was today. I shook off the thought. This wasn't about me. This was about my best friend, my brother, and saying good-bye.

"You got Rim now," I replied. "You got responsibilities beyond throwing a ball."

He nodded and looked down at his hands. I knew he didn't want to leave her. Hell, I'd be the same way, especially after everything they'd been through. Just a couple weeks away from Ivy when she went home at the beginning of the summer had tested my patience. I couldn't imagine leaving for months at a time.

"But that don't mean you're walking away. This is for her too. You gotta build a life, bro. And with this job, this opportunity, it's gonna give you both a hella good one."

"She said the same thing." He half smiled.

Didn't surprise me one bit. Rim knew football was in Rome's blood. She'd never stand in the way of that. I clapped him on the back. "My sis knows what she's talking about."

"I need you to do something for me." He looked at me. "Not sure how you're gonna feel about it."

"Dude." I sighed dramatically. "I told you. That was a one-time thing. If I go running across campus in my boxers again, I might give the old ladies in the office building heart attacks." I gestured to myself. "It takes a strong ticker to handle all this."

"I don't wanna see you in your damn skivvies." He flashed a smile. "Though I'd pay to see Ivy's reaction to that shit."

"Hell," I muttered. "I'd never hear the end of it."

Romeo's smile grew wider into a shit-eating grin. "Rim says Prada has taken quite a liking to you."

"Damn rat," I spat. But then I smiled. It was hard not to love her when she'd come prancing up to the door in a stupid pink outfit when I walked in. And okay, yeah, maybe I let her sleep with us.

"Who's whipped now?" Romeo laughed.

"You kiss your momma with that mouth?" I cracked.

He laughed and pushed off the railing to sit in the row of seats behind us. I dropped down beside him.

"What do you need?" He had to know I'd do it. We had each other's backs like that.

"I rented a house." A ring of keys appeared in his hand, and he spun them around his finger as he spoke. "It's not too far from campus. Nice neighborhood, fenced-in yard, security system, garage…"

"But you're leaving for training in like a week."

He glanced at me.

Ah. He was leaving, but Rim wasn't.

I laughed. "You rented her a house? She's so pissed, isn't she?"

The grimace on his face said it all. "She wasn't too happy. Took some work to get her to come around."

I didn't need to know about the kind of "work" he was talking about.

"I thought she had to live on campus, you know, as part of her scholarship?"

He shrugged. "I called the dean."

That was the Rome I knew. Rules didn't apply to him. If he wanted something, he had the rules bent. It got my respect.

"You sure her living alone is a good thing, though? Might be better on campus or at your place."

"She won't stay at my place, not with Mom right next door," he answered. "I asked Ivy to move in with her."

My eyes shot up to his. "What?" I wasn't sure how I felt about that. "She never said anything to me."

"I asked her not to. Told her I wanted to talk to you myself."

I started shaking my head. "Them two alone in a house?" I thought about what happened to Ivy not that long ago, what she didn't even know. I thought about the way she sometimes still called out in her sleep. I didn't want her alone. "I don't like it."

Romeo nodded like he already knew my reaction. 'Course, he couldn't possibly know how sick it made me to think of Ivy alone in a house, vulnerable. He didn't know everything. I didn't even tell him.

"That's where you come in," he said.

And then I knew what he was asking. Romeo wanted me to move in with them. He wasn't just renting Rimmel a house. He was renting a place for all of us.

"You know damn well I can't afford rent on a three-bedroom home. You probably rented it over in the Palisades," I muttered.

A smile played on his lips. "It's four bedrooms."

"You totally fucking did!" I accused. "My mom can't even afford that neighborhood, Rome."

"This ain't about the money."

I laughed. "Says the guy with a fat fucking bank account."

His eyes narrowed and the look behind them was hard. "You know I ain't about money. We ain't ever been about it either."

I scrubbed a hand down my face and cursed. "No, we ain't. I'm not about to start now."

"I get it," he said low. "You're a man. You got a lot of pride. I'm not trying to take it from you. But you know full fucking well if you had the cash for this, you'd do it too. This is best for them. Ivy can't keep hiding that rat in her dorm. With the new semester, her and Rim'll probably be assigned new roommates. I don't want my girl rooming with some bitch I don't know. And I know you don't want Ivy doing it either. People aren't gonna forget too easily about all the shit the #BuzzBoss said about her. I wouldn't be surprised if *she* reminds everyone of it the first week back."

"If Missy knows what's good for her, she'll stay the hell away from Ivy," I growled.

"They'd never admit it, but they need someone looking out for them. I can't leave here knowing Rim isn't taken care of. I'm asking you to move in with her. I'm asking you to watch out for her."

"I've got some cash saved up, and I'll be working all summer, all the way up 'til training camp." I hedged.

"Rent's paid for the next year."

I shook my head. Of course it fucking was. Romeo always had money; his parents always made sure he had the best of shit. But he wasn't the kind of guy who ever seemed to think about it. It just was. He didn't act all ate up, like he was in some expensive, exclusive club. When we were kids, he hung at my place just as much as his. He ate dinner at our kitchen table, and not even once did I see a look of anything but acceptance in his eyes.

But that didn't mean I wanted him paying my way.

"It's just money, B. We're family," he said, almost like he could read my thoughts.

I groaned, and Romeo slapped me on the shoulder. "Thank God. I really thought you would say no."

"I'm doing this for the girls." I clarified.

"That's why I'm doing it too."

I knew it was. I'd be lying if I said I hadn't thought about what the fall semester was going to be like for Ivy and who she was going to be stuck rooming with. At least this way she could keep the rat, and I knew she'd have somewhere to go where eyes weren't constantly following her.

"I'll pay as much of the utilities as I can."

"Rim and Ivy have insisted on pitching in too," he added.

"I can't believe she didn't tell me," I muttered, thinking about my girl.

"I just talked to her this morning. I asked her not to."

"She wanted this too?" I asked. I wouldn't do it if she had any kind of reservations. We hadn't been together very long, and now we were moving in together. I needed to talk to her. Make sure this was what she wanted.

"Honestly, I think she was relieved. I don't think living on campus was very easy for her at the end of last semester."

I knew better than anyone—even better than Ivy herself—why that was. "I should have figured it out sooner," I muttered.

"Missy had everyone fooled," Romeo said.

"Shady bitch," I slurred.

"You know it's not just Rim I don't wanna leave," Romeo said, his voice candid and low.

I looked over at him. Romeo kept me grounded. Life hadn't always been easy for me, but he was always there. Sometimes he kept me together. I guess I understood why he was worried about leaving me.

"I'm straight, honestly." I promised.

"You talk to him?" He looked me in the eye.

He was talking about my father. The abusive man who used to make mine and my mom's life a living hell.

I hadn't seen him since he was arrested for almost killing her when I was ten. But then he walked into the diner one Sunday morning just a few weeks ago. He came right up to the table like he had every right to my time. Like I would just talk to him, accept his presence as if he hadn't totally fucked me up.

"No." My voice was final.

"So you aren't going to?"

I blew out a breath and stood, pacing a little. Talking about him always made me edgy and frustrated. "I don't know."

I didn't want to. I could have lived my entire life without seeing him ever again. But I did. And he was dying. It changed things. I might not want to talk to him now, but what about in five years? What if I felt different then? My mom talked to me about closure, about dealing with it all once and for all.

Deep down, I knew closure would probably do a lot for me.

But sometimes closure was hard to accept. It was hard to grasp. How did you wrap up something so ugly all neat and tidy and put it away? How did you forgive someone for not being the man they should have been? How did I not feel the effects of his abuse?

I didn't have five years. I might not even have two. If I thought I would ever want closure from my father, it was something I had to act upon now, before he died.

"If you decide to call him, if you want me there, I'll be there."

"Thanks," I said, feeling a little relieved he wasn't going to push what he thought I should do onto me. This was something I had to figure out on my own.

He stood and stepped up to me. His eyes met mine. "I mean it. Just call. I'll come home. Football means a lot to me, but family means more."

I let his words sink in. I felt them for a few seconds. I didn't think he'd ever know what they meant to me, and I wasn't ever going to try and explain. I made a sniffing sound. "You got a tissue, man? I think I'm gonna cry."

He shoved me and laughed. "Asshole."

I caught him off guard with a hug. His laughter died in his throat, and he returned the embrace. We both pulled away and glanced around like we wanted to make sure no one witnessed our moment.

"I'm parking the Hellcat in the garage," he said and palmed the keys that I now knew were to my new place.

"Wouldn't want it to get dust on it," I cracked. "Or are you just hiding it from Rim? Hoping she won't get any ideas about driving it while you're in training?"

Romeo groaned. "Much as I worry about her ripping the transmission out, I'd almost be relieved if she drove it and not that damn bucket of bolts her dad bought her."

Since all the drama went down with Rimmel and her family, her dad sold almost everything he owned to go into treatment and satisfy the courts for his part in her mom's death and the extortion of Romeo. And with what little he had left, he bought her a car. It was an old Honda Civic SI model. A white two-door with a hatchback. It looked like a weird bubble on the road.

Like I said, Rome wasn't eaten up about money. But he didn't like his girl driving around in a car that was well over ten years old. If he had it his way, she'd be driving a Mercedes or some shit.

But she wouldn't have it. My sis was stubborn as hell when she wanted to be. So she drove the Honda, and Rome hated it.

"I've been over that car with a fine-tooth comb. It's safe for her to drive." I assured him.

When she drove it home and we stepped out of the house, Rome about shit his pants. I thought I was gonna have to give him CPR to keep him going. I admit I didn't care for the car either, but one of us had to keep chill, and since he was wheezing on his feet, it had to be me.

So I kept my trap shut about it and got under the hood. I replaced all the shit that needed replacing, and Rome took it for a "test drive," and while he was out, he put new tires on it. We didn't tell Rim and she didn't notice.

"Women," Romeo muttered.

"I hear ya, bro." I sympathized.

We both laughed, and Romeo turned away from the field. "C'mon, I need help moving my gym out of my place and into the new one."

"My own private gym? Da-yum," I sang. "I could get used to this."

"I plan on being around a lot. Every second I have off, I'm coming home. You're gonna have to share."

Turns out it didn't matter I sucked at good-byes.

This wasn't even close to a good-bye.

This was a whole new beginning.

TO TELL OR NOT TO TELL...

(AKA PART ONE)

CHAPTER ONE

#24 isn't here, but his little #nerd is. Moved her off campus into a lovenest.
#FavorFromTheDean
#ISmellSpecialTreatment
#BuzzBoss

IVY

Summer wasn't long enough.

It never was. I thought maybe as I got older, summer would hold less appeal, but here I was entering my junior year of college—almost a full-blown adult—and I was still suffering from the end of summer blues.

Just before finals last semester, summer was a blissful promise. Long, sunny days without the stress of schoolwork, without the burden of getting up far too early in the morning and having to go to bed before it was too late. But most of all, summer had been the promise of long stretches of time absent of all the people who made it hard to breathe.

Not the literal type of breathing. I mean, really, pulling air into my lungs was automatic, except of course when I was in Braeden's arms. Then I had to remind myself to breathe.

I mean all the people who whispered, the people who talked. The people who were liars posing as friends. I beat myself up for weeks, hell, *months*, for things I'd done, when all along, people were doing worse right behind my back.

But summer broke its promise. Those long sunny days went by way too fast. Summer hadn't given me enough time. I still wasn't completely over everything that happened.

It was starting to scare me. Why did some places deep down inside me still feel shaky? What if I never fully got over what happened?

Even as I thought it, I shook my head. That wasn't an option. I was being ridiculous. Sure, things last semester got pretty shitty but nothing so terrible it would leave permanent marks.

Man up, Nancy. That's what my brother always said. He'd say it to my other brother when they acted like crybabies and he'd say it to his friends. He even said it to me, even though I was a girl and calling me Nancy wasn't much of an insult.

A small smile curled my lips just hearing his words echo in my head. It made me feel stronger. A little less scared. I hated feeling afraid; it made me weak and vulnerable. I hadn't told anyone lately, but I felt that way a lot.

Scared.

Vulnerable.

Weak.

I couldn't understand. I wished I could just know why. How could my own feelings be a mystery to me? Wasn't it like some unspoken rule that a girl know what was going on inside her own mind?

Things had been going so great. I was happier than I'd ever been.

So what was with me?

The bell above the door in front jingled, and I blew out a breath. I stuffed my disturbed thoughts down deep and mentally stomped on them with the heels I was wearing. I left the boxes in the back and moved around the corner out into the shop and painted a smile on my face.

Figures someone would come in this close to closing. I really didn't want to stay late tonight, I wanted to go home and shower and get ready for Braeden to get back from training camp. *God, I miss him.* These last two weeks had felt like an eternity.

My irritation was short lived and the "work" smile on my lips turned genuine when I saw a familiar set of jean-clad legs step around a rack of long maxi dresses. My heart lurched as his hips swiveled in the most enticing way, but it was the intensity of his stare that drew my eye.

It had been a couple months since Braeden turned my dorm room into the beach and made our relationship official, but even the passing of many weeks couldn't dull the effect he had on me.

It was just as strong right here, in the center of a clothing boutique, than it had been that first night we went up in flames on the beach.

"You look hot as hell, Blondie," he growled as his espresso-colored eyes raked over me from head to toe.

I shivered a little because the way he looked at me made me feel delicious. His white teeth flashed knowingly as he reached for me. I melted against him with a drawn-out sigh. I wrapped one arm around his tight waist but tucked my other hand between us, pushing my palm flat against his chest.

Both his arms locked around me, molding my body even closer against his. My eyes fluttered closed as a feeling of relief washed over me.

Have you ever dropped a book in the center of a dusty table? The second it hits, the dust scatters out into the air surrounding the book. Like a big cloud, it puffs out and then disperses, disappearing like there was never any dust at all.

That's how Braeden made me feel. He was the book. I was the table. And the dust… that was the fear coating my insides. He made it disappear. It was one of the things I loved so much about him. He made me feel safe. Safer than anyone had ever made me feel before. I belonged in his arms, and that would never change.

It didn't matter how uncertain anything else became; of him I would always be sure.

Braeden pulled back slightly, enough so he could look down and I could look up. He grunted softly and lowered his head to capture my lips. He kissed me tenderly but thoroughly. He coaxed me open with his tongue and swept inside to explore every inch.

That's how it always was when I kissed Braeden. Like every time was the first time, like every time his lips captured mine, he worked to gain even more access, as if he didn't know he would get it automatically.

His kisses took nothing for granted. His tongue never rushed. He owned me with every single touch, but the ownership was earned, never forced.

He used the pad of his thumb to softly stroke the underside of my jaw as he kissed me continuously. It was a gentle onslaught of emotion, and soon everything fell away. Soon there was nothing in this entire world but him.

When at last he pulled back, it took me a moment to find my way back to reality and open my eyes. When I did, he was watching me. Braeden's intensity was something I wasn't sure I'd ever get used to. I sort of hoped I didn't. I loved the slightly tilted feeling it gave me when he stared at me like I was all he saw.

"You totally missed me," he surmised arrogantly, the corner of his mouth curved up into a sexy smirk.

I rolled my eyes but didn't pull away. I didn't want to. "Eh, I thought about you once in a while."

His eyes narrowed into dark slits. "Care to rephrase your answer?"

I pretended to consider.

Braeden growled and caught me around the waist, lifting me off the ground. I squealed and clutched his shirt. He dumped me over his shoulder like I was a sack of lumpy potatoes, and I screeched again.

"What are you doing?" I yelled and gripped his waist.

"Punishing you."

One strong arm clamped around my thighs and held me in place while he smacked my butt with his free hand.

"Well, that really isn't a punishment," I suggested.

He chuckled as his fingers slid up beneath my skirt and his palm stroked over my butt.

I sighed because I really had missed his touch. And even though all the blood was draining to my head and making me feel woozy, I didn't complain. I'd hang here for an hour if he was gonna keep touching me.

With one last pat to my cheeks, he quickly pulled me around. But instead of standing me on my feet, he sat me on the nearby counter and fit himself between my spread thighs. His hands caressed up the top of my legs and slipped beneath the skirt once more so he could cup my hips.

"I didn't like being away from you, Blondie."

My stomach did a little somersault at his words. I dragged my fingers through the short strands of his dark hair and let my palm slide around the back of his head.

"Me either."

Our lips were like magnets being pulled together. There was no way to stop it. The need was just too strong. One of my legs wound around his waist and pulled him as close as he could get, and we went at each other's lips like we'd never kissed before.

It had been a long couple weeks. I knew I'd miss him when he was away at training camp, but I honestly didn't realize how much of an emptiness his absence would leave in my life.

Behind the counter, the phone started ringing, and I jumped back, startled. Crap! I was at work! Anyone could walk in the boutique, and the first thing they'd see was me on the checkout counter, making out with my boyfriend.

Good Lord, my boss could have walked in!

"I'm at work," I hissed.

Braeden swiped at my lower lip with his thumb and then stuck it in his mouth to suck. "You taste good, baby."

Well, damn.

That was worth getting fired for.

I sighed. I was such a sucker every time he called me baby.

He laughed beneath his breath because he knew the effect he had on me and then leaned over the counter to snatch the ringing phone off its base and press it to my ear.

"Say hello, baby," he instructed.

I cleared my throat and spoke into the line. "AU Boutique, how can I help you?"

As I listened to the person on the other end of the line, Braeden's fingers started exploring beneath my skirt again.

My breath caught and I smacked his hand away because this wasn't good for my focus.

"Let me just check on that for you," I stuttered when the customer was done speaking. I pulled the phone down at gave Braeden a hard look. "Stop it."

He wagged his eyebrows, a promise he hadn't even started.

It made me want to kiss him again.

Since I knew he wasn't going to step back, I spun on the counter and hopped down on the opposite side to check the outfits on hold on the nearby rack. When I found the one I was looking for, I spoke back into the line. "Yep, it's here! We close in about ten minutes, but you can stop in tomorrow morning."

After a few other brief exchanges, I hung up.

"Have you been home yet?" I asked, reaching under the counter for the keys to lock the front door. I didn't expect him home 'til later.

"Came straight here," he replied, then gruffly added, "You know how I feel about you locking up here alone at night."

I groaned. Oh, I knew. I didn't want to get into that now with him. I just wanted to be with him for a while without wanting to throw something at his head. When I straightened, there was a small box with a white bow between us on the counter. I looked between Braeden and the gift, a slow smile pulling at his mouth.

"I got ya something," he drawled.

"You got me a present?"

"You're a present kinda girl."

I totally was.

Excited, I scooped up the box and hugged it against my chest. "I love it!"

He laughed. "You wanna see what it is first?"

I shook my head vehemently. It didn't matter what it was because it was from him. "It could be empty and I'd still love it."

His eyes softened. "Come here."

I hurried around the counter to his side. He lifted me once again so I was sitting on the counter in front of him. "Open it."

"It's so pretty." I sighed, staring at it. It was from Tiffany and Company. The square box was the signature Tiffany blue and the white hand-tied ribbon was satin. There was a small white envelope on top, so I lifted it and set the box in my lap.

The card only said three words.

They were my favorite three words ever.

I lifted my eyes to his. "I love you too."

Carefully, I set aside the card and picked up the box. The ribbon gave way easily, and I lifted the lid. Inside was a suede Tiffany-blue pouch with their name printed neatly across the front in black.

I loosened the drawstring and Braeden took the pouch and dumped out the contents in my palm.

It was a silver necklace. The pendant was shaped like a star and had the words *I love you* engraved in script over the front. Tears filled the backs of my eyes, turning my vision a little blurry as I stared down at it.

"It's beautiful." I glanced up, blinking back the tears. "It's too much," I whispered.

"It definitely isn't." He shifted closer. "If I had known it would put that look on your face, I'd have bought it sooner."

"But we have the house," I objected. The rent was paid, but the rest of us were taking on the utilities and everything else. Even still, it wasn't a very convincing objection. The thought of giving this up was actually painful.

"It wasn't that much, baby," he said and reached for the pendant lying against my palm. "Besides," he said as he flipped it over, "I can't take it back. It's engraved."

I laughed. The sound turned a little watery when I saw what he'd put there.

B's

Girl

"I guess Romeo isn't the only one who wants to mark his territory," I quipped, brushing a finger over the engraved words.

"I know you aren't gonna wear my shirt all over campus. You like clothes too much. But this—"

"This I will never take off." I finished for him.

"That's the idea." He plucked it out of my hand and lifted me off the counter. I walked over to the large mirror near the dressing rooms. Braeden came up behind me, and I lifted my hair so he could fasten it around my neck. When it settled against my skin, it felt right.

Before I could turn and hug him, he wrapped his arms around me from behind. His chin settled on my shoulder, and I stared at him through the mirror.

"Thank you."

He kissed the side of my neck. Chills raced across my arms.

"You still wanna live with me?" he asked.

I made a sound. "Have we been living together? The bed's been awfully empty."

"Aw, don't be like that, baby," he murmured and spun me in his arms. "I'm back now."

When the semester was over last year, I went home like I always do in the summer. It only lasted two weeks. I missed Braeden so much that I came back for a visit. Since he was at his mom's, I stayed with Romeo and Rimmel, and the day after I got here, Romeo announced he rented a house and asked me to move in.

I said yes because it was my solution to sneaking Prada around on campus. It was also a way for me to keep Rimmel as my roommate. I'd been dreading whoever I'd get stuck with this year. And yeah, maybe the appeal of sleeping with Braeden every night was a little too enticing to pass up.

After I said I'd move in, though, nerves took over. I began to worry it was too soon for Braeden and me to live together. We'd only been together a couple months. I thought maybe he'd hesitate or feel like I was trying to push him into something.

I was well prepared to back out of the house so Rimmel and Braeden could room together, but he wasn't having it. In fact, he seemed more than happy to have me in his bed every night. So I stayed and I got a job here at a clothing boutique where a lot of the college students shopped.

Right after we moved in, Romeo left for training camp. Just as I started to feel settled, Braeden left too.

So even though we were "living" together, we really hadn't been.

"I painted our room pink," I lied.

He gave me a look that probably should have made me scared. "Woman, I love ya, but I draw the line at pink."

"Purple?" I tried, squinting at him.

"Oh, hells no."

I kissed him swiftly and pulled away. "I'm gonna lock up so we can go."

He pulled me back against him. "Good. I'm horny as hell."

As if to prove his point, he tilted his hips into me. The rigid length inside his jeans wasn't to be ignored. My lower belly loosened and familiar heat filled me.

His eyes darkened as if he sensed the change in me. "I hope you didn't plan on sleeping tonight."

I rubbed against his stiffness and purred, "Sleep is overrated."

He groaned. "We got a week before classes start, Blondie. I plan to take full advantage of that week."

I hurried to go close up. The picture he painted was exactly what I'd been hoping for almost from the minute he left.

I guess if summer had to end, if reality had to return, spending my last few days of freedom with Braeden was definitely the way to go.

And all my worries, fears, and unknowns could wait.

CHAPTER TWO

BRAEDEN

Since I could remember, green had always been my favorite color.

But when I walked into the store tonight, her sapphire eyes lit up when she saw me, and the way they looked…

Maybe blue was my favorite color now.

I was prepared to miss Ivy while I was gone, but I'd missed her a hell of a lot more than I thought I would. Training camp for the Wolves wasn't that long, and it usually flew by. It was usually something I looked forward to. But this year, I looked forward to being done.

Don't get me wrong. I loved football. I probably always would. But Ivy was rivaling the way I felt about the sport. Ivy was rivaling for first place in my life.

Hell, she already had it in my heart.

When she saw me tonight and I watched her face shift and the emotion flood her eyes, I felt like *the* fucking man. I always thought being wanted, being eye candy to a bunch of girls, was as good as it got.

I was wrong.

Being the center of one girl's—*the right girl's*—universe was incomparable.

But…

Even through the bliss of the moment, of finally getting her back in my arms, I still noticed. She had dark circles beneath her eyes. And just before she looked up and saw me, I noticed something else.

Something was weighing on my girl.

That wasn't okay with me. Ivy wasn't the kind of girl to be weighed down. She was light. She was bright.

I thought about demanding to know what was going on, but I didn't. I kept my trap shut. I wasn't going to let it get in the way of us finally being in the same room together.

Not like it was very hard to let it go. The way she looked when I gave her that necklace, the same way the sky shone when the sun broke out from behind a cloud, it chased away all thought of everything else.

I always thought Ivy was high maintenance. That she was the kind of girl who would exhaust a man just by breathing.

I was a damn idiot.

Ivy might appear that way. She might give that impression with her light-blond locks, glossy lips, and sassy little outfits, but Ivy wasn't what she appeared.

Deep down, she was simple. It didn't take much at all to make her happy. All she really wanted was to be important to someone, for someone to think she was special.

I could give her that with no effort at all. But I wanted to give her more. She deserved it, and I fucking loved to see the look on her face when I did something she didn't expect.

I also loved to see the look in her eye when I moved inside her.

As if she could feel the rousing within me, the rush of heat through my limbs, her body stirred in my hold. Her leg slid across my skin, fitting itself between mine. Her cheek was against my chest, but her head tilted back, and I looked down into her sleepy bedroom eyes.

"I fell asleep," she murmured.

I pulled her just a little closer. "Well, I have kept you busy."

She smiled. "You didn't sleep?"

"For a while," I whispered and brushed the hair off her face. I let my fingers travel down the length of her spine and then back up again.

Truth was I didn't want to sleep. I wanted to be here in the moment with her. I wanted to listen to her breathe soundly and enjoy the way her skin brushed against mine. What I had with her, what I felt with her, was something I never thought I'd have. Something I never thought I wanted.

But she changed all that, and now I couldn't imagine my life without this.

I glanced back down at her. "You sleep okay?"

"Mmm." She arched against me. "Better than I have in weeks."

Was she still having nightmares? Was she still dreaming about Zach?

"Go back to sleep." I pressed my lips to her forehead. "I'll stay here with you." My words were a lot gentler than my thoughts. Goddamn, when would they stop? When would what he did stop haunting her? She was probably so confused.

"I'm starving." Her hand brushed across my abs and seemingly distracted her from food. "You're even more muscular than before you left."

"You like?" I rumbled.

I felt her smile against me. "Mm-hmm."

My eyes drifted closed as she caressed my waist. "Training was tough," I murmured. I pushed myself hard, harder than usual. There wasn't one reason; there were many.

She leaned across me, her wheat-colored silky strands spilling across my chest like ribbons. Her lips were warm and her tongue was soft as she pressed kisses along the ridges of my abs and down the muscles on my hips.

I had the urge to fist my hand in her hair and direct her hot little mouth exactly where I wanted it to go. But

I curbed the urge. I curbed a lot of my urges around her; not all of them, just the ones I thought would be too rough.

"Whatcha doing down there?" I rasped.

"Kissing it and making it better," she murmured between well-placed kisses.

My stomach muscles contracted, and she licked around my belly button. I groaned. I was gonna ask what she was making better, but who the fuck cared?

"Are your muscles still sore?" she asked, looking up at me.

It took a minute for the question to penetrate my sex-fogged brain. She thought my muscles were sore from training. I guess they were. Hell, I hadn't noticed.

"Nah, but I got an itch that only you can scratch." My smile was lazy, and I wagged my eyebrows at her.

She giggled. The action caused her bare chest to rub against me. Ivy slid down my body a little farther and prepared to pull the sheets up over her head. I grabbed the ends and yanked them away.

Her blue eyes rounded and glanced up.

"I wanna watch," I explained.

A seductive smile curved her full mouth, and her hand reached for my hard cock. I'd already had her four times since last night, but it still wasn't enough. I thought momentarily about pulling her up and anchoring her on my shaft, but the thought died the second her lips wrapped around it.

She was probably sore by now anyway…

This girl gave a blowjob like nobody's business. She used her lips, tongue, and teeth simultaneously to create some kind of vortex that sucked me right in.

And when she looked up at me while she moved, blond hair around her face and sapphire eyes full of passion, I had to remind myself not to come right then.

"Damn, baby," I moaned, tipping my chin back and closing my eyes. I surrendered to her completely, something I never used to do.

I was no stranger to sex, to women and getting my knob slobbed, but I always held part of myself back. I always stayed in control. But with Ivy, the sensations she brought over my body using her hands and mouth made holding back impossible.

Release came too fast, but it could not be derailed. I felt myself explode into her mouth, and I covered my face with a pillow to muffle the sound of my satisfied shout. My sis was in this house after all.

Even after I emptied, she still stayed between my legs. She worked my now semi-hard cock, massaging it with her lips and making sure she claimed every last drop of pleasure I had in me.

I tossed the pillow away and blew out a breath, staring up at the shadowed ceiling. It was covered in glow-in-the-dark stars. The ones I filled her dorm room with last semester. They were dim now, but I could still see their outline. Gently, Ivy laid my relaxed manhood against me and patted it.

A chuckle vibrated my chest. "He's not a dog."

"But he's a *very* good boy."

She collapsed on top of me, and I wrapped my arms around her. A second later, she stiffened and looked up. "Where's Prada?"

Usually that dog tried to squish herself between us the entire night. "She heard Rim moving around down in the kitchen and was scratching at the door. I let her out, so she's probably downstairs."

"I'm gonna take a shower," she said after a few minutes. "Then go feed her."

"You have to work today?" I asked, not wanting to get out of bed.

Her head shook against me. "I took it off 'cause I knew you'd be home."

"You mean you're all mine today?"

She grinned over her shoulder as she bounced out of the bed. "Yep." I enjoyed watching her shake that naked ass around the room as she went to drawers and pulled out some clothes. When she was done, she bent over—if her ass wasn't the finest on Earth, then I'd never seen an ass before—and picked up my T-shirt.

It fell past her thighs once she had it on. Then she grabbed up her clothes. "Have I mentioned how much I like not sharing a bathroom with a bunch of other girls?"

I smiled lazily, thinking about all the naked ladies in the same room together. "Couldn't have been that bad."

She threw her socks at me, and I caught them. "Now, baby," I admonished. "You know you're my favorite girl."

"I better be your *only* girl," she cracked and reached for the door handle. She tossed her hair over her shoulder and looked back. "I'll be in the shower. *Alone.*"

"Was that an invite?" I called after her.

She slammed the door against my words.

I grinned. I loved pissing her off.

I figured if I jumped up and followed her right away, she'd throw something else at my head, and as tempting as that was, I decided to give her a few. Besides, lying around in bed was hella nice. At camp, we were up before the damn roosters and worked our asses off 'til dark.

It had been weeks since I had the chance to lie in bed just because. Not that I would want to at camp. Those beds were rock hard. Besides, lying around would have given me too much time to think.

It was weird enough without Rome at camp. First time I'd been to football camp without him. It helped a little knowing he was at camp too, just a different one. But I still missed his presence.

So I stayed busy. I tried not to notice the Romeo-sized gap on the field and worked hard not to think about all the other shit that chained itself around my neck at the end of last semester. I pushed myself. I ran drills. I worked in the gym.

All the mental distraction sure was good for the physical part of me.

'Course, I knew eventually there wasn't gonna be anything left to distract me.

Oh, and by the way, the walls in here weren't pink. Or purple.

My girl knew better than that.

She just wanted me to spank her ass.

Naughty thing.

The walls were still the same color they were when I left, a neutral shade of light tan or something. On the back wall, there were two large windows that overlooked the driveway and front yard, covered with white wooden blinds. And while I was gone, Ivy hung curtains.

Curtains were for women. We never hung that shit in the dorms. Hell, I wouldn't even have them in my old room at Mom's if she hadn't hung them.

At least these weren't lace or covered in hearts or something equally girlish.

I knew my girl liked pink, but thank God she kept it under control in here. The curtains had wide white and green stripes on them. It was a girly green, kind of like a bright shade. But it wasn't so bad I would complain.

The bed was done up in mostly white. White sheets, blankets, and pillows. Of course, there were a million pillows we didn't even sleep with. She tossed them on the floor when we got in bed at night. What the hell was the point in that?

She said they made the bed look pretty.

All I needed to make it look pretty was her naked ass in it, but whatever.

Some of those useless pillows were the same color as the green stripes on the curtains, and then there was one (I counted to be sure) hot-pink pillow. And it was furry.

She tried to tell me it was for Prada. I knew damn well she just liked it.

But I wasn't gonna complain about that either.

I'd rather eat toenail clippings from a guy who never washed his feet than admit I kind of liked her girly shit. I liked anything that reminded me of her. I liked walking into this room and seeing her everywhere. Most of all, I liked knowing she was mine.

The running water in the shower across the hall caught my attention, and I smiled.

I threw on a pair of basketball shorts before heading toward the door. I was momentarily distracted from my destination when a ball of fluff came racing down the hallway toward me.

I grunted and looked down at the rat.

Her light-colored ear hair was all over the place and sticking out wildly, her entire butt was wiggling with the force of her tail wagging, and her dark eyes were intent on me.

"Hey, Gizmo," I called, using the nickname I'd given her, which drove Ivy nuts.

Giz put her two front paws up on my leg and wagged her butt some more. I laughed and scooped her up to scratch behind her ears.

"Good looking out this morning," I told her as I scratched. "Giving me some alone time with my girl."

She licked me.

"Dog breath," I muttered and set her back down on the floor. She raced off into the bedroom, no doubt toward the mountain of toys Ivy bought her.

I let myself in the bathroom and turned the lock silently. I could see Ivy moving around behind the curtain, and I shucked my shorts and tossed them on the floor.

The air in here was moist, almost humid, and the mirror was already fogging up. She was humming to herself. I went to the edge of the shower and slid the curtain back barely enough for me to step in.

She had her face under the spray, and ribbons of water cascaded down over her shoulders and back.

She was just way too sexy not to touch.

I reached out and grabbed her by the waist, meaning to tow her back against me.

But she never made it.

Ivy's body went rigid so fast it was almost like her body spasmed. A low shriek vibrated her throat, and she lurched forward.

"No!" The protest was almost a moan, the fear in her voice real.

I jerked back immediately, letting go. I must have been too rough. I must have hurt her.

I started to apologize, but the words died in my throat because the force in which she pulled away and the fact she was soapy and standing in water wasn't a good combination.

Ivy slipped forward, plunging toward the shower wall and the large silver knob that jutted out.

"Whoa," I gasped and quickly recovered the space between us. I caught her just before she fell and would likely smack her head on the knob.

Her body went rigid again, but I didn't let go this time. This time I was ready for her. I pulled her back, bringing her body up against mine, and stepped so we were out of the spray.

I could feel her trembling in my arms, and it scared me.

"Easy now," I said in her ear. "You're okay. I'm not gonna hurt you."

"Braeden." She said my name on a relieved sigh and went boneless against me.

"Right here, baby," I whispered. "I'm right here."

She turned, pressing herself as close to me as she could get, and when I didn't tighten my arms (for fear I'd freak her out again), she whimpered. "Tighter."

I tucked her as close against me as possible. She buried her face in my chest, and another shiver worked its way down her spine.

I stared at the falling water over her head, right through it and at the wall.

Concern, alarm, and anger warred within me.

I wasn't exactly sure what the fuck just happened.

But I was pretty sure all those distractions I'd just been thinking about were long gone.

I was pretty sure this wasn't just a case of her being startled.

No.

It was much, much more.

CHAPTER THREE

IVY

I didn't hear him.

I didn't think.

I just reacted.

People get scared every day. Things happen to startle everyone. But even those with the most focused concentration don't ever react that way.

Violently.

Almost like they're being attacked.

There was something wrong with that reaction.

With *my* reaction.

It threw me, and I stood there pressing myself as close to Braeden as I possibly could until the feeling of sheer panic went down the drain with the water.

I pulled back enough to apologize. He probably thought I was certifiable. Yet when our eyes met, he wasn't freaked out. He seemed almost scared. It wasn't a look Braeden often wore. It threw me off balance even more.

He cupped my cheek, and without thinking, I turned my face into his palm.

"Did I hurt you?"

"No," I replied immediately. Braeden was gentle when he touched me, and just then had been no different. "I—" I glanced away and then back. "I don't know why I acted like that."

His brown eyes studied me, like he was trying to see everything I wasn't saying. But there was nothing to see because I honestly couldn't understand why I acted that way. It was like my body went into flight mode and only wanted to get away.

Only there wasn't anything to get away from.

"I'm sorry," I whispered, confusion and a little despair in my tone.

Both his hands took my face and held me firm so he could stare at me intently. "You didn't do anything wrong. You don't need to apologize."

Goose bumps rose across my skin. Standing here out of the spray of warm water was making me cold.

Braeden turned us and stepped back so he was far enough under the water to warm us both, but his broad shoulders kept it out of my eyes.

"I should have told you I was in here," he muttered, almost like he was scolding himself. He ran a hand across my shoulder and down my arm. "I'll get out and let you finish."

"No." I protested, feeling a little steadier. I wasn't going to let some freak reaction ruin his first day back from training. "I need someone to wash my back."

"You sure?" His eyes searched mine.

I stretched up and kissed him. "I want you to stay." I reached around and grabbed the white loofah I used with my body wash and held it out.

We took turns washing each other. He seemed a little more withdrawn than usual, and it made me worry. But once it was my turn with the loofah, my touch seemed to relax him, so I took my time and made sure my hands were extra bold.

By the time I was done, he was back to his normal alpha male self. I wrapped my legs around his waist when he picked me up and pushed my back into the shower wall. Before descending upon my mouth, he hesitated. "This okay?"

My heart squeezed at his genuine concern. "Anytime you touch me is okay," I whispered.

We made out until the water turned cold, but he never tried for more. He seemed content just to explore the inside of my mouth with his tongue and make me squirm against him.

When the water was off, he wrapped a towel around me before himself and rubbed my shoulders vigorously to get me warm. He didn't dry himself until after he'd lifted me out of the shower and stood me on the fluffy rug I'd bought for the floor.

Once he was dry, he pulled on his shorts and then watched with hooded eyes and I blow-dried my hair. It was gonna have to be a braid or something kind of day because I didn't feel like going to all the trouble straightening or curling it.

Once it was dry and I applied lotion to my face, I reached for my clothes, but B beat me to it. The attentive way he helped me dress bruised my heart in some weird way. His tenderness was almost unnerving.

"Are you okay?" I asked.

He paused and glanced up. "I'm straight."

I rolled my eyes. Lord, he was talking in bro code. "I'm a girl."

His smile flashed. "I'm well aware." To punctuate his sentence, he grabbed my boob.

He was so stupid I smiled. "What the hell does 'I'm straight' mean?"

Braeden stepped closer and slid his palm along my waist, caressing the dark-green silk halter-top I wore. "It means everything's all good."

"I'm sorry I freaked in the shower. I guess you just scared me." It seemed like a dumb explanation, but it was the only one I had.

"Are you still having nightmares, Ivy?" His tone was a little grim.

I glanced away. What did that have to do with anything? "I don't know if I'd call them nightmares," I hedged. Of course, the dreams were about Zach and the horrible mistake I made of sleeping with him, and any dream about Zach could be considered a nightmare.

"Ivy," he growled, a note of warning in his tone.

This was clearly something that bothered him, so I fessed up. "Sometimes."

I pulled back and picked up the white shorts I matched up with my top and slipped them on. They were super cute, made of loose material with extra white fabric around the waist that tied into a big white bow. I concentrated extra hard on tying that bow instead of the way Braeden crossed his arms over his chest and stared intently.

"If you ever need to talk about it, I'm here," he said.

A laugh bubbled out of my throat. Right. Like I was going to talk to him about the guy he hated and that one time I had sex with him.

But he wouldn't be deterred. Gently, he grasped my wrist and pulled me away from the mirror. "I mean it, Ivy. You can talk to me. Even about this."

I nodded. "I'm fine, honestly. They're just dreams. It's probably just karma making sure I get what's mine because I was so stupid and slept with him."

"You're not stupid," he said, harsh, and paced away. He couldn't go very far because the bathroom wasn't that big. When he turned back, emotion burned behind his eyes. "I hate that you beat yourself up over this."

I didn't say anything because I did regret it, and nothing was going to change that.

He reached out and fingered the necklace around my neck. "I love you, Blondie."

Why did it seem like he was trying to say a lot more than just those three words?

"I love you too."

The air in here was thick, so I opened the door to let in some fresh. "Go get dressed. I'm starving."

I heard him in the bedroom, talking to Prada, as I styled my hair in a messy bun on top of my head. The entire time, I couldn't stop thinking about what happened in the shower and just now when he asked me about my dreams.

Why did it feel like he thought the two were connected?

What was I missing?

CHAPTER FOUR

BRAEDEN

Her body remembered.

It remembered exactly what her mind wanted to forget.

It made perfect sense now. The dreams, the weight I sometimes noticed on her shoulders, and just now in the shower… Her body knew exactly what happened.

The mind and body were connected in ways we would never understand. So even if Ivy's brain didn't know why it was reacting, the body told it to anyway.

Did I make the wrong decision? Should I have told Ivy about the pictures I found, about the proof of her being sexually assaulted?

I felt like I was being shown two roads to travel, but neither of them led to my destination. I was damned if I did, damned if I didn't.

Maybe it seemed exaggerated now because I'd been gone. Maybe all the changes of her moving into this house, getting a job, and me leaving were just a lot to deal with all at once. Now that I was back, I could be around more. I could make sure she felt safe. Maybe things would calm down.

School would be starting back up, we would all fall into a routine, and her body's memories would fade. The fight or flight response surely would too.

Right?

God, I fucking hoped so.

I couldn't stand to watch it. To see her body react and her eyes fill with jumbled emotion, then guilt. She thought her torment was punishment for having sex with that dirt bag.

I'd never in my life hated someone as much as I did Zach.

And that was saying something, because I was such a hothead. I didn't even hate my father the way I hated Zach.

Hate was a dangerous emotion. It could drive a man to do things he might not ordinarily do.

But love was just the same.

This was the reason, up until now, I kept women in a neat little box wrapped up in a *just for fun* bow. Deep down inside was this place, a place I always sensed was there. I hid it behind a smile and sarcasm. I posed as a guy who didn't have what I did inside.

Darkness.

A place where anger lived but so did fear. Fear and anger made a deadly cocktail.

My love for Ivy was so strong it had the ability to unleash that darkness.

So did my hate for the one who hurt her.

Ivy was still fussing with her hair and face when I was done throwing on a T-shirt and tan cargo shorts. Why women fussed so much over themselves I would never understand. Ivy was fucking gorgeous the second she rolled out of my bed in the morning. She didn't need to make such an effort.

But Ivy didn't see herself the way I did, the way most other people did. She thought she needed to do all that to make herself look better. I could tell her it wasn't necessary until I was blue in the face. Still, it wouldn't matter. The thing I learned was putting herself together was something she needed to do, if only for herself. Makeup and shit was sort of like her happy place, like football was mine. I wasn't gonna bitch or argue about it. I'd love her no matter what.

I stopped in the bathroom doorway and admired the way her silky green top rode up on her midsection, exposing a smooth patch of skin as she fussed with her hair. "I swear to God, woman, you take longer in here than it took all the founding fathers to create the Declaration of Independence."

Just 'cause I wasn't gonna argue over her hobby didn't mean I wouldn't tease her about it.

She shuddered. "Ew. Did you see those men's hair? If I were making history, I wouldn't have looked like that."

I snickered and crossed my arms over my chest and leaned in the doorway. "I bet they were studs back in the day."

She lowered her arms, shirt falling back into place. So I admired her round ass instead.

She made a rude sound and turned from the mirror. "If they were studs, then the women back then had no standards." I liked the way her nose wrinkled with distaste and the way her eyes took on a shade of green to match her top.

"You look hot," I told her.

She rolled her eyes, but I knew she liked the compliment. Girls like compliments.

"Such a way with words," she mused.

I caught her around the waist and pulled her into the doorway with me. I leaned back and spread my legs, bringing her up against me. "I told ya I'm not good with words."

"The way you kiss makes up for it." She leaned in, but I turned my face.

"Is that all I am to you?" I joked. "A piece of man candy?"

She licked me.

Took that wicked tongue of hers and slid it right up the side of my face.

"Man candy? No. Sour Patch Kid? Totally."

I wiped my face with the back of my hand. "Have I ever told you what a good kisser you are?" I deadpanned. "The best."

"I have been told that before…" she mused.

I lunged at her, catching her around the waist and turning us so she was against the doorframe and I was in front. I moved fast, lightly digging my fingers into her sides, getting all the spots I knew would make her squirm.

"Stop!" she shrieked and jerked, trying to avoid my tickling. "Braeden James, stop it!"

"Ooh, someone means business."

She laughed and collapsed against the doorframe. Prada came racing out into the hallway and started barking at us. When Ivy kept laughing and screeching, Prada jumped on my leg like she was going to attack me and save her favorite girl.

I relented and pulled back slightly. Ivy's cheeks were pink from the commotion and her top was slightly askew.

Prada chewed at the end of my shorts and pulled. Ivy laughed and scooped her up. "Good girl," she crooned.

"That vicious thing tried to attack me, and you tell her she's a good girl?"

Ivy pushed out of the doorframe, carrying the dog. "Oh, you poor thing. You could have been seriously hurt." She stuck her lip out in a pout but slapped me in the midsection as she moved past. "Man up, Nancy."

I grinned and swung around to follow her. "If I were a woman, my name would not be Nancy. I need something with some sass."

Ivy turned and glanced at me over her shoulder as she walked, her eyes amused. "This is quite an interesting conversation, but I need coffee." All her attention moved toward the fluff ball in her arms. "And this little princess needs some breakfast."

The entire way downstairs, I admired the view of her behind. What happened in the shower was seemingly forgotten. There was no trace of it in her eyes just now.

But I knew better. I knew it was possible to hide stuff way down deep.

I did it all the time.

I had a feeling Ivy did too.

CHAPTER FIVE

IVY

My favorite sport was shopping.

But if anyone asked, I'd say football.

Wouldn't want to offend Braeden and Romeo, you know.

Seriously, though, what was better than the thrill of finding the perfect outfit? A hot sale? Going into a store and seeing nothing but racks of possibility lining the walls was exhilarating.

The colors, the fabrics, the shoes… the makeup.

Yep, shopping was where it was at. I even liked grocery shopping.

But there was one kind of shopping I didn't like.

It was basically the black sheep of the shopping world.

Textbook shopping.

Ew. Like who wanted to go into a stuffy old store that smelled like must and mold and sort through piles and piles of books that contained knowledge about chemistry? Or math.

Now I'm not talking about a nice little bookshop with coffee and romance novels. Those were fun. I liked a fun beach read just as much as the next girl.

But school books?

Boring.

And because I disliked the chore so much, I put off buying my books as long as humanly possible… so the campus bookstore was out of one of the ones I needed. That meant I had to go off campus to this little bookshop a few streets over from the boutique.

At least Braeden went with me. Being with him made the task a lot less torturous. The place wasn't busy, and it didn't take long to get what I needed. Not like the campus bookstore. We'd been there for like two hours.

The place was flooded with college students, some of them clearly freshmen, looking fresh faced and frazzled at the same time. But then there were the regulars. The students who'd been attending Alpha U just as long as I had.

Seeing them all answered a question I'd had since classes ended last year.

Would everything the #BuzzBoss said about me (aka Missy, aka my backstabbing friend) be long forgotten? Or would my unwanted status as a #slut still haunt me?

The second I walked in, I'd known.

People didn't forget as easily as I'd hoped.

And it seemed that me being on Braeden's arm made me even more interesting.

I caught the stares, the casual double glances. I noted the way a few cellphones came out and the people attached to them started typing furiously.

Great.

Just what I needed.

Everyone sending Missy a report on my every move. I could only imagine what would show up later on the Buzzfeed.

Braeden acted like he didn't notice, but I knew he did. Just the way he angled his body toward mine while we were getting books and the set of his shoulders spoke volumes.

He saw, he understood, and he didn't like it. He acted like my personal living, breathing shield.

Just knowing that caused two reactions within me:

1) Safety. I felt safe because I knew with him in my corner, things couldn't possibly get as bad as they did last semester. Now that Romeo was gone, Braeden had a lock on the most popular guy on campus. People would be more afraid to harass me, for fear of his retaliation. Not only that, but he loved me. It's amazing what the love of the right man could do for a girl.

And

2) Fear. Yes, this was the complete opposite of the first reaction. What could I say? Braeden always had a way of bringing out extreme feelings in me. I liked—*no*—I loved knowing B was here for me. I loved knowing he was my anchor. But. He had a temper. I

hadn't always understood why, but now that I did… well, it wasn't something I could just forget about. I knew Braeden would never hurt me. He'd literally injure himself first, but that didn't bode well for others. He was extremely protective, extremely territorial… and he wasn't going to just sit back and let rumors fly. I was honestly afraid he might do something that would come back and hurt him later.

However, bringing all that up to him in that moment was just bad timing. So I didn't. I smiled and pretended I didn't see the sideways looks as we got books and supplies. Of course, we could barely walk two feet without people approaching Braeden. Most of them were football players, and everyone was nice.

It made me relax some. Maybe I was just overreacting.

Too bad that feeling was short lived.

After we went to the old, creepy bookshop to get the one book the campus store didn't have, we walked over to a nearby café.

It was a total college place. A lot of the students hung out here, especially the upperclassmen because they all had cars.

The café sat high on the sidewalk, so much that you had to walk up about five steps to get to the courtyard that led to the front door. Down the center was a regular sidewalk, but on either side were flagstone patios with black wrought iron tables and chairs.

The building itself was made of brick. It sort of looked like a cottage, not like a modern café, as the name suggested. The windows in front were arched and the front door was painted black with a bright green symbol in the center. The words *LOTUS: Coffee with Atmosphere* were spelled out in small letters beneath it.

Funky music played through the speakers and filled the outside space. People milled around and talked over coffee and food.

I was tense.

I hated being tense. Going on campus today and facing everyone for the first time since last semester totally frayed my nerves. Usually, I was good at hiding any insecurities, but not right now. Right now I felt like a long length of perfect rope…

That had been hacked off halfway with a pair of dull scissors.

The ends were coming undone, tattered and messy.

I really hoped my hair didn't look the way I felt.

As if he could sense the frazzled way I felt, Braeden draped his arm across my shoulders and pulled me into his side as we walked toward the door.

"B!" some guy yelled from a table off to the right.

"Yo!" Braeden swung around, pulling me with him.

Toward the back of the courtyard was a round table full of a bunch of the Wolves. It was almost funny the way their huge bodies took up so much space and made the table seem insufficient.

"Bring that girl over here," the guy hollered.

I swallowed and Braeden chuckled. "Ready to meet the fam?" he said low as we started toward the table.

"Do I have a choice?"

"Nope. You know they all want a look at the girl who brought me down."

I felt my hackles rise. It was a welcome feeling. A familiar feeling. I wore that spunk like a great-fitting leather jacket.

I glanced around the table and my eyes fell on Trent. He winked, and I grinned.

"Trent!" I said and pulled away from Braeden.

He was already getting up and coming around to greet me. Before I thought better of it, I flung myself at him, giving him a hug. He hesitated for a second but then returned the quick embrace.

"Have a good summer?" I asked.

"You bet. Looks like summer agreed with you," he said, taking in my face. To his credit, he didn't look me up and down.

I beamed. Maybe I didn't look so frizzy after all.

"You hitting on my woman?" Braeden quipped. He said it good-naturedly, but I heard a hint of steel beneath his tone. Trent made a rude sound (was that supposed to be a no?) and held his fist out to Braeden so they could pound it out.

"Maybe," Trent replied when they were done, glancing at me and winking.

I smiled but slid a glance at B, hoping he knew Trent was only kidding.

Braeden angled himself slightly between Trent and me with a glint in his eye I didn't really like. So I slid my hand up the small of his back and let it rest there. My touch worked. He said nothing and turned to address the rest of the table.

* * *

"Y'all know Ivy, right?"

"Oh, we know her all right," one of the guys cracked.

Something in me stilled and my breathing lurched. He seriously wasn't going to say something about that picture Missy released of me and Zach, was he? Surely he wouldn't dare… The Wolves wouldn't be so callous to one of their own…

Would they?

Around my waist, Braeden's arm tensed, but he didn't say anything.

"This girl here is a legend on campus," the player went on. "She's the girl who managed to shackle the least dateable guy at Alpha U."

Relief and amusement caused me to burst out laughing. Braeden released his hold on my waist to give everyone at the table the finger.

"I don't know if shackled is the right word here, guys," I joked. "I think *trained* is a better choice."

Everyone howled.

Braeden leaned over and whispered, "You're gonna pay for that later, *baby*."

That was the most delicious threat I'd ever been served.

I batted my eyes at him innocently.

"Where's your dog tags, B?" one of the guys ribbed. "Did you get your rabies shot yet?"

I laughed, finally feeling at ease for the first time today. At least I was being accepted by Braeden's friends.

Trent caught my eye and smiled. I returned it, glad he didn't seem to hold a grudge that I pretty much brushed off his attempts at dating me to be with Braeden. He said it wouldn't get in the way of our friendship, but then school ended and summer began… and no one heard from him at all.

But that didn't matter, because he looked good as ever and there wasn't the slightest hint of anything but kindness in his eyes when he looked at me.

Braeden's arm returned and spun us around. I couldn't help but wonder if he'd done it on purpose, to break my eye contact with Trent.

"You guys are funny as hell," he said sarcastically. "But we came here for coffee."

"Grab your stuff and come sit with us," Brady, the one who called me a legend, offered. "We can talk football, get to know your trainer better."

To my surprise, Braeden hesitated. His eyes slid to Trent. It looked like he was debating on whether or not he wanted to sit with him.

Trent noticed. Hell, I think the entire table noticed.

An awkward silence descended.

I cleared my throat. "We'd love to!" I offered a big smile. "Can I get anyone a refill?"

Everyone shook their heads. Trent stood slowly from the table and picked up a half-empty iced drink. "I actually have somewhere I gotta be. But thanks for the offer, Ivy." He said my name but still looked at B.

"Oh, okay. Well, it was good seeing you. I'm sure we'll see you around campus."

"Totally." He finally looked away from Braeden and smiled. "See ya."

Everyone was silent while Trent walked away.

I looked up at Braeden with a question in my eyes. "What the hell is wrong with you?"

He grunted. "C'mon."

We turned from the table toward the sidewalk that led inside. I was still kind of surprised by the strain between Braeden and Trent.

Surely he wasn't jealous Trent and I almost went out last semester?

I mean, seriously. He knew he was like the be-all, end-all for me.

I hadn't even kissed Trent!

I opened my mouth to tell Braeden what I thought about his ass-like behavior, when someone very familiar stepped out the café door.

Missy.

I stopped in my tracks, like someone poured instant super glue right there on the pavement.

Braeden took a couple more steps before realizing I was no longer at his side. He swung around. "Blondie." He sighed. "It's just guy shit." But his words cut off when he noticed this wasn't about him and Trent.

Missy saw me and stopped as well. The door to the café slammed behind her.

The large latte gripped in her hand complimented her outfit perfectly.

Her cropped jeans were artfully ripped up, the nude suede wedges on her feet made me want to find a pair online, and the lacey white loose top paired perfectly with the destructed denim. She had on several colored necklaces, a large chunky watch, and her fingernails were painted dark plum.

Just looking at her pissed me off.

Not only because she was a backstabbing traitor who literally slut-shamed me to the entire Alpha U campus… but because she cut her hair.

In the exact style I was planning on getting for fall.

Bitch.

Her dark, glossy locks no longer hung past her chest. She'd gotten many inches cut off so they ended around her collarbone. It was slightly layered to give it a playful look, and she curled it in loose waves.

It was the perfect lob.

(Lob = long bob)

The total "in" haircut for fall.

I'd never admit it, but it looked good. Too bad she couldn't just cut off the shitty parts of her personality too.

Braeden seemed surprised to see her and looked between us for long seconds like he wasn't sure what to expect. Like maybe a catfight would break out and I'd claw out her eyes.

Please.

I was too good for that.

I gave her a withering look, hoping it conveyed the way I felt, and hefted my Marc Jacobs bag a little higher on my shoulder.

Something shifted behind her eyes, almost like regret, but I wasn't about to fall for that. Missy was a great actress, something she'd proved many times over. If she wanted me to think she felt bad for all the shit she pulled, it wasn't going to work.

I noted several people watching the quiet scene between us, and I pulled in a breath. The last thing I was going to do was give people more to gossip about. Especially with the #BuzzBoss standing right here.

Braeden backtracked to me and wrapped his hand around mine. His fingers squeezed, offering me silent support and comfort.

I looked at him and smiled.

When my eyes went back to her, I could have sworn the bitter bite of jealousy was written on her face, but I couldn't be sure with only a quick glimpse. Braeden moved gracefully, once again angling himself in front of me so I couldn't study her facial expressions.

Missy seemed to shake herself and start moving. Even with B blocking me from view, I felt her scrutinizing eyes staring at me through him.

Our paths neared, the distance between my old best friend and me closing by the second. I looked off to the side.

"Ivy."

I glanced over.

She'd somehow gotten herself in view of me. Her perfectly glossed lips parted—to say what, I didn't know.

Braeden made a sound and tucked me behind him. He really needed to stop with all the macho protection, but in the moment, I was grateful for it. I still wasn't quite ready to face her. Deep down, I had a lot to say to her… I just wasn't sure what it was. It was like all my feelings had yet to be transposed into words.

"Walk away," he growled low. "Walk away right fucking now."

Missy's gray eyes widened slightly. She glanced at me like I was going to help her.

I looked away again.

A heartbeat went by, and then she brushed past, leaving behind a cloud of her signature scent, *Clinique Happy*.

Yes, I thought that was ironic.

Braeden relaxed and took my hand again. "Coffee, then home?"

I nodded, still recovering from our almost confrontation.

Funny how someone that used to make me feel so comfortable and relaxed now had the power to twist my guts and make me feel sick inside.

As we stood in line to order, I stared at the door, surprised she wanted to say anything at all. The last time we talked—when I found out everything she'd done and confronted her—she couldn't get away fast enough.

She had nothing to say then.

What could she possibly have to say now?

CHAPTER SIX

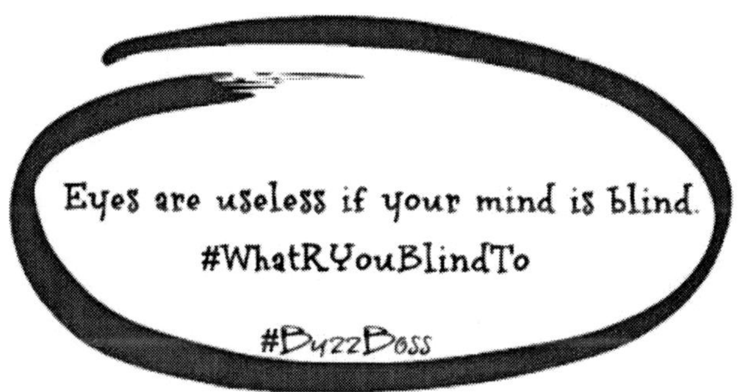

BRAEDEN

Life is heavy.

Secrets are costly.

The lines between right and wrong get blurred.

But the reason for it all…

Still remained.

As clear as ever.

I gazed at her in the quiet early light of the room. The pillow she lay on cradled her head gently while sun-colored strands cascaded across her shoulder and trailed over the white sheet. She looked more vulnerable like this. Asleep and with her guard down, her face scrubbed free of all makeup and expression. The thick, soft lashes of her eyes fanned out over her milky complexion and kissed the tops of her cheekbones.

Her lips were naturally pink, parted slightly as she breathed easily. Her body turned toward mine; it always did when I was in bed. Even if I came in late, the second my body hit the mattress, it didn't matter how she was lying. She turned to me.

Gizmo somehow squirmed between us. She lay stretched out on her back lengthwise against Ivy's side. Her paws were tucked against her chest and her face was turned into the blankets covering Ivy.

My girls.

Never in a million years did I think when I had two girls in my bed, one of them would be a dog that looked like a gremlin.

Never in a million years did I think I'd ever feel this happy.

But I was.

Things were trying to steal that happiness. Things were preventing me from feeling like my life was completely full.

Even though I tried not to think about seeing my father months ago, I did.

And…

What I didn't tell Ivy was eating me alive.

The choice I made was the right decision. At least I'd thought so at the time. Now, even as I lay here watching over the reason for which I'd done so many things, doubts haunted me, like the echo of a bird's song on a clear day.

I couldn't forgive him for what he'd done. The image of my mother, bloody and bruised, lying in a hospital bed would always be there—like a snapshot of the past that would never fade.

My father was an abuser. He was violent and had no respect for women.

I had no tolerance for men like him who lorded their superior strength over the physically weaker sex.

I realized now those feelings influenced my decision to not tell Ivy what really happened that night with Zach. I decided to carry the abuse she'd suffered within me, tucked right beside the abuse my mother had endured.

I only wanted to protect her from the horrible truth.

But what if my protection was hurting her?

With one last gaze upon her sleeping form, I slid out from under the covers. I picked up a pair of basketball shorts on the end of the bed and stepped into them. My T-shirt was close by, but I didn't put it on. Instead, I turned it right side out and laid it beside Ivy so she'd have something to reach for when she finally woke up. It wasn't the shirt she'd basically stolen last spring at the beach. She wore that thing more than I ever did.

But she'd still like this one. I wore it yesterday so it smelled like me. She liked that.

I liked that she liked it.

Gizmo cracked one eye and glanced at me as I moved. I pressed a finger to my lips, and the dog's eye closed again. I didn't think she actually understood what I'd done, just that she was too comfortable to move.

The house was silent as I moved downstairs into the open kitchen. This place was spacious and nice. Hell, I thought I'd be thirty-five before I could even think about affording something like this. Even though technically I wasn't paying the rent, it still came to feel like home. We all pitched in like we said and took care of the utilities. I even cut the grass. It was a pain in the ass, but someone had to do it.

Rimmel and Ivy would probably kill themselves trying to operate a lawnmower.

I worked all summer waiting tables, using my witty personality to charm ladies out of big tips. I managed to save up some, enough to live and not have to work during football season. 'Course, it helped that I had a football scholarship that paid for school. There was even some money left over every semester that I got to keep, so it was sort of like being paid to play football. It was nothing like what Rome was getting paid, but it was enough.

Mom tried to give me money all the time. I seldom took it. I didn't want to be her responsibility. She'd shouldered that enough when I was growing up. She was the parent, yes, but I still felt like it was my job to care for her. Sometimes the cash would just show up. She would have the bank transfer it into my account and not tell me. I never said anything and neither did she, but I think she knew I was grateful.

I glanced at the antique-white cabinets and stone tiled backsplash before stepping up to the black granite countertop and looking out the window over the sink into the backyard. The trees outside would soon be full of color; they were just now starting to turn. The outside didn't hold my attention long, just like the interior hadn't.

My attention once again turned inward.

I thought getting out of bed early would allow me to escape from my thoughts, but the soundless morning only encouraged them.

Instead of thinking about my father, or Ivy and all the things I didn't say, I thought about my future. Here I was a junior in college, almost graduated, but I had no idea where I'd be in two years.

I wasn't like Romeo. I wasn't intent on the NFL. I certainly wouldn't turn down an offer, but I guess a voice in the back of my head always told me that was Rome's dream, *his* goal… It wasn't mine.

It never bothered me before that I wasn't sure what I'd do. But now it did.

Now everything seemed to weigh ten pounds more than it had before.

Maybe I couldn't see past the right now because so much was unsettled. I needed to get my shit together, not just for me, but for Ivy. Because even if I had no idea where I'd be in a few years, I knew without a doubt I wanted her right there with me.

I turned from the window and glanced at the coffee pot on the counter. I looked under the lid and smiled. Rim had it set already. All I had to do was press start.

Damn, I loved that girl.

Seconds ticked by, and then the thick scent of brewing coffee filled the room. I breathed deep, enjoying it.

I heard a key in the lock at the front of the house, then the opening and closing of a door. Seconds later, Rimmel walked around the corner carrying a big box of donuts with a brown paper sack on top.

Her steps faltered when she saw me standing there, but then she smiled. "Is the house on fire?"

"Yes, Rim. Thought I'd stand here half dressed and watch everything burn," I retorted.

She snorted, the action making a strand of thick, dark hair fall over her glasses and shield one eye. "I don't think I've ever seen you get up this early when you didn't have to be up. I figured there had to be an emergency."

I shrugged and pushed off the counter to take the stuff out of her hands and put it nearby on the island. "Must have donut radar." I joked and opened the box to snag a glazed donut.

I shoved half of it in my mouth. Then I paused. "These for me?"

She shook her head and rolled her eyes. "You have terrible manners."

I grinned so she could see the pastry in my teeth. "Thanks, sis."

"Romeo told me donuts and coffee was your tradition with him before classes started every semester."

The mention of Rome and the shit we always did made the donut a little harder to swallow. I missed him, and it made me realize maybe his absence was also one of the reasons I felt so conflicted about everything. We didn't talk heavy shit too much, but he was still my sounding board and I was his.

"Yeah, we pretty much eat everything after training camp and before the semester starts. Once it does, I'm gonna have to really cut my diet for the season."

Rimmel leaned against the counter and smiled. "Well, I know Romeo isn't here, but I'll eat donuts with ya."

I shoved the rest in my mouth and licked my fingers. "I guess you'll do."

"Gee, thanks." She poked me in the stomach.

"Bring it in," I said and opened up one arm while I reached for another donut with the other. Rim stepped into my embrace and wrapped her arms around my waist. She hugged me a little longer—maybe just one second more—than usual. I tossed the food down and pulled her back in, wrapping both my arms around her.

"How you doing, sis?" I said over her head.

"I'm good."

I pulled her back and held her shoulders. "That's a lame-ass reply. And you shouldn't lie to your brother."

Behind us, Murphy materialized and jumped up on the counter. "I'm straight," Rimmel said, this time in a low voice, which I think was meant to be like mine.

I shook my head sadly. "That's just terrible."

She smacked me and turned to grab Murphy and hug him to her chest. "I'm not lying. I really am fine."

"But…" I cajoled.

She looked away as she stroked the cat without thought. "But I miss him."

I nodded. Rim kept herself busy with the shelter, prepping for class, and working part time this summer on campus at the business office, but I knew not even all that was enough to distract her from Romeo not being here.

"It's just weird." She went on, setting the cat down at her feet. "He just became like the sun to my planet, and while I'm so happy he's living his dream and I'd never ask him to come home… it's just weird here without him."

"Yeah." I agreed, understanding perfectly. "Planets need their sun." *I miss him too.*

Rimmel smiled slightly and picked up the paper sack. "I got you a couple breakfast sandwiches."

"Hells yeah." I grabbed the bag and stuck my face inside to inhale the scent of greasy bacon and cheese.

Clutching the bag, I dropped low, scooping her up, and spun her in a circle. "Best sister ever."

She laughed. On the counter, her cell chimed with a text. Her attention abruptly switched to the phone.

I put her down with a chuckle. "Tell Rome I said hi."

She snatched the phone off the counter and leaned against the island, completely focused on the message he'd sent. I knew from the smile that instantly graced her face whatever he said made her happy.

Thinking fast, I grabbed my cell, snapping a pic of her standing there all engrossed and in love with her phone. I shot it off to him in a text with the message: *She still loves ya. Every time U text, she looks like this.*

I set my phone aside and turned to the coffee maker. "You want some?" I hollered over my shoulder.

"Uh-huh."

I poured two mugs, got out the creamer, and then sat at the island with my sugar and grease for breakfast. It went really good with caffeine.

Rimmel looked up a few seconds later, her face still all smiley.

"Come on." I patted the stool beside me. "I'll share my bacon with ya."

Rimmel took the coffee I poured her and climbed onto the seat beside me and went about adding in some creamer.

"He doing all right there?" I asked, setting the food aside.

She nodded. "I think so. At least he acts like it to me. How do you think he sounds when you talk to him?"

"The same." I agreed. "Maybe a little stressed about his arm."

She nodded, concern dimming her features. "His arm is going to be a worry for a while still," she said softly. "He's been throwing, though. Says his arm is almost as strong as it was. And he's gotten even better throwing with his left. He's pushing himself too hard." She paused. "But he says he thinks he'll get to play this season."

He did push himself, but that wasn't ever gonna change. I did talk to him, mostly about football and guy stuff. I asked about his arm once, and he said it was fine. I hadn't asked recently because I figured if there was a problem, he'd say so. I also never asked him about his schedule. I figured he'd come home when he could. "When's he coming home to visit?" I asked.

Rimmel's face lit up. "He thinks he can come home next weekend."

"Hells yeah," I said and grabbed a donut to hand to her. When she took it, I snagged another and held it out. "Cheers."

We bumped the pastries together and then took a bite. My bite was like three times the size of hers.

I polished off what was in my hand and then grabbed up my coffee. Rimmel was still pecking away at her breakfast, her phone screen having gone dark a few minutes ago. I took that as a sign Rome wasn't still texting.

"Hey, so how's Ivy been?" I couldn't help the tentative nature of my tone. I'd been wanting to ask since I got home from camp. Just hadn't gotten the chance. The three of us were usually together, or Rim was at work when Ivy was. This was the first time we'd actually been alone in a couple weeks.

I wondered if maybe I was the only one that thought Ivy seemed a little on edge. That maybe I felt that way as a product of my own emotions and not actually the way Ivy was behaving.

What happened in the shower was all her. I shook the thought away and glanced up.

Rimmel tilted her head to study me. "Why do you ask?"

Damn, she was perceptive. Why couldn't she just answer the question?

I shrugged like it was no big deal. "With classes starting up, I think she's been kinda nervous. You know, after all the shit that went down last semester." I didn't mention seeing Missy at Lotus or the way Ivy acted when we first approached the table full of my teammates.

Rimmel gazed at me with knowing eyes. "You're worried about her."

"It's my job to worry about her."

"It's your job to love her," Rimmel corrected but then allowed, "and yeah, maybe worry about her some too."

I drank some more coffee and waited for an answer to the original question.

"But I've never known you to worry so much it keeps you awake. Is there something specific that has you so concerned?"

"What was in that donut?" I intoned. "You sure are full of questions this morning."

"I'm naturally inquisitive." She used her finger to push the black-rimmed glasses up on her nose and gave me a stern look. "And you seem to be empty of answers."

I wasn't about to tell her what was really going on in my head. Hell to the no. But I had to give her something. If I didn't, I'd never hear the end of it.

I sipped the coffee and sat back on the stool. "She still has nightmares about him." I couldn't keep the harshness out of my voice. I hated just mentioning that fucking menace to society.

Rimmel frowned and looked into her cup, like maybe the answers would just float right to the surface and tell her exactly what to say.

Shit, I wished it were that easy.

I had a corny as hell thought and tucked it away for later… I might need it.

"I've noticed," Rim replied softly. "She's more subdued than her normal bubbly self. But I guess that's not really all that recent. She's been that way for a while."

"Yeah, like since Missy dragged up all the shit she'd been through and hung it out there for all to see."

Rimmel shook her head. "No. It's been longer than that. Since it happened…" She cleared her throat and her gaze slid away. "You know with—"

"Don't say it." I cut her off sharply. "I know."

The apology in her eyes was real, but I barely noticed it because guilt and a little side of self-loathing was all I had room for inside my head.

And in my chest.

I hadn't been there. Ivy and I were still doing the spiteful song and dance around each other when Zach took advantage of her. Back then, the only words we ever said to each other were sarcastic and mean. At the time, I thought it was entertaining.

But now…

Now it made me feel like a shithead.

If I had been willing to really look at her back then, to really accept why it was she drove me so insane, maybe this never would have happened. She wouldn't have been at that party that night without anyone to keep an eye on her.

He wouldn't have had the chance to drug her and get her back to the dorm.

I'd have killed him then. He'd be dead and Romeo's arm never would have been broken. Rimmel wouldn't have been strung up like a piñata, and Missy… well, she never would have gotten the chance to act like a raging bitch with a case of inflamed butt rash.

Well, damn.

When I thought of it all like that, it was even worse. I could have stopped all this before it even got started.

Slight cool fingers slid around my forearm and gripped lightly. "Hey," Rim whispered. "Where'd you go?"

"I should've been there." The regret fell out of my mouth before I could shut it down.

"Braeden," Rimmel admonished and slid her hand down my arm to link our hands. "What happened between them was no one's fault. It was a mistake. What would you have done, burst into our room and stopped them? You and Ivy weren't even together then."

She thought I was just jealous. She thought I just didn't like the idea of my girl with someone else.

God, I wish it were that easy.

I nodded, like her words were true and made me feel better.

What was really going on inside me, the conscience-eating virus that was the truth that robbed me of sleep and sometimes logic, was my personal cross to bear. It was something I chose to carry, a solitary burden no one else could know.

The thought of Ivy knowing she was raped… I was terrified of what it might do to her.

And yeah, what it might do to us.

"She loves you so much, Braeden. I think if Missy hadn't betrayed her and put what happened all over the school social media, she'd be past it all by now. But knowing everyone knows…"

"Fuck everyone," I said vehemently.

Rimmel squeezed my hand. "But everyone includes you."

I felt like I was standing in a pitch-black room and someone suddenly turned on a flashlight. I darted a look at my very smart little sis.

She nodded knowingly.

"I think she beats herself up so much it haunts her because she feels like she betrayed us… especially you."

"I don't expect a saint," I reasoned. "Hell, I'm no choir boy."

Her voice was dry. "You definitely aren't."

I glowered at her, and she snorted but soon turned serious. "But you hate him. And he's done terrible things. And the way you reacted when you found out…"

"You mean punching out a window, shattering my phone, and calling her a slut wasn't the best way to handle the situation?" I couldn't even deliver the words with a sardonic twist. I grimaced and rubbed a hand over my face.

I hadn't even thought of things like this before. I'd only seen them from my perspective, which was angry, murderous, and closed off.

And yeah, Ivy might be having a hard time dealing because deep down, she knew something bad happened. But on the surface, was Ivy ashamed and afraid I saw her in anything but the best light?

I thought back to months ago when she dropped a bomb in the middle of the confrontation with Missy.

I felt like third best…

If I thought so low of myself, then what would everyone else think?

Fuck.

Just because I apologized and filled her bedroom with stars didn't make everything okay. I might have showed Ivy how I felt about her. I might have told her I loved her… but I never told her I didn't care she "slept" with Zach. I never told her it didn't color the way I looked at her.

"I didn't mean to make you feel worse," Rimmel said, pulling me back. "I know you love her, Braeden. Sometimes it surprises me how much." She twisted her lips into a rueful smile.

I growled like the jab pissed me off and tossed my arm around her shoulders and pulled her against me to rub my fist lightly over the top of her hair.

Rimmel shrieked. “You’re gonna mess up my hair!”

“Please, woman. We both know you haven’t even combed it.”

She laughed, and I messed up the dark mane even more.

“Stop!” she squealed.

When I relented, she pulled back. Her cheeks were bright pink and her hair looked like she stuck her finger in a light socket.

She smoothed her hands over it like that was gonna help, and I cackled.

“Talk to her.” Her voice was emphatic and cut through my moment of teasing. “You’d be surprised how much your words can smooth things out.”

Words. Those things gave me a bad taste in my mouth. Rimmel was right, though. I couldn’t lay it *all* out on the table for Ivy to see, but I could a little.

Maybe a little was all she needed to start healing.

For the first time in a while, I thought maybe everything was going to be okay.

I grabbed Rim by the shoulders and yanked her against me for a hug. She was practically in my lap, but she didn't protest. "Thanks, sis," I said into her hair.

"I've missed you too, you know," she murmured.

"I'm always here for you, Rim. That's what BBFLs are for."

"I know. But I also know you have a lot going on right now."

I pulled her away so I could look into her face. "I always got time for you."

Her lips softened and pulled into a smile.

Some movement at the edge of my vision caused my head to swing around. Ivy was hovering in the kitchen doorway, Prada tucked against her chest.

She was watching Rim and me. There wasn't a spark of jealousy in her eyes. But there was something else.

A little bit of sadness. It squeezed my chest.

I set Rimmel back in her chair and turned all my attention toward Ivy. "Hey, baby."

She blinked, clearing her expression. "Morning!" she chirped.

I stood to go to her as she bustled into the kitchen to get Giz her breakfast. The dog was dancing around at her feet, impatiently waiting.

"Coffee and donuts," Rim said, and Ivy grinned. "You know I'm all about that life."

The sadness in her eyes was gone, replaced with her usual happy demeanor. It made me incredibly tired.

And no, not because I hadn't gotten much sleep last night.

But because there was so much between us. So many feelings. So many secrets.

Ivy set the small pink bowl on the ground, and Prada dove in. I hooked a palm around her waist and pulled her up against my chest. "Hey," I breathed in her ear.

Goose bumps rose up along her arms.

She tilted her head back and looked up at me. Her eyes were looking more green than blue this morning. "Hey."

"Can we talk a minute?"

A little bit of apprehension shone on her face. "Sure."

Just as I was about to lead her out of the kitchen, the doorbell rang.

CHAPTER SEVEN

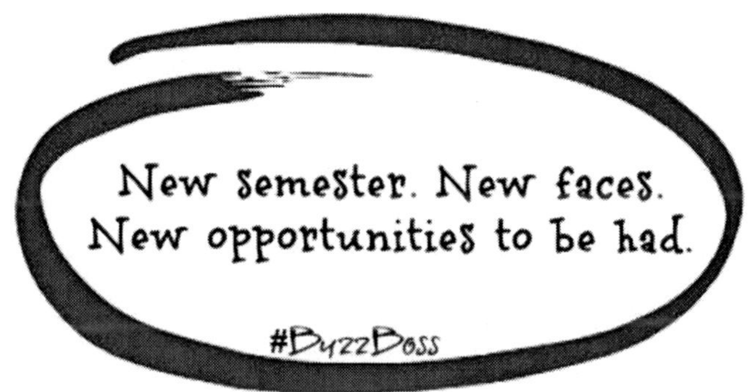

IVY

I heard her laughter from all the way upstairs.

It was a distinct laughter, not because it had a notable sound quality, but because the only time Rimmel laughed that way was when she was with Braeden.

B and Rimmel were close, a lot closer than I realized at first. I'd always known B had a soft spot for his "little sis," and she was always more inclined to defend him when I would say rude things about him when we lived at the dorm. Still, I hadn't really seen just how protective and even thoughtful he was with her.

I wasn't jealous, but perhaps I was tinged with a bit of envy.

There was nothing between Rimmel and Braeden but the kind of feelings family had for each other. It's not like I suspected or even worried something might happen between them when they were alone.

It wouldn't.

Braeden loved me. I saw it in his eyes. I felt it in his touch. I loved him. I loved him so much sometimes it made me ache. Sometimes I walked around with a pit in my belly, this hollow place that gnawed at my insides, because just the idea—the threat—of not having him in my life was too much to fathom.

And I didn't know why, but the sound of Rimmel's laughter this morning brought that feeling out in me. When I stepped into the kitchen, I saw them sitting together at the island, breakfast and mugs laid out before them. They weren't eating. He was hugging her. His arms were wrapped around her, making her look small against his chest.

Well, okay. Her hair didn't look small. I seriously needed to help her with that today. I hoped she hadn't scared anyone when she went to get donuts.

She didn't seem anxious to pull away. She appeared comforted by him and he by her. There was no barrier between them. It was as if I walked in on a moment when they were both completely open…

And that's where the envy came in.

There was a barrier between Braeden and me. I didn't know what it was. I didn't know why it was there. But I felt it.

It wasn't always present. Sometimes I could fool myself into thinking it had vanished.

But then it would reappear and bring with it that hollow ache.

I knew I was responsible. It amazed me how one night, one mistake could cast a cloud over everything. I sort of felt like I was in a constant state of anxiety, like I could never fully relax.

Sure, there were those moments when everything inside me eased. Most of those moments came when I was in bed with Braeden and his body was covering mine.

It wasn't enough.

I longed for what I saw between them. I wanted the kind of vulnerability that scared the shit out of me.

I just didn't know how to get there. Why was it so hard?

When Braeden asked to talk to me, I worried maybe he saw what I was feeling. Or maybe I'd done something to make him get out of bed so early this morning.

When the doorbell rang, I was all too eager to go answer. It was the reprieve I needed to compose myself. Composing oneself before coffee was quite the task.

I slipped away from B and out of the kitchen fast, Prada hot on my heels. Since we'd only been living here a few months, not many people rang the doorbell. Okay, no one did.

Except for a couple nosy neighbors who seriously just wanted a look at the newest Maryland Knight quarterback (Romeo).

Obviously, I expected to find another middle-aged woman on the other side of the door when I flung it open.

But it wasn't.

Surprise made me gasp when I saw who was standing there. Then the rush of familiarity hit me.

He noted my shocked expression and chuckled, the sound bringing back so many memories. His dirty-blond hair was wild, probably because he always drove with his windows down, and a pair of mirrored aviators shielded eyes I knew were blue just like mine.

"Surprise!" He spread his arms wide. The car keys in his hand dangled from one finger and made a clattering noise.

"Drew?" I stuttered.

"In the flesh." He wiggled his arms, reminding me not to leave him hanging.

I bolted out of the doorway and rushed him. His smirk turned into a full-fledged grin, displaying his seriously perfect teeth. I launched myself against him, and with an oomph, we collided, his arms closing around me like a vise.

He gave the tightest hugs I'd ever known. Almost to the point sometimes I thought I might break. But I never did. He'd never break me.

"What are you doing here?" Even though I screamed the words, they were barely audible against his chest.

"Did you really think when I got home to find you gone—moved in with some douche canoe none of us have ever met—I'd *not* come?"

I pulled out of his firm embrace and looked up to roll my eyes, making sure he saw the expression.

"Don't give me that shit, Ives," he growled. "You might have Mom and Dad wrapped, but you sure as hell don't me."

I was used to his bossy pants attitude. He'd acted like he was my ruler almost from the day I was born, so his hard tone didn't offend me at all. In fact, I barely noticed it.

But someone else did.

"Who the hell are you?" Braeden demanded from behind.

I felt my eyes widen, but before I could say anything, Drew did.

"Who the hell is asking?"

I groaned. *Oh Lord. Here comes a pissing contest.*

Braeden moved with the graceful speed he always did when he thought something needed his immediate attention. Clearly, he thought this wasn't a good situation because he slid in front of me like some kind of shield.

"I don't owe you an explanation," B spat. "You're on *my* property, ringing *my* doorbell, and talking to *my* girl like you wanna get a mouthful of my five fingers in the form of a fist." As if to punctuate his words, he flexed his hand.

Well. That escalated quickly.

"Braeden!" I admonished, stepping around him. But being the complete doody head he was, he held out his arm like he was my personal seatbelt keeping me from slamming into a windshield.

Drew was not a windshield.

He was my brother.

I grasped the granite-like side of his waist, as if I could restrain him. "You're misreading the situation."

Drew glanced at me, his brow arching way up so I could see it behind his glasses, and aimed his words at me. "This him?" He hooked a thumb toward B. "Seriously? I thought I taught you better taste."

Braeden tensed and stepped forward. I ducked under his arm and rushed between the guys, feeling like I was the mayo in a macho sandwich.

"Stop!" I pushed on B's chest, and he glanced down at me. Then I turned back to Drew. "Like you're any better," I spat.

Over my head, the two men glared at each other. I noted Rimmel hovering in the doorway, holding a wiggling Prada. I sighed.

"Braeden, this is my brother Drew. Drew, this is my boyfriend Braeden."

"Your brother," Braeden said coolly, looking over Drew again, this time with a little more interest.

"Yes. My older brother. I told you about him." I removed my hand from his chest. Now that he knew who he was, surely he would stand down.

"Funny, I haven't heard shit about you," Drew said, staring directly at Braeden.

I groaned and spun toward him. "Oh my God, Drew! Shut it!"

I turned back to Braeden, and he was looking at me, searching my face like my idiot brother's comment somehow hurt his feelings.

A lump formed in my throat.

"He's just being an ass," I said loudly. Then I quieted my voice. "Of course my family knows all about you. I have nothing but good things to say about you."

I pressed my hand into his bare chest. Braeden brushed the pad of his thumb across my lower lip, and the corner of his mouth slid up. "I know, babe." His lips brushed over my hairline, and the worry I felt eased. "Takes more than that to ruffle these guns," he said, flexing his bicep between us.

I laughed.

Behind us, Drew made a cackling sound, and I tensed, about to yell at him again.

"And who is this?" He turned his attention away from us, and I looked as he started toward Rimmel.

Rimmel stepped out of the doorway and came forward, smiling. "I'm Rimmel."

"Ahh, the roommate." Drew gave her a charming smile. "I hear you like animals. A lot of ladies think I am one."

Rimmel snorted.

Braeden practically snarled. "She's off-limits to you."

"Just me? Or everyone but the quarterback?" Drew said, winking at Rimmel.

Braeden's jaw flexed, and I squeezed his hand, silently asking him to calm down. Good Lord, why did guys have to be so territorial?

"I'm pretty sure you know the answer to that," Rimmel said, and Prada barked at him.

"Prada," Drew said and ruffled the dog's ears. "The little troublemaker." He glanced over his shoulder with a rueful smile. "Mom still misses this dog."

I still couldn't believe he was here. I hadn't seen my oldest brother since last Thanksgiving. He wasn't in town when I went home at the beginning of summer. It was true. Drew was a pain in the ass, but I loved him.

He swaggered over to my side and threw an arm around my shoulder. "What's a guy gotta do to get some coffee around here?"

"We just made some." Rimmel motioned and was the first back inside. She set Prada down, and she pranced around everyone's feet before racing back to the kitchen where her food was.

Braeden gave me one last glance, then went in ahead of us.

Drew and I started for the door, when he pulled back and looked down. "How ya doing, kid?"

"I'm good," I said generically.

"He's a real hothead, huh?" He motioned with his chin toward the direction Braeden went.

"Only when he thinks the people he loves are being threatened," I replied. Then I poked him in the stomach. "Or when people like you goad him."

He held up a hand in surrender. "I'm on my best behavior." He made an X over his heart.

That meant he most definitely wasn't.

"Drew," I sighed.

He chuckled and tugged the ends of my hair. "C'mon, Ives, I need some coffee, and I wanna see your place. Gotta report back to Mom, you know."

"I sent Mom pictures," I pointed out. "And FaceTimed her."

"Can't a guy just make sure his baby sis isn't living in the ghetto?"

I laughed. "This look like the ghetto to you?"

He glanced around the front yard and at the house. "It's pretty nice digs," he allowed and spurred us toward the door as he slid the aviators up on his head. "Now. About that boyfriend…"

I made a choking sound and halted my steps. I was dead serious when I looked into my brother's eyes. "Be nice to him, Drew. I'm not in high school anymore. I love Braeden. Like seriously. I want you two to get along."

"Like seriously?" he mocked. I swear he did the perfect imitation of a Valley girl.

I stomped on his foot, and he howled.

Prada came racing into the entryway and tried to attack the sandal on his foot.

"I'll be nice." He held up his hands. "Geez, I'm starting to feel bad for the guy. Living with you, this vicious beast, and his sister? Poor guy probably needs a couple beers."

Hah! No one said anything about Braeden thinking of Rim as his sister. He totally proved I did talk about Braeden to my family and he was only saying different to be a jerk.

When I crossed my arms over my chest to glare at him, he smiled slyly. "Damn, it's good to see ya, Ives." He pulled me back in for another one of his famous bear hugs.

I closed my eyes and relaxed against him. This had been the longest I'd ever gone without seeing him. I hadn't realized until he was standing outside just how much I missed him. Most girls were Daddy's girls.

But not me.

I was always Drew's girl.

My brother was one of the most important people in my life. Braeden was also at the very top of that list.

I just hoped my two favorite guys would get along.

CHAPTER EIGHT

BRAEDEN

I didn't need to be an art major to see this guy was a piece of work.

When I first walked around the corner and heard some guy talking to Ivy like she needed a good scolding, I almost went out swinging.

It's probably a good thing I didn't. Wouldn't want to send the guy home packing a bloody lip. That wouldn't buy me any points with Ivy's parents.

I shook my head as I poured some coffee down my throat. I'd never been the type of guy to worry about what a girl's parents would think. But Ivy changed all that. She changed so much in my world it was a wonder I didn't have whiplash.

"You know he was coming?" I said low to Rim.

She smiled and shook her head. "He seems nice, though."

I made a rude sound. "Did we just meet the same guy?"

She giggled.

My phone beeped and I held it up to glance at the text message. It was from Romeo. He got the pic I'd sent him of Rimmel. *I love that face. Coming home next weekend.*

Good. Might need backup.

Romeo replied quick. *What's up?*

Ivy's bro was on the doorstep this AM.

Douchebag?

I snickered to myself. Sometimes Rome just got things. *Possibly.*

Be strong like bull.

I laughed out loud as Ivy and Drew came into the room. *Will do.* I shot the text back and then slid the phone into my pocket.

***

"What's so funny?" Ivy asked.

"Just Rome being Rome," I said.

She went about pouring two cups of coffee while Drew made himself at home with the donut box.

"How long you staying?" I asked him.

"Braeden!" Ivy and Rimmel scolded at once.

"What?" I shrugged. "It's a legit question."

Drew polished off his donut. "Not sure yet. I'm in no hurry to leave. Haven't seen my sister in a long time."

"Where are you staying?" Ivy asked.

Drew shrugged and took the coffee she offered him. "Don't know yet. Didn't think about it. Just got home and Mom said you'd shacked up with your friends and boyfriend."

"I'm not shacking up," Ivy retorted.

"Well, how was I supposed to know that? Mom and Dad haven't even met him yet. I can't believe they just let you move in with him."

This guy was a real piece of work. I straightened off the counter, but Ivy didn't seem to need help telling big bro how it was.

"I'm an adult, Drew. I don't need their permission. But even so, they gave it. No one has a problem with my living arrangements but you."

"I didn't say I had a problem," he rebutted. "I just wanted to see for myself how you were."

"You can stay here," Rimmel offered from her seat at the island.

I gave her a *WTF* look.

"Are you sure Romeo won't mind?" Ivy asked.

"Nah. He won't care," Rimmel replied.

"I do," I chimed in.

Everyone ignored me.

"Awesome. Thanks, ladies." Drew picked up another donut and took a bite. "Nice place," he said, glancing around while chewing.

I grabbed my mug and started toward the opposite end of the island from him.

Ivy stepped into my path. I tried to give her an irritated look, but I didn't quite succeed. Her chin was tipped back, her face still free of makeup, and her hair hung like a waterfall following the curve of her back.

Thank you, she mouthed.

I reached around her back and let my fingers play in the loose ends of her hair. Her body swayed toward mine just slightly. I lowered my mouth, ignoring everyone else in the room, and kissed her softly.

It wasn't a terribly long kiss, but it was satisfying.

I hope it also showed Brother Dearest I wasn't going anywhere.

When I pulled back, I took her hand and led her around to where I was sitting and pulled her into my lap. She cradled her coffee with both hands and turned toward her brother.

Rimmel got up and set her cup in the sink. "I wish I could stay, but I have to be at the shelter in an hour."

"Girl," Ivy said, "it's gonna take me that long just to fix your hair."

Rimmel glared at me, and I grinned.

"I'm going to wash it. Maybe you can just braid it for me before I go?"

"Sure! I'll be up in a bit. I have to shower too."

When Rimmel was gone, Ivy turned back to Drew. "So what have you been up to? How was the internship?"

Drew sat back in the stool and sighed. "It went well. Dad's thrilled."

I studied him as he told Ivy about the internship he had over the summer at some big software company. Ivy's dad was some big computer programmer or something, and he was hoping at least one of his sons would follow in his footsteps. Apparently, that son was going to be Drew.

I guess he and Ivy looked somewhat alike. He had blue eyes like her (but hers were better), his hair was a darker shade of blond and cut short, almost like it had been buzzed off but was slowly growing back.

He was a big guy, not quite as big as me, but if he wanted to, he could bulk up. He was probably just under six feet and gave off the impression of a carefree surfer dude. But I knew better. This guy was not a pushover.

Part of me was glad for it; the other part of me didn't like it.

After he talked a little about his internship and how their dad was pushing him to apply at the same company he worked at, I interrupted. "So you saying you don't want to work in computers?"

Drew shrugged. "I like technology. I'm good at it. But sitting behind a desk all day doesn't seem all that appealing. I have a feeling you know what that's like."

"What makes you say that?" I asked.

"Aren't you a football player?"

"Thought you hadn't heard shit about me."

Ivy laughed.

Drew grinned. "Touché."

I grunted. "I play ball. You play?"

Drew shook his head. "Not my thing."

"What is your thing?"

Ivy seemed excited to tell me. She sat up and looked over her shoulder. "Drew likes cars!"

Interesting.

He seemed to pick up on Ivy's excitement. "You like cars?"

I shrugged one shoulder. "It's a hobby."

"Braeden does all the work on my car when it needs it."

That earned me a look of interest. "Does he?"

"I'm not having my girl driving around in a car that ain't safe."

Drew nodded thoughtfully, and something seemed to shift in the air. I'd just earned my first piece of respect from him.

Not that I cared.

"Drew fixes up cars too," Ivy said. "Did you see his car in the driveway? It's beautiful."

"Muscle cars are not beautiful, Ives," he said, exasperated.

I shook my head. I hadn't seen it. I was too busy watching him. "What kind of car is it?"

"Vintage Mustang. I restored it."

"It took him almost the whole four years of college," Ivy added.

"Sweet. I'd like to see it." Well, if the guy could restore a Mustang and keep its integrity, then he might not be so bad after all.

"That your truck in the driveway?"

"Yep."

Drew nodded.

Ivy sighed loudly. "You guys are like a pair of cavemen standing around beating your chests."

I set aside my coffee and wrapped both arms around her so her back was firmly against my front. "You love it," I whispered in her ear.

Her hand covered both of mine and she giggled. "No, but I do love you."

I kissed the side of her neck and enjoyed the slight way she shivered.

"So what do you guys have planned today?" Drew asked.

"I don't think anything. It's our last free day 'til classes start."

"Sweet," Drew said around a yawn.

"Did you drive straight through to get here?" Ivy asked.

He nodded. "Yeah, I might crash for a bit."

That was a long-ass drive to make alone, from North Carolina all the way to Maryland.

"I'll get the extra room ready for you."

"I get a room?"

"Of course!" she said.

From upstairs, Rimmel called down to Ivy. She jumped up from my lap. "I gotta go help her with her hair. Be right back." She leaned around and pressed a quick kiss to my mouth and whispered, "Be nice," before rushing out of the room, Prada chasing along after her.

"You drove a long way just to check me out," I said, blunt.

"Judging from the way your hackles rose when I was flirting with Rimmel, I think you'd do the same for her."

"Flirt with her again and I'll kick your ass." I meant it.

"Don't think I won't do the same for my sister."

I sorely wanted to point out I'd done way more with Ivy than flirt. But I wasn't about to kiss and tell; there was no way in hell I would disrespect Ivy like that. "You don't need to worry about Ivy. I'll make sure she's taken care of."

Drew studied me like he had something to say. So I called him out. "Just say it."

"Something's off with my sister. She might not say it, but I know. She fed our parents some lame excuse about being all stressed about finals last semester, but I don't buy it. Ivy doesn't stress about tests. And then I got home to find her moved out and in with you."

"You haven't seen her in a while. Maybe you're reading her wrong." He wasn't reading her wrong.

"Maybe you're lying to my face." Drew challenged.

"End of last semester was hard on her. Someone started some rumors. Made it tough," I said, keeping my words close.

"Thought this was college," Drew muttered.

"Have you met women?" I cracked. "They're vicious."

"Word." Drew agreed. Then he glanced at me. "Look, I know Ivy's outgoing and quick to throw out a sarcastic line, but that's all on the surface. She was sheltered growing up. She's the only girl out of three kids. We watched out for her. We protected her. She didn't have a lot of freedom in North Carolina because one of us was always there, watching…"

I swallowed thickly. I knew she posed as the party girl. She acted the way she thought she should to fit in here. I knew she had a big family. I knew her parents were strict. But damn if hearing all this from her brother didn't make everything she'd been through worse.

It also explained a lot of how this could happen. How it could happen to a lot of girls. They just didn't think about it. Or they didn't understand people could be so calculating and cold. They hadn't been taken advantage of before, so they had no idea what the signs were when it was happening…

Until it was too late.

"Look." My voice was hoarse and I cleared my throat. "I might not have looked hard enough when I first met her, but that's since changed. I know underneath her blond hair, cute-ass clothes, and smile, she has the heart of a marshmallow. I'll do anything." I paused for effect and stared him in the eye. "To make sure no one hurts her again."

Drew nodded. "I believe you." He ruined the words with a smirk. "But you won't mind if I stay for a while? Another set of eyes on her wouldn't hurt."

Unless he saw the things I didn't want anyone else to see.

"It's cool," I said. "But we're busy tonight. I got plans."

"What kind of plans?"

"Plans that only she needs to be privy to." I might have decided he wasn't the giant jerkwad I originally thought, but that didn't mean he needed to know my business.

"Dinner?" he bargained.

I nodded once and stood. "Sure. Dinner. But after that, she's mine for the night."

CHAPTER NINE

IVY

He said he had something planned.

A surprise.

Braeden was good at surprises, at planning things.

Maybe that was the biggest surprise of all.

He totally wasn't the kind of guy anyone would think of as the type to make big gestures.

But I had a room full of stars that said otherwise.

I had no idea what to expect. After Rimmel left for the shelter and Drew was snoring in the guest room, he kissed me and said he'd see me later.

The entire time I was in the shower, I wondered if maybe it had something to do with whatever he wanted to talk to me about before Drew showed up. I hoped whatever it was wouldn't make the barrier I felt between us stronger.

The truth was I needed Braeden. I needed the connection between us. I needed the feeling of being safe I always had when I was with him.

After my shower, I took my time getting dressed and doing my hair. Drew was asleep, and Prada was attacking a brand new chew toy. I wasn't sure what B had in mind for tonight, but I knew whatever it was wouldn't be fancy.

Braeden wasn't a fancy type of guy. Whatever he had planned would be a product of who he was, and it would be genuine.

I settled on a pair of destructed white jeans that cuffed at the ankles. On top, I added a loose A-line tank top in a silky soft material that floated around my waist and hips when I moved. It was in a graphic turquoise leopard pattern. For my feet, I found a pair of pale-pink wedges and set them by the door.

I left my hair down but curled it in big, loose waves. It had grown over the summer and now fell past my bra strap. I kept my makeup simple, a natural glam look with glowing skin and eyes with a little bit of sparkle. Instead of perfume, I smoothed on some body lotion in a blackberry mojito scent, and I piled a few stackable bracelets on my wrist. The only other jewelry I wore was the silver star necklace B gave me. I never took it off. The low neckline of the tank showcased the gift perfectly.

Braeden got home a little while after that while Drew and I were sitting in the living room, catching up on everything since we'd seen each other last. When Rimmel got home, we ordered some takeout (big, fresh salads and a few pizzas), and the four of us sat around eating and joking.

It wasn't until the sun had gone down and the sky was dark that Braeden reached for my hand. I thought Drew might be upset about us leaving on his first night here, but he didn't seem to mind at all. In fact, he yawned loudly and said he was going back to bed.

Braeden drove for a while, turning on roads I'd never traveled before. When we were about forty-five minutes away from campus, he slowed and turned onto a road I never would have seen had I been driving.

It was a one-lane road that made a path through a bunch of trees. It went up and curved around the hill, seemingly without end.

I was a North Carolina girl. I grew up near the mountains, so this wasn't anything new to me. But it was the first time I'd been somewhere like this in Maryland. I stared attentively out the window as we passed clearings and trees, even a few homes, until finally the road leveled off and straightened.

Out the windshield, a sweeping view literally spread out before us. It was like we were on the edge of a precipice that overlooked a valley of trees rising up to never-ending mountains. It was hard to appreciate the view fully with just the light from the headlights and the moon, but what I could see was beautiful, and I knew in daylight, it would be breathtaking.

"What is this place?" I asked, my voice reverent.

He drove slowly as he spoke. "We used to come here as teenagers to go mudding or just hang out. Lots of people came here to park."

His teeth glinted in the dark, and with the glow of the dash, I could see his eyebrows wag in suggestion.

I laughed. "You brought me parking?"

"Something like that."

A few minutes later, the truck slowed even more and he pulled to the side of the road, on the edge of a large clearing. "Stay here a sec," he instructed once the truck was in park.

"Where are you going?" Suddenly, whatever he had planned didn't seem like such a fun idea.

Braeden slid across the seat and brought his body right up against mine. "I'm not going far, baby." His voice was as smooth as dark chocolate and soft like cotton. "Just wait here, 'kay? I'll keep you safe."

"'Kay," I whispered, lifting my fingers to brush over the side of his jaw. He caught my hand and kissed it.

I was left in a little bubble of warmth and watched him walk around to the bed of the truck. The sound of the tailgate being released and the jolt of him jumping into the bed made me smile.

Braeden had totally brought me parking.

A few minutes later, the passenger-side door opened and his hand appeared in front of me. Without hesitation, I placed mine in his and allowed him to guide me out of the cab.

It was incredibly dark, but he seemed to know exactly where to step. With his arm around my waist, I made it to the back of the truck. B's arm left me and he leapt up into the back.

Seconds later, the space illuminated.

Once again, Braeden surprised me.

The entire bed of the truck was filled with blankets and pillows. It was layered with a thick comforter, blankets that looked filled with down, and ones that appeared so soft my hand flexed with the desire to stoke them.

There had to be at least fifteen pillows. Some were huge and fluffy, while others were smaller and round.

Everything was colorful, not like circus colors, but muted, soft ones.

Braeden sat in the center holding an electric lantern. It cast an amber glow over everything, creating an intimate space.

"You did all this?"

"I wanted some alone time with my girl."

My stomach turned over and danced with butterflies. He set the lantern off to the side, next to a bottle of wine and a couple plastic cups.

I smiled.

He leapt down and practically lifted me into the bed. The second I was there, I kicked off my wedges and buried my feet into the piles of blankets.

"This is amazing, Braeden."

The air was crisp and cool. Technically, it was still summer, but up here on the mountain and without any trace of the sun, there was a definite bite of autumn in the air. The weather was going to start cooling down fast, but tonight it was perfect.

I breathed in deep and lifted my chin a little to let the air caress my cheeks. I missed this, being out in the open, surrounded by nature. Everything seemed a lot smaller when you stood in such a sprawling space, and oddly, it was comforting.

Braeden flipped back the edge of some blankets and sank in the center, crooking a finger in my direction. I sank down right beside him and leaned back against the piles of pillows to gaze up at the sky.

"The sky is filled with stars," I whispered.

Braeden tucked the blankets around us and pulled me into his chest. "They're our stars, Blondie."

I leaned back into him and sighed. "I like that."

"Everything seems easier for us when we're under the stars. Ever notice that?"

"Yeah, I have."

"You know why?" His voice was a mere rumble against my ear. I felt his breath with every syllable he spoke, like my personal lullaby.

"Why?" I snuggled in closer against him, and his arm tightened around my waist.

"Because the stars don't have rules. Anything goes out here beneath them. There is no right or wrong. They twinkle and shine no matter what. The stars see everything, baby. They see us for exactly who we are."

"And who are we right now, Braeden?" I whispered.

Gently, he lifted my chin so his eyes could connect with mine.

"We're two people drifting, like a boat without its oar. I don't want to drift anymore, Ivy. I want to drop anchor. I want to make sure you don't drift away from me."

"I'm sorry." I tried to look away, but he wouldn't let me. Instead, he straightened and swung around so he was facing me.

"I'm the one who's sorry. Can you forgive me, baby?"

I felt my nose wrinkle and my brows draw down. I sank back into the pillows, almost like they were a net that caught me from the shock of his apology.

"Why on earth would you apologize to me?"

A soft breeze floated through the night, and without breaking his gaze on my face, he reached behind him and tugged a furry blanket over my lap and tucked it around my legs and arms.

"I saw the look in your eyes this morning. When you walked in and saw me and Rimmel in the kitchen."

I started to shake my head, to deny, deny, deny. I wasn't going to be *that* girl. I was not going to be the kind who got upset when her boyfriend showed affection to another girl—to his family. I was sorely regretful he'd caught any look at all in my eyes. I should have worked harder to hide it. To lock it down.

I was incredibly tired of hiding things. For some reason, it seemed like so much was hidden lately. Even my own feelings seemed to hide from me.

He grasped my hand and gave it a squeeze. "Don't do that. Don't pretend with me. I wanna know everything. Remember, out here there are no rules. You can say whatever you want."

I relented and nodded once.

"Does it bother you to see me with Rim?"

"No!" I said quickly. "I swear it doesn't. I totally understand the whole brother/sister bond. I have it with Drew."

"That guy is a piece of work," B muttered.

"He's my brother." I defended.

"He loves you so he must be pretty decent."

I rolled my eyes.

"So," he began, bringing back the conversation. "What was it this morning?"

I sighed and glanced up at the stars, hoping they would lend me some strength. "I could just feel how close you two are. How you were so open with each other. I guess it made me sad. I want that with you."

"I thought we had that." He glanced down at our joined hands. "It's not so easy, though, is it?"

That hollow feeling I sometimes got was threatening. I tried to push it away. I wouldn't let it in. Not here. Not tonight.

I looked around at the blankets, the pillows, the wine. The stars overhead were brilliant, and B was holding my hand. It might not be easy with Braeden (with any relationship), but that didn't mean what we had wasn't good.

Things with B were good. *Better* than good.

He was all I ever really wanted. And easy or not, he was worth the struggle.

"I realized something today, something I never said but should have." As he spoke, his thumb stroked over the back of my hand. "Something I think is creating this unidentifiable, unspoken thing between us." He motioned between our bodies with his hand, as if to punctuate his point. "Something that's making it hard for you to move past *that night*."

My breath caught and everything inside me stilled. I didn't want to talk about Zach. I didn't want to drag him into this beautiful moment. I started shaking my head, shoving away the painful thoughts, the guilt and the self-loathing.

Braeden reached out and grasped my hips, sliding me so I sat so close our knees bumped. "It's okay, baby. I know you're scared to talk about it and to hear what I have to say, but I swear on every star up in that sky tonight, nothing is gonna change how much I love you."

Tears threatened at the backs of my eyes. My chest squeezed with unnamed emotion. I drew in a deep breath and nodded.

"I never told you. I don't care."

It's a good thing he already said how much he loved me, or that statement might have damaged my ego. "Honey, your grand gestures can make a girl swoon, but we really need to work on those words," I told him with a patient tone while wearing a slight grimace.

His teeth glowed bright against the dark backdrop of night when he smiled. "We've already established I'm not real good at explaining how I feel."

I slid my fingers between his and linked our hands. “As long as whatever you tell me is the truth, then I don’t care how ugly it sounds.”

I thought the jab would make him laugh. Or at least result in a quick comeback. Silence stretched between us, more eerie than anything I might hear rustling in the nearby trees.

It scared me.

“Braeden?” My voice was tentative.

“I’ve never done this before.” The strain in his words was undeniable. It didn’t ease any of my disruptive feelings. “I’ve never been in a relationship. I’ve never been in love.”

“You’re my first love too.”

He made sound, a cross between a groan and a growl, and cupped my face to stare at me intently. “You’re not my first, Ivy. You’re my *only*. There’s never gonna be another you.”

I bit my lower lip. So badly I wanted to believe that. So irrevocably did I want his heart and his future. But there was this little voice deep in my head that whispered I wasn’t good enough.

“Listen to me,” he intoned, shaking me gently.

I fixed my eyes on his face.

"I don't care that you slept with him. It doesn't in any way, shape, or form control the way I see you. Fuck, it isn't even a factor. I should have told you that months ago. I should have made sure you knew in my eyes…" He picked up my hand and laid it against his chest. The strong beat beneath my palm seemed to accentuate his words. "In my heart, you are on a level no one else will ever reach."

"Braeden…" A tear tracked down my cheek, followed by another. Lord knows I wasn't proud of that night. It was honestly the biggest regret of my life. The self-loathing I felt knowing I allowed Zach to touch my body chipped away at pieces of me until it felt like I might shatter at any moment.

And yes, I worried maybe Braeden thought less of me. I worried everyone on campus looked at me and saw a slut.

I wasn't going to worry anymore.

"It doesn't matter who came before me as long as I'm your last." He continued, the pads of his thumbs brushing away my tears. Then he closed the distance between us and kissed me tenderly.

Channing Tatum himself could show up at my door (he's so totally hot) and it wouldn't matter.

Braeden owned me.

He would until the day I died.

CHAPTER TEN

BRAEDEN

As long as whatever you tell me is the truth, then I don't care how ugly it sounds.

Were her words a sign?

A sign that everything I'd done to protect the girl I loved more than my own life was wrong?

Was my protection getting in the way of us being as close as two people could be?

I brought Ivy out here so we could talk, so we could address the stuff we neglected to talk about, but stuff that was there nonetheless.

I thought the stars, the blankets, the pillows, and cool night air would make it easier. I guess in some ways, it did. It sure as hell bought me a lot of brownie points in the romance department. When I lit up that lantern and watched her eyes round at everything I'd done, my inner jock hollered, *Touchdown!* Because clearly, Blondie liked what she saw.

What I said to her was the truth. I didn't judge her about what happened with Zach. Yeah, I was pissed off and hurt when I first found out, and I experienced an unfortunate case of diarrhea of the mouth, but I never thought badly of her.

Then I found out it wasn't consensual. I found out it was rape.

How does a man digest that shit? To know the most vile, horrific act was done to the woman he loved?

My God, when would the abuse toward women ever end? It seemed like every single woman in my life was the victim of a man.

My mother, Rimmel, Ivy.

To see how it ripped them apart, to watch them try and hold it together, was fucking hard as shit. It might be the hardest thing I'd ever had to witness.

* * *

I wasn't able to help my mother. I was too young to step in and stop my father from beating her. And when he did, he'd hurl hurtful words at her that seemed more painful than any punch, kick, or slap could ever be.

I'd likely hear those words in the back of my mind forever.

I wasn't able to stop the pain Rimmel endured from her own family, from Zach, and from the people who wanted revenge against her father. And she had Romeo, my best friend, a man I knew without a doubt would shelter her as best he could.

But who did Ivy have?

She was a victim who didn't even know she was.

I could protect her. I could make sure her pain didn't have to be any deeper than it already was.

And that's why I hid the truth. That's why I beat myself up on a daily basis, wondering if the choice I made was right.

"Is that wine I see over there?" Ivy asked, sniffling a little.

She cried when I told her I didn't care about Zach. Her tears were just proof that those were words she needed to hear.

"Girl, you know I ain't gonna drive out to the middle of nowhere for some private time without a bottle of the good stuff," I drawled and leaned back so I could snag the bottle.

She giggled. "So what kind of *good stuff* is that?"

"Fuck if I know." I shrugged. "I never drink wine. You know this. I got it from one of the guys on the team."

"Let me see." Ivy held out her hand. Her lips were pursed, but I could see her trying hard not to laugh.

I surrendered the bottle so she could pull it into her lap and turn the label around to face her.

Her laugh burst out almost immediately, and she clutched the bottle against her chest as a bad case of the giggles rocked her body.

I frowned. "What the hell's so funny?"

Ivy laughed even harder, like me not knowing was somehow the cherry on top.

"Blondie," I growled.

She sat up and wiped a tear out of her eye and cleared her throat. Amusement shone in her eyes when she turned the label around to face me.

"What?" I shrugged.

"It's Boone's Farm."

"Is that like a bad brand or something?"

"Well, we are sort of in a cornfield. It's actually totes appropriate."

"*Totes* what?" What the fuck was she talking about?

Her teeth flashed white, and she practically hugged the bottle. "Boone's Farm I guess is technically a wine. I wouldn't necessarily call it the good stuff."

"Why?" I asked dubiously.

"I can't believe you've never heard of this stuff. Every high school girl drinks this."

"I'm not a high school girl," I pointed out, sort of disgruntled yet slightly amused.

"Well, surely you went to high school parties. You know the ones where the girls all acted super tipsy even though they smelled like cherry lip-gloss but swore they were drunk."

I grinned. "Yeah, I remember those days."

Ivy smacked me.

"What?" I demanded. "You asked."

"This has barely any alcohol in it." She snickered. "I didn't even know they still made this. Where did you even get it?"

Okay, so did me bringing this totally amusing girl drink take away any bonus points I had racked up? Or was she secretly pleased I had the shit?

"I told ya. I got it from one of the guys on the team. I told him I needed something other than beer that my girl would like." I glanced down at the bottle. "It's pink. You like pink. I thought it was like that blush-colored wine women drink."

Ivy laughed again. She pointed to the label. "It's watermelon flavored."

I squinted at the label. It said watermelon. I scoffed. "It can't be that bad. Hand it over."

She did, and I unscrewed the cap (yet another clue that perhaps this was some cheap-ass shit) and poured it in the two plastic cups Ivy held out.

I took one of the cups and sniffed the contents. It smelled like some bad air freshener you could buy at Wal-Mart that promised to make your car smell great, when what it actually did was make you nauseous. “Fruity.”

Ivy grinned and took a sip. Her eyes sparkled with mischief. “Try it.”

Oh, what the hell? I’d already forgone my manhood to drink Smurf Balls; this pink shit couldn’t possibly be any worse.

I took a drink, letting the flavor spill across my tongue. I pulled it back and looked down.

Was this supposed to be alcohol or soda?

I guess I could see why they named it watermelon… Okay, no I couldn’t. It didn’t taste like watermelon at all.

It tasted like a giant Jolly Rancher.

“Well?” Ivy asked.

“Too much of this shit might give us diabetes,” I quipped. “I mean, seriously. Did you want some wine with your sugar?”

“Aww, but it’s pink wine!”

I made a rude sound. “The shit I do for you, woman.”

Ivy drank some more of it. I made a face, but oddly, I was thinking about taking another sip too.

"I kinda like it," she confided.

"Drink up." I held out my hand like it was a formal invite.

"You just want me to get drunk so you can take advantage of me," she teased.

My body jerked. "That's not fucking funny." My voice was hard and loud.

Ivy sucked in a breath and straightened. All traces of fun were wiped from her features. "I was just kidding. There's like three percent alcohol in this. I wouldn't even be drunk if I had the entire bottle."

I swore under my breath and rubbed a hand over my hair. "I'm sorry. I guess just the suggestion I would ever do something like that to you makes me sick."

She tucked the cup in her lap and reached out with both hands, laying them on my knees. "I know you wouldn't, B. I feel safer with you than anyone I've ever met. Even Drew."

I blew out a breath and drank some of the Kool-Aid masquerading as wine.

"You mean that?" I asked. For some reason, that statement meant a lot to me. Almost as much as when she told me she loved me for the first time.

It was like it somehow validated everything I'd done.

"I swear on every single star in the sky," she spoke, echoing my own words back to me. "I know you would never hurt me, Braeden James Walker. I am safe with you."

"Bring those fine-ass lips over here, woman." I opened up one arm. She leaned over, and I tugged her into my lap. She laughed, but I caught the sound with my lips and used my tongue to claim the rest.

She tasted sweet and her tongue was cool. I sucked it farther into my mouth, deepening our kiss. The cup in my hand made it hard to touch her the way I wanted, so I tossed it over the side of the truck. It landed with a barely audibly thud on the grass below.

My hands delved deep into the soft strands of her long hair and got lost, kneading in farther until the tips of my fingers caressed her scalp.

She made a purring sound that vibrated both our tongues, and I groaned.

She pulled back, and my eyes narrowed. I wasn't done kissing the shit out of her yet. I followed, trying to pull her back, but she shook her head.

"We came here to talk."

"We talked." My voice was strained. "And now our bodies want to have a conversation."

Her smile was slow, and it made my loins tighten. "My body has lots to say to you."

A groan ripped from deep in my throat. I leaned toward her again, but she leaned away.

"But I actually do have something I want to talk to you about. And judging from the way you almost chewed off my head a minute ago, it's something we should talk about."

Have I mentioned I hate words?

I do. Like really.

Still, this was the main reason I brought her out here (I mean, yes, of course I planned on some sex; that's why I brought so many blankets), so it seemed I should listen to what she had to say.

"That was about your father, wasn't it?"

All thought of hanky panky time went flying off into the distance.

"Ivy," I warned. My father wasn't a subject I liked to talk about.

She held her ground. "You made me talk about *him* when I didn't want to. And you know what?"

"What?"

"I actually feel better."

"I'm glad, baby." My voice gentled.

"So now we're gonna talk about this. And then you'll feel better."

Not bloody likely. "There's nothing to say, Blondie. My father is scum. He abused my mother half my life until he almost killed her. Now he's dying and he thinks death should somehow earn him a forgiveness card."

"So you don't plan on talking to him at all?" she asked.

"No," I growled.

"I think you're wrong."

I blinked. "What?"

She crossed her arms over her chest. "You heard me."

"Whose side are you on?"

"Yours. Even when you're being a giant doody head and are wrong."

"Did you just call me a giant doody head?"

She nodded. "Mm-hmm." I opened my mouth, but she lifted her hand. "Why are you so afraid to talk to him, Braeden?"

"I'm not," I ground out. I was getting all mixed up inside. The darkness and anger deep down was getting all riled up. I didn't like it. Not at all.

"Is it because you're afraid that if you do—"

I cut her off. "I will not ever forgive him."

Her face gentled even though my tone was angry and slightly mean. "That isn't what I was going to say. I don't think he deserves your forgiveness, B."

"You don't?" Just hearing her say that calmed me down.

"No. I don't. But I do think you're afraid if you talk to him face to face, you might see some things in him that remind you of yourself."

Her words hit their mark.

I didn't need to sit down beside him to see those things. Sometimes when I looked in the mirror, he was all I saw.

"You're nothing like him," she vowed.

"How do you know?" I asked, the words the closest I'd ever come to saying out loud my biggest fear. "You've never met him."

"I don't need to meet him because I know you. You aren't capable of that type of violence. You don't have that mean streak in you."

"Yes, I am. I do."

She tilted her head. "Maybe," she allowed.

Her honesty only helped me. I admired that she didn't try to sugarcoat everything she said.

"But those parts of you only surface when you feel like you have something or someone to *protect.* You don't use those qualities against people, Braeden. You don't use them to tear people down. You use them to guard people you love."

She made me sound like some comic book character.

"I'm no hero, Ivy."

"No, you aren't. You drink bad wine, cuss too much, and let very few people in."

"A guy gets one bad bottle of wine…" I muttered. "And he never lives it down."

"You're real. You have real feelings, real emotions, and the things you do reflect that. I'd take you over a hero any day. Even Spider-Man."

I made a scoffing sound. "Superman would kick Spidey's ass."

She gasped. "Bad wine and bad taste in superheroes? You're just pushing it now."

I laughed. "Honestly, sometimes I wonder if I'll regret not talking to him before he dies. Mom says I will. She thinks I need closure."

"Do you?"

"I don't know. Maybe."

"Talking to him doesn't mean forgiving him," she pointed out.

Such a simple statement, but it held so much power.

"No?"

She shook her head. "You do it for you. Not for him. Maybe just telling him you can't accept what he did all those years ago will help you close that door."

Maybe she was right.

All this time, I was thinking if I talked to my father, it would be because he asked me to. I never thought about it being something I would do for myself.

And yeah, maybe that's what Mom was trying to say all those times she urged me call him. But she was too close to the situation. Maybe this was something I needed to hear from someone else, like Ivy.

"I'm gonna tuck that right in here." I tapped on my head. "Think on it some."

She looked insanely pleased with herself. I pulled the cup out of her lap and tossed it over the side to join mine. "Talking's over."

Gently, I pushed her back against the pillows and leaned into her.

"Tell me yes, Ivy," I intoned, hovering my lips mere centimeters above hers.

"Yes," she whispered.

It was all I needed to hear.

CHAPTER ELEVEN

IVY

His need seemed urgent.

His hands were anything but.

I was pressed into the pillows, cushioning my body like they were made just for me. Slowly he kissed me, dragging his mouth down the side of my neck and latching onto that sweet spot, the one that always made me shiver.

I didn't even think about the sounds I made as he licked and sucked because I was too caught up in the feel of his mouth.

When at last he continued down along my collarbone to nip at my shoulder, my fingers were digging into his flesh, impatiently demanding more.

He chuckled and pulled back, taking his weight off mine and reaching for each blanket, peeling away the layers one by one with aching tenderness, like he was unwrapping a gift.

When I was lying there with nothing covering me, he pulled my hand so I could sit up. With ease, my tank top was lifted off my body and tossed aside. My bra joined the fabric, and the cool night air brushed against my bare skin.

If my nipples weren't already hard, they would have puckered instantly.

B pushed me back down and fastened his lips around one of my breasts. He didn't go directly for the bud in the center. Instead, he sucked and kneaded the flesh around it.

My back arched, lifting myself up and offering him even greater access. One hand cupped the fullness to hold it in place so he could assault it even more with slow and gratifying kisses.

Only when I started to shake did he suck the nipple deep into his mouth.

I moaned loudly, and he repeated the action.

I reached for him. My fingers met shirt and not skin.

I tugged at the fabric because it was in the way. He left my breast long enough to rip the shirt over his head and toss it aside. Then he was back, lavishing the same amount of unhurried attention on the other breast.

I spread my legs so he could settle between my thighs. Both of us were still wearing jeans, but I wrapped my legs around him anyway as his lips trailed down my stomach and around my navel.

The button on my jeans gave way easily, and he dipped his fingertips in the waistband, delving beneath my panties.

I gasped at just the skin-on-skin contact and looked up at the night sky.

Soon, I was completely naked, nothing but the soft blanket at my back. Braeden knelt between my legs and stared down at me. I couldn't make out his expression in the dark, but the way he touched me said it all.

I'd never had anyone be so attentive, so tender and gentle.

I gave myself to him totally, offering him almost anything he could want. But he never took advantage of me. When I sat up to reach for him, he sank down and mumbled incoherent words that only urged me on.

He liked when I dragged my nails up the inside of his thigh.

He liked when I nipped at the spot just below his ear.

He especially liked when I took him deep into my throat and lightly pinched his nipple at the same time.

I kissed and sucked until he swore and gently lifted me aside. I reached for his cock, wanting to guide it toward my entrance, but he shook his head.

"Not yet," he murmured and lowered his mouth to my inner thigh.

He licked upward, almost to my most private place, but then he drew back.

I gasped.

"Is this okay, baby? Can I touch you here?"

"If you don't, I'll cry."

He laughed, the sound hoarse. "Just tell me if you want me to stop."

"I'm never gonna want you to stop."

He used two fingers and slid them inside my opening. My knees fell open and a sigh took over my body. As his fingers worked, he sucked gently at the already swollen bud.

When his tongue started lapping and his fingers moved a little faster, I gasped and arched up. He paused, and I urged him on. Seconds after he started up again, I splintered into a thousand pieces. It was like Fourth of July inside my body; everything exploded into a finale of lights.

I was still floating from the pleasure when he came over me. I felt his insistent length at my opening, and I sighed and tilted closer.

With a groan, he slid inside me.

Both of us cried out. Braeden's body went rigid.

"Fuck," he whispered into my ear. "You're so warm and slick."

In response, I tightened my walls around him, flexing against his cock. He made a sputtering sound and then slid out, only to delve right back in.

It felt so good. It felt so right.

I clutched him against me and swiveled my hips. "You feel incredible," I murmured.

He pumped his hips again, his eyes going wide. He propped himself up on his hands and stared down at me.

"Shit," he ground out, like speaking was hard. "I forgot to wrap it."

That explained why this time felt a little different, a little more raw.

"It's okay," I said as he pulled out. I could tell he was upset. "I'm not mad. I'm on the pill."

"It's not okay," he spat, sitting back and reaching for his jeans. "I got so caught up in you that I freaking forgot a condom."

I sat up and pressed my hand to his lower back. "I've been tested. You don't have to worry about anything."

He laughed.

He actually threw back his head and laughed.

"What?" I grumbled. Some of the sex-induced bliss I was feeling floated away.

He turned back with a condom clutched in his fist. "I know you're clean, baby. I don't care about me. I care about you. About respecting you."

"But I'm not upset."

"I know you aren't, and I love the shit out of you for it. But when we go bareback, I want it to be something you agree to when you aren't under the spell of my touch."

I opened my mouth to say something sarcastic, but he stopped me. His hand flattened on my shoulder and pushed me back down. "Now, baby," he cajoled. "I'm just as deep under your spell too. It's the reason I forgot."

He ripped open the foil packet and slid it down over his still-rigid length.

"Have you done that with lots of girls?" I asked, suddenly self-conscious.

Braeden lowered himself so the front of our bodies touched completely. He brushed the hair away from my face and kissed me. "Never."

My eyes popped open.

He nodded. Before I could say anything else, he kissed me at the very same moment his length slid home.

Braeden was so gentle. He was so thoughtful. It almost seemed the longer we were together, the more careful he became.

I'd always thought maybe it was the other way around. That a guy would be more careful in the beginning until he really got to know a girl.

The thought didn't last very long because pleasure took over all thought. Only after, when I was tucked into his side, securely in his arms, did I think about the way he always asked my permission, how he was never rough, and how he spoke about always wanting to respect me.

He loved me. Irrevocably.

But was there something more?

CHAPTER TWELVE

BRAEDEN

"Can I ask you something?"

That question was pretty much the kiss of death for a guy. There was no good conversation that began with those words.

But if I said no, all hell would break loose.

If I said yes, then I'd have to think very, very carefully about whatever answer I needed to give.

There was also another factor here: the after sex fog.

It was a real thing. Oh boy, was it ever. Ask any man and he'll agree. See, there's a window of time in the minutes after a man has awesome fucking sex that he's at his most vulnerable.

A time when his body is in a relaxed, blissful state. One might compare it to being high, just not the chemically induced kind. The orgasm kind. It's during this window when a man is so satisfied he doesn't think before he responds.

Well, that and he's pretty fucking pleased with the woman in his arms.

I was currently suffering from ASF. My brain didn't even warn me I was stepping into dangerous territory.

"Hmmm?" I answered, dragging my fingertips up the length of her spine.

Ivy moved slightly and the blond strands of her hair tickled my bare chest. "You're always very gentle with me."

"Precious things should be handled gently."

And that is *exactly* what I'm talking about. I, Braeden J. Walker, was no good with words. But those were some mighty pretty ones. I would get the credit for saying them; however, those words weren't courtesy of me.

It was the after sex fog.

I meant them. No truer words had been spoken. But if I'd been in my right mind, I wouldn't have been able to say such a thing so eloquently.

"Is that all it is?" she asked.

Something inside me shouted a warning.

"Wait," I said, sitting up slightly to lean against the bulkhead. "What are we talking about right now?"

Ivy flattened her palm over my chest and propped her chin on top. "The first couple times we had sex felt a little different."

The fog blew away. Like it literally disappeared. "Are you saying you aren't satisfied… in bed?" I had to practically croak out the words. It was blasphemy! I was a *legend* in bed.

Ivy's gorgeous cerulean eyes widened and she sat up with a gasp. "No!" The tops of her porcelain cheeks turned bright pink, and she tugged the blanket up around her bare skin.

I wrapped an arm around her, pulling her against my chest. "Tell me you like my cock."

A laugh bubbled out of her chest. "I am not saying that."

"Why the hell not?" I demanded.

Ivy stretched up and kissed the corner of my mouth. "You're the best I've ever had, Braeden. I didn't even know it could feel like this between two people."

I studied her.

A slow smile split her lips. It made me want to kiss her.

But I had to stand firm.

Giggling, she pushed away and sat crossed-legged at my side. Her pinky finger appeared in front of my nose.

"Ivy." I mock-gasped and pressed a hand to my chest. "*No*, I will *not* pull your finger."

She hit me in the head with a pillow as I guffawed.

"Pinky swear!" she demanded once I chucked the pillow away.

A pinky swear to girls was the equivalent of a fist bump for guys. I couldn't leave my girl hanging, so I wrapped my pinky around hers.

As she shook our hands, she vowed, "My best. My last. My only."

If I were stranded on an island somewhere, with no food and no water, it wouldn't matter. I could live off those words.

Pulling on our joined fingers, she fell forward and I kissed her. "I like that," I whispered against her lips.

She was slow to sit up, but when she did, I saw the question in her eyes. "It was rougher the first couple times, more…" I watched her search for the word she wanted. "Urgent."

So she noticed.

She noticed the *before* and *after*.

I guess I should have known this would happen. Ivy was more perceptive than people gave her credit for.

Caressing the top of her cheekbone with my thumb, I replied, "It was different, baby. There's a difference between having sex and making love. Our first few times was sex, but everything afterward is love."

Her eyes softened. I let out a silent breath. I made it through the questions without any injury.

"Sometimes I feel like you're scared to touch me."

So softly spoken yet so incredibly loud.

Just like a true battle. Just when a man thinks he's home free and a landmine goes off.

"Ah, baby." I pushed up and pulled her into my lap. I breathed in the scent of her hair, felt the familiar weight of her in my lap. "I'm not scared to touch you."

I didn't know what to say. This was a time words couldn't fail me. She needed them; she needed reassurance. The only way I could give her that was to reach deep.

"I've never been in love before. You stir emotion in me I didn't know was there. The thought of hurting you in any way makes me physically ill. I would die for you, baby. I would kill for you. I would give you the last breath in my body just to give you another heartbeat of life. Of course I'm going to be careful when I touch you. You're basically my beating heart walking around outside my chest."

The sheen of tears in her eyes was unmistakable. I watched with bated breath as she chewed her lower lip.

Well, shit.

Clearly, when I reached deep, that's what I unearthed. Shit. And now she was crying.

"Don't cry." I spoke softly as I wiped a tear trailing over her cheek.

"I seriously love you." The words came out in a cross between a moan and a wail. "That was so beautiful."

She collapsed against me, and I smiled into her hair. I guess it wasn't shit after all. Ivy sniffled, and I couldn't stop the laugh escaping my chest.

"Don't laugh at me!" She poked me in the ribs.

"Let me hold you," I scolded her, even though it didn't hurt at all.

Exhaling, she surrendered. Her breathing turned even and deep after a while. I still held her close.

Even though everything I said tonight was the truth, I hadn't admitted it all.

I used a beautiful truth to conceal an ugly lie.

The lies weren't getting any easier to tell.

In fact, they were getting harder.

The truth stuck there right in my throat, just waiting to be set free. I couldn't help but wonder how much longer I was going to be able to keep it locked away.

CHAPTER THIRTEEN

IVY

We spent the night right there in the bed of his truck, curled under the blankets, beneath the glittering stars.

We woke up to the sun rising over the mountains, staining everything with a blush-pink shade. We stopped for lattes on the way back to campus and we rode in silence, but he held my hand. It was the best night we'd ever spent together—well, except for maybe the first night we came together during spring break.

Or the night he turned the dorm into the beach.

Braeden and I might not be perfect, but I felt closer to him than I had in a long time. Nothing could interrupt the glow of happiness inside me.

At least I thought.

Then the new semester started.

Classes resumed.

I was reminded there was life outside of the boutique, my friends, and Braeden. It was a part of life I had to allow.

After all, summer couldn't last forever.

I made it the whole first week without seeing Missy. Actually, I almost made it two. But near the end of the second week, my luck ran out.

Of course, I knew she was around. Her stupid Buzzfeed notifications hit my phone several times a day. I thought about deleting the stupid app and not following her at all.

But a girl had to be prepared.

I'd rather see her hate coming at me than walk around campus and hear snickers only to wonder if they were about me.

Her notifications weren't so frequent during the summer, but as the start of the semester neared, she started up again. It was almost like she wanted to remind people of the #BuzzBoss so she would have the same kind of "cult" following during the New Year that she had before.

I just didn't understand it. As more time passed, I was afraid I never would. How could she? How could she do so many terrible things to the people who called her friend?

She was the worst kind of poser there was.

At least with Zach, you knew he was an asshole. But with Missy? She pretended to like you. She pretended to be your friend.

I saw now it was only a ploy to get gossip for her stupid feed.

I stepped out of the building, grateful my final class for the day was over. I glanced down at the letter that had been given to me by my professor. It was from the school. The pressure to declare a major was officially on. I needed to do it like right now. So said the entire staff of Alpha U. If I didn't, I wouldn't graduate at the end of next year. I needed time to fulfill the credits focused on my field of study.

Too bad I had no idea what that was going to be.

I opened the flap of my crossbody and stuffed the paper inside. I'd deal with it later.

A group of kids (probably freshman) came blasting right by me like they were being chased, and I had to swerve to avoid being taken out. When I looked up again, *she* was standing not so far away, her gaze locked on me.

I gave her a frigid look, one I hoped would tell her in no uncertain terms where I wanted her to go. I tossed my head so my hair would flip behind me, a total mean girl move, but I didn't care. She deserved a lot more than a nasty hair flip.

I yanked my eyes away, not letting them linger. I wanted her to know she wasn't worth the effort. I passed beneath a large black iron clock sitting near the sidewalk, with several benches around it. It had a lot of character, with a lantern-style shape at the top, a large white and black face on it that had yellowed slightly with time. The base tapered down into a thick black pole that sank directly into the ground.

It was still early afternoon, but I had stuff I wanted to do before my shift later at the boutique, so I was anxious to get off campus.

"Ivy." The familiar voice made my shoulders tighten. *Ugh!* Didn't she get the memo? I didn't want to talk to her.

"I'm busy," I said and kept moving.

"You don't have five minutes for your old best friend?"

I stopped and pivoted on the heel of my leather short boot. "Old," I emphasized. "As in no longer friends. If we ever actually were."

She was dressed in a pair of dark skinny jeans, silver flats, and a gray slouchy boyfriend sweater I saw online at Victoria's Secret. Her hair was still looking cute in the lob style. Today she had one side pinned pack behind her ear while the other waved around her perfectly made-up face.

"I honestly thought you'd have a lot to say to me. I didn't expect you to just cut me off," she said as she approached me, closing the distance between us and stopping right in front of me.

"Last time I tried to talk, you slammed out of the room faster than a cat being given a bath."

"You weren't talking to me," she said, the look on her face pinched and kinda dark. "You were talking to him, feeding him a line of bull just so you could wrap him further around your finger."

Oh. My. God.

She was still jealous. It was totally killing her that Braeden was in love with me. Last semester, the thought would have killed me. I would have done anything not to hurt Missy, but not anymore.

Yeah, I hurt Missy. But it wasn't intentional. What she did to me? That was totally thought out.

I snorted, not caring a bit that I sounded like Rimmel. There were a lot worse people I could be like.

For example, the one I was looking at.

"Clearly, my version of that day is a lot different than yours, Miss," I said, wincing a little when the nickname I used slipped so easily off my tongue. "I have no words left for you."

"Not even a why?" She lifted her chin in challenge.

Sadness overcame me all of a sudden. It seemed like she cared about explaining herself a lot more than I did. Didn't she understand? "Sure, I've wondered why you did it lots of times. Why you stabbed me in the back. Why you hurt Rimmel—"

Missy rolled her eyes dramatically. "Please. I helped her. I practically made her a campus celebrity."

I shook my head. How I never sensed this side of her I would never understand. It made me feel like maybe I was a lousy friend because I hadn't known her as well as I thought.

Nope.

Stop.

Don't do it to yourself.

Missy's psycho behavior was *not* my fault. Not even a little. She and she alone was responsible for the shattering of our group.

"I might have wondered why," I began, meeting her eyes and staring at her directly. "But in the end, no reason you could give would ever be enough for me to forgive you."

Hurt flashed across her features. "You act like you're the only one who got hurt."

"No." I refused. "I know I'm not." This conversation was totally bringing me down. "I have to go." I moved away.

"This conversation isn't over," she called behind me.

I turned around, still walking backward away from her. "Just put it on the Buzzfeed. It's what you do best."

That shut her up.

Could it be? I thought sarcastically as I turned away and headed toward the parking lot. *Could my forgiveness not be as important as keeping her true identity a secret?*

I laughed out loud. It was a sardonic, amused sound. I felt a few stares turn my way. I didn't care. I was too busy being shocked and, okay, maybe slightly hurt.

I should have known by now to expect this of Missy. Shouldn't I? After all, I learned the truth about who she was deep down last semester. Still, this small part of me remained shocked every time she did something to prove it all over again.

When I first saw that flash of hurt in her eyes, the way she seemed to genuinely want to talk to me today, I thought maybe it was sincere. That maybe the girl I'd spent so much time with the past few years really was in there somewhere.

But the more she talked, the more I realized Missy was still angry at me for becoming involved with Braeden. She was like a professional grudge holder.

It only served to remind me that her hurt and anger gave her motive. Motive to hurt me all over again.

My phone buzzed, and I pulled it out and looked down.

My steps faltered. She took my advice and put up a new notification. I knew exactly who she was talking about. She was trying to goad me, to get a reaction.

It wasn't going to work.

If she thinks I'm fake, she should take a long look in the mirror.

I planned to stay as far away from Missy as I could get.

CHAPTER FOURTEEN

BRAEDEN

Football was in full swing.

The Wolves were holding their own so far this season, and morale was high amongst the team. I'd never say it out loud, but I wondered how camaraderie and even performance would fare with the absence of our leader Romeo. The new quarterback wasn't really new; he'd always been on the team. He just never got to play because Rome did. He wasn't a bad guy or a bad player. He definitely wasn't as good, but he still played well enough.

A couple of the guys remarked that maybe the new quarterback wouldn't be doing as well if I hadn't been there all the time to stop the other team from rushing him and taking him down. I was aggressive and a lot more ruthless this season, or so they said.

In my opinion, I was always aggressive, but maybe I was just a little more ruthless. Football was a good outlet for all the shit I felt and couldn't express otherwise.

It was after a game, and all of us were sweaty and sore. I was stripping off my gear when the coach passed by and patted me on the shoulder. "You've been playing hard, Walker. It looks good on you."

"Thanks, Coach." I grunted and turned back to my stuff. He meant it as a compliment, but for some reason, it didn't feel like one.

I glanced in the small mirror hanging inside my locker and studied my face. It seemed like an insult that aggression looked good on me. Hell, I knew I wore it, but I tried to hide it. I thought I was the only one who saw my father when I looked into the mirror.

Did everyone else see him too?

Sure, they would have no idea who they were seeing, as I still technically looked like me. They'd never seen my father before, but I had. His face was branded in my mind. More and more, I saw him when I looked at myself.

More and more, I felt like a poser.

Pretending to be a good guy when who I really was deep down was the guy Coach saw on the field. I was the guy my teammates were starting to refer to as The Incredible Hulk.

After I showered off the residue of the game, I fished around my bag for some clothes. Everyone was going to Screamerz tonight to celebrate the successful start of the season. It was the first time since the semester started that we were all hanging out together.

After tonight, our traditional bonfires out in the field would be an every weekend thing.

I couldn't say I was especially looking forward to them this year, and it wasn't because Rome wasn't here.

It was because of what happened at the last one I went to.

The one where Ivy was almost gang raped.

Just thinking about it made adrenaline and hatred spike into my chest. I hadn't seen any of those guys since that night, which led me to believe maybe they went to a different school, but if I did see them, The Incredible Hulk would be out in seconds flat.

The party scene had always been my jam. And then I got serious with a girl. My priorities shifted, and I realized the party scene I loved so much was dangerous for a girl like mine. It was all too easy to look at her and assume she'd be willing.

I used to not think so much about the double standard women faced that guys were exempt from. Hell, if I were honest, I'd sometimes enjoyed it.

But now?

Now it made me want to smash faces.

As if on cue, a face I'd like to smash dropped a shoulder against the locker beside mine and regarded me like he had something to say.

I never had a problem with Trent.

Hell, I liked the guy.

Until he left my girl alone at the edge of the woods at a party.

Until he walked away without any thought to her safety.

Now he was on my shit list, along with Missy, Zach, and my father.

The list was filling up…

There were some bad bitches in this town.

"You got something to say?" I asked, shoving my dirty shit in my duffle. I'd left my shirt at home. All I had to wear to the club was my jeans. Guess that meant I needed to get my ass in gear so I could swing by the house and get one.

"Thought maybe you might," Trent said.

I abandoned my bag and straightened. "Nope."

"I thought we were friends," he said.

"Guess you thought wrong."

Trent straightened from the locker, his body becoming rigid like he expected a fight but wasn't going to back down. I had to admit I respected that.

And it only served to piss me off more. A guy like him should have known better.

"This about Ivy?" he said, his voice deepening. "Because I asked her out?"

I laughed.

He bristled further. "That a joke to you?"

"No, it's just ridiculous. I admit it made me crazy as hell to watch you sniffing all around her last semester, but that was a long time ago. She's with me. I know how to keep my girl happy."

"So what? You don't want us to be friends?"

I wiped a hand over my face. "If Ivy wants to be friends with you, then its cool with me. But don't think I won't keep an eye on you."

An angry looked crossed his face. "You make no fucking sense," he growled. "I get its kinda part of your charm, all smiles and high-fives off the field and then morphing into a giant green monster on field, but you're giving me goddamn whiplash."

"Put on a seatbelt and get the fuck out of my way," I growled back.

"I've been putting up with your frosty attitude and barely concealed pissy-ness at me since training camp. I haven't complained. But I'm tired of it. We got lots of games left this season. Parties and shit on top of it all.

The Wolfpack is family. I gave you the respect of coming to you. The least you could do is give me the same in return."

He was right.

He'd been loyal even when I gave him reason not to be.

I slammed my locker shut and looked him in the eye. "You just left her there," I said.

"Who? Ivy?"

It made me mad he had no clue what he'd done. How anyone could be so careless with her was beyond me.

You used to be the same way, a voice inside me whispered.

Fuck.

"That night at the bonfire, the send-off for Rome?"

He nodded. "I don't remember much of that night. I got shit-faced."

"You remember talking to Ivy?"

"Sure, that was before I got wasted." Then he grimaced and looked at me quickly. Yeah, I knew what that meant. He got so wasted because she told him she wanted me, not him.

"You left her at the edge of the woods, away from the crowd, man," I explained. "By herself."

His eyes widened. "Did something happen to her?" His arms went rigid at his sides and his fists clenched like it was something he wouldn't allow.

"Almost." Some of the anger I felt toward Trent was draining away.

Okay, all of it. Clearly, the guy hadn't meant any harm. I was being an ass.

"Four guys jumped her from the edge of the trees. They towed her back into the darkness. They were drunk as hell and wanted to have a sample of the campus slut," I spat.

Trent reared back like I'd buried my fist in his face. The look of absolute horror in his eyes got rid of whatever residual harsh feelings I had toward him. "Oh fuck."

"If I hadn't seen from across the field, she'd have been raped. Repeatedly."

"You stopped them? She didn't get hurt?" He was genuinely worried.

"I beat the shit out of every single one of them."

"Who were they?" he demanded. "That kind of scum shouldn't be allowed to walk around campus."

"Haven't seen them since. I'm starting to think they don't go here."

"You see them, call me. It'd be a pleasure to help you kick their asses again."

The side of my lip curled up in a smile. "Will do."

"I guess I can understand why I always felt like you wanted to deck me."

I sighed. "I might have overreacted."

"I get it. Ivy's worth it."

I felt my eyes narrow. "You still got a thing for my girl?"

He met my stare. "No. But I still consider her a friend."

Relaxing, I slid my jacket over my bare arms and picked up my bag. I was shocked Ivy wasn't blowing up my phone, asking where I was.

"Look, I'm sorry I acted like a dick. I get a little… protective where Ivy's concerned."

Trent grinned. "It's cool. Next time maybe just say something instead of making me sleep with one eye open."

"Shit," I cracked. "You're a pansy ass."

He laughed and held out his fist. "We cool?"

I bumped mine against his. "Yeah, we're cool."

"I'll see you tonight at Screamerz?"

"Hells yeah."

On my way out to the truck, I glanced around the lot. Ivy's car wasn't here. Usually, she waited for me. An ounce of worry tingled the back of my neck. I reminded myself she was a big girl and was probably fine.

Inside the cab, I found my phone and lit up the screen. I had a missed call and text.

Romeo is here. Going 2 house 2 get him. Meet there.

A grin cracked my face, and I fired up the engine. He slid into town early on the sly. Of course they didn't wait. Rimmel probably threatened to run home in the dark if Ivy didn't drive her there.

I tore out of the lot and down the road toward the house we all shared. It was going to be good to see Rome again. It had been a long time since we'd all been in the same room.

Tonight was gonna rule.

I didn't slow down 'til I pulled onto our street. The last thing we needed was the neighbors bitching about the way I drove. I stared ahead, though, scanning the driveway, expecting to see the Hellcat already out of the garage and ready to roll.

But it wasn't the Cat I saw.

It was another car.

A familiar one.

Distaste curled my lip, and I forgot all about making sure the uppity bitches in the neighborhood didn't have something to twitter about over coffee. My foot hit the gas and I sped up to the house.

People were standing outside on the walkway.

They were arguing.

I took one long look and my blood pressure went through the roof.

Aww, hells to the no.

CHAPTER FIFTEEN

IVY

I thought Rimmel was going to bounce right out of her seat and through the roof of my Toyota. When Romeo texted her cryptically and asked why her car was home but she wasn't, she all but fell out of her chair.

"He's here!" she squealed and leapt up.

"What?" I asked, looking around the stands for whoever she was shrieking about.

Her hand grasped my arm as she bounced and tried to pull me up. In true Rimmel fashion, she fell over, but my brother managed to stop her from hurting herself.

"Rim." I laughed. "What's gotten into you?"

Her phone went off again.

She read the screen and laughed. "I knew it!"

Drew glanced around her at me. "Should we be concerned?"

I snickered. "Nah."

She was typing off a response and said, "We have to go!"

"Go where?"

"Romeo is at the house!" She hurried past me into the aisle. "We have to go!"

"I thought he wasn't getting here 'til really late?"

"He got in early!" She was hopping from one foot to the next. She bolted down the steps, and I grabbed Drew's arm and followed suit.

While we hurried through the parking lot, I texted Braeden quickly to let him know what was going on. The game was ending in just a few minutes, so he wouldn't be very far behind anyway. Drew had my keys, so he slid into the driver's seat, and Rimmel practically dove into the back.

"Better step on it," I told him, amused.

I forgot how literal he would take those words. He drove to the house like he was on a NASCAR track and he was in first place. I held on to the door handle as if my life depended on it and told him to knock it off, but usually shy and cautious Rimmel only laughed.

When he slid into the driveway, the front door swung open and Romeo's large frame stepped out.

Rimmel fell out of the car.

Like literally forgot how to work her feet and hit the ground. Before any of us could do anything, she was up and moving again, heading straight for Romeo.

I could hear his laugh drift through the car door she left open, and he planted his feet, bracing himself for her to launch herself at him.

Which she did.

He caught her and her legs wrapped around his waist.

"There's my girl," he said.

They didn't say anything else because they started kissing right there in the grass. Drew glanced at me and raised an eyebrow.

"Totally normal for them," I said and opened my door. "C'mon. I'll introduce you to Romeo."

"He doesn't expect me to jump in his arms, does he?"

I laughed as I came around the hood. The pair still hadn't come up for air. I knew from experience they would likely be in bed half the weekend. I thought back to how good it had been to be back in B's arms when he came home from camp. And that had only been a couple weeks. It had been almost a month since Rim had seen Romeo.

"Maybe we should just give them some space," I murmured and took Drew's arm to steer him around them and into the house.

Just then Romeo lifted his head. "Nah, it's cool," he called out, his voice hoarse.

Another minute passed as he glanced back at Rimmel and slid his thumb over her lower lip. She smiled and buried her face in his shoulder. Romeo shifted all her weight into one arm and held out his fist to Drew.

"Ivy's bro?"

"Drew." He confirmed and hit his fist against Romeo's. "Thanks for letting me crash here while I visit my sister."

"I hear you been throwing some money at the bills," Romeo remarked, respect in his tone.

It made me relax. I had to admit I worried that Drew and Romeo might get off to a rough start like B and him had.

"I pay my way," Drew replied.

Romeo nodded and swung his attention to me. His blue eyes crinkled at the corners and his teeth flashed. "Blondie," he said, using Braeden's nickname for me.

I smiled. He stepped forward and gave me a one-armed hug, pulling me into his side. "How ya been?"

I returned his embrace and replied, but my answer was muffled against him. I liked Romeo. He was a really good guy, and I had to admit I was glad he liked me too.

"B still at the field?" he asked.

Rimmel lifted her head. "Yeah, but I'm sure he'll be here as soon as he can. Ivy texted him."

"Sweet."

I wasn't sure if it was just me, but he seemed bigger. Taller. Stronger. Maybe it was just because I'd forgotten how big his presence really was, or maybe he really was just bigger. After all, training this year had put some bulk on Braeden. Maybe it was the same for him.

"I'm gonna catch some alone time with my girl before he shows up and gets all needy on me." Romeo joked and winked at me.

He turned and carried Rim into the house, her laughter floating behind them as he went.

Drew started toward the house, but I caught his arm. "Let's give them a few."

I knew how important alone time was. My cheeks heated and desire curled low in my belly just thinking about the last bit of true alone time B and I had together. The night in the bed of his truck was something I was never going to forget.

A few minutes later, I deemed it safe to probably make it to the kitchen without seeing anything we didn't want to, and we made our way inside.

Halfway up the steps to the front door, a car pulled up. My heart leapt, expecting Braeden to be there when I turned around. Seeing Rimmel and Romeo together made me even more anxious to see him tonight.

All anticipation drained from my chest, replaced with annoyance when I saw it wasn't Braeden at all.

It was Missy.

What the hell was she doing here?

"My date's here," Drew said from behind and stepped around to jog down the steps.

"What!" I gasped.

He tossed me a sheepish grin over his shoulder, but then his attention went right back to his "date." I watched with open contempt as she threw one long leg out of her two-door car and then the other. She was totally playing up the fact she was wearing knee-high brown boots and a short jean skirt.

"When the hell did you have time to get a date for tonight?" I demanded.

"When I was getting us drinks." He couldn't tear his eyes off her. It made me want to pour bleach in my own.

"Funny thing," Missy said as she drew closer. "Someone totally body checked me when I was walking by the concession stand at the game. If Drew hadn't been there, I'd have face planted right there onto the hard, sticky floor."

Somewhere in hell there was a Golden Globe with her name on it. *Biggest Manipulator Ever.*

Her top was tight, accentuating her model-like form, and her hair floated around her face along with large gold hoops in her ears.

I glanced at Drew. He was gazing at her like he might be her next knight in shining armor. I was sorely disappointed in him. I thought he had a better bullshit meter than that.

I smacked him in the ribs.

"Ow," he complained and looked at me. "Why did you do that?"

"You know why," I intoned.

He looked at Missy. "I really don't."

The bewildered tone in his voice had me choking back a laugh. Missy nodded emphatically.

My teeth snapped together. Drew might not know what he did wrong, but Missy totally knew what she was doing. She'd seen pictures of him before. Hell, she probably saw us sitting with him during the game.

Missy knew this was my brother. What the hell was she sniffing around him for?

"How the hell do you even know where we live?" I asked, stepping down off the steps and back onto the sidewalk.

"I know lots of things." She smiled secretly.

Reminding me about her alter ego, the #BuzzBoss, wasn't a good way to start this conversation.

"I texted her the address," Drew said, as if he hadn't just heard her be all shady.

"Well, you can leave."

"I was invited," Missy said, her tone turning frosty.

Here come the claws.

I smiled.

Drew looked between us. "Do you two know each other?"

"The name Missy didn't strike you as familiar?" I asked with a total duh expression in my tone.

His blue eyes widened. "You're *that* Missy?" He looked between us again. "Ivy's best friend Missy?"

"We are *not* best friends," I snapped.

"She won't talk to me," Missy told him pathetically.

So that's the way she was going to play this, huh? Total victim mode. I knew it was for my brother's benefit. It was to make me look like the cold, heartless one and her the poor, misunderstood beauty.

"What the hell do you want?" I burst out. "Why are you here?"

My explosion finally seemed to penetrate Drew's thick skull. "Whoa."

"I was invited," Missy purred and sidled up to Drew.

Oh no she didn't.

"Don't even think about putting your grimy claws on my brother." I snarled.

"Or what?" She challenged, her voice sickly sweet.

"Girl," I warned. "I will kick you in your cooter."

Drew seemed shocked (what was with him tonight? He was being a total idiot) and swung around to face me.

At the same moment, Braeden's truck skidded to a stop at the end of the driveway. His door popped open before the engine was even fully off. In one leap, he was on the ground and rushing forward.

If Missy didn't seem nervous before, she did now.

CHAPTER SIXTEEN

#Poser

In the end, the person you really are comes out.

#NotEveryoneIsFooledByYou

#BuzzBoss

BRAEDEN

I didn't know exactly what was going on here.

But the angry look on Ivy's face told me all I needed to know.

I sorely wanted to yell. Like my throat was fucking itching to throw out hostile words at an alarming speed.

That's why I swallowed the need.

The darkness inside me was too close. Way, *way* too close.

Instead, I pulled Ivy's side against my chest and leaned down to speak into her ear. "I leave you alone for five minutes, Blondie."

Her body was tight, like a tension rod that had been given way too much weight. I could tell by the set of her jaw and the look in her eye that she didn't want Missy here. That the bitch just showed up. Probably ambushed her.

I wasn't okay with that. This place, our house, was supposed to be a safe zone. It was the reason Romeo rented it. It was the reason I moved in. We wanted Ivy and Rim to feel like there was a place the drama wouldn't knock on their door.

Her blue eyes, which looked more green than blue tonight, met mine. She smelled good. A combination of chocolate and vanilla.

Like a dessert I wanted to taste.

She didn't say anything at all, anger still prevalent on her face.

But I felt the give. The slight shift of her weight toward me, like I was exactly what she wanted. I was exactly who she needed.

That feeling was like a drug. It kept me coming back for more, just one more fix. I'd never get enough of being the one that made Ivy feel whole.

I tore my attention away and looked at Missy, my stare growing hard. "I told you to stay the fuck away from her."

"I'm sensing a lot of tension here," Drew said. It was a shitty attempt at a joke.

"You have no right to tell me who I can and cannot date." Missy sniffed.

My hand spasmed around Ivy's waist. She glanced at me out of the corner of her eye. "My brother seems to be suffering from the serious illness of idiocy tonight," she cracked. "Missy here batted her eyes at him at the game, and he asked her out."

"Whose side you on?" I asked him.

He stiffened. "I didn't realize there was a side."

"Let me give you some advice. This chick right here? Total head case. You don't want what she's offering."

"You didn't seem to mind what I was offering last semester," Missy remarked, sly.

Ivy jerked in my hold, and I felt the muscle in my jaw jump. I stepped forward, angling myself in front of Ivy. She didn't need to hear this kind of shit.

"One of the biggest mistakes I ever made was sleeping with you," I said, cold. Usually, I didn't try to hurt women's feelings.

But this chick had it coming.

It was her or Ivy.

There was no freaking competition.

"You slept with my sister's best friend?" Drew ground out.

Ivy tried to step forward. I gently held her back.

"I know you're late to the party, man, so let me sum this up for you: Ivy or her."

Missy made a sound like I was being ridiculous and flipped her hair. "Please, this is—"

I gave Drew a subtle nod, letting him know this was do or die for Ivy. Without hesitation, he crossed his arms over his chest and stepped up beside me. We created a wall between her and Ivy.

Missy sputtered. "You've got to be kidding me."

"You're hot and all," Drew said. "But family always wins."

Ivy tried to get around me, and I blocked her again.

"He isn't your family." Missy glared at me.

Ivy gasped and tried to shove around me. "For God's sake, Braeden. She's not a bullet, and you aren't a bulletproof vest."

She stumbled past me, and I caught her around the waist.

"Yeah, well, the damage she inflicts could match a bullet," I drawled.

A mean look crossed Missy's face. She pinned Ivy with a gray stare. "You're so convinced I'm the bad one. Have you ever wondered who else around here kept secrets and told lies?"

"What?" Ivy said, confusion in her tone.

"I wonder if you would be as quick to condemn them as you did me."

I've never in my entire life wanted to hit a woman. I *hated* men who abused women. But as I heard the suggestive words leaking out of her mouth and saw the cold, calculating look in her eyes, I wanted to.

Fuck. I wanted to.

It shook me all the way to my core.

"Get the hell off this property and don't ever come back," I warned. "This is the last warning you're gonna get from me, Missy. The next time, everyone is gonna know *exactly* who you are."

I saw the fear drift across her face, but then she shrugged one shoulder like I didn't worry her at all. "Just remember if I go down, I'm taking you with me."

I lunged forward, catching everyone off guard. Missy flinched backward, but my hand shot out and closed around her upper arm. "Let's go," I growled and forcibly directed her toward her car.

"You're hurting me!" she yelled, the dramatic bitch in her coming out.

"Takes a lot more than an escort to hurt someone as hard as you," I snapped. Even so, I made sure my hand wasn't too tight around her arm.

"Let go of me!" she yelled again.

God. All the little biddies in the neighborhood were gonna have a week's worth of gossip after tonight. I could practically feel them all staring out their windows.

I let go of her but didn't step back.

"What the fuck is going on out here?" A new, familiar voice cut through the night behind us.

I was too pissed off to be happy.

"Romeo," Missy said, surprise in her voice.

"You're not welcome here." His voice was soft but held that note of steel everyone knew lay at his core.

He was so controlled. It was a lot more effective than my hot, wild anger.

Missy's mouth opened and then snapped shut. Romeo stopped right beside me, and for a second, it felt like everything was as it was supposed to be again.

Rome and I were strong apart. We could each hold our own. But together…

Together we were damn near unstoppable.

As if we had some kind of freaky psychic connection, we both crossed our arms over our chests at the exact same moment.

Missy turned tail and rushed to her car.

"Don't worry," Drew yelled after her. "I won't be calling!"

Romeo glanced at me and grinned.

Behind us, Ivy muttered something about men and imbeciles.

We watched her car in silent partnership until Missy's taillights disappeared around the corner. Only then did I turn to my best friend.

"Dude. How do you survive without me?" he cracked. The shit-eating grin he always wore appeared.

I guffawed. "I was just wondering the same shit about you."

We laughed and pounded our fists together, but it turned into a hug.

"Missed you, bro," Romeo whispered.

"Times two," I replied.

Realizing we had an audience, we jerked back. Everyone was watching us with amused expressions.

Rimmel came running out of the house. "What's going on?" Her words were rushed and concerned.

She was clearly late to the party.

And her shirt was on backward.

"Dude." I groaned. "No one wants to see that."

Romeo laughed.

Rimmel skidded to a stop and blinked at us. "What?"

Ivy cleared her throat and motioned at her shirt. Rimmel looked down and even in the dark, everyone could see the cherry color bloom across her face.

"Oh."

"Everything's fine, Smalls," Romeo told her and walked to her side. "B was just taking out the trash."

She wrinkled her nose. "I thought you were going to Screamerz?"

"Party?" Romeo said, interest in his face.

"All the Wolves are gonna be there," I answered.

"Hells yeah!" he yelled and scooped Rim up and dumped her over his shoulder. "Let's go fix your shirt, baby. We're going out tonight."

Drew turned to Ivy. "I knew something was up with you. I'm guessing that girl has a hell of a lot to do with it?"

"I need a minute with my girl." I cut in.

"I have just one question," he said, serious.

"Ask," Ivy said.

"What the hell is a cooter?"

Ivy burst out laughing. I glanced at her with a raised brow. I knew exactly what a cooter was.

I pressed a hand to my chest like I was offended. "Ivy." I gasped. "Did you threaten that girl's cooter?"

"Maybe," she replied nonchalantly.

"Well, damn. I'm sorry I missed it." My voice was forlorn.

"Y'all are so weird," Drew said and then went in the house.

I closed the short distance between Ivy and me.

"The thought of you and her makes me feel sick inside." The confession rushed out and her voice cracked. When I glanced down, I saw the sheen of tears in her eyes.

It was like a punch in the gut. I never thought my partying ways of the past would ever become a regret. Live and let live. YOLO and all that shit.

But seeing the way it clearly hurt her made me wish I could take back a few things.

I couldn't.

I searched for the words, for beautiful words to say that would totally erase the effect Missy had on her tonight.

There were none, but the emotion in me swelled up like the ocean in a storm. It burned just beneath my ribcage, an almost unpleasant feeling. It was like my brain had no clue what to do, but my heart…

My heart knew exactly.

Slowly I reached out and cupped her waist. I wanted her to know I was coming. I wanted her to anticipate my touch. I knew she craved it, because I did too. I stepped up close, so close our toes bumped together and I could feel the breath leaving her lips.

I felt like a cloud wrapped around us, like we entered a place of our own making, a place no one else could touch or see.

I lowered my lips to press gently to her hairline, then lower to her forehead. Her head tipped back and her eyes slipped closed. I pressed a kiss to one eyelid and then the other. When she sighed, I pressed one to her nose.

My hands left her waist to reach for her hands, cradling them in mine. I dropped a kiss in the center of one palm and pressed it beneath my jacket to my chest, just over the place where my heart beat. I was sort of glad I wasn't wearing a shirt just then. It brought us skin to skin.

I held her there and allowed my lips to feather over hers.

"You're the only one who's ever been in here. You're the only one who's ever had the most important part of me. You're the one who turned a man who vowed to never love into one who loves completely."

"How do you do that?" she whispered, not pulling her face away from mine.

"Do what?" I stroked the backs of my fingers across her cheek.

"Pull me back in the second I start to drift away?"

I smiled. "I told you I was dropping anchor."

"Don't ever let me go, Braeden."

"Oh, baby." I vowed, "Never."

Still holding her palm against my chest, I took her mouth with mine. Even though it was a kiss filled with tenderness, the impact was like a 10.0 earthquake. I didn't have to kiss her hard and fast or deep and long. It didn't matter that our bodies weren't molded together in every place.

What mattered was I loved her so much it turned the simple kiss into something much more.

But I was a guy.

I liked being close too.

So after a long, soft kiss, I picked her up and she wrapped her legs around my waist.

"Braeden," she murmured against my lips.

I grunted and palmed the round lushness that was her ass.

"Why aren't you wearing a shirt?"

I smiled and she kissed my chin. "Forgot it."

"I want to go to the kitchen." She patted my shoulder like I was her personal taxi. 'Course, I'd carry her anywhere.

"Baby, you know we have roommates. We can't be doing it right there in front of them all."

Her giggle filled up the dark sky. "As interesting as you, me, the kitchen counter, and a can of whipped cream would be, that's not what I was talking about."

I pulled back, totally intrigued. "That's it. We're getting our own place."

"Promises, promises," she sang, teasing me.

Her hair was long and straight tonight. It floated around my shoulders as I walked us into the house. Just before I stepped inside, she pulled back and looked into my eyes.

"I love you so much, B."

"Times two, baby," I murmured. "Times two."

She sighed and rested her chin on my shoulder as I carried her the rest of the way into the house.

It seemed everything else Missy said to her had been forgotten in the moment.

I wasn't fool enough to think she wouldn't remember, that those taunting words Missy used to imply someone around Ivy was keeping something from her would stay forgotten for long.

And now I was faced with an impossible dilemma: to tell or not to tell.

Should I tell her before someone else did in hate?

Or…

Should I keep my mouth shut and pray to God my lie didn't take away the only woman my heart would ever beat for?

CHAPTER SEVENTEEN

IVY

I heard everything Missy said.

Everything she implied.

The energy around him electrified the second she spoke.

Not in a good way.

Oh God, Braeden, what have you done?

Please, don't let it change us forever.

CHAPTER EIGHTEEN

BRAEDEN

She made me brownies.

And not just any brownies. Ones with sprinkles.

No one ever made me brownies except my mother.

That explained why she smelled like chocolate and what she'd done with her time before the game.

She was so damned cute about it too. The second I set her down in the kitchen (as requested), she shyly picked up a glass dish with a lid and held it out. Ivy never did anything with bashfulness, so I knew this was a big thing for her.

I took the container and ripped off the lid. "Baby, you baked."

"I've never baked before. I don't even know if they'll be good. But I added extra sprinkles!" The enthusiasm in her voice made me smile.

I never would have told her about my love of sprinkles. I mean, come on. That was like the least macho food a guy could love.

My mother told her. I'd been pretty annoyed. Now I was kind of grateful.

"Best brownies I ever ate," I announced.

"You haven't actually eaten them," she pointed out.

"So?" I quipped. "I got brownie radar. I know good ones when I see 'em."

Her teeth sank into her full lower lip, and I was distracted from the sprinkle goodness in my hand.

"Do you want to try one?" she asked, her voice tentative.

"Does a cow have tits?"

"That's disgusting." She made a face.

"Hand me a fork, woman!"

"You're gonna eat them right out of the container?"

"Hells yeah. I ain't sharing."

She was nervous when she held out the fork. I dug it right into the center, noting the extra-thick layer of sprinkles. She probably dumped an entire container on here.

It made me love her even more.

I shoveled a huge bite in my mouth and chewed.

They weren't as good as my mother's, but they were pretty close. Considering this was her first try at making anything, I was damn proud of her.

When I didn't say anything right away, her face fell.

I made a sound and shoveled another huge bite in my mouth. "Best ever," I said as I chewed.

Her eyes rounded and looked up. "They aren't terrible?"

"They're the bomb." I gave her a toothy smile I knew was full of chocolate.

Her face lit up, and my chest warmed.

Rome came in the kitchen behind us. "Oooh." He looked over my shoulder. "Brownies."

His hand shot out, and I stabbed him with the fork. "Hands off the goods!"

"Vicious!" He jerked away.

I shoved another huge bite in my face. The sprinkles were the perfect amount of crunchy and melty.

"I'm gonna go change so we can go," she said, laughter in her voice. "I'll bring you a shirt, 'kay?"

"Thanks, baby," I said around another mouthful.

Romeo watched our display of domestic bliss with amusement.

Prada was dancing around my feet, begging for a bite. "No chocolate," I told her.

She kept begging, so I pulled out the bag of dog treats and gave her one.

"Whipped," Rome mocked.

"Where's your *cat*?" I countered.

He gave me the finger. After another bite, I put the lid on the container and slid it back onto the counter. I'd eat the rest later.

"Everything cool around here?"

"For the most part." I shrugged.

Drew stepped into the room, and our talk was cut short. The three of us shot the shit while we waited for the girls to appear. When they did, Rome and Rim took the Cat, and me, Ivy, and Drew followed in the truck.

Screamerz was packed.

It was the prime hangout spot for everyone on campus. 'Course, the Buzz that went out almost right after Missy hightailed it out of our place probably added to the crowd.

I hoped she wasn't here, but I wasn't stupid enough to think she'd stay home. She was lurking somewhere, collecting gossip and secrets to expose on her feed.

The second our group walked in, people zeroed in on Rome like he was some kind of tracking device that had been lost but was now found.

People started chanting his number, and the Wolves started howling.

He only laughed and shook his head.

We didn't have to wait for a table because we had a place with the team. While Rome went around and talked to everyone, I guided Ivy toward our seats and picked up a beer. I needed one. Today had been hella long. I was looking forward to some chill time with my best friend and maybe a little after-hours action with my girl.

Ivy was looking like an eleven on a one-to-ten chart. It seemed her outfit (or attitude) had a little extra sass in it tonight.

The jeans she wore were skintight and so dark they almost looked black. She was wearing a bright-orange tank top with another looser shirt over it. It was white, cropped, and long-sleeved but had big cutouts at the shoulders, exposing her skin. The neckline was decorated with some kind of colored design and had two strings hanging from it with orange tassels on the ends.

Her hair was straight and fell around her shoulders. It was my favorite on her. The way the silky strands caught the light made me want to touch it.

Trent sat across from us, and she gave him a little wave. He grinned at her and saluted me with his beer.

Romeo and Rim finally made their way over, and he took up residence right beside me, pulling Rim into his lap. "Damn, it's good to be home," Rome yelled, and a beer appeared in front of him.

We clinked the glass together and chugged. Rimmel wrinkled her nose. Ivy leaned around me, and I slung an arm across her shoulders.

"Where's your brother?" I asked.

She pointed on the dance floor. He was already out there and surrounded by women. He saw us and turned his smile up a notch.

Or ten.

"He's got some game." I admired that.

"He's incorrigible," Ivy said fondly and motioned for him to join us at the table. He disengaged himself from the ladies with some experience (clearly, he wasn't new to the rodeo) and made his way over.

The seat beside Trent was open, and he pulled it out.

"Trent, this is my brother Drew." Ivy made the introduction. "He drives a Mustang too."

Drew took up residence in the chair and gave Trent an interested look. "A fellow gear head?"

Trent lifted his hands in surrender. "Only when I have some spare time. Which isn't often."

"Football?" Drew guessed.

Trent smiled. "That and a fraternity."

"Sa-weet. You know enough about cars to hold a conversation, don't you?" Drew asked.

I almost choked on my beer. I fucking could talk about cars all damn day. But since I didn't drive a Mustang, I wasn't considered worthy.

"Does a bull have balls?" Trent countered.

I laughed, but Ivy groaned.

Drew slapped him on the back. "I like this guy, Ives."

"Of course you do," I muttered darkly.

Drew looked at me, then Trent. "You and my sister?"

My eyes narrowed on Trent, waiting to see what he would say.

"Nah, man. It's always been B for her."

I relaxed. Ivy poked me in the ribs, and I kissed her bare shoulder. Drew and Trent dove head first into a conversation about Mustangs and car parts. Over my head, a tray of shot glasses full of blue liquid hit the table.

"Smurf Balls!" Ivy exclaimed.

Rimmel laughed.

"What is it with you two and these damn blue drinks?" I intoned. Beside me, Romeo groaned.

Ivy picked one up and tossed it down her throat. Rimmel wasn't as fast to get hers down, but she was working on it.

Ivy stuck her tongue out, and it was already stained blue.

A current pop song started playing loud as hell, and Ivy got up and grabbed Rimmel's hand. "Come on."

Rimmel groaned, but she followed, and soon the pair was out on the dance floor, moving to the beat.

Rim was still a terrible dancer.

"How's the team?" I asked Romeo.

"It's good. Not the same without you."

I nodded. I knew what he meant. Even halfway into the season, I still wasn't used to playing on the field without him.

"How's the arm? You getting some play time?" I knew he had yet to start a game, which was why I hadn't been to one yet. Rimmel traveled to a couple of his first games, where he basically sat on the sidelines. I would have gone too, but with my own football practices, the scheduling had been tight.

But the first game he started and was on the field for more than a few plays, I was there. The Wolves be damned.

Romeo flexed his right hand and made a fist. "Arm's good. Their therapists and trainers are top notch. I can't complain."

"Play time?" I pressed.

He shrugged. "Not as much as I'm used to." He gave me a rueful smile. "I'm a small fish in a big pond over there."

"People giving you problems?" I asked, my eyes narrowed.

"No, everyone's cool. I just gotta prove myself. You know how it is."

I did. I also knew that soon, Rome would be dominating the lead position of quarterback on the team.

"You're getting lots of press." His name was practically a mainstay in the papers and in the state. The title "Comeback Quarterback" was seriously sticking.

Ron Gamble, owner of the Knights, was probably tickled shitless.

He flashed his teeth. "Press isn't hurting."

I chuckled. Rome was the golden boy of football in this state.

"How 'bout you?" he asked. "How's the Wolves doing this season?"

"Kicking ass and taking names," I said. The guys around us all howled.

"How could we not be with The Incredible Hulk intimidating the shit out of all the other teams?" cracked the guy right next to Trent.

Rome lifted his eyebrow.

"Shit," I muttered. That name was ridiculous.

"That you?" Rome asked.

Trent looked up from his in-depth bonding session with Drew and nodded. "He's like a damn bouncer out there. All aggressive and shit."

See, that's the thing. All the other guys might have thought it was cool. They admired the way it helped the team.

Romeo knew better.

He knew my "Incredible Hulk" status was likely the product of shit going on inside me.

"We should talk," he said so only I could hear.

"We should drink another beer!" I hollered. Everyone agreed.

After all our glasses were full, everyone went back to their own conversations. Romeo turned to me. "You talk to him? See him?"

"No. That ain't what this is about."

"Then what?"

I shook my head once. Not even Romeo knew the secret I carried around. I never told him about Ivy and Zach. I thought about it, but I couldn't. Just thinking about it was hard enough. And I couldn't do that to Ivy. I was loyal to Rome, but I was to Ivy too.

Plus… what if when I did, he said I did the wrong thing?

I didn't think I could handle my best friend telling me how wrong I'd been.

"I decided to call him." I hadn't really meant to say that. I only wanted to turn the conversation away from him getting too close.

Hell, I hadn't even realized I decided to talk to my father. I barely had time to think about it. But I guess the things Ivy said to me that night under the stars, about talking to him for myself, really resonated with me.

I probably made the decision that night, just hadn't wanted to say it.

Romeo clapped me on the shoulder. "I think it's good."

"Yeah?" I asked. Up until this point, he'd kept his personal opinion out of it. As if he knew he'd influence me and didn't want that.

"Hells yeah. Put it to bed, man. Once and for all."

Now that I declared my intent, it felt right, and for the first time, I felt ready to face him.

I hoped to hell it wasn't the beer and when I woke up tomorrow, I'd feel the same.

A couple ladies came up to the table, making eyes at Drew. It was a few of the girls he'd been dancing with earlier. "We need some company," one of them said. She had long, almost-black hair.

"The ladies want what they want." Drew sighed and stood. "Ladies, you know my bro Trent?"

"Of course." They smiled, and he was pulled out onto the floor with them.

That used to be Rome and me. Before we fell in love. Funny, I didn't miss those days at all.

Out on the dance floor, Ivy and Rimmel were laughing and having fun. It was good to see her smiling and just living in the moment. I watched a couple guys dancing nearby. I saw the way they watched her, and I knew they wanted to slide right up behind her for a dance.

So far, they'd kept their distance.

They'd remain where they were if they knew what was good for them. This far into the semester, everyone knew she was taken and they knew by whom.

Drew and Trent moved through the crowd and appeared beside them. Ivy hugged her brother fast, then went back to dancing.

"What's his deal?" Romeo hitched his chin in Drew's direction.

"Don't worry. I threatened his life if he even looked at Rim."

Romeo's body stiffened. "He hit on Rimmel?"

"Hells no. I'd have kicked his ass out. But I sure as hell made sure he knew he better not."

Romeo relaxed a little, but I noted the way he watched them all on the floor a little closer. "What's he doing here?"

"Came to check me out. Came home from his summer internship to find his little sis moved in with some guy."

"Her mother's approval wasn't enough for him?" Romeo took a chug of beer.

I made a rude sound. "Guess not. Made his panties twisted that her parents haven't actually met me, only through FaceTime."

Romeo laughed. "Dude. You FaceTimed her 'rents?"

"Fuck you." I grinned. "I had to, man. She asked me to."

Romeo nodded solemnly, then busted out laughing.

"Anyway, he showed up, said he missed her. But when she left the room, he made it clear he was here to check us all out, make sure we're good enough for his little sister."

"What aren't you saying, B?"

I turned my eyes on him. "What makes you think I'm not saying something?"

The look on his face was one of a guy who smelled the worst fart ever. Since it didn't stink in here, I knew he was calling bullshit.

I drained the rest of my beer, basically stalling for time, trying to think up some smartass comment that would change the subject. Or hoping one of his many fans would come over here and take the heat off me.

A distraction.

Any kind of distraction would be good right now.

Except for the one I got.

"No!" a female shrieked. The sound was so loud and panicked it carried over the music and through the crowd.

I knew that sound.

I jerked upright and looked toward Ivy. Some guy had come up behind her, grabbed her, and had his arms locked around her waist.

"Don't touch me!" she yelled.

I saw the panic in her face, the way her body locked up.

It's happening again. Just like the shower.

I let out a string of curses and dropped my empty glass. The crowd around our table was massive, and I wasn't about to make my way around. By the time I got to her, she'd be in a full-blown panic.

I jumped up on the tabletop, my feet knocking over some beers and baskets of peanuts. I didn't pause. I kept going and jumped off the table and onto the floor on the other side.

By that time, Drew had yanked the dirty bastard off her but was handling the situation entirely wrong.

Hell.

He was handling it like any brother would, but not the way Ivy needed. It wasn't about that guy, the fucker; it was about Ivy. Her body was having a flashback.

Drew had the guy by the shirt, and as I shoved people out of my way, he plowed his fist into the guy's jaw, sending him flying backward.

Right into Ivy.

The two of them fell to the ground in a heap, Ivy on the bottom.

Pinned to the floor, beneath a complete stranger.

She started to scream.

CHAPTER NINETEEN

IVY

The hands came out of nowhere.

The body forced itself right up against mine. There was something dirty and unwanted about the way it felt.

One second, everything was fine. I was having fun and laughing.

And then it wasn't.

In the span of two seconds, my heart rate tripled, a sick, dizzy feeling washed over me, and I felt sweat break out over my forehead.

"No!" The protest literally clawed out of my chest and burned my throat on its way out.

I have to get away from him.

I don't want this.

"Don't touch me!"

I felt the body ripped away. We spun with the force of it. I was still reeling, still trying to pull myself back from the anxiety that had completely taken over.

I blinked enough to clear my vision and see Drew ramming his fist into the face of the man who grabbed me.

I didn't have time to think or move.

The stranger knocked into me, both of us crumpling to the floor.

The smell of booze hit my nostrils, and I gagged. The guy was so drunk he couldn't even control his own body.

He was lying on top of me, his weight so heavy, his skin so sticky.

Oh my God. No.

It became excessively hard to breathe. Black spots swam before my eyes. I wanted him off me. I wanted him—

He groaned and tried to get up. All it did was push his body closer into mine.

I started to scream.

Seconds later, all the weight was gone and the sound of a familiar—yet angry—voice floated above me. "Don't you fucking touch her."

"She's my sister," another voice argued.

I started to shake. The adrenaline in my system was too much to handle so fast. "Ivy," Braeden said. "Baby, I'm gonna touch you."

His gentle hands lifted me off the ground. I barely registered the crowd around us or the music playing through the club.

"You're okay," he promised, his voice soothing and close to my ear.

A sob ripped from my chest, and I pushed my face into his shoulder. He picked me up and held me against him.

I liked the way he felt. His arms didn't feel like panic. They felt safe.

We started moving through the place. A minute later, the cool night air brushed across my skin and lifted my hair.

"We're going home," Braeden said, and I heard the sound of gravel crunching under his feet.

It was soon joined by more of the same behind us.

"What the fuck happened back there?" Drew yelled.

Braeden stopped, his body tense. I concentrated on breathing. "We're going home," he said, tight.

"I want a fucking explanation for what just happened!" he roared.

"I'm fine," I said, my voice weak and my throat raw.

Braeden's hold tightened around me. "Hush."

"Now is not the time." Romeo cut in, his voice the only reasonable one.

"That's my sister," Drew growled.

"I get it. She's like one to me too," Romeo replied. "Which is why you need to let B handle his shit and take her home. Standing in a parking lot and arguing isn't good for her."

Braeden started walking again. In the truck, my head started to clear a little. I was able to hear my own thoughts.

"Braeden," I whispered.

"You don't have to say anything, baby." He tucked me closer into his side.

"What's happening to me?" My voice broke.

He didn't say anything, but I knew he saw it too.

Something was wrong with me.

I was scared.

CHAPTER TWENTY

BRAEDEN

Right before I carried her out of the club, the crowd parted.

She was standing right there at the edge, staring.

Our eyes locked.

The threats she made to take me down had been just that, threats. Words she never intended to follow through with.

How did I know?

The stark, unbridled fear in her eyes.

Missy knew I was at my snapping point. She knew the unspoken truce between us to not say shit was crumbling.

This was my final straw.

Something had to give.

I wouldn't watch Ivy suffer this way.

It was time I told her the truth.

MEANWHILE, AT THE MENTAL WARD...

(AKA PART TWO)

CHAPTER TWENTY-ONE

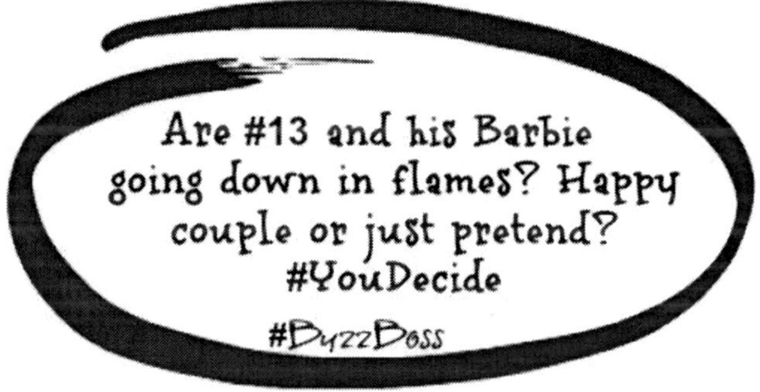

ZACH

Dope me up.

That's all they wanted to do to me here. They wanted to cram pills down my throat to "fix" me because it was easier than trying to change who I was—who I would *always* be at the core.

They didn't need to know that, though.

All these people in their white coats with understanding smiles and happy, positive outlooks could keep living in their fantasy world. I'd play along. It pissed me off more than anyone would ever understand, more than they would ever see. I was good at hiding what was really inside me.

The best, actually.

I walked through these halls in my designer slippers and pajamas. Frankly, it made me feel like Hugh Hefner, like I was at some spa, and I often wondered if these people really believed they were any better than the prisoners here (prisoners = patients).

We were all liars. I was just more honest about who I was than the rest. My honesty got me locked up here, in this cushy treatment center where they could fix me and tell the courts I was no longer crazy. That I was a functioning, contributing member to society.

Though, I always was that. I just wasn't what everyone else deemed appropriate. I just didn't behave the way everyone else thought I should.

Screw that and screw them.

But I could play their game. I could pretend to be exactly who they wanted. I could sit in my therapy sessions across from my grossly inadequate therapist who cared more about her Botoxed forehead than anything that came out of my mouth.

I said what she wanted to hear, and she made the appropriate noises and asked me how I felt.

The truth was I felt like laughing.

Sometimes the laugh would bubble up inside me, rising up like a tidal wave in the center of a violent storm. It would threaten to burst out, escaping into the room, and turn from one single giggle into an ongoing, high-pitched laugh that made me sound like a hyena.

A few times, I actually choked trying to force the reaction back down. I used it to my advantage too. I turned it into a sob and was "overcome by emotion." Remorse for what I'd done. Guilt for the pain I caused and agony from the effects of my childhood.

The doctor bought it every time. Hook, line, and sinker. Sometimes she even handed me tissues and looked at me with pity in her eyes.

Maybe when I left here, I would take up acting. God knows I was good at pretending.

In actuality, I didn't feel any of those emotions. No remorse. No guilt. No agony. I did feel resounding anger and satisfaction. I never really set out to do the things I did. But I didn't regret them either. Those people deserved what they got, and I deserved to be the one to give it to them.

Sometimes life wasn't fair, so you had to level the playing field. You had to make sure people knew you weren't buying what they were selling.

Did I take it too far?

Only in the respect that I got caught.

I'd do it again, but this time I'd be a lot quieter about it.

This time I was gonna be smart. I was gonna pose as the man everyone wanted me to be.

Posers gonna pose after all.

Jokers gonna joke.

This time, the joke would be on them.

CHAPTER TWENTY-TWO

ZACH

Months. That's how long I'd been locked up here.

Of course, they preferred to call it "visiting."

It's only a visit if you choose to come here and then walk out whenever you feel like it. I didn't choose this place. I was ordered here by a court of law. Even my lawyer father couldn't keep me out. But this wasn't his fault. He'd done the best he could. He got me sent here instead of a jail cell.

I was getting weary of this place, of the doctors and the staff. I felt like an expensive toy shoved in a box with a bunch of broken rejects. I watched them day in and day out, shuffling around this center with glassy eyes and slack mouths. The minute I started to see some actual signs of life behind their vacant stares, an orderly would come by with a plastic cup full of meds.

It's like they'd just given up. Like they preferred being here to the outside world. I had too much ambition inside me for that, for this life.

I'd never make it in here an entire year. I'd snap. The last time I snapped, I ended up here. The next time…?

They'd send me somewhere worse.

I needed to get out. I needed some kind of contact with the outside world. I needed an exit plan. What does a guy do when he wants to get to the outside? Make friends with a guy on the inside.

I could have gone the route of paying off an orderly, but that would have been too obvious. I didn't trust the people who worked here. They'd accept my money, tell me one thing, and the next thing I knew, I'd be locked up even longer.

That wasn't going to happen. The way to go here was to make friends with another inmate. Another patient. I'd been watching since the day I walked in. When I wasn't participating in group activities, misleading my therapists, and pretending to read the books they offered here in the library, I was sizing everyone up.

Like I said, a lot of the patients here were basically just filling space, going with the motions. But not all of us. It took a while to pick them out, to know the ones who were as lucid as me, but I did. All I had to do was watch, wait. It made me wonder why none of the orderlies ever picked us out. Was it because they just didn't care as long as no one caused trouble? Or was it that they honestly just didn't see what I did?

Perhaps like recognized like. Perhaps I saw because it was familiar.

Every evening before bedtime, the patients were given an hour of free time. Free time meant herding us all into one large room and allowing us to play board games, participate in art class, or read.

It was totally lame.

I longed for a beer, a cold tall one. I wanted to sit at a frat party, surrounded by guys I ruled. What a high it was to be in charge.

This hour of "free" time only served as a reminder of why the hell I wanted out so bad. I would be at the top again one day. I would be in charge. Guys like me weren't followers. We weren't minions. I was a king. I was meant to rule.

Like all my other true feelings, I stuffed those down deep and acted like this hour of free time was my time to reflect and show how I could function normally in a room full of people.

Shane was sitting at a table by himself when I walked in. There was a checkerboard in front of him, and he concentrated on putting the red and black pieces on the board where they belonged. The seat across from him was vacant.

It was like he knew. Like he knew I was ready to approach him. Up until this point, we'd only exchanged a glance or two. Being too friendly too fast was like waving a red flag in front of a bull. I was here to work on myself, not make friends.

My slippers were silent as they padded across the hardwood floor, and I took the seat across from him. Without saying anything, he made the first move on the checkerboard. I made one after him.

This went on for a few turns, just two patients playing a friendly game of checkers.

"How long you been here?" I asked after I moved my black piece again.

"Two years."

My fingers stilled on the table. That long? I must have misjudged him. I didn't do that very often. Being in here was making me lose my edge. This conversation was over. He was the wrong guy for me. I started to get up.

"You want out?" he said, ignoring the fact I was leaving and making a move to counter mine.

"What would you know about it?"

He shrugged. "Plenty."

I settled back in. "If you knew that much, you wouldn't still be in here after two years."

"To some, this place is preferable."

I didn't know why he would rather be here than out there, and I didn't care. All I cared about was information.

"How long you in for?" he asked.

"A year."

He nodded like it was standard. "You got family?"

"Yeah."

"Focus on Doctor Becks. She has a thing for family support and shit. She's been known to spring people for home visits."

Bingo.

"Visitor's day is coming up. You in yet?"

Visitors were allowed to the facility once a month. Each visitor had to register and be approved by the staff before they were permitted to see the patients. So far, I hadn't had visitors. The first few months of treatment were focused solely on me, but good boys get rewarded.

I'd been a very good boy, and now I was authorized to have a visitor.

"Yes. My father will be here."

"The lawyer, right?"

I wasn't surprised he knew that.

"Yeah." I moved my piece on the board and jumped one of his.

He retaliated by jumping two of mine. "Might be a good time to tell him how you want to spend the holidays with him. Put his *persuasive* background to work."

I made a sound and kept playing the game.

"'Course, you'll probably have to come back," Shane said.

I didn't care about that. I just wanted a way to get out, cause a little trouble, and then come back before anyone could even suspect it was me. All I needed was enough time to let the debauched boy inside me off his leash for a while before I let the choirboy in me shine again.

A little bit of balance. That's all a guy could ask for.

I made it to the other side of the board and slid my black chip into place. "King me," I said.

Shane looked up and smiled.

I smiled back.

CHAPTER TWENTY-THREE

ZACH

Dr. Becks was a schmuck.

But she was an educated schmuck so that made her dangerous. She was also one of the people who stood between the door and me.

I had no doubt I would be able to bring her around to what I wanted. I just had to make it seem like it was her idea. I could do that, but it wasn't going to be easy. Doctors like her were trained to read between the lines. They were trained to see what other people didn't.

So…

To get around her education and training to the heart of the schmuck, I was going to have to bring it. Enter the not so easy part. You see, the best way to make people do what you want is to give them something they want.

And Becks wanted a breakthrough.

She wanted to think all the time she spent in classrooms, wearing that stupid white coat, and walking the halls of this fancy prison was worth it. She wanted a stroke to her ego. She wanted bragging rights around the water cooler.

I'd give it to her.

I didn't want to, but it was the only way.

After my talk with Shane, I started laying the groundwork. Dropping hints, contributing vague omissions I knew would lead her to think all her yapping was finally starting to build back up whatever was broken inside me.

I couldn't just walk into her office one day and spill my guts. Especially not so soon after being seen with Shane. Maybe no one noticed, but I wasn't about to risk everything on maybe.

I knew I was on the right track when Dr. Becks added a second session to our weekly meetings. She was becoming more eager for the breakthrough she thought she was drawing out of me.

Like I said, she was a schmuck.

The more time passed, the more eager (okay, desperate) I was to get out of here. Hawks weren't meant to be caged. Lions weren't meant to be trapped. Kings were meant to reign.

I walked into her office and adjusted the scrubs I wore. I longed for a polo and a pair of dark jeans. I wanted to feel human again, not like some patient that was only ever trusted to wear pajamas or standard issue scrubs. And shoes. I'd like a pair of damn shoes. The real kind, with laces. I still wasn't allowed that luxury (which was ridiculous), so I still wore slippers. Frankly, it seemed like a hardship I couldn't dress the part of the man I was trying to portray.

Appearance was everything after all.

If I wanted Dr. Becks to see me as less of a patient, then I had to look and act like one. Walking around in a robe like I was ready to crawl into bed and sleep away the rest of my life wasn't the kind of attitude that would get me out of here. I needed to look put together and confident, but not too confident.

I still needed vulnerability.

So, yeah, maybe the scrubs would help me with that.

Women loved vulnerability, even doctors who were trained to see it as a weakness.

Sometimes nature trumped training, and nature created women (well, *most* women) to soften when they saw someone who appeared injured or down on their luck.

I left my face unshaven—that wasn't by choice. They wouldn't let me have a razor either. So between my un-gelled hair, unshaven face, and slippers, I figured I still looked vulnerable yet with the appearance of *trying* to pull it together.

Can we just take a minute to bask in the genius that is my mind?

… … …

Okay, we're back.

"Right on time, Zachary," Dr. Becks said as I stepped toward the chair I was to sit in.

It annoyed the hell out of me when she called me that. I mean, seriously. I told her I don't know how many times it was just Zach. She didn't listen. I don't know why she expected me to concentrate on any fool thing that came out of her mouth when she couldn't even comprehend the way I asked to be addressed.

Only one other person ever called me that. I hated her too.

My fingers curled into my palm and squeezed. I felt the too-long nails cut into the skin, and it gave me a high. I liked that little prick of pain. The sick satisfaction.

She couldn't control me. She could call me whatever she wanted, but it didn't matter. In the end, I would always do what *I* wanted.

"Punctuality is a sign of respect," I said, reluctantly unclenching my fist. It wouldn't do for her to see my display of controlled anger.

The doctor indicated toward the chair and I sat. I felt agitated. What I knew I had to do, what I thought was going to be easy, was clearly not as simple as I thought.

I hated this place.

I hated Dr. Becks.

I hated her.

My knee started bouncing up and down as energy filled me and I couldn't manage to keep it in.

I felt the sweeping stare of the woman across from me, and I wanted to snarl at her for her judgmental gaze. But I didn't. I held in what I could.

"You seem anxious today," she observed. "Would you like to tell me why?"

Fuck no, I wouldn't.

When I didn't answer, she set her pen down and focused solely on me. "I thought you were ready for more frequent sessions. Perhaps it's too much right now."

The mental vision of bars slamming in my face snapped me out of it.

"No," I said quickly. Then I slumped forward a little and smiled internally. This wasn't how I imagined this session going, but I could roll with this.

In fact, it would be better this way.

"I'm just, well..." I paused for effect. "I've just been thinking a lot lately."

She nodded that I should go on.

"I don't like it when you call me Zachary," I admitted.

"Why is that?"

"It reminds me of *her*."

"Her?" Dr. Beck's tone shifted ever so slightly. The underlying note of interest was hard to miss. "By her do you mean your mother?"

Who else would I mean? Certainly not the woman everyone thought was my mother—the woman my father moved into our house like she would make us normal again, like this stand-in would fix everything *she* had broken.

I nodded and looked away at all her diplomas lining the walls. She was clearly an egomaniac.

"You've yet to talk about her during your stay."

"I don't like to talk about her." The familiar rush of anger flushed my veins. I probably shouldn't allow so much truth into my voice when I spoke of her, but it would only serve to be more convincing.

"Maybe talking about her might help," the doctor suggested. "It's quite possible a lot of the anger and resentment you have stems from whatever it is you hold inside. Perhaps it's a driving force behind your behavior."

"You mean the reason I hung that girl from a goalpost and then ran her boyfriend down with a lawnmower?" I said it matter-of-fact and with a straight face. I even managed to infuse a little regret in my tone.

Inside, I was high-fiving myself for my own epic-ness.

I ran down Mr. Quarterback himself with a lawnmower.

Ha!

"That was probably the most terrible thing you've done," Becks said without any hint of judgment. Her acting was almost as good as mine. "But it certainly wasn't the only thing you did to get yourself in here."

Yeah, yeah. Poor nerd and poor Mr. Popularity. I'd just tortured them. Blah, blah, blah. Wonder what she'd say if I told her about the things I did that no one knew about.

She cleared her throat and waited for me to disagree with her statement. I didn't say a word.

"Why don't you tell me about your mother?"

"She's quite the pillar of society." I began. "She's very active in charities. She always dresses for success, and she's always poised under pressure. The perfect qualities for a lawyer's wife. Wouldn't you agree?"

"I'm not asking about your stepmother. I think you know that. Though, we can talk about her if you like?"

Talking about that phony was almost as unpleasant as talking about my real mother. Except talking about stepmommy wouldn't earn me a get out of jail free card.

"I'm surprised you don't have everything there is to know about her in that file." I motioned toward the folder lying in front of her.

"Facts written on a page are one thing. How they make you *feel* is completely different. I'm more interested in how she makes you feel, Zachary."

God! Did she call me that on purpose? Did she want my head to explode?

I pulled in a deep breath.

Long seconds ticked by, filled with silence. She reached down and opened the folder, revealing a stack of papers and charts inside. But there was something else clipped to the front flap.

Photographs.

Dr. Becks slid the top one out from beneath a paperclip and held it up so I could see it. "This is her? Your mother?"

I fought to keep my upper lip from curling in disgust.

But even as unpleasant as the image was, I still stared at it. I couldn't look away.

My mother, Jennifer Anne Marshall-Bettinger, was a bona fide piece of work. My father should have dumped her back where he found her when she decided to hyphenate her last name instead of just using his.

She was a small woman with a delicate frame and not much of anything on her bones. It gave her the appearance of being weak, of looking like she needed to be protected. I hated women that looked frail.

Her hair was a deep shade of brown, very long and thick. It was perfectly styled in the picture before me, but I knew it had the ability to be unruly. Her skin was pale, which made her large dark eyes stand out behind the glasses she wore.

Jennifer was good at appearing innocent.

She most definitely wasn't.

"That's her." I nodded.

Dr. Becks lowered the photo, laying it on the desk and out of sight. Yet I still saw her face. The hate she made me feel still pulsed just beneath my skin.

"Why don't you tell me about her? All that pent-up emotion must be difficult to manage." Her gentle words prodded me.

And so I did.

CHAPTER TWENTY-FOUR

#BuzzOnTheFieldIS
#13 has a new nickname. The Incredible Hulk is not a good name for our resident hottie.
#NominationsAreOpen
#BuzzBoss

ZACH

They were fighting again.

But it wasn't the kind of fighting anyone could hear. Or even the kind you could see.

Still, I felt it. It permeated the house, the very air I breathed. With every tick of the clock, with every light sound the housekeeper made, I heard.

Sometimes silent battles were worse than the knock-down, drag-out explosive confrontations. It was like the quiet just before a storm, the angry gray of a rain-heavy sky. The anticipation that hung in the atmosphere was worse than any screaming match could ever be.

I wished they would just yell. I wished they would throw things. I wished I could hear her cry.

Something.

Anything.

The silence was stifling, like I imagined a sarcophagus would be. Buried alive, gasping for breath, waiting, waiting for death to claim you.

Is this what marriage was like?

On TV, it always looked so happy, so fun. The couples on the screen would smile at each other and hold hands. They would stare lovingly into one another's eyes. They would have lively conversation around the dining room table every evening with their perfect children.

I tried to be perfect.

I always wore matching clothes, and even though I never wanted to, I showered every single day. I styled my hair exactly like the boys on TV, and I worked hard in school.

Perfection wasn't enough.

I was beginning to think perfection was just a lie, an ugly promise no one could ever achieve.

Our dinners were filled with silence, except when I scraped my fork across the plate. My mother would tell me not to scratch the china, and Dad would pretend we hadn't spoken at all.

My parents were cordial to each other. So cordial it was as if they were passing strangers at a train station. There was no familiarity between them, no warmth.

I tried to remember a time when it was different, when they were different.

I searched every corner of my mind for a shred of what it used to be like, but the way it was now was all I ever found.

So one night during the heavy yet polite silence at dinner, I asked a question.

That question turned out to be a catalyst.

The match that started the fire.

The words that changed everything.

"Am I adopted?"

The silence was shattered by the sharp clatter of a fork being dropped on a plate. My mother's gasp didn't cover the sound; it seemed to enhance it.

My father's fork froze halfway to his mouth. The bite of steak on the end sat poised to be devoured.

They sat on each end of the table, the two farthest points possible. I sat in between them, like the filling of a sandwich.

Everyone knew the thing that held the sandwich together was its filling.

A white tablecloth draped over the wooden table and the corners just skimmed the floor. The high-backed wooden chairs we all sat in were formal and hard.

My mother, who was always poised, seemed to let her composure slip, like those three words shocked the hell out of her.

I watched as she lifted her dark eyes to my father and stared straight at him from behind the glasses she wore. In her expression was more animation than I'd seen between them probably ever.

It gave me hope.

My father set down his fork, abandoning the steak. "Zach, why would ask such a thing?"

I shrugged. "Because I want to know."

"Of course you aren't adopted, Zachary." My mother spoke up.

"Then you must have liked each other once… if you made me." I'd learned about baby making in health class. It was gross. My friends and I laughed about it the rest of the day.

But even as I made jokes, in the back of my mind, I realized for two people to do stuff that would make a baby, they must really have to like each other.

Mom's hand went up to her neck. "Of course we like each other." She glanced at my father and then back at me. "We're in love."

"Then how come you never smile?"

I glanced to the other side of the table at Dad. He seemed uncomfortable and caught off guard.

Mom paled. "We smile."

I shook my head. "I thought maybe you were sorry you adopted me or that you thought you picked the wrong kid."

A strangled sound cut through the silence, and Mom pushed out of her seat and dropped on her knees beside my chair.

I turned toward her, and she took my face in her hands. "Zachary, my darling boy. I could never be sorry you're ours. There could never be a more perfect son."

"I try to be perfect for you, Mom. Maybe someday it will make you smile."

Her eyes glistened with unshed tears, and I realized the animation I saw in them moments ago wasn't the kind of emotion I probably wanted to see. She was filled with sorrow. Sadness seeped from her very pores.

Her graceful arms wrapped around me and folded me close. I breathed in deep the scent of lilac that always seemed to cling to her skin. "I'm gonna work on that smile," she whispered in my ear.

I pulled back and gave her one of mine.

More tears pushed into her eyes, and she cleared her throat and stood. "I just remembered a phone call I need to make. If you'll excuse me." She glanced at the dinner table. "Go ahead and finish without me. I wouldn't want your meal to get cold."

She left the room quickly and didn't look back.

I ate the rest of the meal with just my father. Mom never returned to the table.

That night, the silence was interrupted.

For the first time ever, I heard her crying when I was supposed to be asleep.

She said it wasn't me. She told me I was the perfect son.

This was his fault.

My father was the reason Mom never smiled. He was the reason she was crying right now.

I hated him.

One year later…

What a difference a year made. Three hundred and sixty-five days, each one a new chance to make him pay. I was good at it, better than I thought I'd be. It seems I had this well inside me that was filled with unfettered anger and resentment. It never dried up, no matter how much trouble I seemed to cause.

I was good at trouble. I was perfect at it.

It was all in appearance, really. I kept up the outward appearance of impeccable breeding. I still styled my hair perfect. I still dressed like a real-life Ken doll. I got good grades in school, because no less could be expected from such an affluent, well-to-do family.

That was the key.

The key to putting my father through silent hell. I posed as the perfect son, all the while causing all kinds of havoc, which he quietly went behind me and cleaned up.

I'd give the guy points. He seemed to pose as well as I. The perfect little family. The picture of domestic bliss.

After that night at dinner, I started out small. I'd "forget" to give him messages when someone called. I'd move his car keys into random places and then watch him rush around the next morning, searching. It was especially amusing when it made him late for work. I'd come home late from school, chew loudly at dinner, and then backtalk when he told me to stop.

He tried to talk to me about it once. He came into my room and sat down. The second he brought up Mom, I told him to go to hell.

That night I snuck in his office when everyone was in bed. I wrote all over the deposition he was going over with black marker in random scribbles and words. The sections he'd highlighted I made sure to mark out so they weren't legible.

A few nights later, I heard my parents arguing in their room. I listened outside with smug satisfaction.

My father wanted to send me to boarding school. He thought it would be a better environment than the one I was being raised in now. Of course, my mother wasn't having it. For the first time ever, I heard her stand up to him.

"He's the reason I stay here. You know that!" she yelled.

"Well, if he's gone, then you won't have to be here anymore," my father muttered. Something inside me sort of paused. He sounded so weary, almost beaten down.

It wasn't how I expected him to sound. He was too cold for that. Too calculating and self-centered.

"I've put up with a lot over the years, Jennifer. I've done everything I could to make sure you have everything you need."

"Money can't buy happiness," she said.

He sighed. "No. It cannot."

He never said anything about the papers I ruined, and he never brought up boarding school again. But he did start going on more business trips. He spent more and more time away.

My mother started smiling. The life started coming back into her eyes.

I knew it was because I'd made him pay for her unhappiness. I knew it was because I'd pushed Dad away and he wasn't around so much.

We didn't need him anyway. I could be the man of the house. I could make sure Mom smiled.

Sometimes she'd send the housekeeper home and we'd order pizza and sit in the kitchen to eat. Other times we'd hop into her Roadster and go shopping. She'd never been much of a shopper, and I knew now it was because Dad wouldn't let *her go.*

But she was making up for it now. By the time we were done, the car would be so full of bags and packages she'd have to have some delivered home or we both wouldn't fit in the seats.

We were happy.

I was making her happy.

Then I realized happiness was a lot like perfection. A lie.

Dad was once again on a business trip, and Mom forgot to pick me up at school. I had a driver responsible for taking me everywhere I needed to be, until Mom let him go just a few weeks before. She told me we didn't need him, that she'd be the one to drive me.

It made me happy.

Well, until she forgot me.

I caught a ride home with a friend, having them drop me off down by the gate at the end of the driveway. I walked along the perfectly edged stone, my steps quick because I was worried maybe Mom was sick or something.

If she was, I was going to have to call Dad. I liked when he wasn't home, but if something were wrong, he'd fix it.

My steps faltered when I saw an unfamiliar car parked near the house. Something flashy and sporty. I knew it wasn't my dad. He'd never drive something so… loud.

It was bright yellow and had a spoiler on the back. The rims were back and silver. The engine was running and the windows were rolled down.

Fear skittered down my spine because this must have been why she never came. She must have been in trouble. But just as I thought the words, the wide front door opened and Mom came rushing out.

I blinked and looked again just to make sure it was her. She was wearing a pair of jeans with the knees ripped out. Her black T-shirt was a little slouchy, and she had sneakers on her feet.

I would have denied it could be my mother—a woman I'd never seen wear anything ill-fitting or with holes. But there was no denying her identity. Her long dark hair floated behind her as she ran, and the unmistakable black-framed glasses were perched on her nose.

God, she looked so young like that.

Mom jumped in the passenger seat of the waiting yellow car, and I heard a woman giggle.

My mother never giggled.

Seconds later, the sports car turned away from the house and in my direction. I thought about hiding behind some of the landscaping nearby, but I was rooted in place by shock.

They drove right by me. Mom didn't even seem to notice I was there. She didn't glance my way once. But the man driving did.

He smiled. He had perfect white teeth, blue eyes, and very blond, messy hair.

CHAPTER TWENTY-FIVE

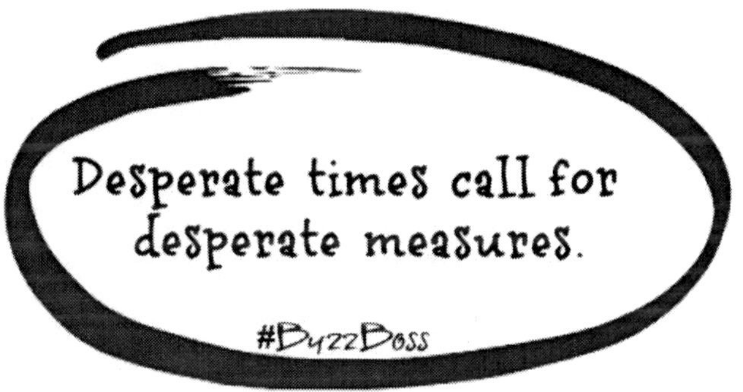

ZACH

"So your mother was having an affair?" Dr. Becks's voice broke into the memories that seemed to pour right out of me.

I snapped back to reality. I didn't like how easy all that was to recall.

Familiar feelings of betrayal and anger resurfaced. "Well, she wasn't having tea and cookies with the guy."

"It must have been a hard thing to see. Her with him."

"He was taking advantage of her," I replied.

"In what way?"

Her nosy question irritated me. "Using her innocence to get what he wanted. She was lonely and sad. He used it against her."

"Did you ever consider the fact that maybe he made her happy?"

"If she was happy, she wouldn't be dead."

Becks didn't react to my harsh statement. She remained calm. She had to be taking some of the drugs they passed out in here like candy. "You blame him, the other guy, for her death."

"Guys like him think they have a right to anything they want. They're arrogant and conceited. They're users."

"That's a blanket statement, don't you think? You're punishing *all* men you perceive to be like the man your mother ran off with because you assume they'll be just like him." She was trying to bring this conversation around to Romeo, trying to make the connection to why I hated him so much.

I didn't want to talk about Romeo.

"She didn't run off," I gritted out.

"Not in the literal sense. But she did leave your father, move out and in with the new guy, correct?"

She knew it was correct. It was all in my file.

But I played along. I'd told her this much. I might as well give her the rest. Let her think I was really opening up and spilling my deepest torment.

This conversation was just a means to an end.

Besides, it was about time I told someone how I got here. Hell, she'd probably recommend an early release by the time I was done. Everything I did was justifiable.

"He started hanging around more… Brett." I snarled. "The guy with the sports car. I hated my dad, but Mom bringing some other dude into his house wasn't cool. Some lines just shouldn't be crossed, you know?"

She made a noncommittal noise, and I ignored her and got up and paced to the window overlooking the parking lot.

"I thought I was the one making Mom happy. I thought I was the reason she was smiling. But it was him. She'd been seeing him for a while. No one knew. But the more time Dad spent away, the less secretive she became. It was like she just stopped caring who knew, like she no longer valued the perception of others. Of what her own son thought."

"This wasn't about you, Zach." Dr. Becks cut in. I took the fact she didn't use my full name as a good sign all my gut-spilling was working. "This was about your mother's demons. What she was feeling. Manic behavior oftentimes blurs the line of appropriate behavior."

I ignored her.

"I got tired of it. Of *Brett*." Just saying his name left a sour taste in my mouth. "Her whole world revolved around him. All the years of silent dinners, tense conversations, and being the perfect son… it was all for nothing. The only thing that seemed to make her happy was him."

I swung around and looked at Dr. Becks. "I got sick of it, so when my father came home, I told him. I told him about everything that was happening right there in his own home."

Dr. Becks nodded. "It wasn't your responsibility to keep that secret."

Mom never asked me to keep her relationship a secret, even though I said nothing for a while. I thought she'd see I was still the perfect son by not saying anything.

But when *he* came along, she didn't see me at all.

"Dad didn't even seem surprised. He acted like he already knew. The hate I had for him went away that day. I'd realized how misplaced it had been. He and I were a lot alike. I just never realized it. We both wanted her love. All the ways he'd tried to make her happy failed, just as I had failed."

"You must have been very confused," Dr. Becks interjected.

I nodded, lost in thought. I was. Everything I thought I knew about my parents was wrong. I'd punished my dad for years for mistakes I thought he made. But he'd remained loyal to my mother. He'd cleaned up my messes and kept the trouble I got in at school off the record so I'd have a fresh start at the new school I went to. He took the anger I directed at him without complaint.

And that time I heard him talking of sending me away?

I realized much later he wanted to do that because he thought I'd be better off away from *her*. Away from my own mother.

"So what happened once you told your father?" Dr. Becks prodded.

I felt my upper lip curl. I was tired of talking about this. I didn't like to think about my mother.

"He confronted my mother, they fought, and she left him," I summed up.

"Your mother filed for divorce?"

I shook my head. She never did. And my father never did either. He said it was better she keep his name. I learned later, if he'd divorced her, she would have lost all insurance. She wouldn't have been able to afford the medication she was on. Not that she was taking it.

He took care of her. Even after she moved in with another man, he tried to take care of her. I think he thought it was only a phase, that she'd wake up one morning and go back to who she really was. She'd go back on her meds.

"It's why she never smiled," I said to myself.

"What was that?" Becks asked.

"The medication she was on, it made her numb. She never smiled. She was vacant inside."

"So you understand it had nothing to do with you?"

I glanced at the doctor. "Of course." Then for effect, I added, "Of course, knowing that doesn't make it any easier."

"Of course not. But acknowledging the way you feel will go a long way."

I sat back in my assigned chair. There. It was done. I handed Becks my inner thoughts and my deepest pain. My bipolar mother, my lonely childhood, and my rocky relationship with my father.

"I know." I agreed with her because that's what she wanted. "And something good did come out of it all."

"What's that?"

"I bonded with my father. We have a very close relationship now. Through everything, he's always been there."

She smiled. "You are very lucky to have him as part of your support system. And your stepmother as well."

I forced down the urge to curl my upper lip in distaste. My stepmother Anna wanted nothing to do with me. I think my father thought he could replace my mother with a better version, a woman who would act like a real mother should: loving and kind.

She might be that way toward my father, but to Anna, I was just someone to tolerate, a visible reminder that she wasn't my father's first choice.

I didn't care much, because the feeling was mutual. I didn't like her either. But my father did, and I figured after everything he put up with for so many years, if Anna made him happy, then I'd tolerate her presence.

At least she wasn't blond. It was her saving grace.

"I just wish…" I started, then trailed off.

"You wish what?" Becks encouraged, just like I knew she would.

"This will be my first holiday without him." I looked down at my lap and focused on sounding forlorn. "Ever since Mom…" I paused for effect again.

"We always made sure we were together for the holidays."

"But this year you'll be here," she supplied.

I nodded.

"Why don't you tell me about how you got here?"

"I just did." God, didn't this woman ever stop? I might as well take out my damn brain and hand it to her on a platter so she could dissect it.

"Not necessarily. You told me about how you grew up, what shaped you into the man you are today. While, yes, what you have told me has shed some light on recent events, you have to tell me about the catalyst."

"The catalyst for what?"

"For the way you treated your victims, Romeo Anderson and Rimmel Hudson."

I sighed dramatically. "Don't you see? Romeo is just like Brett. Thinks he's God's gift to women. Preys on the ones who are too innocent to protect themselves. He doesn't care about anyone but himself and being the best."

"And Rimmel reminds you of your mother?"

"I think my mother was probably a lot like her before she met my father. Innocent, small, kind of fragile. My father saw those things in her. He wanted to protect her. He loved her and was loyal to her. Then Brett came along and took her away.

"I tried to warn her. I don't know how many times. Outside her class one day. In the haunted house. She wouldn't listen. She was so blind to him." I felt myself growing agitated. Just picturing the way those two walked around campus like they owned the place. It made me want to—

"So you punished them, because you can't punish your mother and Brett." Dr. Becks cut off my thoughts.

Fishing. She was always fishing for what she wanted.

"Yes. I punished them. It was wrong. I see that now. I let my past and my anger cloud my knowledge of right and wrong."

"Do you think your medication has helped you keep those impulses in check?"

"Of course." I lied. I never took that shit. I'd become an expert at hiding it in my mouth and waiting until no one was looking to get rid of it. Like I'd ever let myself become vacant and empty like my mother used to be.

There wasn't anything wrong with me. I just wasn't who everyone wanted me to be.

"And the fog you talked about your mother experiencing, the way her medication made her not smile." She glanced at me, assessing. "Do you feel that way?"

"No." That was the truth at least. Couldn't get foggy from something you never swallowed.

"Well, you are on a different brand and dosage," the doctor said, almost to herself, as she looked at my chart.

I glanced at the clock. Was this shit almost done? I might crawl out of my skin if I had to sit here with her any longer.

"Dr. Becks," I said impulsively. *Stupid!* I yelled at myself. Now was not the time to bring this up. But I' already spoken. I'd just tread lightly.

She glanced up.

"The thought of my father being alone for holidays is very painful for me."

"How so?"

"I feel immense guilt that my selfish ac going to cause a man that has been there

entire life—a man who has lost so much—to have no one to share the season with."

"Are you forgetting about Anna? He won't be alone."

God! She was insufferable!

"But *I'm* what makes them a family. My father…" I paused because I was losing focus. I just wanted to be finished. I sighed. "Maybe it's me who doesn't want to be alone."

Her reply?

"I'm sure he'll come here for visitor's day."

I looked at the cup of pencils on her desk. One of them was freshly sharpened and pointy. I thought about stabbing her right through the hand with it. I didn't just dredge up all these personal memories and thoughts to not get what I wanted.

Let me out of here!

I forced a smile. "It will be good to see him."

"How do you think your victims would feel if they aw you?" She turned the tables.

"I'm sure they're glad I'm locked up here."

"How would you feel if you saw them?"

I couldn't lie about this. She'd see right through it. "I'll never like Romeo or Rimmel. They will always represent something painful that I'll never forget."

"It's more than just your mother leaving, though, isn't it? It's more than her having an affair. There's more to the story, isn't there, Zachary? There's the way it all ended."

I stared at her without blinking for a long time. She didn't seem to mind the way I studied her. I could read between the lines. I knew exactly what she wanted.

She wanted it all. The entire story.

It was the only thing that would give me a chance of getting out of here for a couple weeks.

She wanted to know the end of my childhood. The part I'd never spoken of out loud. She wanted to know what finally pushed me over the edge.

The catalyst.

The catalyst that broke me.

#

Betrayed. That's how I felt.

Everything I'd believed was wrong.

Dad wasn't the enemy. Mom wasn't a victim.

Well, yes, she was, just a victim of someone other than my father.

Mom moved out, packed her stuff and sped off in that bright-yellow car. I asked her only once if I could come with her.

"I thought you said the reason you stayed here was because of me. Now you're leaving me behind," I told her as she threw things in a bag.

"I'm not leaving you behind," she said. "You can come visit me whenever you like."

If it weren't for him, the blond-haired, blue-eyed womanizer, this wouldn't be happening.

She'd see. She'd leave here and miss us—miss me—and then she'd see him for what he really was.

Months passed.

She didn't see.

If anything, she seemed to get further and further away.

My father stopped trying to call her. He stopped trying to reason with her. It was like he'd given up.

I wasn't ready to give up, so I kept going to visit her. She and Brett were living across town, in a house on the lake. I wasn't sure who was paying for it all. Obviously Brett had some money, because he paid for that car and all his clothes. But Mom had money too. Dad never cut her off. He still supported her; she still had access to accounts and credit cards. I knew because when I visited her, she'd take me shopping and use Dad's black card.

I couldn't understand why he would pay for her to live another life, a life without us.

With him.

Brett didn't like me much. I didn't care because the feeling was mutual. He seemed pissed when I would come around, like having a kid was an annoyance. I pretended he wasn't there.

Well, except when no one was looking. I might not act out toward my father anymore, but that part of me was still alive and well. So I directed it all at Brett.

I poured vinegar in the milk he used for his coffee and watched as he spit a mouthful out all over the table. I drilled a hole in the canoe he used for fishing and watched him get to the center of the lake before he realized the boat was taking on water.

None of the stupid pranks made him want to leave, though.

I had to kick it up a notch.

So I put a lace thong in his glove box and paid a girl at school to call my mom and tell her she was sleeping with Brett.

Mom of course didn't believe her, so she told her to go see the proof in car.

I lay in bed that night and listened for the fireworks. Come Monday morning, Mom would come home.

I didn't know then that Mom was severely bipolar. I didn't know she had manic ups and downs. I didn't know my father was talking with specialists in Switzerland to get her an exclusive room at a top-notch facility.

I didn't know my actions would ruin everything.

I was just a teenager, a fucked-up one.

No yelling ever came that night. No crying. No accusations. She didn't come into my room to tell me we were going home. She didn't come in my room at all.

But Brett did.

He opened the door and strolled right in. I still remember the sound of the latch on the door as it closed behind him. He stood over my bed and stared down at me. I tried to scramble up, but he shoved me back down.

"You think I don't know you're doing all that shit?" he asked.

I didn't answer.

"You trying to get rid of me?"

"I don't like you."

His white teeth flashed in the dark. Something twisted in my stomach.

"Here's the thing, kid. Your mom and I have a good thing going. I'm not going anywhere. You, on the other hand…"

"I'm not going anywhere either."

"Then I think you owe me an apology."

"I don't owe you shit."

He grabbed me up by the front of my shirt and lifted me partially out of the bed. "If you don't want me poisoning your mother's mind against you, then I think you do."

He couldn't do that!

Could he?

He chuckled and let me go. I fell back on the mattress. "I can and I will."

I felt my shoulders slump a little. I believed him. My mother would probably take any excuse to get rid of me.

"Sorry," I mumbled.

"What was that?"

I said it again, louder.

"If you think that's an apology, then you've got something to learn."

I looked up. "What do you want?"

"I want to make sure I'm not gonna have any problems with you again."

"I already said I'd stop," I growled.

"Yeah, but I don't trust you."

He popped the button on his jeans and reached for his fly.

I felt my eyes round and I crawled backward on the mattress. "What are you doing?"

"Showing you who the boss is around here." He pushed the jeans down so he was standing there with them around his knees and only a pair of red boxers covering him.

I scrambled toward edge of the bed. This guy was a fucking freak! I had no idea what the hell he was doing, but I wasn't staying around for it.

He caught my shoulder and shoved me back. I fell but quickly sat up. He rubbed the front of his boxers, right where his junk was, and my stomach churned.

"I've always wondered what it would be like to have another guy suck my dick. So I'll tell you what. You do it right now, and I'll forget about all the shit you've pulled lately and I won't say anything to your mom."

"Fuck no," I swore and tried to get off the bed again.

Once again, he stopped me and pushed me back. Before I could say anything, he pulled his cock free of the boxers, pushing the fabric down just far enough to reveal his shaft and balls.

"Make it up to me," he demanded, low. "Or I'll make sure you never see her again."

This guy was seriously sick and perverted. I started to yell, to scream for help. He grabbed the back of my neck with one hand and slapped the other over my mouth. "Don't even think about it, you little fuck. This is a lesson you need to learn."

He straightened and pulled me with him, positioning my face right in front of his still swollen member. Bile rose in the back of my throat.

"I'm gonna let go of your mouth, but if you try and scream again, it's going to get real ugly. Understand?"

I was so shocked I could barely think. Was this seriously happening? Did stuff like this actually happen in real life? Did he really think I was just going to suck him off as an apology for what I'd done? That it would somehow teach me a lesson to never cross him again? God, he was so twisted. What in the hell did my mother see in him?

"Answer me!" he demanded and shoved the tip of his head against his hand that was still plastered against my mouth.

I nodded once.

He left one hand on the back of my head but slowly peeled the other off my mouth. The second his hand was free, he pressed his flesh up against my lips.

I gagged. He took advantage of my open mouth and slipped the tip between my lips.

Adrenaline surged through my body along with the fight or flight response. I didn't even think it through. I just reacted.

I bit down hard on the spongy flesh intruding upon my lips.

The metallic taste of blood shot across my tongue, and Brett howled. He jerked away and hunched over, and I gave a loud shout and leapt off the bed.

"You bit me, you little fucker!" Brett yelled, but it sounded more like a groan.

I heard a commotion outside the bedroom door and then it swung open. I was gathering up my backpack against the wall and picking up my shoes.

"Zachary?" Mom said. Light from the hallway spilled into the room and landed like a spotlight on Brett and his hunched-over form.

"Brett? What happened?"

"That monster attacked me!" he howled.

Mom gasped and looked at me.

Wide-eyed, I shook my head. "He shoved his cock in my face, so I bit it."

Her face paled, stark white in seconds. "What?"

"He's a perv, Mom."

Brett roared and stood up. I followed Mom's stare down to his crotch where his softened pecker was smeared with blood.

"Oh my God," she whispered.

"You left me and Dad for that*!" I yelled.*

"Come here, you little son of a bitch!" Brett stumbled toward me, and I took off.

Out in the hall, I heard a loud thud, and even though I was scared out of my mind and disgusted beyond belief, I stopped.

I turned back.

As badly as I wanted out of here, I didn't want Mom to take the brunt for what I'd done.

She wasn't. Brett had gotten tangled in his pulled-down pants and fell over. He was lying in a heap on the floor. When he saw me looking around the doorway, he started cussing and vowing all kinds of bodily harm. When he managed to get to his knees, Mom grabbed my arm.

"Run, Zachary. Run and don't look back."

"Come with me," I said.

Her eyes were sad when she patted my cheek. "My perfect boy."

Brett was back on his feet and lunged into the hallway.

"Run! I'll be right behind you!"

I ran as fast as I could. I rushed out into the night and down the street. It was only when I looked over my shoulder to make sure she was following that I noticed my footsteps were the only ones. I turned back toward the house, debating.

Going back there was the last thing I ever wanted to do.

The distinct sound of a gunshot filled the night.

It was followed seconds later by another one.

My lower lip wobbled in the still of the night. I stood there in the center of the dark street, utterly alone.

Not another sound came.

I knew.

I knew then my mother was dead.

CHAPTER TWENTY-SIX

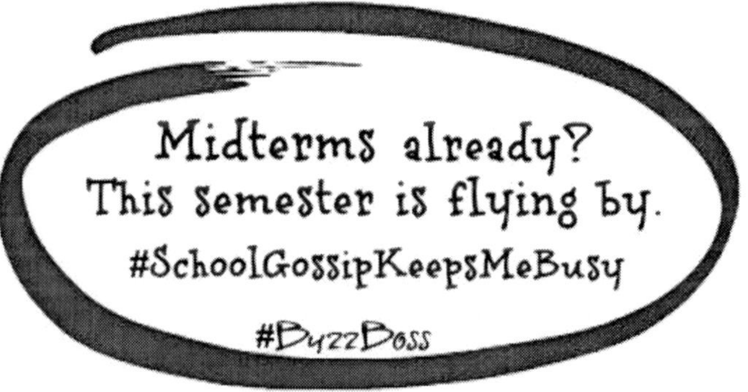

ZACH

She shot Brett and then she shot herself.

It was considered a homicide-suicide, which is what it was. But to me, it couldn't be summed up in two words.

That incident seemed to flip a switch inside me. It turned on a part of me I hadn't known was there. I kept it hidden mostly. I never let it get out of control.

My father knew what really happened that night. He told me the bite marks on Brett's cock weren't consistent with my mother's jaw.

He asked me one time.

He asked me if it had been me, if Brett tried something and I'd defended myself.

I only nodded.

We never spoke of it again.

I assumed he told the police, the ones who questioned the bite marks. I was never interrogated. It was never in the news.

My father made it all go away.

Except for the damage he couldn't see inside of me.

To his credit, he sent me to therapy. I would merely sit in the chair until my hour was up and then leave. I never spoke about that night. I wouldn't. Some things couldn't be explained in words, especially not to a stranger sitting behind a desk.

The effects of my mother's suicide and the incident with Brett were shoved down deep… way into the darkest corner of my mind.

And then I met Romeo.

Alpha U star. Mr. Perfect himself. He wanted to rush my frat. I shut that shit down. He was everything I hated about the man who was the downfall of my mother. He thought he was untouchable. He thought he was a god among men. Him and that sports car of his could go to hell.

I kept him out of the frat. I kept my hatred for him under wraps.

And then Rimmel came along.

Dark hair. Glasses. Fragile. She reminded me of my mother. It wasn't a memory I was prepared to see every single day.

I saw her looking at Romeo one day. I knew that look. I knew she was weak and would fall for him too.

That part of me I kept buried?

I unearthed it.

Seeing them walking around was far too tempting. Seeing the way they looked at each other. Out of respect for my mother, I warned her. I thought maybe

Rimmel would listen, that maybe in a sick way, my mother could have another chance.

But she was stupid too.

So I tried to ruin Romeo's reputation. That would show her she needed to get away from him.

The little bitch was far too loyal and too far under his spell.

So I tried to get her expelled. I'd have her sent away and my problems would be solved. She'd be gone and Romeo would be far away from my frat. I could bury these feelings once again and move on.

But it didn't work out like that.

They loved each other. They had too many friends. It seemed everything in the universe worked to keep them together…

And it made me fall apart.

But no matter.

I made a breakthrough here today. At the mental ward, with Dr. Becks.

I spoke of the unspeakable.

I admitted all the feelings inside me.

Becks was so impressed she said I was on my way to total healing. Whatever that meant. Hopefully, it meant I'd get sprung sooner rather than later.

In fact, she was so happy she seemed to "fix" me, she didn't notice the things I didn't say.

The new unspeakable.

I would say anything to get out of here.

Time spent locked away had allowed me to rebuild. To realize if I wanted to take someone down, I had to do it indirectly. I had to do it quietly. I also realized I didn't have to hate Romeo and Rimmel because they reminded me of people in my past.

I could hate them without any excuse at all.

CHAPTER TWENTY-SEVEN

ZACH

I was starting to think he wasn't coming.

I sat there at visitation, watching patients greeted by family or whoever it was that gave enough of a damn to come see them. Last month was the first time I was allowed a visitor. My father came, and it was good to see him.

My father was a lot of things. A successful, feared lawyer. A pillar of Maryland society. A son. A father. A widower. A husband.

I spent a lot of time in my early years hating him. But as a child grows, as a boy becomes a man, he sees a clearer picture of the people who raised them. He isn't so much blinded by the identity of *mother* and *father* and learns to see the individuals behind those titles.

My father wasn't a perfect man; he made a lot of mistakes. He married my mother out of love, but he wasn't able to hold on to it. Their love, their relationship became about codependence. My mother needed my father like a sapling needed water. Instead of getting her the help she truly needed before it was too late, he enabled her. I think he liked being needed by her.

He let her become overmedicated, a mere shell of the woman he married, and they settled into some plastic existence. He never bothered to look around and see how that affected me. He wasn't affectionate and he didn't give praise often. Frankly, it was probably good they only had one child.

He did what he thought was right. I blamed him for that for a long time. But I couldn't hold him at fault because he'd always been there for me.

Even when I didn't think he was. Even when I didn't understand.

Even now.

My mother took the easy way out and killed herself. My father stayed and picked up the pieces.

So where was he? Why wasn't he here?

Just as I started getting annoyed, a door off to the side opened. It led to the administrative wing where the doctors kept their offices and therapy rooms.

My father stepped into the doorway and turned to say something over his shoulder. When he turned back, the door opened a little wider and I caught Dr. Becks's profile.

Well, this was interesting. My father had a meeting with her?

His eyes scanned the room until they landed on me. He moved with ease as he made his way over. He was dressed impeccably in a dark-grey three-piece suit and tie. His short, graying hair was combed neatly and his face was clean-shaven.

He was starting to age, with fine lines around his eyes and a deeper one across his forehead. He always looked a little tired, though he tried not to.

Approaching the table, he said, "Son."

"Dad," I said as he sat down. I didn't bother to get up. We never hugged. "I didn't think you were coming."

"You know I wouldn't miss a visitation."

I nodded.

"So how're you doing?" he asked, looking me over.

I knew I looked well. I made sure of it. "I'm fine."

He nodded slowly.

"You had a meeting with Dr. Becks?" I asked, not wanting to wait around.

"Yes, I did. She seems rather impressed with the progress you're making. Said you've really opened up lately."

I nodded sagely. "I feel a lot better, more in control."

"She mentioned you're having some anxiety about me being alone for the holidays."

"We've been together every holiday since Mom…"

He nodded quickly. "I'm going to be fine, son."

My chest deflated a little and my mood spiraled downward. That didn't sound like I was getting out of here.

"She asked me how I thought you would do with a brief home visit over the holidays."

I looked up and grinned. "And you said?"

He smiled slightly. "I said it might be good for you."

"Thanks, Dad!" I tried to keep the enthusiasm down a notch, but it was so hard. The thought of getting out of here was enough to make me salivate.

"Not so fast. It's not a done deal. It depends on the next few weeks, what the judge says based on Dr. Becks's report and arrangements for your outpatient care."

"What kind of care?"

"You're still in treatment, Zach. Therapy sessions, medication monitoring, etc. All that will need to be done at home."

I didn't care. I just wanted out of here.

"There's talk of you wearing an ankle bracelet."

Well, that wouldn't do.

I tried to hide my anger and annoyance. "It's not like I killed anyone. Geez."

"Need I remind you what you did?" Dad took on a stern tone. "I saw that girl at the hospital, Zachary."

I resisted the urge to sneer. How dare he judge me! Rimmel deserved everything she got.

"There just isn't an excuse for what you did to her."

I wanted to yell and argue. I certainly didn't want to sit here and be contrite. Not with my own father. It was bad enough I had to play that game all day long.

Still, I sucked it up. "I know and I'm ashamed of what I've done. I'm on medication now. It keeps me level."

His shoulders deflated, and he patted my hand. It was as close to a hug as I would get from him. "I know, son. It's clear you've been working hard. I'm going to make sure you get all the help you need. If I had done that for your mother…"

"I'm nothing like her," I insisted, my voice hard.

"Of course not." He glanced around to see if anyone noticed my distress. "I just want to make sure you're feeling your best."

I wanted to laugh at how quickly he made it sound like I was at a spa.

Dad cleared his throat and glanced at the clock on the wall. "Well, I know I didn't stay as long as last time, but Dr. Becks wanted to speak to me."

"It's okay. I appreciate you coming."

"I'll always be here for you, son. And Anna sends her love."

That was a lie.

He stood, and I did the same.

"You'll follow up with Dr. Becks about the holidays?"

"Of course. Hopefully, this time next month, we'll be watching football and eating turkey."

Football. Ugh. "Sounds great!" I lied.

After he left, I sat at my empty table and watched some of the other people a few more minutes before going back to my cell—I mean room.

When I stood up to leave, one of the orderlies motioned for me to sit back down. As I sat, he came over. "You have another visitor."

"Me?" I asked, confused. There was no one that would come here other than my dad.

"Yep. Time's almost up. Keep it brief."

I stared at the entrance where the visitors were ushered in. A few seconds later, the door buzzed and opened.

Someone familiar stepped into the room.

Well, well, well…

This was going to be interesting.

CHAPTER TWENTY-EIGHT

ZACH

I watched her long, slim legs as she approached me. They didn't make her brand in this place. After all, any woman who looked like that wouldn't spend a second in here. Even if somehow someone like her was sent in, she wouldn't walk out the same.

So I took the time to appreciate the fine eye candy headed my way without thinking too much about what this could mean.

I knew it was going to be good whatever it was, but first, I was going to enjoy the view.

She was wearing a short skirt and heels. I didn't notice the color; all I saw was skin. Her top wasn't overly tight, but I still looked at her tits. They weren't large, but they were perky. Definitely better than anything in here.

She stopped at the table, and I lounged back in my seat and slowly looked up. I wanted to give her an official onceover. I wanted to smirk and say something inappropriate.

But I couldn't.

People were watching.

Doctors were watching. Those who signed papers that would let me out of here. Instead, I settled for a polite smile and folded my arms across my chest. "How'd you get in here?"

"I have my ways," she replied and perched on the chair across from me.

"Do tell." I leaned forward in interest.

She shrugged one thin shoulder. "No rules against a girl checking up on her poor, sick former classmate."

I stared at her another minute. She was hot, the best looking one out of the ragtag bunch that hung in her social circle. Her dark hair was sleek around her shoulders and framed her made-up face and watchful gray eyes.

Funny, I never really noticed how much those eyes actually saw. There was something shrewd deep in them, like she missed nothing.

"Are you here to tell me how terrible I am, Missy?" I asked.

"I'm pretty sure you don't need someone to tell you. Especially not in here." She glanced around with distaste.

It amused me. In fact, this entire conversation was amusing. It was the most entertainment I'd had since I walked through the doors of this prison.

"Then why are you here?"

She reached down beside her and pulled up a basket. "Thought you'd like a few things to make your stay here more comfortable." She slid it across the table.

I glanced down. It was filled with designer soaps and lotions. Much better quality than what they provided in here. There were also a few bags of candy and some business and men's magazines.

"What, no fashion mags?" I asked like I was unimpressed.

"Oh, did you want to read your horoscope?" she mocked. "Here, let me just sum it up for you. You're going to hell." Missy's glossy lips pulled into a sweet yet sardonic smile.

I smirked and let out a full-on laugh disguised as a chuckle.

"I'm here to give you information," she said, her smile disappearing and a more business-like tone taking over her voice.

"You mean giving me this totes adorbs basket wasn't why you came all this way?" I batted my eyes and tried to speak her native tongue.

Okay, I just wanted to mock her.

She rolled her eyes and gave me a disgusted look. "Get real. But you of all people know how it works. Gotta play the part."

Ah, yes, I knew very well. I was just surprised she seemed to know.

"What information could you possibly have that I would want?" I asked, my interest growing.

"I know about what you did to Ivy."

Well now. I sat back and narrowed my eyes. "I don't know what you're talking about."

She laughed like I said something funny and smiled like this was just the bestest visit ever. I'd hand it to her. She was good at playing the part.

"I think you do," she said in a much lower, serious tone after her display of friendliness.

In truth, I knew exactly what she was talking about.

The night I roofied Ivy and had my way with her.

#

I did it as a means to an end. A way to get access to Rimmel's room.

But I guess if I were being totally honest with myself, I would admit maybe there was more to it than that. I wanted to take a blond-haired, blue-eyed looker for a ride. I wanted to know what all the fuss was about with her kind.

She was basically the female version of Romeo. *The female version of the type my mother left me and my father for. The type that was her ultimate downfall.*

What was it about these fun-seeking, laidback blond bombshells that made everyone so crazy anyway? They had no substance. It was all about status with them. All about a good time.

Couldn't blame a guy for wanting a sample of the stock.

I hadn't set out to drug her. I thought she'd fall right into my bed. Everyone knew she was easy. Everyone knew she got around.

At the party that night, Ivy was looking fine and living it up. Drinking too much and laughing loud. She was constantly surrounded by people, the life of the party. Guys checked her out from all angles, and she seemed to like it.

So I watched her that night. I waited until she was pretty drunk, worked my way into the crowd around her, and cracked a couple jokes to make her drunk ass laugh.

Then I made a move on her.

Stupid bitch acted like I had some kind of disease. She didn't want anything to do with me, like I was somehow lesser than every other guy in the house. Romeo *thought I was scum, so that must mean I totally was.*

It pissed me off.

How dare she act just like the rest of them! Like she was too good for me. Didn't blondes like any attention they got?

When she was in line for the bathroom, I approached her. I pinned her up against the wall and kissed her. She smacked me across the face.

People nearby laughed at me.

I played it off and laughed too. Made some comment about how I liked it rough.

Inside, I was fuming, but I kept it contained. When she locked herself in the bathroom, I went and found the drug. That shit was so easy to find on campus; they might as well set up a station for it at the food court.

I grabbed a pill, dropped it in a beer, and let it dissolve.

When she was back in the crowd, surrounded by her followers, I sidled up to her. She rolled her eyes and told me to get lost. I swallowed my nasty comeback and apologized for trying to kiss her.

Her drunk, clueless ass thought I was sincere. I offered her the beer as an apology. She stared at me so long I thought she was suspicious. I started to freak out a little, thinking she somehow knew what I was up to.

But then she shrugged and snatched the cup. Ivy downed that beer like the bad little girl she was.

She was so wasted it didn't take long at all.

I got her back to her room, used her keycard, and let us in. The first thing I did was dump her on the bed. She had no clue what was going on. She actually thanked me for bringing her back home so she could sleep off the liquor.

I accepted her thanks, of course. I was a gentleman after all.

While she lay there out of her mind, I hurried to find Rimmel's laptop. I did everything I needed to do and left the trail behind on her hard drive so I could get in later.

When I was done, I almost left. Okay, I didn't almost leave. I thought about it for a passing second. And then I laughed.

At first, I thought she was passed out. The drugs made Ivy practically boneless. But when I stood over her and looked down, her eyes fluttered open and barely focused on me.

"What are you doing?" she slurred.

I smiled and pulled off my shirt. "Giving you exactly what you want."

I reached down and grabbed her boob. She had nice full ones.

"No!" She tried to slap my hand away but didn't have enough control.

I yanked off her shirt and bra, letting her half-naked body flop back down on the bed. Her blue eyes widened and I saw fear in their depths. It made me feel high, gave me a rush.

"Don't touch me!" she moaned.

I grabbed her face with my hand and squeezed. "You think you're too good for me?" I spat. "You're not. I'm too good for you. *You should think of this as a gift."*

I shoved her face away and pinched her nipple.

She whimpered.

I reached for my jeans and unbuttoned the top.

A clear memory of years ago when Brett had done the same thing flashed through my mind. He was trying to show me he had the power and he was the one in control.

It didn't work, though, because in the end, I won.

I always won.

I'm the one who taught him *a lesson, just as Ivy was gonna get one right now.*

But I wasn't like Brett. Not really. He was a sick pervert. Ivy wanted this. She just didn't want to admit it. And at least she was a girl. Trying to prove dominance over another man through sex was just nasty, but dominance in the bedroom with a female…?

That was different.

Romeo thought no one could touch him. He thought he was above us all.

Well, he was going to find out just how wrong he was. I was going to penetrate his inner circle. I was going to take away everything he held dear.

But first, I'd start with penetrating this blonde. The female version of him.

"No, please," she begged when my clothes were gone and I climbed on the bed.

"Just lie there and enjoy it. It's the best you'll ever have," I told her. "Shame you won't remember this tomorrow." I sighed regretfully. I leaned down close, and she tried to turn away. It didn't matter. I knew she could hear my whispered words. "Deep down," I said, shoving my hand down her panties and cupping her sex, "deep inside, you'll know…"

After I had my way with her, I took a couple pics. By that point, Ivy was practically passed out, so she didn't even protest. These pictures would just be one more way to show Romeo I could take what I wanted, that his perfect existence wasn't so perfect after all.

I knew exactly what I would do with them too.

I'd send them to the campus gossip hound, the #BuzzBoss himself. He'd post them up for everyone to see.

Then everyone would know who the true alpha of Alpha U really was.

#

"You're really just going to sit there and pretend you don't know what I mean?" Her voice brought me out of the memory, and I glanced up.

"What?"

She made a huffing sound. "I saw the pictures."

I sat up straighter in my seat and stared her down. She looked back without blinking. "How?" I said slowly, trying to understand.

"I have my ways." She smirked.

"Did the #BuzzBoss post them recently?" I asked, panic making my leg jump underneath the table. I tried to remain calm, to appear unruffled. It was fucking hard. Those pictures couldn't get out.

Not now. Not ever.

"One," she replied. "A very naughty one of you two in bed. The whole campus was atwitter at the sight of Ivy's naked chest."

Wait a minute.

There was more to this. Missy was like Ivy's shadow; the two went everywhere together. It took a while to get Ivy alone at the party that night just so I could get her back to her dorm room. And if Missy knew what I'd done to Ivy, then she wouldn't be sitting there all calm and collected.

Wouldn't she be outraged?

Wouldn't she be pointing a finger and yelling, "Rape," for all to hear?

Did Missy think what Ivy and I did was consensual? Is that what everyone thought? This was good. This could work in my favor.

I'd been on a high that night. I hadn't been thinking straight. I was pumped up from pulling off breaking into Rimmel's room and starting my next plan to bring down Romeo. I was also pretty keyed up over the hot sex I'd just had.

So I did something stupid. I sent the pics I took throughout the night (with the help of a couple of my buds) to the #BuzzBoss.

At the time, I thought of those pictures as trophies. Of proof of how good I was.

But I didn't see them that way now.

Now they were evidence. They were nails in my coffin. If word got out, proof that I assaulted a girl after slipping her the date rape drug, my cushy cell here might be exchanged for something a little less cozy.

If I thought this place was bad, I'd never survive prison.

There are probably guys just like Brett there. Men waiting to assert their dominance over guys like me.

But Missy said she knew what *I* did. Not what *we* did. That implied she knew Ivy wasn't exactly wanting what I gave her.

And…

She said she saw the pics—plural. If the #BuzzBoss only posted one, then how did she know there were more?

I looked at her sharply.

Her glossy, painted lips stretched into a slow smile.

It was the kind of smile I sometimes saw in the mirror (minus the gloss, of course).

"You're the #BuzzBoss?" I asked in equal parts awe and shock.

"In the flesh."

"Well, I'll be damned," I crooned and stuck out my hand. "I need to shake your hand. You're a goddamn genius."

She looked at my outstretched arm, then back up at me. "I'm not touching you." She sniffed.

I wasn't offended. I was still too awed by her fucking brilliance.

"So all this time, you've just been pretending to be friends with those status freaks?" I asked, warming up to this conversation.

I finally felt like I was amongst equals. That I'd finally met someone who was at my level.

Damn, it felt good.

She half shrugged. "I wouldn't say that."

I pursed my lips and studied her. Missy didn't seem put off by my stare. In fact, I think she kind of liked it. She probably felt relieved she was finally around someone so similar to her level of genius.

"So," I surmised, "if you hadn't planned to take them all down from the beginning, then what, or should I say *who*, caused you to snap?"

Beneath her white top, her shoulders tensed. It told me I was on the right track.

"I didn't come here to talk about my personal feelings," she snarled.

"I think you did." I disagreed. "I think you needed to talk to someone who understands what it feels like to be their victim."

Her nose wrinkled. "You are not a victim."

"Only because I wouldn't let myself be. Just like you. So tell me, Missy. Why did you post that picture of Ivy and me after months and months of sitting on it?"

"She slept with Braeden." The words rushed out.

"Ahh," I sang and sat back. She squirmed in her seat. "So the blond swooped in and took away the one you wanted."

We had so very much in common. She had no idea.

"She knew I wanted him," Missy snapped.

"So you posted a picture that would totally ruin her reputation and make Braeden regret falling into bed with her." I rubbed my hands together. "Brava."

Oh, the things I've missed while locked up in here.

Her grey eyes shifted away as if she were embarrassed and her arms wrapped around her middle. She didn't exactly appear to be a woman vindicated. And if she'd gotten back everything she wanted, she wouldn't be sitting here with me.

"So what happened?" I asked. "Didn't your big reveal work? Did your choice of meat move on to better pastures instead of coming back like you planned?"

The look on her face appeared reminiscent of sucking on an entire lemon. Sour, bitter, and slightly pissed off.

My eyes widened, and the words bubbled out of me almost with glee. "Don't tell me. She batted those big blues of hers and he stayed."

Missy made a choking sound. "He says he loves her," she muttered. "The guy who never wanted to settle down."

"Once again, the power of the blond wins."

Missy looked at me like I'd lost my mind. "What?"

"Forget it." I brushed aside the words and leaned my elbows on the table. "As much as I've enjoyed this little visit, I must ask. What does any of this have to do with me?"

"I'm not the only one who knows about Ivy. He saw all the pictures too. He knows what you did."

"Who?"

"Braeden."

I slapped my hand down on the table. "How could you let this happen!"

She jumped a little at my sudden movement. "I didn't *let* it happen," she hissed. "He broke into my laptop and went through all my files. He found me out."

"What about Ivy?" I asked. "What does she say?"

Just then, an orderly came over to the table. "Five minutes."

Missy looked up at him and smiled deliciously. "Thank you, sir. I'll just say my good-byes."

The orderly was also taken with her exotic beauty and never-ending legs. He cleared his throat and walked away.

Missy leaned close. "She doesn't know."

"You mean the guy who professes to love her didn't tell her?" This just kept getting better and better.

"No. He doesn't want to hurt her." I saw the flash of regret in her eyes, and I knew now why the #BuzzBoss never posted the pictures when I first sent them. She didn't want to hurt Ivy either. Until the blonde got in the way of what she wanted.

Missy was a woman after my own heart, the devious little minx.

"This is serious." She snapped her fingers in my face. "He is beyond pissed. Braeden has a bad temper."

I shrugged. "What do I care? He can't get to me, and he isn't going to say anything, because if he does, he'll have to admit he's been lying."

"He's waffling." She seemed way less convinced that our secret was safe. "I think he's going to tell her."

"What makes you think that?"

"Because I've seen him. It's eating him alive." The emotion in her voice when she talked about her old flame made me angry. It made her sound like she still had feelings for him.

I started to push away from the table. This conversation was over. I had my own agenda. I couldn't be bothered with hers.

"Wait," she said and reached across the table to take my hand.

I looked down where she touched me. Her olive-toned skin looked warm and inviting next to mine—which hadn't seen the sun in far too long.

I lowered back into my seat.

"I'm pretty sure it would be bad for you if what you did gets out. They might lock you up longer."

She didn't remove her hand as she spoke. She still touched me, still wrapped her fingers around mine. I couldn't remember the last time someone voluntarily touched me.

"I'm getting better," I said. "They think I'll get out soon. I'm even getting to spend the holidays at home with my father."

Missy gave my hand a light squeeze. "So you definitely don't want this to get out."

No, I really didn't. But I didn't say it. "I would think if he tells all, it would be pretty bad for you as well. You'd become the campus pariah pretty quick. You'd be ostracized just like me."

In the depths of her stormy gray eyes, I saw something I hadn't seen since she sat down.

Fear.

"Probably even kicked out of Alpha U," I added just because I wanted to see more of that look in her eye.

I liked seeing her frightened. It was like she looked to me to make it better.

Her hand jolted at my words.

I flipped my hand over so they were palm to palm. "What do you want, Missy?" I asked softly.

"I don't know what to do. How to stop him from telling Ivy. Because once she knows, they're going to tell the entire world."

Maybe she wouldn't. Maybe being violated like that would be the last thing she'd want anyone to know. I had first-hand experience with something like that.

But I didn't say that to Missy.

But then, of course, there was Braeden. He was a lot like Romeo. He wasn't just going to let this go. He would want to see me punished. Maybe even see Missy punished.

"You want me to help you, don't you?" I asked.

She nodded. "It would be bad for both of us if what you did came out."

Indeed it would.

Visitors started getting up and filing out of the room. I glanced down at our joined hands.

"All right, Missy. I'll help you. I'll see what I can do."

She let out a relieved breath and gathered up her bag. Reluctantly, I let go of her hand. "Thanks, Zach."

I wrapped my hand around the handle of the basket she brought and watched her walk away.

Fascinating things were happening on the outside.

So fascinating that now, more than ever, I had to get out of here.

IT'S ABOUT TO GO DOWN IN ALPHA TOWN...

(AKA PART THREE)

CHAPTER TWENTY-NINE

IVY

I didn't want to think I was slowly losing it.

I wanted to deny I suspected there might be something wrong with me.

After the incident at Screamerz a couple weeks ago, I did everything I could to shut it all down. Talk about embarrassing. It wasn't the first time I'd been grabbed from behind on the dance floor by someone wanting to dance. It wasn't a big deal, yet the way I reacted, you'd think I was being attacked.

I freaked out so bad Drew punched the guy right in the face. 'Course, that only made things worse. When I fell to the ground, it's like all reason and logic fled from my brain. My body totally took over and a panic attack took control.

I wasn't a person prone to panic attacks and anxiety. I was usually laidback and a go-with-the-flow type girl.

I changed, though. Lately, I was a lot less laidback and a lot more rattled.

Braeden drove me home that night. He held me through the trembling that wracked my frame, and he wouldn't let me apologize. Not even once.

In fact, as I was drifting off to blissful sleep, I heard him tell me he was sorry.

What could he possibly be sorry for?

He hadn't done anything but be there to help me get through.

The next morning, my body was tired and sore, like I'd run a marathon. I drank coffee in bed, hiding from the entire house, afraid to come out, afraid to face the questions and the stares.

I told B I heard his apology. I never asked him why he felt he should be sorry.

He never asked me for an explanation. He didn't ask why I flipped out that way.

I kept thinking about that morning in the shower and how I'd basically reacted the same way, just not quite as extreme. He hadn't pushed me then either. I remember thinking at the time it was like he sort of understood.

But how could he when I didn't?

I was afraid to ask that too.

When he told me he wanted to talk, I shot him down.

I wasn't ready to talk. I wasn't ready to uncover the doubts in my head or in my heart.

I loved him so much it hurt.

And I was terrified I was going to lose him.

Braeden didn't push me. He gave no reason for me to think our relationship was in danger.

The heart didn't need reason.

The heart had a mind of its own.

The space between us I thought we reclaimed the night under the stars was back, wider than ever.

I never quite understood how paralyzing and all-consuming fear could be. How it turned you into an alternate version of yourself. I became someone I didn't even like.

I wanted the old me back. The makeup-loving, fashionista, happy girl who wasn't afraid of her own shadow.

Braeden probably wanted that me back too. He didn't strike me as the type of guy who wanted to date a head case.

I did my best to hide the darkness within me. I tried not to let anyone see. No one except Drew asked me about that night. I laughed it off and told him I had too much to drink.

He said he believed me, but deep down, I knew he didn't.

I was starting to wonder if perhaps he sensed there was something wrong with me all along and that was why he was really here.

Everyone got busy fast, which also made living in denial a lot easier. The football season was heating up.

Braeden had training and practice before and after classes. I picked up some extra shifts at the boutique, and we all started cramming for midterms.

Thanksgiving break was almost here, and once that was over, we would be on a downhill slope to the end of the first semester.

The declaration of a major letter lay open on the dresser in our room. I stared at it almost every day. Braeden had one too, right beside mine.

Sometimes we laughed about our poor decision-making skills. Other times it made me worry how we would hold on to the decision of each other if we couldn't decide on anything else.

It was cold outside now, the crisp bite of autumn gone and the cold promise of winter in its place. I was at the boutique, unpacking a few shipments of more winter clothes to stock on the floor. As I went through the boxes, I set aside some extra cute combinations so I could style the mannequins around the store.

That was probably my favorite part about this job, mixing and matching pieces to make complete ensembles.

The owner of the place let me run with my creativity. She said I was better at it than she was.

I reached into the box and my hand closed around a stack of shirts I'd yet to unearth. I pulled them out and plucked one from the top and held it out.

"Oooh," I said to myself. It was a soft, flowy material, a lot thinner than most winter shirts should be, but that's what coats were for.

And staying inside.

The front was completely white with a rounded hem, but the long sleeves were a sheer gray with yellow polka dots. I turned the top over to look at the back.

"O.M.Geee," I squealed to no one but myself (the shop was empty). "I need this."

The back was in the same style as the sleeves and there was a big V-shaped opening up the back. It would be totally adorable with a coordinating tank beneath it and a pair of destructed jeans.

I found my size in the pile and put it beneath the register. I was totally using my discount to buy it.

What?

Yes, I had changed, but some things never would.

And besides, this just proved the old me—the real me—was still in there somewhere.

The bell above the door chimed, and I looked up from the boxes as Rimmel came into view. "Hey, girl!" I called. "You're back!"

She smiled, her cheeks red from the cold outside. "Just got back in town," she replied, a large garment bag draped over her arm. "I figured I would bring this back before clumsy me lost it or somehow spilled something on it."

I laughed. "You know you're allowed to keep it all. The owner said so. It's the least she can do for all the free promo you're giving the store."

"I like my sweats." She laid the bag across the counter, and I unzipped it to reveal the pile of clothes inside.

Romeo was a newspaper staple in Maryland these days, so of course, his girlfriend was getting some press time as well. She hated the attention, but because it made Ron Gamble happy, which in turn reflected positively on Romeo, she played along and sat in the stands, in very open view, at all the Knights games she could attend.

After her first two appearances, there was mention in one of the magazines (a total gossip rag) that she was too frumpy for the *Comeback Quarterback*, and a few of the other headlines started following the way she looked.

So far, she got lucky and they only ever photographed her when she was at Romeo's games or something having to do with the team. The reporters caught her and Romeo out on a date once when she was visiting him, but that never happened again.

Romeo was fiercely protective of her privacy and he hated what the media had started to say.

But of course, there was a solution. If the press wanted to talk about Rimmel, then we'd let them talk. She just needed to put a positive spin on it.

So I stepped in and helped her.

Now before she went to visit Romeo, she came to the boutique. I would choose outfits and style her. I matched everything up and put it together, including accessories. Now when she sat in the stands, the papers wondered who she was wearing.

They'd begun calling Romeo's father's office to request a statement about the "first lady" of football's fashion.

And where she was getting her clothes was always mentioned. Business had picked up, and as soon as Rim stepped out in an outfit styled by me and it hit the paper, students would come in and buy the pieces until we were sold out.

I reached into the bag and pulled out a purple faux leather motorcycle jacket. "Did you wear this one yet?"

She shook her head.

I always packed extra because I never knew if they'd have to go out on the town. I handed it back to her. "Keep it, then. We don't have any left in your size, and since it's the primary Knights color, it's a good piece to have." She reached for it. "Plus, it's a great color on you."

"Okay, I'll pack it for next week," Rim said.

I raised an eyebrow. "You're going back next week? That's fast." Usually she only went once a month.

Behind her glasses, her eyes lit up. "Romeo's starting in a game!"

"Ohmigod," I rushed out. "It's about damn time! Braeden is gonna freak!"

Rimmel nodded vigorously. "I talked to Ron. I got extra seats. I was hoping you guys would come too? Support Romeo?"

"Of course we'll be there!" I exclaimed. "I have outfits to pick out!"

Rimmel laughed. "I'm gonna stay there with him through the Thanksgiving break. His parents will be there too."

"Oh boy," I muttered. "Time with Mother Dearest."

Rimmel didn't seem so thrilled. "Yeah. But she's been okay. She's making an effort to get along."

"You mean kiss your ass and make up for all the shit she did to you?"

"That too." Rimmel giggled. "Are you going home for Thanksgiving?"

I frowned. "I'm not sure." I hadn't even thought about it. I'd been too busy just trying to be normal and stay afloat.

"What's B doing?"

"I don't know that either," I admitted.

"Everything okay with you two?" Rimmel inquired gently.

I gave her a brilliant smile and hoped she didn't see through it. "It's great! We just haven't talked about the holiday." *Or about anything else important.*

"Well, I'm sure if you want to stay and have the holiday with us, there will be plenty of turkey." She offered.

"Thanks, I'll let you know." I went back to pulling new inventory out of boxes.

"So how were things while I was gone?" she asked, leaning her elbows on the counter and putting her chin in her hand.

She looked small behind the tall countertop. I could only see from her shoulders up. She was wearing Romeo's Alpha U hoodie. I swear it was like a permanent part of her body.

Without thought, I reached up and fingered the star necklace B gave me. I guess I could say the same about this necklace. "Good! It was a pretty quiet weekend. There was a game Friday night. Drew went with me. Then B had football every day. I worked a lot, and Drew's been hanging out with Trent."

Rimmel grinned. "Those two hit it off."

I groaned. "If I have to endure one more conversation about engine size and car parts I know nothing about, I'm going to run off into the night screaming."

She laughed, and then I showed her the top I was going to buy before I left. She hung out for a while, helping me go through clothes and just chatting about girl stuff.

It was really fun. A lot like it when we shared a dorm room. Rim and I still saw each other every day and we still went to football games, ate lunch together, and hung out when we could, but it was still nice to have this time with her.

It felt normal.

A few customers came in, made purchases, and left. I set up a new jewelry display.

Rimmel glanced at the clock and groaned. "I better go. I have to make sure I have everything done for classes tomorrow, and I want to see Murph. Plus, if I don't call Romeo and let him know I made it home, he'll send a search party."

I gave her a quick hug. "Thanks for hanging with me. I like girl time."

"Me too." She pushed her glasses up her nose. "Will you be here Thursday afternoon?"

I went and checked the schedule. "Yes!"

"Okay, I have a free afternoon. I'll come in before I go to the shelter and you can style me for the break." She stuck out her tongue. "Heaven forbid the paparazzi see me in the same outfit twice!"

"Like you care," I teased, taking in her half falling-out bun and sweatpants.

"I don't, but I won't have my unfashionable nature reflect badly on Romeo or the Knights. Ron Gamble has been really good to him."

"Stick with me, girl. I'll never lead you down a bad fashion path."

It was dark out when I walked her to the door. Her little white hatchback that all the guys hated was parked at the curb a couple shops down. The sidewalk was lit up, but I still stepped outside while she walked to the car.

Leaving her alone out there in the dark stirred a queasy feeling in my stomach. Once she pulled out onto the road and waved, I turned to go back inside.

As I turned, something caught my attention down the street. The shop right beside us was closed so the windows were dark, but the one on the other side was still open. Light spilled from the windows across the sidewalk.

I thought I'd seen someone standing there, just inside the dark section, right in front of the light.

I blinked and looked again.

I must have been wrong; nothing was there.

You are totally losing it.

The doorbell jingling startled me. I jumped, pressing a hand to my pounding heart, and then laughed at my ridiculousness.

I rushed back into the shop to greet the customer. "Hey! How can I help you?"

No one was there.

The boutique was empty, exactly as I left it.

Hadn't I just heard the bell?

No one was walking out when I turned. That must have meant they were going in.

Maybe they were in the bathroom. Or the dressing rooms.

I passed by the counter and shoved open the small two-piece bathroom door. The light was off and no one was in there.

I turned the light on and looked behind the toilet.

A crazy girl could never be too careful.

Backtracking out of the bathroom, I went to the nearby dressing rooms and pulled back the heavy curtains to look inside.

No one was there either.

I stood in the middle of the clothing racks, confused. Maybe I was hearing things. Maybe I hadn't heard the bell at all.

The wind! I thought. It was probably the wind that rattled the door and made the bell jingle.

That was totally possible. Feeling ten times less like a crazy britches, I grabbed a stack of shirts I already put on hangers and carried them to a new rack near the front of the store.

A blur of movement rushed around the corner of the window and out of sight.

Anger eclipsed my alarm, and I dropped the clothes and rushed out onto the sidewalk. The air seemed a lot colder than it had just a minute ago.

"Whoever you are, don't come back!" I yelled around the corner into the dark.

I swear, some people had no lives. They got a kick out of lurking around and scaring people.

I let out a frustrated growl and ignored the shaking of my hands. With force, I spun back around to go inside.

My body slammed into something hard, and I let out a shriek.

CHAPTER THIRTY

BRAEDEN

"Whoa!" I said, catching Ivy by the shoulders when she slammed into me. "You trying to take me out?"

"Braeden!" she gasped. "You scared me!"

I frowned and gentled my fingers on her shoulders. "You okay?"

"Yes," she sighed. "Some kid was playing a prank. Making the bell on the door ring."

I looked toward the end of the building. "Want me to find him?"

What kind of douche played pranks on women in the dark?

"No," she said firm and laid her hand on my chest, gentling her voice. "But hi."

Both hands slid up and wound around my neck. She rose up on tiptoes and pressed her lips to mine. She tasted like coffee, sweet and warm. I licked into her mouth with a sigh and kissed her deep.

"Hey," I rumbled after I pulled back. "How's my girl?"

"Glad to see you."

I scrutinized her face, looking for signs that maybe she was more scared than she let on or that she was feeling anxious. I should have been here earlier. Before it got dark. I hated her working these closing shifts. The idea of her alone in this shop so late made my skin crawl.

But practice ran over and I didn't get here as early as I wanted.

I made a note to ask Drew to start coming in and staying with her 'til closing. Just the thought made me want to grind my teeth, but I would do it. He was extra suspicious of me since that night at Screamerz. He tried to interrogate me more than once. It pissed him off that I never folded.

It was none of his damn business. I wasn't telling him jack. I hadn't even told Ivy, even though I'd made up my mind to.

She didn't want to know. She hadn't said those exact words, but she might as well have. I knew she was scared. I knew she was upset and confused. Sometimes the words were right there on the tip of my tongue, on the verge of spilling out into the open.

But how did you just tell someone they'd been raped?

Would that make her worse? Could she handle it? My God, she seemed so fragile sometimes. Like a light wind might snap her in half.

And then there were other times, like right now, when she was the Blondie I always knew. Strong, kickass, and stable.

"Rimmel was here!" She went on, taking my hand and leading me into the store.

The place reeked of Ivy, so naturally, I liked it. It was all bright and colorful. Clothes lined every wall and jewelry hung on every table. There was a furry rug by the checkout counter and a huge free-standing mirror near the dressing rooms.

"She's back in town?"

"Yep, just got back. She brought in some clothes I styled her in."

I chuckled. Ivy would style the damn cat if it would let her. Hell, she already styled the dog. Poor Gizmo. I came home last night and she was wearing a leather jacket with tiny boots.

"She told me Romeo's starting next weekend."

"Hells yeah!" I said, pride puffing up my chest. "About fucking time."

"She got us seats at the game. I told her we'd go."

I nodded. Of course we'd go. I'd tell Coach I was gonna miss a couple practices. He'd probably be pissed, but whatever. The Wolves weren't gonna be in the championships this year anyway. It wasn't do or die. We had a damn good season, but not as good as last year. Hell, if I got lucky, he'd cancel all practices the week of break and then I wouldn't have to worry about it at all.

I looked up at Ivy, who had a huge pile of clothes in her hand as she walked by. I stepped forward and took it from her.

Her smile was grateful, and she led me to the rack where she started hanging them. She was quiet a minute as she worked, but then she paused and glanced up at me.

"Rimmel asked me about Thanksgiving."

"She gonna put up with his moms?" I asked. Poor Rome, having to play mediator between his mother and Rim. I got lucky. My mother loved Ivy. And Ivy loved her.

Ivy nodded and added the rest of the clothes in my arms to the rack. "She wanted to know what we were doing."

Why did she seem hesitant to bring this up?

"I told her we hadn't really talked about it…"

Ahh. She thought I didn't want to spend it with her.

"Bring those B handles over here," I said and caught her around the waist.

"B handles?" she echoed, a bewildered expression on her beautiful face.

I palmed the place where her waist dipped in on each side. My hands fit there perfectly. "These right here," I explained, giving them a little squeeze. "They were built for my hands. That makes them B handles."

"You think my waist was built just for you, huh?" She smiled. I could tell it pleased the shit out of her.

It should. No one else was built for me. "Of course."

"Does that mean I can call something of yours an Ivy handle?" Her voice was sly and deep.

A slow smile spread across my lips. "Baby, you know exactly where that is."

The lightness in her eyes dimmed just a little. She kept her tone easy and teasing, but I'd already felt the change. "I don't know. It's been a while."

Well, shit.

I was just racking up mistakes tonight.

Having a girlfriend was a lot of fucking work.

And being a gentleman was getting me nowhere.

But she was worth it.

I'd backed off on the sex. Not totally. I mean, damn, she was sexy as hell and when I touched her, she never pulled away. But still, I wasn't on her every single night, multiple times a night, like I usually was.

I couldn't.

My conscience wouldn't let me. I felt like I was taking advantage of her. Not really with the sex, because I loved her. I loved her so damn much, and making love to her was just another way of showing it.

But a part of me wondered if she'd want me if she knew what happened to her.

I thought maybe backing off the physical stuff would give her body and mind a chance to work some of itself out. Maybe all the sex we had kept what happened to her from really fading away.

Clearly, it was just making her feel like I was pulling away.

And the fact that I just assumed we were spending Thanksgiving together instead of asking made it worse.

It was a classic case of me not using words when I should have.

"Hold up just one second, Blondie." I picked her up, and she wrapped her legs around my waist. I carried her over to the door of the shop and turned the sign over to closed and flipped the lock. I made my way to the counter and sat her down, fitting myself between her spread thighs and cupping her face in my hands.

"I don't like the things I'm hearing out of this damn kissable mouth." I leaned in and kissed her once. Twice.

She started to say something, and I kissed her again.

"I was trying to be a good guy. You've been under a lot of stress with work, midterms." I paused. "Other shit." Her eyes darkened a little, but I pushed on. "I don't want to put any added pressure on you, Blondie. I don't want to overwhelm you. If you want more of all this…" I gestured to myself, and she giggled. "Just say so."

"I thought maybe you missed your old life," she confessed. Her eyes looked everywhere but at me.

"My old life," I echoed. "You mean the one where I was miserable and grouchy without you?"

"Well, you were grouchy."

I growled like I was mad even though I wasn't. "*You* are the life I want."

"Even if I act crazy?"

I could have made a joke here, but this wasn't fucking funny. This shit here was why I needed to man up and blurt out the truth even if she didn't want to hear it.

I grabbed her face and spoke fiercely. "You are not crazy. Stuff happened. A lot of it. You're dealing with it." I took a breath and then muttered, "And I'm not fucking helping at all."

I started to pull away, but she clamped her hands around my wrists and held me in place. "You're the only thing that's helping."

I stared in her eyes and saw openness. I saw willingness to talk. Relief poured into me. "Am I really?"

"God, yes. I'm terrified I'm going to lose you, that one day we'll be miles apart."

"That's not gonna happen." *I'm your anchor. You are mine.*

"But it is. It already is."

"No," I protested and pressed my forehead against hers. "I think we should talk, baby. Like really sit down and just lay it all out."

"I'm scared to."

"Believe me, so the hell am I."

After a minute, she nodded. "Okay. But not tonight. Tonight I just want to be with you. In every way."

I groaned. "Thank God. I want you so bad it's killing me. I played like shit at practice tonight. Coach rode my ass."

"I wanna go home," she whispered. "Make love to me."

I wrapped an arm around her waist and pulled her fully against me. Our tongues twisted together in perfect rhythm, and I could practically hear the crackle of electricity between us. My cock was so hard it throbbed, and Ivy's hands were impatiently exploring my back beneath my jacket, already tugging at my T-shirt.

When I tore my mouth away, I shuddered with need. "We need to go."

She nodded, eyes wide.

"Give me your keys. I'm gonna pull your car right up front and get the heat going."

She leaned around the cash register. The way she draped her body across the counter to do so had me biting down on my lip. Then she tossed me the keys.

"Close everything down. I'll be right back," I ordered, thoughts of her in bed literally all I could see in my head.

I kissed her again, having to forcibly peel myself off her before rushing out the door.

We hadn't even talked about Thanksgiving yet. But I'd make sure we did. After.

I walked to her car down the block. It was close to where I parked the truck. As I approached, I noticed someone standing at the hood. Irritation was like a bee sting through my body when I realized who it was.

I walked to the back of Ivy's car and stopped to call out. "What the hell do you want?"

Missy bristled and stepped forward. She was holding a cup of ice cream in her hand, one with the logo of the place right nearby, and I couldn't help but wonder if she was only using that as an excuse to watch me and Ivy.

"Did you tell her?" she asked. At least she didn't waste my time with stupid talk.

"I thought you didn't care," I snapped. "I thought you said if I did, you'd just make sure I went down with you."

"Did you or not?" she demanded.

"Guess you realized how much you had to lose, huh, *Boss*?"

She made a rude sound. "Obviously you didn't. If you had, she wouldn't let you anywhere near her."

A jolt of panic hit me because I often thought the same thing. But I didn't let her see it. "Don't be so sure," I said.

"So she will forgive you, but not me?"

"Wow. You almost sound hurt," I quipped. "You finally realizing what you lost when you totally trashed your friendship?"

Her eyes slid away.

She totally regretted what she did.

A mean streak cracked through me like a bolt of lightning. I knew it was courtesy of the darkness curling in the depths of my soul. But I didn't feel bad for her. Not one bit, so I said what I wanted to say. "There's a difference between what you and I did, Miss."

Her eyes snapped up.

"What I'm doing is out of love. I'm trying to keep her from getting hurt worse than she already has. But you? Everything you did was to hurt and humiliate her. Shit, you were there that night. You could have *stopped* him. *Why the fuck didn't you?*"

She recoiled like a snake bit her.

It was a question I'd asked myself over and over again. Why had Missy not realized Ivy was being taken advantage of? Why had she not seen Zach pulling her out of that party? Sometimes in my darkest moments, I wondered if she knew all along and just let it happen.

"It's not my fault what he did to her." Her voice shook.

"No, you didn't give him the drug, but friends look out for each other. You weren't ever Ivy's friend, were you? The only thing you've ever cared about is your status, and you had a lot of it when you were friends with Ivy, because she came with Rimmel and Romeo."

"You're a son of a bitch."

"No, I'm just an asshole. But you? You're way worse than I'll ever be."

She dashed a hand up by her eye. Was she crying? I didn't know. I didn't care. "I didn't tell her. Not yet.

But I'm going to because she deserves the truth. I won't lie for you, Missy. So you might want to start thinking about what you're going to do when everyone knows what kind of person you really are."

I turned away but then glanced back.

"At least I'm giving you a warning, to know what to expect. Ivy didn't get that courtesy when you blasted her all over the Buzzfeed and branded her a slut."

"I'm sorry!" she yelled as I was getting into the Toyota.

"It's too little, too late." I slammed the door, turned over the engine, and drove the short distance to park in front of the store.

When I got out of the car, I saw Ivy standing at the counter, gathering up her things. I looked back down the street.

Missy was gone.

CHAPTER THIRTY-ONE

IVY

With Black Friday just around the corner, the boutique was gearing up for a big sale. Several of us girls were working today, helping prep. I was in the back, putting signs into display cases to be clipped onto the racks the morning of, when the phone rang. I knew the girl out front was busy. I could hear her talking to a customer. So I dropped the sign I was working with and rushed to answer the phone.

It was one of the girls that had been in here yesterday that I helped style an outfit. Word had gotten around that Rimmel's fashion successes were because I was picking her clothes. Occasionally, someone would come in and ask me to pick stuff out for them too. It was fun, so I did it.

Anyway, I put together a totally adorable sequined skirt outfit with black tights and a silk top because she wanted something to wear to some fancy dinner her parents were having over the holiday. She loved it but didn't have enough money.

So I promised I'd hold it for one day so she could get what she needed and come back.

"Is Ivy there?" she asked after my usual greeting.

"It's me!"

"This is Sarah. I was in yesterday," she said.

"Hey, girl, you coming back in for the outfit? It's waiting right here." I glanced over my shoulder at it hanging behind the counter.

"I can't," she practically wailed. "My ride totally bailed on me, and it's way, way too cold for me to walk over. Can you hold it 'til tomorrow?"

I made a noise. "I'm sorry. Per our policy, we can only hold things for twenty-four hours."

She acted like her life was over. I had to suppress a laugh.

"Okay," I said after I composed myself. "How about I bring it by the dorm? Like a delivery service. You have the cash for the outfit?" I read her the total just to be sure.

"Yes! I have it right here."

"Okay, what dorm?"

"Cypress Hall. Second floor, room 202."

Rimmel and I used to live on the second floor, and it made me smile. "I know the place. I'll be there in a bit!"

After I hung up, I told the other two girls where I was going and offered to make a coffee run while I was out.

It was cold today, in the thirties. I wrapped up in my plaid pea coat and ran out to my car, grateful I was wearing boots today. It only took a few minutes to drive to Cypress Hall, and the second I pulled in, I remembered all the fun we used to have here.

Missy had been part of almost all of it.

Pushing away the thought, I grabbed the garment bag with the boutique logo on it and ran to the door. One of the residents was coming out, and she let me in so I didn't have to stand there and wait for Sarah to buzz me in.

I saw a few girls I knew, so I stopped to say hi (not stopping would be rude) and then I passed by a few who only wanted to look at me and whisper. You'd think people would be over it all by now.

Geez.

Didn't Alpha U have a new campus slut yet?

Ugh.

Being slut-shamed had been almost worse than sleeping with Zach. Hell, at least I couldn't remember some of that.

As I walked by all the little Miss Gossip Pants of the floor, I gave them a bright smile and wave. They only stared in return.

I jogged up the stairs like I had thousands of times before and pushed through the door onto the second floor. The second I was inside the hallway, I stopped.

Missy was standing there. Her room was one of the closest to the stairwell. Well, I assumed it was her room because she was standing in the half-open door, staring down at something.

Her hair was in a super-short (and, I grudgingly admit, cute) ponytail, and she was wearing yoga pants and a long-sleeved T-shirt.

I hesitated because she had yet to see me, and I really didn't want her to. I didn't feel like dealing with Missy today. Actually, not any day. Especially not here where she pretended to be my friend.

I watched as she bent down to pick up what she was staring at. It was a single red rose. She put it up to her nose and inhaled, a small smile playing on her lips. Then she pulled it back and looked at the plain tag hanging from its stem.

Whatever she read there made her smile slightly. Then she smelled it again.

God, she had a boyfriend? I freaking felt bad for him. Someone should warn him. Poor guy was gonna end up the subject of the Buzzfeed.

But wait? Missy had a boyfriend? It didn't seem right. That day on campus when we traded hostile sentences, she still seemed jealous about Braeden and me. A girl who was happy and in love wouldn't be jealous of someone else's relationship.

Would they?

Did she have a secret admirer?

I must have stood there staring too long because she turned in my direction and we locked eyes. Surprise danced across her face, and she lowered the rose a little so it was against her chest.

I cleared my throat and started moving. How unlucky for me the room I was delivering to was just two doors down from hers.

This was gonna be the last time I offered to do a good deed and deliver an outfit.

I walked past without a word, and she watched me unabashedly. I knocked on the door and in two seconds, it was flung open and Sarah was standing there with a huge grin on her face.

"Thank you, thank you, thank you!" she exclaimed and flung her arms around me for a big hug.

I laughed. "You're welcome."

She bounced back and took the garment bag to her bed. "Let me grab the cash," she sang out.

Aware of Missy still staring, I stepped a little farther inside the room.

Sarah handed me the exact amount she owed, and I handed her a receipt. She promised to come back after break to get some more outfits, and she promised this time she'd have more money.

After we chatted for a few minutes about which shoes of hers would work best with the skirt, I waved bye and backtracked out of the room, closing the door behind me.

There were a few more girls in the hallway now. I felt them watching me, and it made me so incredibly glad I didn't live here anymore.

Missy was still standing in her doorway, like she was waiting for me.

I flicked her a glance and then started walking.

"Hey," she said like I was her friend and she was glad to see me.

"Hey," I echoed in a way less enthusiastic tone.

"You have a minute to talk?"

I stopped in my tracks, aware some people were watching us. I realized then people probably wondered why we didn't hang out anymore. I wondered how she explained that around here. I wondered if the #BuzzBoss ever got any questions about that, since he was so "on point" and "in the know" with the gossip.

"Can't," I said brusquely. "I'm on the clock."

"You work there?"

"Yep," I replied. *Like she didn't know.* I pushed through the door and into the stairwell. For some reason, I felt out of breath, and I leaned against the wall and sucked in some air.

The stairwell was always colder than the floors in this place. Probably because there were very few heat vents in here and this old building had poor circulation. The lighting in here was kind of crap too, something everyone always complained about, but no one ever fixed.

But the cool felt good against my heated cheeks. It bothered me that it bothered me to talk to Missy. Maybe I should just confront her. Tell her what a bitch

I thought she was and how awful her betrayal felt. Maybe avoiding this situation was only making it harder to get over.

I had told Braeden to talk to his father. Not because he'd asked, but because it would be good for B.

Wasn't that sort of the same concept here? Didn't my advice apply in my own situation?

Sometimes it just amazed me how linear life could sometimes be. Everyone had their battles. Oftentimes, they weren't as different as everyone else's. Just like a Christmas present. Most people got them, but they rarely looked the same.

'Course, everyone liked presents.

No one liked a terrible person.

I snorted and it reminded me again of Rimmel. I laughed and the sound floated up into the stairwell, echoing a little.

You know what? *Screw this. Screw her.*

"Just confront her," I said out loud, an audible push for me to turn around.

I stopped midway down the stairs and turned back around. There were two flights of steps between each floor, and I was at the top of the bottom one. With purpose, I strode back up, stomping a little because it made me feel like a badass.

(You know it does.)

I was almost to the door, reaching out for the handle, when I heard a sound.

Faint.

Elusive.

Creepy.

I paused but didn't turn around. I listened, thinking it had only been my imagination. Above me, there was a faint scuffle. Like someone was up on the next landing.

It was probably someone coming down the stairs, probably a guy who wasn't supposed to be in here and he was creeping around so he didn't get caught.

I rolled my eyes at the thought and started forward again.

"Ivy…"

What. The. Hell?

Did someone just whisper my name?

Was I hearing things?

I spun around so fast my hair whipped around before me and hit me in the face. It stuck to my lip-gloss, and I spit a little and used my hand to pull it all out of my face and clear my vision.

He was standing on the stairwell landing.

His body was only a barely there shadow, but his face, much paler than the rest of him, was unmistakable. I gasped, the sound bouncing off the walls and pressing into me.

It was a face I knew well. One I thought I'd never have to see again.

"Zach," I croaked, my hand going up to my neck.

He smiled.

That's all he did. He stood there in the shadows, looking like a ghost, and smiled. He had this look in his eyes, the kind murderers in movies always wore.

I blinked, thinking it was just my imagination. That my mind was playing some kind of cruel joke on me.

But he was still there.

"I've missed you," he said. His voice was so low I had to strain to hear.

My skin crawled and a cold sweat broke out over my forehead. Completely horrified, I rushed through the door and burst into the second-floor hallway.

Missy was standing there talking to a few other girls.

I stumbled and leaned against the wall, gasping for breath and trying to clear the sound of his raspy voice from my head.

I can still hear him breathing.

It was a god-awful sound. *Why am I hearing it?* He hadn't been breathing like that just now.

I am losing it.

No. I've officially lost it.

"Ivy?" Missy said from just beside me, her voice low and totally concerned. "Are you okay?"

"He's in there." I gasped.

"Who?" Her eyes went to the door.

"*Him.*"

She seemed freaked out, and before I realized who exactly I was talking to and that we weren't BFFs anymore, she pushed through the door and stepped into the stairwell.

I rushed after her, the word *no* forming on my lips, but not making it out.

I skidded to a stop behind her.

Her eyes met mine over her shoulder. "There was someone here?"

Confused, I looked up to where Zach had been standing.

The shadows were just that, dark, empty space with no lurking crazy guy.

Utter relief surged through me but so did embarrassment. I straightened and made sure to look her in the eye. "Just some booty call racing down the steps, trying not to get caught."

Her eyes narrowed like she didn't believe me. "A booty call scared you?"

"His junk was flapping in the wind. He needed some Nair. And some zit cream." I made a face. It wasn't even hard. That was a nasty thought.

Missy made a face too.

If this had been last semester, we'd have both burst out laughing.

But it wasn't.

"Maybe you should post a disclaimer. Give some male grooming tips for the hygiene challenged," I said sarcastically.

Her eyes hardened like she too remembered we weren't friends.

I ran down the stairs and out onto the sidewalk. I didn't relax until I was in my car with the doors locked. I searched all the people walking by, the bushes, and even the parked cars.

No one even remotely looked like Zach.

Besides, it was impossible he was here. He was locked up. Sentenced to time in the loony bin for what he did to Romeo and Rimmel.

No one would let him out. Especially a trained doctor.

I leaned back and let my body relax. My mind was just playing tricks on me. Probably because I was back at the dorm, on the floor where I'd made the huge mistake of sleeping with him.

I would just never come back here again.

Problem solved.

I started the car and pointed it in the direction of the coffee shop near the boutique.

There wouldn't be any coffee for me tonight. I didn't need the caffeine. I'd grab a green tea and hope like hell the calming herbs convinced me of everything I'd just told myself.

CHAPTER THIRTY-TWO

Reports of 2
previously joined-at-the-hip friends, now
not on speaking terms, spotted having a
tense convo at the dorms.
#Did13GetBetweenThem #HosOverBros
#CatFight
#BuzzBoss

BRAEDEN

I wasn't much of a procrastinator.

Except maybe when it came to homework. But even then, when the shit needed done, it got done. I'd been putting this off since the end of last semester. I used every excuse under the sun to avoid it.

The clock was ticking.

My mother reminded me almost every time we talked. The words Ivy spoke the night in the truck haunted me. I knew what I had to do. It was the right thing.

Sometimes the right thing sucked.

I picked up the phone and dialed the number no one else knew I had memorized. I might have procrastinated calling my father, but I thought about it a lot. So much so the number was burned into my brain and probably would be forever.

It rang so long I started to think he wasn't going to answer. Just as I pulled the phone away to end the call, I heard a voice come from the other end.

"Braeden?"

I hesitated, then put it back up to my ear. "How did you know it was me?"

"You're the only person that has this number."

Was I supposed to feel honored? All I felt was sad and shame. Sad he had no one else to give it to and shame because I thought maybe he deserved it.

"I thought about what you said." I got right to the point. "If you still want to talk, I'm ready."

"I've been waiting for you to call. Hoping you would. I'm at the hospital. Been here for a while now."

Shouldn't I feel some kind of emotion when I learned my father was likely in the hospital and would be there until he died?

I didn't.

All I felt was hollow.

"What floor?" I asked, my voice low.

He told me, and then I hung up without saying good-bye. I didn't play the radio on my way to the hospital. I drove in silence. I thought about when he used to live with us. I tried to recall just one happy memory I had with him.

A baseball game. A goofy joke. A moment he hugged me good night.

I searched and searched my memory.

All I could find was pain and fear. He was dying and there wasn't one single moment with him that would make me sorry.

The hallways smelled of cleaning supplies and the dying. I remembered the scent well from when I used to sit beside my mother when I was just ten years old. Hospitals always brought back those memories for me;

they were a constant reminder of the most terrifying time of my life. If Romeo's father hadn't stepped in with the courts, I might have been lost to the system forever, just a number on a piece of paper, a forgotten soul in a broken world.

Thank God for Anthony. He's the one who engineered the deal that if my mother pressed charges against my father and locked him away, I could come home.

I arrived at his room. The door was open and the low sounds of the television floated out into the hall. Nurses bustled around, going in and out of patients' rooms, silently wheeling carts with medical supplies.

I hovered in the doorway, staring at the single bed in the room. He lay in the center, a bump in the blankets, looking a lot smaller than I ever remembered him being.

He turned his head and looked at me. We stared at each other for a long time.

"Are you gonna come in?" he asked. His voice was rough like sandpaper, not loud and harsh like before.

I entered the room and walked toward the bed, keeping back a couple feet. I had no desire to get too close to him. He appeared frail and thin. Weak. His eyes were sunken and dark rings lined their perimeter. His once dark hair was almost completely gone, only a few downy wisps clinging to his scalp in their valiant effort to hold on. His skin looked paper-thin and dry. I could see the blue veins beneath, giving the surface a gray-ish unhealthy cast.

His shoulders were still pretty wide against the mattress, but they looked out of proportion to the rest of his bony frame. The blankets were pulled up past his chest, and what I could see was covered in a generic blue-and-white hospital gown.

I knew cancer was a hateful disease. I knew it silently, slowly killed its victims. And my father was definitely dying. He almost looked like it was hard to live.

I didn't like my father, but even I wouldn't wish what he was suffering through on him.

"Thank you for coming," he said when I only just stood there and stared.

"I didn't do it for you," I replied. "I did it for me."

"And that's okay." He nodded once. "It gives me a chance to say what I want to say. And then you can say what you came here to say."

"I don't think you'll like what I came to say." I couldn't even pitch the words the ominous way I meant them. For so many years, I hated my father. I carried a torch of anger wherever I went. But now, standing here and looking down upon a dying man, all I could feel was sadness.

"What's it like to know you're dying and you pushed away every person who might care?" I asked almost without thinking about it.

It wasn't a very nice thing to say, but I wasn't here to make my words all pretty.

"The biggest regret of my entire life is that I alienated you. That I wasn't the father I should have been."

"What about Mom?" I asked, my fists clenching at my sides. "What about the husband you were supposed to be to her?"

"Your mother didn't deserve anything I did to her."

I made a scoffing sound. "You know, it's so easy to lay there on your deathbed and be sorry for all the shit you've done. You call me, beg me to come. You want my forgiveness. You want to die in peace. Well, why the fuck should you get that? What about us? What about the people who are left behind? We have to live with what you did. Every single day."

"I don't expect you to forgive me, son."

"Don't call me that," I bit out.

"I just wanted to see you. I wanted you to know you deserved better than what I gave you. I can't make up for all those years, but I can give you this moment to let out all the hatred you have for me. Maybe that will make the rest of your life a little more peaceful."

I rubbed a hand over my face and sat in a nearby chair. "I *thought* I hated you. For years and years, just the thought of you made me crazy. But I don't hate you anymore. I don't have room for it like I used to. I feel sorry for you. Sorry that you wasted your life in the bottom of a bottle, taking out whatever demons you had on an innocent woman and child."

"You're a lot stronger than me. Better."

I laughed. It was a harsh sound. "Do you know how long I've lived terrified that I was gonna turn out just like you? When I look in the mirror, some days it was you I saw."

"For that I am sorry."

I snorted. "I can't forgive you. I won't. You took my childhood. You turned it into a nightmare. I don't have one, not even a smidgen of a good memory with you in it. I used to lie in bed at night and wish you'd change. I used to watch Romeo with his dad and wonder why mine didn't love me like that. I thought it was my fault you hated me."

"I don't hate you, Braeden."

I thought I saw tears in his eyes, but I ignored them. I wasn't saying these things to hurt him. If he was hurt, it was because he knew what I said was true.

"Maybe not. But you sure as hell don't love me. You probably never did."

"I used to lie in bed at night and wish I was better too. I'm a weak person. A sorry excuse for a man. I lived by the bottle, and in the end, I will die by it."

I went to the window across the room and stared out across the cold parking lot filled with cars. It felt good to say these things, the thoughts that bounced around inside me for so many years. But it was also hard because it just hammered home that he would never be the man I wanted him to be.

Never.

"I'm proud of you, Braeden."

I stiffened at his words and didn't turn around.

"You're more of a man in your little finger than I ever was. You succeed in life in spite of the way I treated you. You're in college. I've seen you play ball. You're good, son. You're so good."

I didn't need his pride. I didn't want it.

But still, hearing him say those words… It meant something.

Behind me, a nurse came into the room. "Time for your medicine," she said. Her voice faltered when she saw he wasn't alone.

I turned from the window.

"Oh, you have a visitor." The surprise in her voice wasn't lost on me.

"This is my son," he said, and the nurse's eyes widened.

"I didn't realize you had any family."

"He doesn't," I said.

The nurse grew uncomfortable and bustled about giving him his pills. I stared at the machines hooked up to him, at the IV taped to the back of his hand, as she checked a few things and then, without a look back at me, left the room.

"It won't be long now," he said. A cough rattled his lungs.

I walked to the side of the bed and stared down at him. "I hope you get some peace in death, because you sure as hell never had any in life."

"I think maybe I finally will," he said. His eyes drifted shut for long minutes.

My chest squeezed. This was hard. A hell of a lot harder than I even expected it to be. I didn't want to feel sorrow he was dying. I didn't want to feel anything at all. I wanted that hollow sensation back.

I didn't want to feel compassion.

"I have to go," I said. The feels in this place were just way too real.

He nodded like he knew it was coming. "Thank you for coming. For giving me the chance to at least tell you how sorry I am."

The muscle in the side of my jaw bounced.

"I know you're going to do great things, son." He coughed again. "No thanks to me."

I would, if only because I would fight like hell to not end up like him.

"Good-bye, Father," I said.

He smiled wistfully. "Good-bye, son."

I stared at him a moment longer, and then I left.

Out in the hall, I sucked in a deep breath. My chest hurt; my stomach felt tight.

It was good I got to say the things I wanted to. It was good I got a chance to say good-bye.

I just wished it didn't hurt so fucking bad.

CHAPTER THIRTY-THREE

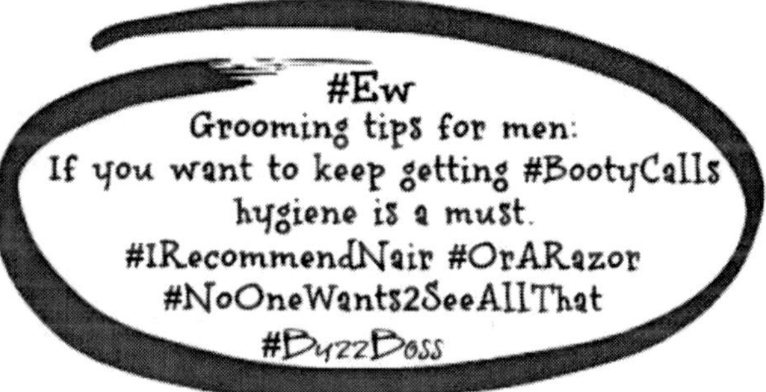

IVY

The #BuzzBoss was at it again.

I should have known my run-in with Missy earlier would end up on the Buzzfeed.

Twice.

The first one was really to be expected. After all, as I stood there talking to her in the hallway, I asked myself how many people wondered why our friendship basically went extinct. I was guessing a lot. If was a betting woman, I would bet every girl that witnessed our exchange had sent in some kind of info to the #BuzzBoss.

It forced Missy's hand. Which, frankly, I thought was poetic.

She was obligated to make a Buzz about herself. Speculating about our relationship, or lack thereof.

But it wasn't that notification that got to me. It was to be expected.

It was the one that came after it.

A recount of the conversation we had in the stairwell. She put up a snarky Buzz about men and their hygiene. Just like I'd sarcastically suggested.

What did it mean?

Was it her way of showing me she could do what she wanted, sort of a slap in the face?

Or…

Was it her way of trying to recapture that second we forgot we weren't friends?

Times like this, I wished I was still five years old and my biggest worry was what my brothers were going to hide in my bed.

* * *

Thankfully, I hadn't had much time to dwell on it because we'd been busy. It was finally closing time, and I offered to be the one to close up so everyone else could go. Going home and replaying the moment I thought I saw Zach wasn't exactly high on my to-do list.

After I texted B to tell him I was closing, I walked around to straighten all the jewelry displays. I found a piece that would look perfect for one of the outfits I picked out for Rimmel, so I carried it behind the counter and dug around for a mesh jewelry bag to place it in.

The bell on the door rang, and my shoulders slumped. I was ready to go.

When I saw who it was, I didn't bother hiding my annoyance. "Why are you here?"

"You know me. I love to shop," Missy said. She was still wearing the yoga pants and T-shirt from earlier.

"Actually, I don't know you," I refuted. "I close in ten minutes, so shop fast."

Surprisingly, she didn't say anything else. She wandered around and started filling her arms with clothes.

"Maybe you should come back tomorrow when you have more time. And I won't be here."

She didn't even look up. "But I'm here now."

Some people just needed hit in the head with a chair.

A few minutes later (and exactly three minutes until closing time) she stepped into the dressing room and pulled the heavy curtain closed.

I sighed. Loudly.

She was totally doing this on purpose.

"I wanted you to know," she said, talking through the curtain, "I had to put up that notification. The one about us."

"Yeah, you just *had* to," I said, sarcastic.

"I don't expect you to get it. But being the #BuzzBoss is important to me." The curtain slid open and she stepped out in one of the outfits. She walked over to the large mirror to look at herself.

"You look fat," I said, bland.

She gave me a withering look. "That was childish."

"Oh? Maybe I should slut-shame you in front of the entire campus instead."

She marched back into the dressing room and yanked the curtain shut. I grinned, thinking she'd leave.

A few minutes later, she came out wearing another outfit. It was a black dress with a low neckline, high hemline, and flirty cap sleeves.

Missy definitely had the body for it. Her legs went for miles and she didn't have too much boob to look offensive. If I were nice, I'd say it looked great and recommend a necklace to go with it.

I wasn't feeling very nice.

"I didn't come here to try on clothes," Missy said.

I just stared at her. I was tired and wanted to go home.

"It was the only way I knew you'd talk to me. You've completely shut me out on every attempt."

I made a face. "You honestly thought I would just forget everything you did?"

"No, but I thought you'd let me apologize."

"That's the stupidest thing I've ever heard." In a mocking voice, I went on. "*Hey, let me totally humiliate Ivy, call her a slut, turn her into a laughingstock, and then apologize. She's so dumb she'll laugh and say it's okay.*"

"It wasn't like that," she demanded.

"No? Then what was it like?"

Her voice dropped and hurt clouded her words. "I saw you."

"You saw me what?" I wasn't going to fall for her sad act.

"Remember that night when you stayed at Romeo's with Rimmel? He was out of town and I had play practice? I was supposed to come late so we could all hang out, have a girl's night."

"You never showed." I pointed out.

"Yes, I did."

I listened intently.

"I was really late, but I came anyway. When I got there, I looked through the window and I saw you—with Braeden."

That must have hurt her. It must have been hard to see. "So you decided to post half-naked pictures of me on the school Buzzfeed? You called me a slut?"

"I was so mad, Ivy. I was so jealous I couldn't see straight."

"Well, you saw well enough to type."

"I regret what I did to you. I never intended for that to happen. I never planned to let it get out."

I frowned. "Let what get out?"

She stiffened and turned back to the mirror. "How angry and jealous I was. I couldn't believe you would sleep with him. You knew I was in love with him."

She was in love with him.

The thought made me sick to my stomach. Not because I'd "gotten" in the way of their relationship, but because I loved him. He was mine.

"I never meant to hurt you. I agonized over that night at the beach for weeks. I beat myself up on a daily basis. I vowed I wouldn't ever do it again," I said, finally getting to say all the things I never did. "I tried to tell you so many times, Missy. I tried to stay away from him. I couldn't. It was like that one night unleashed an entire ocean of feelings inside me. That night you saw us? That was the second time. It wasn't planned, and when I woke up the next morning, I told him I was going to tell you."

"But you never did. You just laughed behind my back."

"I never laughed. And I never said anything because you started putting up all those notifications. I had to hide in my room thanks to you. The ridicule, snide looks, and suggestive comments I got were unbelievable."

She just stared at me like she was trying to decide if I was lying.

I shook my head sadly. "I honestly liked you. You were my best friend. I slept with Braeden, but I never, not in a million years, would have done what you did."

Missy went back into the dressing room and hid behind the curtain. Maybe that meant she was done talking. But I wasn't.

"And what about Rimmel? All those things you said about her. You called her a #nerd. That name stuck, you know."

"Please," she spat. "Being a #nerd is *not* an insult. It made her cool."

"And what about the notifications when you said people should stick to their circle, when you implied Rimmel wasn't good enough? Gah! Then you came to our room and smiled at her and acted like her friend. When you accused her of plagiarism in front of the entire school? She could have lost her scholarship."

She didn't say anything.

"And what about Romeo? You practically made him the star of the Buzzfeed. You gave Zach even more ammunition to come after him. God, it's like you were obsessed with all of us!"

"That's not true!" she burst out. The curtain didn't muffle the sound of her shriek.

I must have hit a nerve.

She came out of the room, her ponytail partly falling out. She was dressed in her own clothes and holding the black dress.

I stared at her red cheeks for minute and then gasped.

She looked at me sharply.

"It was Romeo you really wanted, wasn't it?" I prodded. "Right from the start of freshman year. You created the whole #BuzzBoss persona so you would have a legitimate reason to watch his every move. Then we met. I thought we hit it off, but you just hung out with me because I always got invited to the same parties as him."

Her face turned redder as I spoke.

"Then Rimmel came along and you didn't like her. I always suspected, when I first started inviting her to sit with us, you didn't like her. But then Romeo started coming around more. He liked her, and it drove you crazy. That's why you posted all that stuff about her. But it backfired. He fell in love with her anyway."

"You're crazy," she protested.

But I wasn't. For the first time in a long while, I knew what I thought was exactly right.

"Once he was taken, you had no choice but to accept Rimmel because now you were in the 'in crowd,' part of the inner circle. My God, you had access to all the information and we never suspected you." I shook my head. She'd played us all perfectly.

"So what about Braeden?" I pressed. "Was he your consolation prize?"

"I fell in love with him," she whispered. "He's so good-looking and charming. He always made me laugh, and the way he kissed me…"

I made a sound. I did not want to hear about how she felt kissing my boyfriend.

I didn't care he was hers first.

I didn't have to feel bad anymore. I didn't have to feel anything about her at all.

A hundred-pound weight lifted off my shoulders. Its name was Missy.

"We hurt each other. You took things way too far. I'm honestly sorry for how I handled things with Braeden, but I'm done apologizing to you. We aren't friends. We never will be again."

Her eyes were rimmed with red when they met mine. "He isn't as perfect as you think."

I laughed. "Are you kidding? Of course he isn't. But neither am I. We're a total mess, but together, we make sense."

"I wonder if you'll still feel that way later," she intoned.

I thought back to all the stuff she implied that night at our house. I thought about all the things I knew needed to be said between B and me. It scared me. If what he had to say had anything to do with her, it was going to be bad.

Really bad.

"I think it's time you leave," I said. "I need to lock up."

"I want to buy this dress." She held up the black fabric.

"Sorry. Already closed out the register. Looks like you'll have to come back."

"What do you think your boss would say if he knew you were turning down a sale?"

"Her name is Monica. She'll be in tomorrow at ten. Why don't you ask her when you come back to buy that dress?"

Missy's mouth opened, then closed.

I walked around the counter and took it out of her hands. "I sure hope it's still here when you come back. This is the last one. I was admiring it myself earlier."

It was a total lie. My boobs would be falling out all over the place in that thing. If Missy were a true friend, she'd know that.

Instead, she huffed. "Bitch."

I smiled sweetly. "Takes one to know one." I went to the door and held it open. "Buh-bye now."

She stomped out onto the sidewalk and turned back. I saw the mean streak in her eyes and knew she was about to say something entirely hurtful. I slammed the door in her face and locked it.

I turned my back and walked away, putting the gown behind the counter. I was tempted to take it home just so she couldn't buy it tomorrow.

My own deviousness impressed me, and I watched as her car sped down the street out of sight.

That confrontation hadn't been as hard as I anticipated, and it turned out I had a lot more to say to her than I thought.

I went into the back and neatly stacked the signs I'd made and then moved a few boxes of inventory to the other side of the room. I was pulling on my coat when I heard a faint sound out front.

I froze.

I really needed to stop hearing and seeing things.

This wasn't some Stephen King movie.

I wasn't a virgin and the first to die.

I wasn't going to cower like a damsel in distress, so I snatched up my bag and held it before me like a weapon. Hey, it was heavy. I could totally take someone out if I needed to.

"Yo, Ives!" Drew yelled. "Where you at?"

I loosened the grip on my bag and slumped a little. I was totally glad it was my brother. "Hey!" I called and went out into the main room. "What are you doing here?"

"Braeden asked me to meet you so you wouldn't be alone locking up."

Of course he did. I couldn't even be mad because it was totally sweet he thought of me enough to ask Drew to be here. "Where is B?" I wondered.

"Dunno. Said he had somewhere to be and he'd call you soon."

I locked my arm around my brother's and turned him toward the door. "C'mon, let's go."

We made it two steps when I stopped. "Wait."

He looked at me.

"How did you get in here?"

He looked at me like I had three heads. "Uh, the front door."

"I locked it."

He frowned. "It was open when I got here."

"No. I locked it."

Seeing I was one hundred percent positive, he freed his arm and went to the door, pulled it open, and tested the lock several times. "Well, it doesn't seem to be broken. Are you sure you locked it? Maybe you just thought you did."

"Maybe," I echoed. I was tired, and I was anxious to get away from Missy.

That reminded me of the dress. I was totally taking it home. I didn't care if it was too small for me or not. Served her right. "I forgot something," I said and hurried around the counter to where I'd left the dress.

It was gone.

CHAPTER THIRTY-FOUR

BRAEDEN

It was late when I finally walked in the house.

Gizmo came rushing up to me, bouncing on her back legs and resting her front paws on my leg. I smiled, the first time since I'd gone to the hospital, and bent to scoop her up.

"Hey, Giz."

She licked my face about a hundred times. Her fur was silky soft and her tail wagged about a mile a minute. Today, she was wearing a white T-shirt with pink trim and a pink rhinestone collar to match.

After I scratched behind her ears for a few minutes, I put her down and she ran circles around my feet. I laughed and tried not to step on her as I went into the kitchen, where I saw a soft glow from the light above the sink.

Ivy was sitting alone at the island, a bowl of ice cream in front of her, hair piled on top her head, and my name and number written across her back.

Just the sight of her eased everything inside me.

"Whatcha doin'?" I asked, coming up behind her and leaning down to rest my chin on her shoulder.

"Drowning my sorrows in fat and calories."

"Uh-oh." I lifted her and slid beneath her, fitting her right into my lap. I glanced in the bowl at the vanilla ice cream.

"That needs sprinkles."

"You ate them all."

Unable to resist, I kissed the side of her neck. "What's the matter, baby?"

"I had a run-in with Missy." Her voice was sour.

"You give her hell?" I hugged her close.

She made a sound and put the spoon in her mouth, pulling it out slowly. It was a terrible distraction from our conversation.

"Where have you been?" she asked, glancing over her shoulder.

"I went to see him."

The spoon clattered in the bowl, and she abandoned it completely. Ivy spun in my lap so we were face to face and her legs were wrapped around me. She leaned back a little, resting on the edge of the counter, and I tightened my hold on her waist a bit.

"Tell me," she demanded.

I half smiled. "It sucked."

She nodded with sadness in her eyes. "I would have gone with you."

I shook my head. "It was something I needed to do alone." Plus, I didn't want her around him. I didn't want his darkness to touch her.

"He apologized?" she asked.

"I told him I couldn't forgive him."

"What did he say?"

"He told me he was proud of me." I met her eyes. "It felt good to hear."

She cupped my face in her hands and made a sound. "Of course it did. You're only human, B. It's okay to not like him, but at the same time want his approval."

I didn't want it.

But maybe deep down I did.

Fuck, I was messed up.

Ivy let go of my face and reached around behind her for the bowl. She scooped up a spoonful of ice cream and held it out.

I opened my lips and the sweet, cold flavor slid down my throat. She fed me the rest of the bowl. Neither one of us said a word. I stared into her blue eyes, and occasionally she would kiss me between bites.

I loved her.

I loved her more than life itself.

Coming home to her after seeing him was exactly what I needed.

"Are you glad you went?" she asked when the bowl was empty and pushed to the side.

I thought for long minutes and then nodded once. "Yeah."

It was good to close the door to that part of my life. It was good to know I said everything I wanted to say.

"Wanna go have sex?" she whispered.

My smile was fast. "Thought you'd never ask."

We left the bowl on the counter, and I carried her up the stairs. Her laughter was exactly what I needed. Her touch was what I wanted.

As long as I had Ivy, everything else was just details.

CHAPTER THIRTY-FIVE

IVY

I didn't tell Braeden about the dress.

About the noises I kept hearing and the night I thought I saw Zach.

He had enough going on already, and I wasn't a hundred percent sure I wasn't imagining things.

CHAPTER THIRTY-SIX

#RandomButTrue
It takes 600 cows to make one full season's worth of NFL footballs.
#FauxFootballAnyone?
#BuzzBoss

BRAEDEN

The pillow beneath my head was yanked away, and my eyes flung open as my head hit the mattress. "What the fuck?" I yelled, my voice half asleep.

"You're turning into a woman," Romeo taunted above me. "Laying in bed halfway through the morning."

I groaned and glanced at the clock beside the bed. "It's six a.m., fucker."

"We got shit to do."

Beside me, Ivy groaned. "Make the bad man go away."

"You're a bad influence," Romeo told her fondly.

"Tell me again why we got adjoining rooms in this hotel?" I muttered.

"Rimmel!" Ivy yelled.

"Whoa," Romeo rushed out. "Don't be waking up the beast."

I laughed.

"I'm going to the field. I want to get some throws in, warm my arm up before the game later today."

His first starting game of his NFL career. We were all in town just to watch him play. He was probably hella excited. And maybe nervous. My eyes opened. "You want me to come?"

"Does a boar have an asshole?"

Ivy groaned again and pulled a pillow over her head.

I shoved my face beneath it and kissed her cheek. "I'll be at the field with Rome."

"Bye," she murmured.

I jumped out of bed and grabbed some sweatpants and a hoodie. It was probably colder than a witch's tit outside, but I didn't care. I got to throw some passes with my best friend, and I got to do it on a field where the Knights played.

"You sure it's okay we're doing this?" I asked Rome on the way to the field.

He nodded. "I don't want to overdo it before the game, but I need to decompress a little, you know?"

I knew. He had a lot riding on today. If he didn't play well this season and show Ron Gamble he could be an asset on the field, his contract wasn't going to be renewed next year.

"Trainers meeting us there?" I asked.

"Hells no. I wanted some time to play, not be instructed."

"Just me and you, then?" I rubbed my hands together. It had been a long time since me and Rome got to fire it up on the field.

He offered his fist and we bumped it out.

The field where the Knights practiced was a lot like Alpha U's. I wasn't a stranger to a football field, not even one that had money to keep it nice.

But there was something majestic to me about an NFL field. Even if it was the place they just practiced. I loved this place in the early morning. It was quiet and open, filled with lots of possibilities and opportunities.

The air was cold, and I lifted my hands to blow some hot breath on them as I gazed out over the green. Everything here was purple and orange instead of blue and gold.

A football appeared in Rome's hand, and he elbowed me. We looked at each other and then back out at the field.

It felt like we were back in high school again, two kids with high hopes, when we laughed and rushed out into the center.

We messed around for a long time, blowing off steam and throwing crazy passes to see who could catch them.

I ran the ball some. It felt good to stretch my legs.

Even as we goofed off, we were in sync. Romeo and I were always like that on the field. We played off each other, like we were connected.

Maybe it was because off the field, we were.

Eventually, the fun turned a little more serious, and I moved in so he could throw me some spirals. He was looking good; his arm had come a long way.

"Okay, man," he yelled down the field. "Let's switch it up. I'm gonna throw with my left now."

I gave him the signal and moved in a little more, thinking his left arm was still a little weaker than his right. His throw was strong and straight. It hit me right in the chest when I caught the ball.

"Da-yum!" I whistled. "You've still been practicing throwing with your left arm?"

"Hells yeah," he called. "I might be right handed, but I'll never be in the position of not being able to use my left ever again."

I admired his attitude. When he broke his right arm, so many people thought his career was over before it had even started. What the hell good was a quarterback if he couldn't throw the ball?

But Romeo didn't give up that easily. He became an ambidextrous quarterback and learned to throw as a lefty.

I thought maybe now that his right arm was healing up nicely, he'd have focused more on it. I was wrong. I should have known he would make sure he never lost the lefty skill.

We threw for a while longer, and then he moved in closer so we were in talking instead of yelling distance.

"You called him?" he said, like he knew.

"How'd you know?"

"You seem lighter."

"I went to see him. He's in the hospital."

Romeo paused. "He in bad shape?"

I nodded.

Romeo threw the ball, and I caught it.

"I told him I wouldn't forgive him."

"He don't deserve it."

"I know." I threw the ball back.

"You okay, man?" he asked, giving up on throwing all together and walking toward me.

"Yeah," I said, wiping the sweat off my forehead. "Yeah, I am."

He nodded. He was wearing a purple Knights hoodie and a pair of black Nike workout pants. His hair was messy and damp around the ears, but he didn't look tired.

"Purple's a good color on you," I teased. "Doesn't look girly at all."

He laughed.

We glanced across the field at the sidelines where Ivy and Rimmel sat. They showed up not too long ago, carrying big coffees and still looking half asleep.

We'd been out here for a couple hours, so it wasn't like it was still the butt crack of dawn.

Ivy saw us looking and waved. I waved back.

"How's things at home?" Romeo asked.

I shook my head. "You know, man. It's hard."

His face turned serious and his body shifted toward mine.

"I got this stain on my favorite shirt and no matter what I try, I can't get it out."

Romeo shoved me.

"Being an adult is hard!" I cackled.

"If I didn't have to play today, I'd tackle your smart ass right now." He laughed.

I turned serious. "You nervous?"

He nodded like he was confiding a secret.

"You got this, Rome. You're ready. It's gonna be fucking awesome."

"Thanks for being here."

"Shit," I drawled. "Did you really think I'd miss your NFL debut?"

Romeo started to say something, then stopped. He looked back at the girls and made a sound. I followed his stare and saw Ron Gamble standing there smiling and talking with Ivy and Rim.

"What's he doing here?" I asked.

Romeo shrugged. "He owns the place."

"He gonna be pissed I'm out here playing on his turf?"

"Nah." Romeo slapped me on the shoulder. "Come on. I'll introduce you."

We jogged over to where the group stood.

"Mr. Gamble," Romeo began and held out his hand for a shake. "Looking forward to starting in today's game."

Gamble smiled. "I like a man who gets up early and gets prepared."

"Just want to make sure I'm ready to play," Romeo replied.

"You're ready," Rimmel interjected. "He's going to be amazing."

"I like your confidence, young lady," Gamble said to Rimmel, fondness in his tone. Clearly, the dude liked her.

Then his eyes turned to me. "You're a pretty good player yourself."

I stood up a little straighter. "Thank you, sir. We were just playing around. I was helping Rome get warmed up."

"You two play well together. Like a well-oiled machine."

"Well, we've been doing it for a long time," I replied.

Gamble nodded. "You play for the Wolves, don't you?"

"Yes, sir."

"He's a free agent," Romeo put in. "He's been kicking ass on the field this season."

"Totally." Ivy agreed.

Gamble chuckled. "Quite the cheering squad you got here."

I shrugged. "They're family."

"Family is important," he mused. "Romeo, good luck today. I'll be watching from my box." He started to turn away but then looked back and offered me his hand. "Good to meet you, number thirteen. Maybe we'll meet again."

He knows my number?

"I'm sure we will," I said. "I plan on being here as much as I can to support Rome."

"Loyalty is a good quality," Gamble said, and then he walked away.

When he was gone, Rome looked at me, speculation in his eye. I just shook my head.

"Come on," I said to everyone. "I'm starving. Let's go eat."

After we ate, Romeo went off to get ready for the game, and I hung with Rim and Ivy. Mostly, I just watched TV. Ivy was busy fussing over what Rimmel was wearing and then what she was gonna wear.

It was a football game, not a fashion show. But I didn't tell them otherwise.

Before it started, we filed into the seats Rimmel got us, and I watched the stands fill to capacity. I knew there was a lot of press there. I knew this game was getting a lot of media coverage, but I didn't care.

I was here for the game and to watch my best friend play.

And play he fucking did.

He smoked that football, and the crowd went nuts. He played the entire first half of the game, throwing a shit ton of completed passes and four touchdowns.

They pulled him out at halftime, and I knew it was because they were afraid to push his arm. But it was cool. He had his moment in the sun, and he proved to everyone he deserved his *Comeback Quarterback* status. I could tell by the blinding bright smile on his face when he looked up in the stands and waved that he knew it too. Gone was the worry that his contract wouldn't be renewed.

It was a damn fine day in football.

It was a damn fine start to Thanksgiving break.

I couldn't wait to see what else vacation was going to bring.

CHAPTER THIRTY-SEVEN

If you think 7 years of bad luck
is bad for breaking a mirror...
try breaking a condom.
#BeSafe
#BuzzBoss

IVY

The Knights game had been the first NFL game I'd ever been to. Honestly, besides having a bigger stadium, it was a lot like going to a Wolves game.

But not to B.

He was in his element, and it had been awesome to see. We had such a good time with Romeo and Rimmel that I almost forgot about everything else.

The second we got home, Braeden kissed me fast and went to the gym. He was meeting some of the other Wolves there to train. I could tell he was excited to get in there and work out, to tell everyone about Romeo's big game.

I made myself some tea and then went up to the bedroom. Prada was dancing all around my feet, having missed us while we were gone. She stayed with Braeden's mom, and I knew she loved it there, but I was her favorite person.

As I drank my tea, I played with her and gave her some extra attention. She made me smile, and when I went to shower, I was completely relaxed.

What was it about the shower that always made a person think?

Wasn't standing under the gentle spray of warm water supposed to be further relaxing and mind numbing?

Maybe that's why my thoughts wandered where I didn't want them to go.

I was too relaxed, my guard too low, and it gave the perfect opportunity for my mind to conjure up all the thoughts I'd been successful at pushing away.

Like the missing dress.

My confrontations with Missy.

Imagining I saw Zach in the stairwell.

I didn't want to think I was slowly losing it.

I wanted to deny and shove away I suspected there might be something wrong with me. But seriously, how long could a girl pretend nothing was wrong?

How long could she pose that everything was fine?

Sleeping with Zach was arguably the worst thing I'd ever done. And it was something I did to myself. Yes, it hurt Rimmel and Romeo, but I was the biggest victim of my choice to sleep with him.

I released a groan and stepped forward, leaning my forehead against the shower wall. I stood so my head was past the spray, but it hit my shoulder blades and cascaded down my back.

Why couldn't I let this go?

No one else was punishing me for it. Hell, no one else even brought it up. But it was still there, like an undercurrent in the ocean. You couldn't see it, but once in the water, you could feel it. It's like my brain wouldn't let me forget.

So much so that now I was starting to see things. People. *Him.*

I heard things and felt things. I'd become paranoid and suspicious. I mean, geez, the bell over the boutique door couldn't even ring without me going tense.

I knew I should talk to Braeden and tell him about the war inside me. I saw the worry in his eyes, the concern. We never spoke of it, but it was there.

The distance between us hurt me. He was the one person I wanted to be closest to. I wanted to give him all of me, even the parts I didn't like.

He'd done that with me. He deserved the same.

I wanted it to be like it was just yesterday, when all we did was laugh and have fun.

I reached up and fingered the necklace that hung around my neck. I'd worn this every single day since he fastened it around my neck.

It didn't matter I knew B loved me. It didn't matter I saw it in his eyes. I was terrified, and it wasn't going to go away until I told him about the turbulence inside me, about the unstable, cuckoo thoughts that just wouldn't leave me alone.

After all, if what was going on inside me was enough to make me doubt even myself, then how could he not doubt me too?

Suddenly, the icy drops racing across my skin felt a whole lot colder. I jerked back from the spray and adjusted the heat. It warmed marginally, but not very much.

Teeth chattering, I rinsed out my hair one final time, then shut off the tap. I was grateful my towel was so fluffy and large. I quickly dried my hair and body, then wrapped myself in the softness.

I'd been so anxious for a shower, when I'd come in, I hadn't taken the time to gather up my clothes and bring them into the bathroom. Not that it mattered. I was the only one home. Well, besides Prada of course.

The comb slid easily through my long hair, and my moisturizer felt like silk against my skin. I went through my routine on autopilot, not really thinking about it at all. I was suddenly so incredibly exhausted.

Exhausted from fighting.

Exhausted from feeling.

Holding the towel around me tightly, I switched off the bathroom vent and opened the door. The sound of Prada's muffled barking immediately filled the air.

I frowned and glanced across the hall at our bedroom door. "Prada?"

When I'd gotten in the shower, she was in our room, dragging out every toy we gave her. She wasn't in the bedroom now. Her barking was coming from down the hall.

Behind a closed door.

A creepy feeling crawled up my spine and goose bumps broke out along my bare arms. The door to the gym at the end of the hall was closed. We never closed that door.

How would Prada somehow shut herself in?

It wasn't even possible. Was it?

And her bark… I knew that bark. It was her warning bark, the sound she emitted when she felt threatened or was approached by someone she didn't know.

Terror skittered across my neck in tiny pricks that felt like stabs from a dozen tiny knives as I slowly padded down the hall.

My fingers ached from the intense grip I had on my towel. This was another one of those times when I could argue with myself about being crazy. About making stuff up or exaggerating things inside my head.

I wasn't going to do that.

I wasn't imagining this.

I was home alone, and somehow my dog got shut in a room behind a door no one ever closed.

"Prada?" I spoke, my voice shaky and a little weak.

Her barking paused and she scraped at the door.

I grabbed the handle, took a deep breath, and flung open the door.

Prada came racing out and danced around my feet. She sniffed me as my eyes searched the gym. Everything looked normal. Nothing seemed out of place.

Without thinking, I glanced down the hall, sweeping every shadow and corner. I'd laugh at my own ridiculousness—it was broad daylight after all—if I could stop the pounding of my heart.

Prada jumped on my leg, and I reached down to pet her. She licked my hand and then went trotting down the hall, sniffing as she went. I watched her pass by our bedroom door and stop at the top of the steps. Her ears perked up and she seemed to stand there listening. What she was waiting to hear I didn't know.

My stomach turned and clenched with nerves.

Was someone in this house?

Was I not really alone?

There couldn't be. I had the alarm set. No one could come inside without the code.

To prove my thought, Prada gave up listening and raced into the bedroom. A second later, I heard the squeaking of her favorite toy.

Odd.

On wobbly legs, I went to get dressed, ignoring the way the ends of my damp hair dripped down my back. I turned the corner and smiled, Prada was attacking her toy with serious vigor and dragging it across the carpet.

"You crazy girl," I told her and stepped into the room.

Something on the edge of the bed stopped me in my tracks.

Rooted in place, I stared, confusion and terror warring within.

After an undetermined amount of time, I took a step forward.

And another.

And another.

I stared down at the red item on the comforter. It looked like blood against the pure white of the bed.

It might as well be blood. The memory it evoked felt like a knife wound, deep and jagged right across my chest.

And what lay beside it was even scarier.

Suddenly, I was bombarded with a flash of memory. And one more.

My stomach lurched. I felt sick, so insanely sick.

Blindly, I reached out and grabbed what was most definitely *not* there when I went to take a shower.

Something someone had to put there.

Something someone had to have all this time.

Someone I thought I'd seen.

I couldn't deny what was in my hand, the horror replaying in my mind. I stumbled across the room, a sob wanting to rip from my chest but never making it out. I slid down the wall until I was tucked into the corner of the room, my knees against my chest.

I didn't cry or yell.

I didn't do anything at all.

CHAPTER THIRTY-EIGHT

BRAEDEN

Something was wrong.

I didn't know what or why. I only knew how off everything felt the second I walked into this house.

The dog wasn't by the door. She didn't race down the steps to greet me like she always did. The silence in here was stifling, almost painful.

My pulse spiked, anticipation or adrenaline pumping through my veins. Maybe a combination of both.

I wanted to call out her name. I wanted to rush up the steps and into our room. Something held me back. I stepped almost with hesitation, with a sort of sticky fear.

Dread formed in the pit of my stomach, so heavy if I'd been in water, I would have sunk to the bottom with no hope of finding my way to the surface. My foot paused midway up the stairs when Prada appeared at the top. I shared a silent look with the dog, and then she took off back into the bedroom.

I burst into action, racing the rest of the way to the top, and nearly catapulted into the bedroom, ready for some terrible sight. I never should have gone to the gym. I never should have let her come home alone…

But everything seemed fine.

Ivy wasn't even in here.

I rubbed a hand over my head and blew out a breath. I opened my mouth to yell for my girl, when Gizmo came around the side of the bed and stared at me expectantly.

I crossed to her, bending to pick her up. But she skirted out of my way and planted herself on the carpet in front of something.

Someone.

Ivy was huddled in the corner of the bedroom, arms wrapped around her knees.

Her hair was wet; her face was pale. She wore only a towel, and the vacant, lost look in her eyes was the scariest thing I'd ever seen.

"Ivy." Her name ripped from my throat.

If she heard, she gave no indication.

I dropped to my knees beside her, sweeping her over for injuries, looking for a reason for finding her this way.

Maybe if I could see a reason, I wouldn't be so sick inside.

I was merely stalling. Going through the motions of trying to make sense of this. Deep down, I knew what happened. I knew why she was basically sitting here traumatized.

She knew.

Maybe she didn't know everything.

But she knew enough. I didn't know how. I didn't know why.

But I knew.

Cautiously, tenderly, I reached for her. My palm hovered over her bare shoulder before I allowed it to gently touch her.

When she didn't flinch away, I counted it as a victory.

"Baby," I whispered. "Ivy. What happened?"

She said nothing, but I felt the way her body trembled. Her skin felt cold to the touch. Slowly, I pushed her wet hair aside and trailed my fingertips lightly across the top of her back. A soft caress to hopefully bring her back from wherever she was. A gentle reminder she wasn't alone.

I shifted so I was sitting down and inched just a little closer. "Ivy, please say something," I whispered.

Her blue eyes shifted toward me. After a moment, they focused, and for the first time since I entered the room, I felt like she saw me.

"I thought I was going crazy," she whispered. "All the things that have been happening."

Alarm jackknifed beneath my ribs. *What things?* I wanted to demand, but I didn't.

"I didn't tell anyone. Not even you." She went on.

"Oh, baby." I said it like a vow. "You can tell me anything."

"Someone was here, Braeden. In this house. In this room."

My eyes sharpened and I felt my hackles rise. "What do you mean?" I said, harsh, all thought of being gentle forgotten.

I winced and quickly looked at her, but my tone didn't seem to scare her. If anything, it seemed to jar her out of the state she was in.

"Someone left me something on our bed." She glanced down.

I noticed the smallest scrap of something red sticking out of her clenched fist.

"What is it?" I leaned in, desperate for answers.

Ivy pulled her arm from around her knees and held out her hand, palm up. One by one, she opened her fingers, revealing a pile of red lace.

CHAPTER THIRTY-NINE

IVY

My lucky panties.

Lost.

Gone.

Never to be seen again.

Until they showed up on the end of my bed. The bed I shared with Braeden.

I loved these little red lacy thongs. They had a four-leaf clover on the right hip in gold glitter. Hence the reason I called them lucky.

The last time I saw them was the night before the big championship Wolves football game. The night I slept with Zach.

I'd woken up the next morning, hung over and partially disoriented. I was dehydrated for days. I was ashamed even longer.

After I'd showered and cleaned myself up, I picked up the clothes scattered around the room. I never found my panties. I was too ashamed to ask Rimmel if she'd seen them. I figured they'd turn up when we moved out of the dorm.

I didn't find them.

I assumed I'd lost them on the way back to the dorm, in a drunken moment of passion.

I shuddered.

Beside me, Braeden tensed.

Oh God, Braeden. He was sitting here beside me, so sweet and concerned. I knew the hollow, almost vacant way I was acting was probably eating him alive. As much as I wanted him right now, a piece of me wished he wasn't here. I didn't want him to see me this way.

I hadn't lost these panties that most certainly were *not* lucky that night.

There had been no drunken moments of passion.

There hadn't even been consent.

"Ivy," Braeden said in a cross between fear and worry. "You're scaring me, sweetheart. Please say something."

How was I supposed to speak when the memory wouldn't stop hounding me? I clung to the hope that maybe it wasn't a memory after all, but just a terrible dream. More evidence that I'd surely lost my marbles.

#

Muddled. Everything around me was so incredibly muddled. Even my own thoughts were unclear. What was happening? I knew it wasn't good because the pit of dread and the feeling of stark horror clung to me. It stuck to my thoughts just like the fog that made it hard to think.

The familiar feel of my sheets was against my back, but I didn't remember coming home. I thought I was with Missy at a party.

How did I get home?

I felt the mattress dip and tilt; my body shifted with the change in weight. But I wasn't the one moving. My limbs felt like lead, too heavy to move.

But I knew I did want to move.

The unfocused image of someone rose above me. He had dark hair, and at first, I wanted to smile. Braeden had dark hair.

The sound of the man speaking blew away just a smidge of the clouds filling my mind. Just enough for me to realize this was not Braeden. This wasn't someone worthy of my smile.

What the hell was Zach doing here? Hadn't I told him to get lost? I was a lot of things, but I wasn't the kind of girl who would come back to my room with someone as vile as him.

Wait.

Zach was in my room.

Panic, strong and sure, clawed at the back of my throat. I pried my eyes open, tried to hold them as wide as I could. Why was I so tired? What was happening to me?

I saw his lips move. I saw him smile. Something was wrong.

Why wasn't he wearing a shirt? Why wasn't I?

I didn't want this. I didn't want to be here with him. I didn't want to be half naked. I didn't want to sleep with him.

My body jerked, and I stared up through hazy eyes at him. He tossed some clothes—my clothes—aside and then stared down at me.

"I just knew you'd have something slutty on beneath those clothes," he said.

"Please, no," I begged. It seemed like maybe I'd said that already.

I felt a touch along my hip and rough fingers probed below the band of my thong.

"No."

Zach didn't act like he heard me. Had I even spoken out loud?

Next thing I knew, my pair of lucky red thongs were dangled over my face.

Those things were soo not lucky.

"You mind if I keep these? A little reminder of the night I owned you?"

I tried to push myself up, to run away.

My body didn't obey.

I tried to scream, to yell.

My voice was silent.

It was like my body was no longer my own to control.

It was like I was a third party, standing in this room, watching something horrible about to happen.

I couldn't stop it.

Rough hands poked at my entrance, and I squeezed my eyes shut.

Maybe being detached wouldn't be so bad after all…

I didn't go to sleep, but I didn't really stay awake.

The statement "out of it" had never held more truth.

I felt the violation in my body. I felt the screams and cries echo inside me.

But even as I started to sob, I'd somehow slip away again…

Into nothing.

Nothingness was preferable to this.

#

I jolted back, hitting against the wall, and the thongs dropped like a weight onto the carpet beside me.

Braeden let out a gruff curse and reached for me.

I was up off the floor in seconds, cradled against his chest. He was warm. I didn't realize I was so cold.

"Say something right now, Ivy, or I'm taking you to the damn hospital," he demanded.

I huddled against him, pushed my cheek into his shoulder, and then I said three words a woman never wanted to say.

"I was raped."

CHAPTER FORTY

BRAEDEN

The words sliced me open and left my insides to spill out.

How did one function with everything he needed on the inside suddenly ripped out?

I knew.

Those three words, I already knew them. Hadn't I just stood there and suspected Ivy finally realized?

It didn't matter.

The shock was unmatched. Sure, on some level I understood my girl knew, but to hear her say those words, to hear out loud a nightmare that up until now only rattled around inside me…

It was like finding out all over again.

The images I found on Missy's computer played through my head like a slideshow.

The violation Ivy experienced was something I knew a man likely couldn't fully comprehend.

I honestly didn't think she'd arrive at such a clear realization. I thought maybe her doubts and questions would slowly reveal a larger picture.

It would have been kinder that way.

Not that there was one fucking kind thing about any of this, but at least Ivy wouldn't have been overcome by the truth.

I stood there in the center of our bedroom. The room where I held her in my arms every night and listened to her sighs when I kissed her skin. This place was supposed to be our sanctuary.

But that bastard invaded it.

He wormed his perverted, sick ass right here.

I stared down at the red lace thongs. They still lay exactly where Ivy dropped them.

Were they the culprit?

Was seeing them the trigger for this?

Holy fucking balls, did she remember that night?

Please, God. I hoped not.

I didn't want her to have to relive that hell for a single, solitary second. But if she remembered, the torment would be endless.

Just like mine had been.

CHAPTER FORTY-ONE

IVY

"Put me down," I said, my own voice sounding foreign to my ears.

The silence in the room was uncomfortable, almost tense. Braeden's arms didn't comfort me. They felt like a vise holding me in place.

I didn't want to be in place right now. I think I wanted to shatter.

Was this how it would be from now on? Would everything feel changed?

He didn't automatically do as I asked. Instead, his dark-chocolate stare shifted to me and flickered with bleakness and pain.

This was going to be hard on him too. I wasn't the only one who was going to be irrevocably changed by rape.

But I couldn't think about Braeden now. I could scarcely think at all. I was too violated, too shocked, too dirty.

How could this happen?

Why didn't I know until now?

My God, I'd been living months and months inside a body that had been invaded, violated, and used.

He used me.

He shoved his… his… I shook my head. *He shoved himself inside my body.*

I didn't want Zach. He was the last man on Earth I'd ever touch. I knew that, didn't I? I'd said as much to myself a million times. I was so shocked I would stoop so low as to let him touch me.

I hadn't at all.

I said no.

"Put. Me. Down." My voice scraped out of my throat, raw and sick. Whatever he heard made him finally listen. The second my feet hit the carpet, I ran. The ends of the towel around me flew open, and I rushed out of the bedroom.

I fell to my knees in the bathroom, hitting the cold, unforgiving tile. Pain jolted my knee, but I ignored it.

Nothing was worse than the pain inside.

Mental flashes of him ripping at my clothes, forcing his hands down into my thong, assaulted me.

They wouldn't stop.

And neither would the sound of my mind screaming, *No, no, no!*

I leaned over the toilet and vomited violently. Over and over again, I gagged and heaved. My back hurt so badly and my chest burned from the force of throwing up.

As I emptied out every last drop in my stomach, my hands gripped the white porcelain. It was cold and smooth, but my fingers ached from holding on so tight. My throat burned from the acid splashing up my esophagus.

I was raped.

"Ivy," Braeden said from somewhere close by.

Tears blurred my vision and shivers racked my body.

"Go," I choked. "Just go."

"I'm not leaving you," he said.

"I don't want you here!" I yelled and started sobbing.

I shoved off the toilet and fell back against the wall. The towel had fallen off of me, and I was sitting there completely exposed.

As I cried, I pulled the towel into my lap, using it simultaneously as a cover and a tissue.

Even though I screamed, he didn't leave. I wanted him to. I didn't want anyone to see me this way. I didn't want anyone to know what Zach had done to me.

I'd rather be a slut than a victim.

But I didn't get a choice.

My no was ignored.

Why? Why hadn't I fought him off? Why hadn't I screamed until someone came running?

Nearby, I heard the lid to the toilet close and the sound of it being flushed. The tap water in the sink ran. It sounded so far away, like I was in another universe.

Beside me, Braeden fell to his knees. I stared at his jean-clad thighs, just staring at the faded blue fabric without really seeing.

"Come on," he said gently. "Let's get you cleaned up."

It reminded me of the first time we'd had sex. He'd brought me a cloth and placed it between my legs. He'd always been so considerate of me. So careful.

Zach had been rough.

Zach had been hurtful.

I started sobbing again. Open weeping and unintelligible sounds filled the small bathroom.

I felt Braeden's hands as he wiped my face and neck. He used care and caution, and every once in a while, through my own sobs, I would hear him whisper it would all be all right.

But how could it be?

The cloth disappeared, but he remained. He used the end of the towel I wasn't clutching to ring out the ends of my still-wet hair.

Then he brushed through it all, coaxing it all back away from my face. The repetitive motion of the brush through my hair calmed me. My sobs turned into heavy gasps and the tears slowed.

When he was done, his large, warm hands lifted me off the floor. I clutched the towel against me, and he didn't try to take it away.

Instead, he held out his old Wolf Pack T-shirt, the one I'd claimed that morning on the beach. "You're freezing," he said. "Put this on."

I stood there shaking, and he pulled it over my head. I dropped the towel and pushed my arms through. The familiar feel of the soft fabric gave me a little more of a solid grip.

Braeden knelt at my feet and held a pair of sweatpants ready for me to step into. I did, and the warmth seeped into my skin once they were pulled into place.

My head felt thick and my eyes were puffy when he took my hand and led me out of the bathroom back into the bedroom. When the lamp beside the bed was clicked on, my eyes zeroed in on the thongs. I stood there and stared at them, shuddering at the barrage of memories tied to them.

"I'm throwing these out," he half growled and scooped them off the floor. When he did, the note that had been beside them fluttered onto the carpet.

He picked it up, uncrumpled the paper, and stared at the crudely scrawled words.

DON'T TELL

"This was here too?" His voice was low and hard.

Anger radiated around him and made me slink back. I wasn't scared of him. I never would be. But there was so much raw emotion already inside me; I couldn't deal with any more.

"That fucking bitch."

My head snapped up. I might have been shell-shocked, confused, and sick inside, but I could still hear. Why would he say bitch? Zach was a lot of things, but a bitch wasn't one of them.

In fact, why wasn't Braeden asking me—no, demanding to know more about my rape. Why did he seem to understand it hadn't been tonight? Why did he seem to know it was in the past?

I stared at him as question after question took bite after bite out of what was left of my insides.

He must have felt me staring. He must have felt my gaze.

He turned.

His deep eyes locked on mine.

Bleak apology was all I could see.

The note in his hand slipped from his fingers and fluttered toward the floor.

"No," I protested. "*No.*"

The guilt in his face turned into fear.

I gasped. "Oh my God, Braeden," I whispered.

"Ivy—" He stepped toward me.

I held out my hand, halting his steps. "Stay there!"

He watched me helplessly as more questions swelled inside me.

The picture on the Buzzfeed. It didn't come out 'til long after Zach was locked away. He couldn't have done it.

It had been done by the #BuzzBoss.

By my so-called best friend.

You're so convinced I'm the bad one. Have you ever wondered who else around here kept secrets and told lies?

Missy's words replayed in my head. I knew she'd been talking about Braeden. I'd known he was likely keeping something from me.

But this?

Never in a thousand years would I have expected this.

Tears blurred my vision once more, and I folded my arms across my waist. I felt like throwing up again, but there was nothing left inside me to purge.

Except for two little words. Words that felt like a grenade and blew up my entire world.

"You knew."

CHAPTER FORTY-TWO

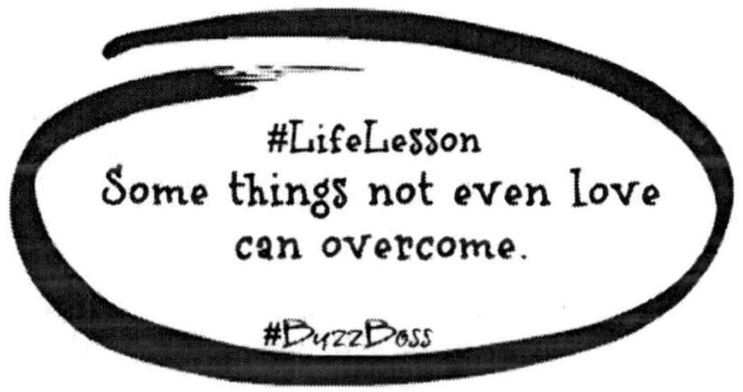

BRAEDEN

And there it was.

The truth.

The secret I wanted to tell, but never could.

Her face was splotchy, her eyes swollen and red. The sound of her sobs in the bathroom would likely haunt my soul long after I was dead.

Was I the cause of this, or was this the reason I never wanted to tell? Everything was blurring together—moments, thoughts, feelings.

I couldn't even fathom how she must feel, what she was seeing in her mind.

I just hoped she didn't remember the details. I just hoped she would be able to find some kind of peace.

She is never going to forgive me for this.

"You knew!" she yelled, as if I hadn't heard her the first time.

I stood there under the force of her wrath and nodded once. "Yes, I knew."

A sob racked her shoulders and she hunched in on herself a little. I stepped forward to go to her, but the second I moved, she straightened and took a step back.

"How?" she demanded. "How did you know I was raped before I did?"

I flinched. I hated that goddamned word. I hated it more than anything. It was ugly, it was violent, and the fact it was now associated with the woman standing in front of me made me want to kill.

"Maybe you should sit down," I said, calm. I felt anything but, but Ivy was enough of a storm. She needed the balance.

"I will not!" she yelled. Prada went under the bed. "I deserve to know!" She angrily dashed away her tears with the back of her hand.

She looked so small and fragile just then, standing there with my clothes hanging off her slim form. Her curves were hidden in too much fabric, and her hair was brushed severely back from her face.

"I'll tell you everything," I vowed. "I've wanted to for a long time."

She sobbed. "A long time? How long have you known?"

"Since the end of last semester."

She gasped. "*Six* months?" She said it like it was a long time, but to me, it had felt like an eternity. "Why the hell didn't you tell me?" she demanded.

"Because I knew it would do this to you," I admitted, weary and filled with defeat.

She stared at me, angrily.

"How could I?" My voice cracked. "How do you tell someone they've been abused in the sickest possible way?"

She flinched.

"Ivy, baby." I stepped forward.

She stepped back. "No! Don't call me that! Just tell me."

I rubbed a palm over my face and started to talk. "I was so pissed when that Buzz of you and *him* went all around the school and after everyone started ridiculing you. I could barely see straight or think straight."

"You called me a slut," she deadpanned.

"Yeah, I did. I'll regret it 'til the day I die."

She fell silent, and the angry look on her face calmed just a bit.

"Anyway, you and I were still trying to figure us out. I was so in love with you even then. I was scared as hell to be in love, and here you were, the one I wanted above everyone, being tortured by the #BuzzBoss."

She started to say something, but I held up my hand.

"So after the night in your dorm and the Buzz with the pic of you and me, I decided to put an end to it. I wouldn't have someone hurting you like that. So I started thinking, started piecing together stuff that no one ever saw before. I went to Missy's dorm room. I charmed her roommate and went inside. She was drunk and didn't pay attention to what I was doing, so I went through Missy's laptop."

"And you figured out who she really was," Ivy said, sounding more like herself.

I said a silent, quick thank you to God, because seeing her fall apart in the bathroom scared me.

"Her computer was filled with files. Files and files full of information, pictures, and texts. She had an email account set up with hundreds of emails full of gossip and speculation. She had enough material on that computer to get her through an entire year of notifications."

I still marveled at how sly she'd been and how well she had us all fooled. Hell, I probably never would have figured it out if she hadn't shared that picture she took off my phone. When I realized she'd been the only one left alone with it, I knew it had to be her.

"What does any of this have to do with me and being raped by Zach?" She wrapped her arms tightly around herself once more.

I could still see her shaking, and I knew she was in danger of going into shock. Hell, I was worried sick she was going to fall over.

Taking a chance, I snagged a blanket off the end of the bed and went to her slowly. She watched me carefully but didn't say a word. I draped the fabric around her shoulders and tugged it across her chest.

Her hands slid up to pin the sides together. "Thank you."

"Please sit down, baby."

She frowned when I called her that, but this time she didn't yell.

"Keep talking," she ordered, and I would have smiled at her cute, demanding ass, but there was nothing cute about this moment.

Nothing at all.

I nodded and backed up to sit on the edge of the bed, keeping my feet planted on the floor.

"Missy had an entire file of pictures from that night, Ivy. Zach sent them to the #BuzzBoss, not knowing it was her. I went through them. They make it incredibly clear what happened to you."

Ivy dropped into the chair near the door, surprise draining the color from her face. "Missy knew?"

"Oh, she knew. She knew almost right after it happened. The file was dated in the fall."

She pressed a hand to her mouth and leaned forward so I couldn't see her face. Her shoulders shook imperceptibly, and I knew she was crying again.

She had a right to cry, and I wouldn't tell her not to.

"Keep going," she said, her voice hoarse, and she didn't look up.

"I couldn't believe what I was seeing. I didn't want to believe it at first. It made me sick, so fucking sick. I should have been there that night. I should have protected you."

The torment I felt ripped right out of my chest. I could still remember that night, the way it felt like someone had punched me with a pair of brass knuckles when I realized what I was seeing.

Ivy was watching me again, her eyes wide. I shook off what I was feeling and pressed on.

"I deleted the file. I wiped it off her hard drive and removed any trace it was there. I didn't want her to get all pissy again and use the pictures on the feed."

"You just deleted them? It's evidence, evidence against him!"

"I emailed the file to myself before I did."

"You have the pictures?"

I knew what she was thinking. I shook my head adamantly. "You're not looking at them. I won't fucking allow it."

"It's not your choice."

"The fuck it isn't!" I yelled. For the first time, my temper got the better of me. "Look at you! You think I'm gonna give you even more shit to be sick over? This is why I didn't fucking say anything to begin with!"

The force of my words and the emotion behind them spurred me up off the bed, and I paced across the room toward the windows.

"It wasn't your decision to make."

"Maybe not," I said, my voice level. "But it was my choice. Perhaps it was the wrong one, but I did what I did because I love you."

It was like she hadn't heard my words, because she completely ignored them. "What was in the pictures?"

I turned from the window. "What do you remember?"

"Not very much," she admitted, her voice forlorn. "Mostly just flashes, memories of how I felt and how I couldn't do anything." She paused, and I swallowed. "I remember saying no, Braeden. I didn't want him." Her voice started rising again.

"I know you didn't, Ivy. I believe you."

That seemed to calm her. "He was rough and sort of mean. I remember the sound of him breathing… the ragged way he… his grunts." She squeezed her eyes together, and I spun around.

I stared at the curtains, but seeing only red, I fought with the urge to put my fist through the wall.

"He taunted me," she whispered. "I remember his words. He seemed to know I wouldn't remember, but he'd told me…"

A beat of silence passed after her voice faded away.

"He told you what?" I ground out.

"He told me that deep down, I'd always know what happened."

A shout forced its way out of me, and I lunged at the dresser, sweeping my arms across it and knocking everything onto the floor. It made a loud crashing sound, and I was pretty sure at least one thing shattered, but I was too busy heaving to even see.

That son of a bitch.

It wasn't enough that he raped her? He had to taunt her too?

Motherfucker was probably the reason she panicked when someone touched her suddenly. No wonder her body lived in the knowledge of what she suffered; he'd practically conditioned it to.

I. Would. Kill. Him.

"I don't understand why I couldn't remember, why I still can't," she said, once again like my outburst hadn't even registered.

"If I hadn't seen those panties, I might not have ever remembered."

I didn't want to ask. But I had to. "Were you wearing those that night?"

"Yeah. I thought I lost them."

A trophy. He took a trophy to remember what he'd done to her.

I took a deep breath and told myself to chill. I needed to get through the rest of this conversation without trashing our house. I forced myself toward the bed to sit down.

"He drugged you. The pictures show him putting a roofie into a beer. You drank it. He took you back to your dorm, and then he... And afterward, he broke into Rimmel's laptop."

"Why would he do this to me, Braeden?" she asked.

The question broke my heart.

I went to her, knelt in front of her chair. "I don't have an answer for that, baby. I don't know how anyone could hurt someone as perfect as you."

"You did too." It was said without heat, without accusation. It was a statement. A fact.

A spear to my chest.

I did hurt her. I wondered if, in her eyes, that meant Zach and I were the same.

"I'm sorry," I whispered. The words weren't enough, but it was all I had.

"I'm tired. I want to go to bed. Alone."

I nodded and moved away from her. I knew she'd want to be alone. It was to be expected.

I'd give her space. I'd give her whatever she needed.

I walked out of the room. When I turned back, she was behind me, the door handle in her palm. Without another word, she closed it, silently, right in my face.

I blew out a breath and leaned against the wall. Gutted, that's exactly how I felt.

I didn't think I could feel any worse.

Until she started crying again.

She tried to hide it in the pillows, but I still heard. I heard every single whimper and gasp.

It was hard not going to her; it was hard not pulling her into my arms. But she didn't want me. I wasn't sure she ever would again.

And so as minutes turned to hours, I stood there in the hall and listened to the woman I loved cry until she was so exhausted she had nothing left.

CHAPTER FORTY-THREE

#HappyThanksgiving
If you can't find something to be thankful for, take a deep breath and be thankful for that.
#BeingAliveIsAGift
#BuzzBoss

IVY

I refused to go to Braeden's mother's for Thanksgiving.

I couldn't pretend that way. I couldn't go sit and smile and pretend while I ate turkey and pie and watched giant balloons pass by on the TV.

I was done with posing. I was done with it all.

I just wanted to be alone.

I wanted to grieve for what was taken from me.

My choice.

My knowledge.

My decision on how I would deal with it.

He told her I was sick, that I must have some kind of flu bug. My temperature wouldn't go down and I didn't want to risk making everyone else sick. I admit I sort of smiled when I heard him arguing with her on the phone because she wanted to come over and check on me. She was a nurse after all.

"I know you love her, Mom," Braeden muttered out in the hall. "But she's resting. She's taken the cold meds and is asleep. If she's not better in a couple days, I'll drive you over here myself."

A few beats of silence.

"Mom," he groaned.

A few more.

"Mom!"

I hoped she grilled him the entire dinner and made him uncomfortable and made him tell even more lies so he could cover up what he'd done.

I was so angry with him. So hurt and confused. Not only had Zach violated me, but so had my best friend and my boyfriend.

It was a triple whammy of betrayal.

As I hid in my room for days, barely coming out, I reasoned out what Missy had done. And why she'd done it.

My guess was she never planned on showing those photos to anyone. She never planned on letting anyone (including me) in on what really happened that night. She probably had the same motive as Braeden; she wanted to keep me from getting hurt.

But then she changed her mind.

She got pissed when I slept with B, so she lashed out and posted that picture.

She probably had no idea it would lead to Braeden finding her out. Angry people make mistakes, and she'd been angry.

No wonder she kept hanging around, kept trying to find a way back into our circle. She wanted to know if I knew. She wanted to know if I was going to rat her out for the shitty stuff she'd done.

Maybe I would.

But really, I probably wouldn't. Ratting her out would only make it harder on me. I was so incredibly exhausted. I slept for almost three days and then hid in the covers with Prada and my thoughts.

I called off sick to work, knowing I might get fired for not showing up on Black Friday. But the second I spoke into the line, my scratchy, hoarse, stuffy voice totally convinced Monica I wasn't faking.

Braeden came and went. He kept his distance just like I asked, but he was still there. He brought me food, which I barely ate. He brought me coffee (I drank that) and made sure Prada went outside and got fed.

He never tried to touch me. He never asked to sleep in here, and he never even grabbed stuff from our closet or the drawers.

I was too hurt to think about how he was feeling. I was too angry to care.

But as the days passed, I found my eyes lingering more on him when he would appear, before I retreated back into the small world I existed in.

Mostly, I asked myself the same question over and over again.

It wasn't why.

I knew why. The why might not make sense to me, but really, it didn't have to. I knew deep down, being raped wasn't my fault. The why wasn't about me. The why was about Zach and whatever the hell was wrong with him.

A single question haunted me most.

Was it better to know the truth or would it have been easier to think it had been a one-night stand from hell?

Some days I felt certain knowing the truth far outweighed the rest.

But then sometimes, usually when I would lie awake in the dark and stare up at the glowing stars B and I put on the ceiling, I would wonder…

Wouldn't it hurt less if I didn't know?

I was torn.

On the fourth day, somewhere in the house a door slammed. Rimmel wasn't due back from Thanksgiving with Romeo until late the next day, so I knew it wasn't her.

It was totally possible it had been Braeden, but he hadn't slammed anything since that night he shoved everything off our dresser. It all still lay broken and scattered.

I heard some raised voices and sat up a little straighter, wondering what was going on.

Footsteps stomped up the stairs, and Braeden's angry voice grew louder. "I told you she's sick! Leave her alone!"

"If she's too sick to see me, then she can tell me herself!" Drew yelled back.

My brother! What in the world was he doing here?

The door burst open and Drew stepped inside.

His footsteps stuttered almost immediately. He took in the dark room, the messy bed, and probably my zombie hair and face in complete shock.

He really hadn't believed Braeden when he said I was sick.

Had he thought I was tied up in here?

"Ivy," he said.

Braeden hovered out in the hallway, peering past my brother at me.

I couldn't tear my eyes away from him. He looked terrible. It was like I hadn't realized until just now. My heart felt bruised, so much so that I pressed a hand against my chest and rubbed.

What was happening to us?

Annoyed, I didn't answer. Drew stalked to the door and slammed it right in Braeden's face.

"Get dressed. You're going to the hospital."

"What!" I shrieked. "No."

"Don't argue with me, young lady," he said, sounding more like my father than my older brother. "I didn't believe you were too sick to call and talk to Mom on Thanksgiving."

Guilt pierced my heart. Braeden called and told them all what he told his mother.

"And I didn't believe you were still too sick to call now, so I came back." He said it like it proved something.

"And?" I asked expectedly.

"And you look like shit. I've never seen your hair look so bad. Your skin is so white you look like a ghost, and this room smells…" He wrinkled his nose. "And it doesn't smell good."

"Rude," I snapped. I had a right to be smelly.

"If you're this sick, then I'm doing what bonehead didn't do." He hitched a thumb at the door, leading me to believe bonehead was Braeden. "I'm taking you to the hospital."

"No." I crossed my arms over my chest.

"No?" he countered like it was a dare.

I stared him down.

He marched across the room like he was going to yank me right from the covers. I prepared to kick him.

His foot crunched over some broken glass and he stopped. Looked down. His eyes rounded at the mess all over the floor.

"What the fuck happened here?"

"Nothing." I sniffed.

Drew's eyes narrowed and a deadly calm took over his body. "Did he do this?" he growled. "Did he hit you?"

My mouth fell open. The fact that he would accuse Braeden of all people of hitting a woman was just ridiculous.

"No!"

"Don't you dare lie for him." Drew whipped the words at me. "Do you have bruises? How long has this been going on?" As he fired questions, he paced the room, his shoes crunching over even more glass. "I'm gonna kill him."

He stormed toward the door.

“Wait!” I yelled.

He glanced over his shoulder.

My body slumped. “Braeden would never do that.”

“Then what happened?”

The only answer I had left was the truth. I wasn’t going to lie. I hated lies. Besides, my brother would see through them in three seconds flat.

“You should probably sit down,” I said and readied myself to say out loud what Zach had done to me.

CHAPTER FORTY-FOUR

Stressed is Desserts spelled backwards.
#ThisExplainsSoMuch
#CakeAnyone?
#BuzzBoss

BRAEDEN

He was upstairs a long time.

The quiet resonating through the house made me nervous.

I hadn't been prepared for him to come storming back here, demanding to see Ivy. 'Course, looking back, it's exactly what I'd have done if it were Rimmel.

* * *

I didn't listen at the door even though I thought about it. Spying on my girlfriend wasn't something I ever planned to do.

I wasn't even sure if she still was my girlfriend.

Four days of nothing.

Four days of her hiding inside her room, only coming out when she had to. I tried to talk to her a couple times, but she was completely closed off, completely lost.

Still, I wouldn't leave her.

It brought up a lot of bad memories from when my mom was beaten and too hurt to get out of bed. The house would turn quiet. I would tiptoe around, afraid to be noticed by him.

I didn't want to live like this. But I didn't know what else to do.

I told myself in a few more days, she'd realize she couldn't hide forever.

True, she might hate me forever, but she couldn't hide. I'd rather fight with her than have nothing at all.

I was basically waiting it out 'til Rimmel came home. My sister would know what to say to her. She would know what to do.

* * *

But then Drew showed up.

And now it was quiet.

What if she went home with him? Would she just pack up and leave like that?

What would I do if she did?

Would I let her go?

No.

I'm letting her go without a fight.

Suddenly, the quiet was disrupted by the sound of heavy footfalls on the stairs. Drew shouted my name, and I knew she'd told him.

I didn't have time to be surprised because he came at me like a frickin' freight train.

"You son of a bitch!" he roared and threw out his fist.

I let him hit me. Hell, I welcomed it. I deserved it.

My head snapped back and I felt my lip split. The warm ooze of blood pooled in the corner of my mouth, and I wiped it away with the back of my hand.

"My sister was raped and you did nothing about it!" he ground out and pulled his fist back again. I moved just before it connected, and he spun.

"Watch it," I growled. One free hit was all I allowed.

And how the fuck dare he say I did nothing?

I'd been killing myself for months, trying to help her heal without making it worse.

"I knew something was wrong. I even asked you. You didn't say jack!" He threw out his fist again, grazing my jaw.

I shoved him back. He hit one of the stools at the island and knocked it over. It made a loud bang when it hit the floor. "Don't hit me again."

The dumbass rushed me. Clearly, he didn't know not to do that to a football player. I sank into a crouch and reversed his rush. I picked him up around the waist, spun him around, and dropped him on his back.

He caught me around the ankle, and I bent at the waist, delivering a rapid punch right to his jaw. Drew rolled, knocking my legs out from under me, and we tumbled on the floor, exchanging blows like we were in the ring.

I was bigger than him. And physically in better shape. He got winded, but I was just getting started. I pinned him to the floor. His struggles to buck me off were useless.

"What kind of man doesn't protect his girl!" Drew shouted.

I saw black. Not red. Black.

I pictured Zach's face. I heard my father's yell and my mother's cry. I felt Ivy lying in bed at night, trembling in my arms from nightmares she didn't even remember the next morning. She had no idea I burst in our room at night. She had no idea she crawled right into my arms.

It was just more shit I didn't tell her.

I drove my fist into Drew's face. I felt his skin split and saw the blood run. In the process of our struggle, we'd knocked down all the barstools and rattled a couple pictures hanging on the walls.

I drew back my fist to hit him again, no longer in control, no longer caring the damage I inflicted.

"Braeden!" Ivy shrieked, terrified.

My fist froze in midair, and I looked over my shoulder.

"Stop!" She rushed into the room, horror on her face.

Drew took advantage of my distraction and rolled, pinning me beneath him. His fist buried into my side, and I grunted but then locked my arms around him to throw him off.

"Don't hurt him!" she pleaded, tears in her voice.

I let out a curse and rolled. Drew landed on his back, his chest heaving. I jumped up and wiped at my still-bleeding lip.

"Oh my goodness!" She rushed forward. "You're bleeding!"

"I'm fine."

"Oh, your face," she crooned and lifted her hand to the tingling spot near my eye.

I held my breath. Was she actually going to touch me? Was that worry in her eyes?

Drew groaned from the floor. "I'm bleeding too!" he whined.

Ivy dropped her hand and went to his side. "You're an idiot. What the hell did you think you were doing coming down here at him like that?"

"Deserved it," he mumbled, his lip already twice its normal size.

"I told you it wasn't his fault."

"You told him?" I asked, still dabbing at my lip.

She glanced up. "Yes."

I nodded. I was fine with it. She could tell whoever she wanted. But I wasn't. That was her call.

Drew groaned like a damn pansy, and I rolled my eyes. I went to the freezer and pulled out a bag of peas. They must have been in there for ice pack purposes, 'cause no one in this house ate peas.

I threw them at Drew and they smacked him in the stomach. Ivy gave me a hard look, and I stared back, keeping my face stony.

"Go sit down," she told her brother, disapproval in her tone. I watched her walk to the freezer and pull out an actual ice pack.

It was blue and flexible. She wrapped a kitchen towel around it and then crossed to me.

"Does it hurt?" she asked, pressing it to my cheek.

"No."

"Liar!" Drew yelled.

I smirked. "I'm used to taking hits. Unlike some people."

Ivy rolled her eyes but was gentle when she lifted the ice and looked at the area. "Hold this one there."

"What if I want you to?" I said so low only she could hear.

"Sometimes we don't get what we want," she said equally as quiet.

I took the ice and held it to my face.

She picked up another towel, wet it, and then started dabbing my lip. It burned like hell.

"I'm sorry he took this out on you."

I shrugged. "I can handle it."

She pulled the towel back and stared up at me. Her eyes were bloodshot and not nearly as vivid as usual.

"You look like shit." Her voice was blunt.

"So do you."

"How come he gets a real ice pack and I get peas?" Drew whined.

"Would you prefer carrots?" I quipped.

"You're an asshole. My sister could do way better than you."

It stung. Probably because it was true.

Ivy gasped and turned away from me. "Andrew Wayne Forrester!"

I smirked at him behind her back. Dude's middle name was Wayne. "You a cowboy in another life?"

He jerked up from the table, the chair clattering to the floor behind him. Ivy jumped, and I reacted, sliding her effortlessly behind me.

"It's like you want me to come at you again," Drew growled.

I held out my arms in invite.

"Shut it right now!" Ivy yelled. "Or I'll punch you both!"

"Damn, sis. Why you gotta be so violent?" Drew asked.

It was kinda funny and my lips twitched. Ivy sighed like all her patience was gone, and for one brief second, Drew and I shared a look. A second of truce.

But then it was over.

"Why don't I give you guys some time?" I said, pulling the ice away from my face and dropping it onto the table in front of him. "Then you can bad mouth me some more in the privacy of *my* house."

I walked out of the kitchen and into the living room.

Ivy rushed after me. It kinda pissed me off. Now she wanted to talk? Now she wanted to make sure I was okay?

"Braeden, you don't have to leave."

"It's cool," I said, like it was no big deal. "I could use a break anyway."

She didn't say anything else. She just stood rooted in place.

I left without looking back.

I might have acted like it was no big deal, but inside…

Inside was a different story.

CHAPTER FORTY-FIVE

IVY

He left and didn't even look back.

I yelled at him.

I blamed him.

My brother punched him, made him bleed.

He insulted him.

Braeden took it all. He didn't say a word.

* * *

He was doing all this for me while I hid in my room.

I was being selfish.

No more.

CHAPTER FORTY-SIX

BRAEDEN

I sent out a text. *I need you.*

Hours after I stomped out of the house, I walked back in. The kitchen stools were cleaned up; everything was in place. No evidence of a punching match between Drew and me remained.

I went upstairs and took a shower, my muscles sore from the way I'd broken them down at the gym.

Even still, it felt good to work out that hard. I needed it. I felt a lot less volatile than I had just hours before.

Since all my clothes were in the bedroom and the ones I had on were way too ripe to put back on, I wrapped a towel around my waist and quietly opened the bedroom door.

Prada was curled up on her side against Ivy, who made a slight bump in the center of the bed. She was sleeping, so I moved around in the closet as quiet as I could until I found a pair of basketball shorts and a T-shirt.

Back out in the bedroom, I glanced back at Ivy, creeping a little closer to the bed. Prada rolled onto her back and showed me her belly. I smiled and scratched her stomach for a few minutes.

The mess I made the night Ivy found out was cleaned up. All the things I'd shoved onto the floor were back on the dresser, minus a couple picture frames and a clock that had all shattered on impact.

There was a candle lit on my side of the bed, making the room smell like vanilla and cinnamon. I couldn't help but notice she'd showered and blown out her hair. She was wearing something other than the same thing she'd been living in the past four days.

I guess Drew's insults hit home.

I wondered what they talked about after I left. He probably tried to convince her to go home with him. Maybe he would be good for her, especially if she decided she couldn't forgive me.

I was glad she had someone; at least she wouldn't be alone.

I closed the door quietly behind me and went downstairs. I stared at the beer for a long time but then grabbed a bottle of water and drained it instead.

I flipped through the TV channels without much interest and then glanced at the clock. It was late and I was tired. Instead of lying down on the couch and passing out, I went upstairs.

I sat down outside Ivy's bedroom door and leaned against the wall. It had become a routine. For the past four nights, this was where I spent my time. It would have been a lot more comfortable on the couch, or hell, before Drew got here, the guest room.

But those places were too far away.

Ivy was having nightmares. I needed to be close by.

I exhaled slowly, rested my head against the doorjamb, and shut my eyes. The workout drained me, and I fell asleep easily for the first time in a long while.

I don't know what caused me to wake. Maybe I heard the alarm code being keyed in. Or maybe it was the fact he was staring at me in my sleep.

I jerked up off the wall like someone blew an air horn in my ear. Romeo was standing above me, staring down with a concerned look on his face. He looked tired. Like a guy who'd been driving several hours without stopping.

"What the fuck are you sleeping in the hallway for?"

"You came," I said, my voice still thick with sleep.

"You texted." So simple but it meant so much.

"Was Rim pissed?"

"Of course not!" she said, appearing at the top of the stairs almost out of nowhere.

Romeo grinned. "Didn't think she'd let me come home without her, did ya?"

"My BBFL needed me." Her eyes found me on the floor and concern darkened them.

"He texted me, Smalls." Romeo reminded her.

"He probably got the phone numbers confused," Rimmel muttered.

"Or maybe he just wanted some manly advice instead of feeling like he was being interviewed for Doctor Phil," he teased.

"Roman Anderson, if everyone wasn't asleep in this house, I'd kick you so hard you'd scream!"

"Now, baby, that's just mean."

Man, I'd missed them. And they also made me realize just how much I missed Ivy. I missed tossing insults at her and getting them right back.

Rimmel snorted and pinned me with a stare. "Why are you sleeping in the hallway?"

"Ivy kicked me out of the room."

"See? It's man business, babe. Take your cute ass to bed. I'll be in later," Romeo told her.

I stood and pulled her in for a hug. She really hugged me back. I liked it. "Thanks for being here, sis," I whispered in her ear.

"Love you," she whispered back.

After she disappeared into their bedroom, Romeo motioned for me to follow him downstairs.

"We got a couch, you know," he said, dropping on it and propping his feet on the coffee table. Rimmel and Ivy spent an entire weekend painting it and two side tables white.

I was pretty sure if either one of them saw his feet and shoes on it, they'd give him a lecture.

Naturally, I sat down and put my feet on it too.

"She has nightmares, dude. I need to be close."

"Can't say I was surprised when I got your text. Shit's been going on with you for a while."

"It's not really my shit to tell."

"Coulda fooled me."

He was right. I might not have been the one to get raped, but I was still dealing with the fallout. I needed someone to talk to. I couldn't just keep being quiet. And I texted him. He came. It took him hours to get here, which meant he left right after I texted. I had no idea what kind of inconvenience this was on him, but he didn't even mention it.

I wasn't going to refuse to tell him now. He showed up. I had to put up.

Romeo waited me out while I struggled internally, folding his arms across his chest, leaning his head back, and closing his eyes.

"Zach raped Ivy."

Romeo's entire body went dead still. One eye opened. Then the other. He turned his head and stared at me. "The fuck you just say?"

I nodded, grim. "The night he broke into Rim's laptop. Ivy didn't sleep with him because she was drunk. He drugged her and then he raped her."

He jackknifed up and his feet hit the floor. The hard set to his jaw and the pissed-off glint in his eye wasn't unfamiliar. I knew that's exactly how I looked when I found out about it too.

"She's been carrying this around all this time," he muttered. "She didn't say—"

"She didn't know." I cut him off. Before he could ask for an explanation, I told him about the pictures, how I found out and never told anyone.

He rubbed a hand over the back of his head and then down his face. "You've known for six months?" he echoed, totally shocked by it all.

"I hoped I'd never have to tell anyone."

He let out a string of curses. “I had no idea. I’m sorry, man. I should have been here. You’ve been dealing alone.”

“Ivy just found out.” I quickly explained about how she had a flashback and I admitted it all. I left out the part about the panties because that opened up too many other questions.

“If he wasn’t locked up,” Romeo swore.

“I’d have already killed him.” I finished, dead calm and serious.

He stared at me. I stared back. He nodded.

“So what can I do?” His voice still held a note of shock.

“I don’t think there’s anything anyone can do. I was just going stir crazy, you know? It’s been four days of silence, silence and listening to her cry. She’s pissed at me. I’m not sure she’s gonna be able to forgive me.”

He waved away my words. “You did the right thing.”

I don’t know why, but his words stunned me almost as much as learning what really happened. “You think so?”

"Hells yeah. If I had been in your shoes, I'd have done the same thing. We gotta protect them."

I let out an uneven breath. All this time, I thought he would tell me what a dumbass I was. I honestly thought Romeo wouldn't have done the same.

I felt somehow validated.

A partial weight lifted off me, and I settled back into the couch, feeling slightly lighter than before.

My newfound peace was very short-lived.

Ivy's scream cut through the house. I jumped up off the couch and rushed up the stairs.

CHAPTER FORTY-SEVEN

IVY

I thought I heard voices, the familiar kind, of the people I'd grown to love. But when I turned over and listened, I didn't hear them at all.

It must have been a dream.

Maybe it was a dream about better days, when we all didn't feel so separated. When we were all here in this house like a happy family.

I closed my eyes and snuggled back into the blankets, determined to go back to sleep. Tomorrow, I was going to talk with Braeden. I was going to start living my life again. I needed rest to do it; the task wasn't going to be so easy.

I dozed off at last, slipping into quiet bliss, away from my racing thoughts.

#

The sound of loud, pounding music had me stirring again. It was so loud it vibrated my chest and made it so everyone had to yell over the bass.

There were a lot of people here. The party was raging, the house packed so tight if the fire department drove by, we'd get slammed for violation of code—too many bodies in too small of a space.

But no one ever thought about that. The beer was flowing and the night was young.

I took a sip of the drink in my hand, fresh from the keg in the kitchen. I liked the way it slid down my throat and hit my tummy, spreading out like a warm blanket.

"This is the best party all semester!" Missy yelled in my ear.

"I know, right!" My voice sounded funny to my own ears. It was a little too loud, a little too bright.

We started dancing right there where we were. People around us started dancing too, and soon we had our own little dance party happening right there in the center of the frat.

As I shook my hips, I glanced to the corner of the room. There was a couple sitting in a chair that looked like a throne. The girl was on the guy's lap; she was straddling him, practically dry humping him right there for everyone to see.

All I could see of him were his large hands gripping her back and helping her move against him. Her long dark hair flipped around and they made out, and for some reason, it made me feel sick.

Why were they just making out right there where everyone could see?

"Someone needs to get a room," said a dry voice beside me.

I spun so fast some of the beer sloshed out of the cup and over my hand, soaking my skin in the thick liquid.

"Careful now," he said. "Don't want to waste any of that. It's got a little something extra in there just for you."

Terror was like a sharp talon that swiftly ripped open my skin. What was Zach doing here? I thought he was locked away, put somewhere he couldn't hurt anyone anymore.

He smiled like a shark that just ate a forty-pound seal. I watched him reach out with a single finger and push the cup up toward my mouth. I didn't fight him. It was like I was hypnotized. Like I was helpless to fight. Warm, yeasty beer spilled over my tongue. This time it didn't taste fresh.

It tasted odd.

There was something in there…

I looked down.

Dozens of white pills floated in the pale liquid.

I spit out what was in my mouth. It flew everywhere but somehow avoided Zach. He watched me, amused, a maniacal look glinting in his eyes. "It's too late for that, Ivy," he intoned, and my vision started to blur.

My eyes grew heavy and I was suddenly so tired.

"You're mine now," he whispered. "To do with as I please."

"No," I slurred.

He laughed and palmed my shoulder. His fingers bit into my skin. "There's no one here to save you," he taunted and then spun me around.

All the people who packed this room just moments before were gone. The only ones who remained were the couple in the chair.

The girl was no longer wearing a shirt, and she was making disgusting noises as she rode the guy's lap.

"See?" Zach purred. "He's already moved on."

As if on cue, the girl turned and looked at me. Her eyes were full of spite.

It was Missy.

And the man whose lap she was sitting in… was Braeden.

The next thing I knew, I was queasy and pinned to a bed. I had no idea where I was or how I got there. But I wasn't alone.

Zach was here. He was ripping at my clothes and saying the vilest things to me. I tried to push him away. I tried to scream and yell.

"I like it when you fight," he ground out and rubbed his erect penis against my body. It protruded through his pants, and I gagged. "Makes me good and hard."

He shoved his face just inches from mine and yelled, "Now shut up and take it!"

#

"NO!" I screamed and jolted up in bed. My clothes were damp and sticking to me, and my body shook so badly I could hear my teeth chatter.

It was only a dream. Just a dream, I told myself over and over. But I couldn't stop shaking. I couldn't stop hearing him scream at me.

I shoved out of the bed. My foot got tangled and I fell. My knee hit the floor first, and I yelped. Pushing up, I stared at the closed door.

I wanted Braeden.

I wanted to feel safe again.

I didn't even know if he was here and, if so, if he would talk to me.

If he is home, his truck will be in the driveway. I went to the window and lifted back the curtain. The blinds were closed, so I slipped a couple fingers between them and opened up just one of the slats.

I pressed up close and peered out into the night, hoping to see the big red truck.

My eyes landed on something else.

Someone else.

I jolted, the blinds clattering against the glass. Doing a double take, I told myself I was still just freaked from the dream.

But he was still there. Zach was standing there in the center of the driveway, looking up at the house.

Looking up at *me.*

Dressed completely in black, his body practically disappeared with the night. Just like before in the stairwell.

I'd imagined that.

Hadn't I?

His hair was perfectly arranged, just like it always had been. I hated it. I hated everything about him. His face was pale and stuck out like a crow in a cornfield. The way he just stood there, unmoving, unblinking, staring right at me…

I shuddered. My mouth opened, ready to scream.

He saw. He knew.

With careful, deliberate movement, a single finger lifted to his lips, pressed in the center, and he slowly shook his head.

Shhhhh.

I started screaming, and once I began, I couldn't stop. I fell away from the window, practically ripping the curtain right off the wall, and fell back into the bed. A blanket tangled around me and the sensation of being pinned down came over me.

I fought against the blanket, screaming even more.

He's here. He's coming for me. He's going to rape me again. I won't be able to stop him.

The sound of the door flying open and banging against the wall barely registered. The lamp on the bedside table rattled with the force of pounding footsteps.

Braeden called my name, but even though I knew it was him, I couldn't stop. He appeared over me, his face terrified. He reached for me, but then his arms fell short.

He turned away.

"Her eyes are open. I think she might be awake. I don't think she wants me." The torture in his voice couldn't be denied, and even as I wanted to tell him it wasn't true and I wanted him, I couldn't stop screaming.

Not even another second passed and someone else was there. The bed dipped beneath his weight, and I was hauled up off the mattress, out of the blanket trying to choke me and against a rock-hard chest.

It felt similar to Braeden's, but it wasn't the same.

"It's okay now," Romeo said, pushing my face into his chest and holding it there. "Just another dream."

Another dream? The thought was so fleeting it was there and then gone.

My fingers clutched at his shirt, holding on so tight. My screams turned to sobs against him, and his arms tightened.

He cursed softly. "I'm so fucking sorry, Ivy." I felt him rocking me gently, and honestly, if I had been in any other state of mind, I'd be embarrassed as hell. But I couldn't find those feelings in me because I was too busy trying to forget what I'd just seen.

I gasped and jerked upright. Romeo held me tighter to keep me from falling off the bed. "He's here!" I screeched.

"Who!" Braeden demanded.

My eyes sought him out in the dark. He was pacing nearby, his jaw tight and shoulders tense.

Drew burst into the room. "What the fuck!" he yelled.

"I think she was having a nightmare," Rimmel said quietly.

I gasped, not even realizing she was in the room, and peeked around Romeo. She was standing just inside the door, her hair wild and no glasses on her face.

I sniffled and went rigid at the same time.

Reality slowly came pulsing back. I looked up.

Romeo's face was so close to mine that even in just the candlelight, I could see how blue his eyes were. He searched me, a hard frown set to his mouth.

"I-I'm so-r-ry," I stammered. My teeth were still chattering slightly. "I—"

I tried to pull away from him. It was totally wrong. I was practically in his lap.

He pulled me back. "It's fine. Just calm down a second."

"Ivy," Drew said, rushing to the bed. "Are you okay? What the hell happened?"

Zach's face and the way it seemed to glow in the dark driveway flashed before me again. "He's outside!" I burst out, agitation working its way through me again. "I just saw him in the driveway."

"Who?" Drew asked, confused.

"Zach." I sobbed and collapsed against Romeo again, forgetting I shouldn't cry all over him and clutching at his chest.

Braeden tore from the room. He was gone before I could even call him back. "No!" I yelled.

The front door slammed and I knew he was outside.

"No," I cried and tried to scramble after him. "He's going to get hurt. Zach's gonna hurt him too."

Romeo stood up swiftly, bringing me with him. He placed me in Drew's arms and then brushed my hair off my wet face.

"Ivy," he said firm, the authority in his voice unmistakable.

A sob caught in my throat. I looked at him with wide eyes.

"Calm down. I'll go get B."

I nodded.

Romeo rushed from the room, and I practically jumped out of Drew's arms and went to the window. When my hand closed around the curtain, I took a steadying breath. I wanted so badly to look outside, but I was also terrified of what I would see.

Seconds later, the door downstairs opened and closed again.

I gripped the curtain, anticipating Romeo yelling for help or the sounds of something indicating more trouble.

All I heard were footfalls on the stairs.

Braeden was the first to come around the corner. A sound ripped from my chest, and I rushed across the room, right into his arms.

Familiar.

Safe.

Right.

"I'm okay," he whispered.

"Zach?" My voice shook.

"No one's out there, baby. It was just your dream. It was all a dream."

"I wasn't dreaming," I insisted. "I had been, but then I wasn't."

"It's okay," he murmured, holding me tight. "You've been dreaming a lot."

"Is that why when I got up to piss earlier, you were sleeping in the hallway?" Drew asked.

Braeden tensed but didn't reply.

I glanced up. "You've been sleeping in the hallway?"

"Don't worry about it," he muttered and pulled my head back down.

Romeo stepped back in the room. Braeden shifted us toward his best friend. "Would you mind sitting with her 'til she falls back asleep?"

"I'll do it," Drew said behind us.

"I think I'd rather it be someone who doesn't like to punch me in the face."

Rimmel's gasp filled the room. "Is that what happened to your face?" she demanded.

"No, tutor girl," Braeden quipped lightly. "I'm naturally this good-looking."

"Now see here, *Mr. I Drive Too Fast*," Rimmel said, taking on a no-nonsense tone. I peeked out from Braeden's shirt to see her stride over in front of my brother like she was some type of badass.

Even though I was still shaking and scared, I half smiled. The sight was ridiculous. My brother outweighed her by at least a hundred pounds and he was like a foot taller than her.

"I don't know how you are with your brothers at your house, but in this house, brothers don't punch each other in the face!"

"Yes, they do," Romeo and Braeden said at exactly the same time.

Drew suppressed a smile, and Rimmel gasped. "You two better not be punching each other!" she snapped.

"He's not my brother," Drew argued.

Romeo stepped forward slightly, and my gaze slid to him. Drew hadn't said it to her with any kind of heat, but just the fact he was arguing with her was enough to put Romeo on alert.

Rimmel pointed her finger at him and waved it around. "Oh, yes, he is! And if you can't accept that, then you better go pack your bags."

"Yes, ma'am." Drew replied, contrite.

I couldn't help it. I smiled.

It made me sorry that I hadn't been present enough lately to lay down the same rules.

God, I'd been such a mess.

Romeo moved forward and caught Rimmel around the waist, lifting her off the ground and towing her back. "Down, tiger."

"I'll stay with her," Drew said. Braeden tensed again.

"No." I stepped back out of his arms and resisted the urge to rush right back in. "I'm fine. Go to bed."

He opened his mouth to argue, and I gave him a death glare.

"Geez. The women in this house need to take a pill," he grumped. On his way past, he kissed me on the forehead.

"If you want to come sleep with me like you did when you were three and there were thunderstorms, I'll leave the door open."

"Thanks." I hugged him quickly. The memory of all the nights he used to make up stories about what caused the sound of the thunder warmed me inside.

When he was gone, Rimmel yawned. "We'll talk tomorrow?"

I nodded. "Sorry I woke you."

Romeo patted her butt on the way past, and then it was just me, him, and Braeden.

"I looked around outside. There's no one there. The alarm is on," Braeden told me, his voice subdued.

"Thank you."

I felt Romeo watching us, and I wondered what he knew. I turned to him. "He told you?"

"Just tonight," Braeden answered instead. "I just needed someone—"

"To talk to." I finished.

The fact B hadn't even told Romeo until tonight, well, that said a lot. He told Romeo everything.

"It's okay," I whispered, even as I felt a little self-conscious about Romeo knowing. Would he see me different now?

Seconds later, Romeo was right in front of me. He pulled me into his arms and hugged me close. My eyes slid closed and I rested my cheek against his chest.

"I'm so sorry I brought him into your life." His voice was so sincere and held a note of pain. I realized Romeo understood what it was like to be Zach's victim.

A victim of a different sort, but a victim all the same.

"I don't blame you," I told him. "I don't blame anyone."

I didn't have room inside me for blame. I hurt too much.

Braeden shifted and cleared his throat. "Thanks for being here, Rome. I'll be downstairs on the couch."

I pulled out of Romeo's hug. "Wait."

Braeden looked back.

"Will you stay?"

"You sure?"

I nodded.

He stepped back into the room, and I felt a little better.

Romeo hugged me again. "See ya in the a.m., Blondie."

"Don't call her that," Braeden growled.

Romeo sighed loudly. "Drew already calls her sis. You call her Blondie. What the hell am I supposed to call her?"

"I do have a name," I pointed out.

Romeo made a face. "Brothers don't call their sisters by name."

He was right. They didn't. My two brothers called me everything but my name. "Brother?" I questioned, as if I just realized what he said and that he was talking about me.

He nodded. "I know you already got two, but I don't have a sister."

A genuine smile lit up my face. "I'm good at handling brothers."

"Sweet." He moved to the door as he talked. "I probably need some practice at having a sister, but I think you're gonna be a good one. We have a lot more in common than I think even you and I realize."

I nodded, thinking he was right.

Braeden groaned loudly. "Shit. I'm dating the girl version of you."

Romeo laughed. "What can I say? You got good taste."

I watched him and Braeden pound it out, and then he was gone.

B went to the bed and began straightening all the blankets. I felt sticky and uncomfortable, so I went in the closet and quickly changed into a fresh pair of satin PJ shorts and top. When I came out, I couldn't help but lock eyes on the window, still shaken about what I'd seen.

"It was just a dream, baby," Braeden said. I spun around, surprised to see him sitting in the chair and not the bed. "You've been having them all week."

"What?" I gasped, totally distracted.

He rubbed a hand over his face. He looked so exhausted. I knew the flickering candle wasn't just creating the shadows on his face. They were there because he'd been sleeping in the hallway. Outside my door.

And now I knew why.

"You start crying out in your sleep. I come in and lay with you…"

I stared at him open-mouthed. I think he took that as a sign I was angry.

"I didn't touch you," he assured me. "Well, sometimes I rubbed your back. Over your clothes," he hurried to add.

"You did?"

"It calmed you down."

"Will you lie with me now?" I asked him.

"If that's what you want."

"I want." I slipped between the sheets and he did the same. "Thank you for being here for me, Braeden," I whispered. *Thank you for respecting me. For giving me my space, but never going too far.*

I scooted a little closer to him. He held out his arm and without hesitation, I slipped against his side and laid my cheek on his chest.

There was no place like home.

"Are you still scared?" he whispered.

"A little," I admitted.

"It's okay to sleep, Ivy. I swear to God, no one is gonna hurt you tonight."

I believed him. There was no safer place than in his arms.

I still couldn't not think about what I saw out the window. Everyone seemed convinced it was part of my dream.

I knew better.

I'd been fully awake when I looked out that window tonight.

CHAPTER FORTY-EIGHT

BRAEDEN

When I opened my eyes, she was staring at me.

The quiet way her eyes took in my face made my chest tighten.

I didn't say anything; she didn't either. We just lay there and watched each other, not a single word spoken.

She was lying on her back, her face turned in my direction. Champagne-colored hair spilled across the pillows and her scent mingled on the sheets.

God, I'd missed her scent.

I'd missed this bed.

I'd missed her.

I wanted to move closer. I wanted to touch her, but I didn't move. I was afraid I'd break whatever this moment was that whirled around us. As my eyes ate up her beautiful face, I noticed a tear, full and glistening, form in the corner of her eye. It hung there, clinging to her dark lashes, as if it were trying not to fall.

In the end, it lost the battle.

The tear slowly slid along her skin, leaving a wet trail behind it.

Without thought, I reached out and brushed it away. I didn't want to see Ivy cry. I didn't want to be the reason.

"If you could go back to the moment you found out, would you do things different? Would you tell me?" she whispered.

"I don't know," I answered honestly. Even knowing how things would end, how everything would come out, I still wasn't sure I would have told her. Sometimes we do things knowing they're wrong, but the motive behind them is pure.

"I don't want to be mad at you anymore."

I felt like there was a vise clamped around my heart and someone was cranking the handle, tightening, tightening until it almost hurt.

But even though it hurt, this wasn't the bad kind of pain. This was exactly what I wanted. A chance to talk to her. A chance to let her hate me. A chance to let her heal.

"You have every right to be." Our voices were so quiet, sort of raspy from being unused while we slept. The moment I feared would be broken when one of us spoke or moved was the opposite. It closed in around us, narrowing until it was just her, me, and the bed.

"You aren't the one who hurt me though. You only tried to protect me."

"I was wrong." I sorely wanted to give in to her words, to allow her let me off the hook. It would be so easy.

I didn't want easy.

I wanted real.

In that moment, I realized something.

I wasn't him.

All these times I looked in the mirror and saw my father…

I'm not him.

If I was, I'd never be lying here, openly, brazenly admitting I was wrong. I'd never have put my heart and soul on the line to keep Ivy from being hurt. If I were my father, I wouldn't care at all.

"Even if you're still mad at me…" My voice was husky. "It's okay. I'll wait for you."

"You slept outside my door."

"I promised you I'd never let you go."

"You're my anchor," she whispered.

"Always."

"I hate what happened to me."

Something inside me cracked. I felt it so profoundly I wondered if she heard the sound. "I know, baby. I hate it too."

That dark place in my center rose up like it was ready for battle. I swear to God, if I ever saw Zach, I'd kill him for what he'd done to her.

"And even though I don't like what you did, I understand."

Just like that, the darkness receded. Like a strong wind came and blew it right away. "You understand?" I echoed, making sure I heard her right.

She nodded once and turned, moving onto her side, tucking her hand beneath her cheek, and hitting me with both her eyes.

They were so blue this morning.

Bluer than I'd ever seen them before.

Blue was definitely my new favorite color.

"I've kept secrets too. I understand the inner struggle that comes with not saying something you know you should, but not wanting to hurt anyone."

She was talking about how she slept with me, knowing Missy wanted me.

"I remember thinking to myself that I had no idea if what I was doing was…"

I finished the sentence. "Was the right thing."

She smiled softly. "Yeah."

She did understand.

Dear God, I have no idea what I did to deserve this woman. But thank you, and I swear I'll never take her for granted.

"Braeden?" The hesitant way she said my name stopped me in my tracks.

"Yeah?"

"I feel kind of relieved." She looked away, closing off her blue-eyed stare. "Like I can finally understand why everything inside me has felt so confused."

"Oh, baby." I itched to reach out and touch her, to pull her against my chest. I wasn't sure she wanted me to do it, so I kept my arms where they were.

"Does that make me a bad person? What kind of girl feels relief when she figures out she was raped?"

Her voice cracked on the last word, and my heart stuttered a bit.

"A tortured one," I swore. "A girl who's been fighting a long time without even knowing why."

I could have prevented that.

"I understand so much now. The distance I sometimes felt between us, the careful way you touched me, why you always put yourself in front of me like a shield."

"Oh no, I'm gonna do that forever."

Her lips kicked up in a half smile. "It's okay. You have a pretty nice butt for a shield."

"I work out," I bragged.

She giggled. It was all light and warm.

The best fucking sound I'd ever heard.

"That's why you pulled back from me physically after that night at Screamerz."

"I thought sex with me was only making you worse," I admitted.

"Anything that brings me closer to you can never be a bad thing." She reached out and touched my face, drew her fingers down the side of my cheek. "I love you."

I closed my eyes. It was so good to hear those words.

"I love you too."

"I want you to touch me, Braeden."

I opened my eyes and stared deep into hers, looking for absolute certainty.

It was there.

I reached for her, but she drew back. My hand paused in midair.

"I want nothing between us. I want it all out in the open. No more secrets. No more barriers."

"No more," I murmured and reached for her again.

She caught my hand and held it. "*Nothing*," she intoned.

Understanding dawned.

"Do you still want me that way, Braeden, after knowing I can't be the one to give that part of myself to you first?"

She wanted to make love without a condom. And she was afraid I wouldn't want to because Zach had raped her without one.

I untangled my hand from hers and wrapped it around her waist, towing her right up against my front. I knew she could feel my erection. I was so hard there was no way she could miss it.

"You will be the one to give me that part of yourself first, sweetheart," I said gently. "Because you never gave away that part of yourself. It was taken."

"You don't care?" The doubt was still in her voice.

"Oh, I care about lots of shit, but none of it is that," I murmured. "I want in you in every single way you'll give yourself to me. He isn't even a factor. He isn't even a thought. The only people in this room right now are me and you."

I felt the give in her body, the relaxation of muscles. All her weight pressed into me, and I accepted it with ease. Ivy dropped her cheek to my chest, and I pressed my lips to the top of her head.

I let my fingers work through the strands of her hair and explored the length of her spine with my fingertips. Her body was all curve and satin skin. I could spend half my life touching her and I'd still find new things about her that I admired.

Eventually, my hands moved down to her ass, which tilted upward when I smoothed my palm over it.

It has been previously stated that I'm an ass man.

And being as such, I had full authority to declare Ivy's ass the best one around.

I massaged the round firmness with both hands, and she purred. Slowly, I massaged farther in, toward the meeting of her thighs, and let my fingers delve down into the slick opening between them.

She was already wet for me.

I flirted with her opening until she started to move restlessly. Carefully, I moved, laying her out in the center of the bed. I took a moment to stare at every inch, committing it to memory and marveling at what a lucky bastard I was.

I took it slow, allowing my tongue and lips to linger on all the parts of her. I was selfish like that. I wanted every inch, especially when I'd been so afraid I'd never have her again.

I kissed the insides of her knees, slid my tongue down her calves and up the sides of her waist. I didn't leave a single inch untouched. She was shaking when I spread her thighs and licked up her center.

She groaned my name, and I went in. I began with one finger, slipping it easily into her drenched core. She was warm, tight, and willing so I slid another finger in and began to pump them slowly. Her hips rocked in motion with my fingers, and I smiled, lowered my mouth to the swollen clit at her center, and pulled it into my mouth.

Her body arched up off the bed. Her hands left my hair and fisted the sheets at her sides. I kept on her, moving my fingers and mouth so the orgasm would go on and on.

After several long minutes, she shuddered and collapsed against the bed. My fingers gentled, but I continued to lick her. Her body still shook and she still moaned.

One hand found its way over and limply rested on my head.

"I can't take it anymore," she murmured.

I lifted my head and looked all the way up her body, the look in her eyes was unfocused and soft. I grinned. "You want me to stop?"

"No," she moaned. "I want more…"

I covered her body with mine, cupped her face in my hands, and claimed her mouth. I wondered if she could taste herself on my tongue, hoped she could. I wanted her to know how fully she was part of me. I wanted her to know how delicious she tasted.

"I want to give it all back to you," she whispered when I kissed down her neck. "But I can't move," she whined. "You totally made me worthless."

Playfully, I bit at her neck and laughed. "I don't need anything from you but exactly what you're doing."

I knew she'd try and talk some more. I was done with words. I kissed her deeply, penetrating her mouth with my tongue, and rocked my hips into her, allowing the hard length of my cock to stroke against her belly.

"Are you sure?" I asked, poised at her entrance, totally bare, my emotions stripped raw.

"Oh yes."

With one surge, our bodies joined together, and I forgot to breathe. For a fraction of a second, my heart stopped.

Everything did.

The sensations rippling through my body were unmatched. Every time I made love to Ivy, from the first time to right now, was the best I'd ever had.

But this was a different level. It was because we'd somehow managed to endure through it all and we were still here together.

There was nothing left lingering between us that could potentially rip us apart.

"Can you feel it?" I asked her.

"More than ever."

I started moving. Her teeth sank into her lower lip. We moved together, slow at first, and all I could think about was what it felt like to be skin to skin.

But eventually, those thoughts were replaced with need. Hot, hammering need. My hips surged harder into her, impatient for release.

She moaned, and I realized what I was doing and slowed.

Her eyes popped open.

"Did I hurt you?" I asked, mentally kicking myself for being so rough.

"I'm not so fragile, Braeden," she answered. "I like it that way. I like feeling like you're losing control."

It'd been so long since I lost control with her. "I don't want to scare you."

"You didn't scare me that first night. You won't scare me now."

I hesitated, and she reached down and pulled my butt in so I was buried deep. A groan ripped from my throat. My forehead dropped to her shoulder and my body shuddered.

"Harder," she whispered in my ear. "Deeper."

I gave in.

Bracing myself on my hands above her, I pounded into her like I hadn't in so long. Her mouth opened, but no sound came out. Her legs fell open; she appeared boneless on the mattress.

I worried I took it too far, but then her nails dug into my back and she demanded. "More."

I went at her like a shark after its prey, holding back my own release until my balls felt like they were going to explode.

Her nails raked into my back, and my teeth grazed her collarbone. When my arms were weak and shaking, when I couldn't hold back any longer, I gave in.

I exploded inside her, my hot seed pumping deep into her accepting body. Ivy grabbed my ass and pulled me in, rocking so I was deeper than I'd ever been.

I swear to God, another orgasm ripped through me. I bucked against her chest like a bull at a rodeo and released a shout into the pillow right beside her head.

"Yes," I think she murmured, rocking in small motions against me. Her hands and arms quivered.

The roaring in my head gave way enough that I heard her satisfied mewling. I'd been so lost in my orgasms.

Two.

I just had two fucking orgasms.

I hadn't even realized she was having one too.

Unable to hold up my body, I collapsed on top of her. I knew I should move, that I was way too heavy for her, but I couldn't. I was completely drained.

Her graceful arms wrapped around me and her hands rubbed the muscles in my back.

I shuddered under her delicate touch.

I was a goner.

So far gone under her spell I'd stay that way even after I was dead.

She could've asked me for anything, and I mean anything, in that moment and I would have agreed.

The after sex fog had been taken to a whole new level.

Hells yeah.

"B?" Ivy said after a long time.

I grunted, still on top of her.

"Did you, um… did you go twice?"

The pillow muffled my laughter.

"Have you ever…?"

Finding the strength, I rolled off her and stared up at the ceiling. "Nope, never before. That was the best sex I've ever had in my entire life."

She giggled.

Then she giggled some more.

"You're pleased with yourself," I drawled, rolling on my side to look at her. I tucked some hair behind her ear. "You should be. You're good for me, baby."

"You're good for me too."

"I know."

She rolled her eyes. "There isn't enough room in this bed for me, you, and your ego."

Goddamn, it was good to have her back.

"Tell me you like my cock," I teased.

"No!" she cried, suppressing a laugh. "You're so gross."

"That's not what you were saying a minute ago."

"Braeden James Walker, do *not* make fun of me!"

"Ooh, pulling out all three names."

She pushed a hand into my hair. It had grown longer 'cause I'd been too lazy to get it cut, so now it could curl around her fingers and she had something to grab.

"Your hair is messy." She tugged at the strands above my forehead.

"You like it?"

"I really do."

I kissed her quickly. "Wanna help me wash it?"

"Does a giraffe have a long neck?" she quipped.

"Aww, baby. That was terrible."

She threw a pillow at my head. "It was good!"

I jumped out of bed and grabbed her ankle. She screeched as I towed her to the edge of the mattress. Then I picked her up, sheet and all, and headed toward the bathroom.

"Braeden!" She gasped. "I'm naked!"

"I've seen it all before," I said, dry.

"We can't go into the hall like this! What if Rimmel sees! My brother!"

"Close your eyes!" I yelled.

She screeched and hit at my back. I kept walking but made sure the sheet covered her up completely. I flung open the bedroom door and stepped out toward the bathroom.

Romeo was coming down the hall, a pair of jeans hanging off his hips. He carried two mugs of coffee, so I figured he was delivering to Rim.

"I'm guessing things are better?" he drawled.

Ivy started screaming and tugging at the sheet.

I laughed.

"Dude, you better not be looking at my woman's naughty bits."

"*Braeden James!*" Ivy yelled.

I cackled and shut us in the bathroom. Romeo's laugh floated down the hall.

I knew she was still gonna need a lot of time heal. Hell, maybe even some professional help. I knew we still had issues to work out, but I didn't think about that stuff just then.

All I could think and all I could feel was…

Damn. It's good to be back to normal.

CHAPTER FORTY-NINE

IVY

My hair was still dripping from the shower when Rimmel knocked on the bathroom door and announced it was pancake Sunday. This would be the first time we were all together for our traditional pancake Sunday since Romeo left for the NFL.

Just the mention of the diner had my stomach growling loudly. It took me a little by surprise because I hadn't thought of food at all for a long time.

"Someone's hungry," Braeden said, coming up behind me and wrapping his bare arms around my towel-clad body.

"I could eat," I murmured, enjoying the feel of him so close. I marveled at the fact that even after everything, it still didn't color the way I felt with him. If anything, I felt closer. I felt safer.

"You need to. My B handles are shrinking away." He kissed the side of my neck, then moved back.

I made a sound. Yeah right, those curves were here to stay.

"You feel up to going out?" he asked, running the towel over his damp hair. When he pulled it away, the dark strands literally stuck out all over the place.

"Yeah. It will be good to hang out. Just like old times."

"They aren't old times," he corrected. "They're current times. Nothing will change with that."

"What the hell is pancake Sunday?" Drew yelled from down the hall.

Braeden made a sound.

I opened the bathroom door a crack and yelled. "Food!"

"Count me in!" he yelled back.

"Is he, like, moving in?" Braeden grumped.

I contemplated myself in the mirror. I was pale, my eyes were kinda puffy, and my lips were dry. I had a lot of work to do just make myself not look like death warmed over.

"B?" I asked.

"Yeah, babe."

I was still contemplating my reflection when I spoke. "I'm sorry."

He fell silent, like he was surprised I would apologize. I turned and leaned against the sink to regard him with an honest stare.

"I'm sorry I shut down. I was so selfish. I didn't even think about how hard it must have been for you. All these months… you haven't had anyone to talk to."

"This wasn't about me. It never was. This has always been about you."

I shook my head. "It's about us."

"I love it when you say us."

"I still feel pretty… raw inside, you know?"

His face turned solemn and he nodded.

"Like all the scabs on a wound have flaked away and left the unprotected skin exposed."

"That's kinda gross, baby."

I laughed lightly. "Yeah, but that's exactly how it feels, and kinda gross is part of that."

"I'll be your really good-looking Band-Aid."

I ran a hand across his chest. "I don't want you to be my Band-Aid. You can't fix this, no matter how hard you've tried. Just like any wound, it's gonna take time to heal. But I don't want you to be careful with me like you have been. I want it to be like this morning in bed, when it was just you and me and nothing else."

I saw the doubt form in his eyes, and I pressed on.

"You don't remind me of him, Braeden. There's nothing about you that frightens me. Except maybe the thought of losing you."

"That's not going to happen."

He was so sure. It made me feel sure too.

"I've been dealing with this—with what happened—for a long time. Yes, some of the facts and pieces are new, but deep down,"—I pressed a hand to my chest—"I've been dealing with this a long time."

"Just tell me what you want, Blondie. You'll have it," he vowed softly, pulling me close.

"I want everything. Don't hold back. Some days I might need a little patience."

"Woman, you've always required patience," he drawled.

I pinched his nipple lightly.

"Was that supposed to be a punishment?" Desire clouded his eyes.

I groaned. He was absolutely incorrigible.

He caught my hand and brought it up to kiss the knuckles. "Go on. Tell me what else you need."

"I guess what I'm trying to say is I don't know where to go from here. Right now I feel stronger. I feel like I want to get back to life. I want to eat pancakes, go to work, be with you."

"But..." he encouraged.

"But sometimes what happened feels like a storm cloud on an otherwise sunny day."

I couldn't quite get out what I was feeling. I couldn't quite put it into words.

"You're still healing. You're still dealing. I got it."

Well, gee. He made it sound so simple.

"I love you." That feeling was so easy to convey.

He kissed me. "I love you," he said against my lips.

I pulled back. "Promise you'll never keep anything from me again, Braeden. Even if you think it would be better for me."

"I promise."

I ran my fingers through his wild hair, trying to tame the strands.

"We good?" he asked.

"We are."

"I'll go feed Giz while you get dressed." After a kiss on the tip of my nose, he left me to try and fix the mess I'd made of my face the past five days.

Thank goodness for eye cream, moisture masks, and lip balm.

And for luminizing foundation, highlighter, blush, mascara…

Basically, I'd like to thank every product in my beauty arsenal, because I had to whip every last one of them out this morning.

Good thing I'd had a lot of practice and was able to pull it together before Braeden threatened to eat the southbound end of a mule or something equally disgusting.

By the time I went downstairs (I was the last one down there, of course. I swear, did no one else worry about the way they looked?), I had my face looking fresh and awake, my dry lips were soft, and my hair was shiny and sleek around my shoulders.

I chose a casual outfit (it was pancake Sunday after all) of dark-green leggings, tall brown UGG boots, and a chunky knit oversized cardigan in soft cream.

The diner wasn't that busy, probably because we were there a little later than we usually were, but it wasn't empty.

I was surprised when we pulled up to see Trent waiting in the lot, but almost just as quick, I was glad he was there.

"You called Trent?" I asked Braeden.

"That would be me," Drew said, sheepish. "Is this like… a family thing?"

"Trent's family," B said.

I was glad to see whatever kind of tension he felt toward Trent was gone. I'd have to remember to ask him about it.

We had to wait for the staff to pull together two tables for us, but once they did, we had coffee, juice, and our orders placed in record time. I sat between Braeden and my brother. Romeo, Rimmel, and Trent sat across from us.

As I sipped my coffee, I thought briefly of Missy, I felt a pang of sadness she wasn't here. But Missy's part in my life was over. It was time I let go of that as well. Finding out she knew about Zach and used it against me was the final nail in the coffin of the friendship we once shared.

She couldn't hurt me anymore. She'd already done her worst.

Under the table, B entwined his fingers with mine. I left my thoughts behind and smiled at him. The waitress brought heaping plates of food and set them in front of all the guys. Then she handed Rimmel and me much more sensible portions.

"So," Romeo said, around a huge bite of eggs, "what's your deal, Drew? I thought you were staying in North Carolina after Thanksgiving."

"I think what he meant to say," Rimmel corrected, "was you are welcome to the guest room."

Romeo didn't bother to agree, but he did smile and wink when he saw me looking at him.

"Why did you come back, Drew?" I asked, picking up my coffee and cradling the warm mug in my hands.

"'Cause I knew you needed me."

"And I love you for it, but I think it's more than that," I said.

"It's the man crush he has on Trent," Braeden announced while shoveling pancakes in his mouth.

Trent choked on the coffee he was sipping, and everyone laughed.

"Man crush," Drew intoned.

"Bromance?" I tried and looked between him and Trent.

"B would know all about bromance," Trent cracked.

Romeo and B both gave him the finger.

Drew guffawed. "I admit it's cool hanging with someone who likes cars as much as I do."

Even though it was super fun to tease him about their fast friendship, I had a feeling I knew the real reason Drew stayed with us so long.

"Did you and Dad get into it over Thanksgiving?" I asked.

My parents were great. I loved them, and my family was super close. My childhood was nothing but amazing, but I wasn't the oldest son. I wasn't expected to swallow my own passions so I could follow in my father's footsteps and become a computer genius.

Drew set down his fork. "We never get into it. You know that. But he certainly wasn't subtle about how disappointed he was that I hadn't picked a company to start working my ass off for."

He'd been hiding at our house and using me as an excuse. I hadn't been a very good sister as of late.

Beside me, B spoke up. "I know something about having a father you feel like you gotta see when you look in the mirror."

Everyone looked at him, frankly surprised he was openly talking about it.

"Take it from me, man. Hiding won't solve the problem. From what I know, your Dad is a good man. He's always been good to you guys. Just tell him you don't want to sit behind a computer. Tell him you want to drive, not just as a hobby."

"How'd you know I want to drive?" Surprise made Drew's voice high.

"I listen when you talk, man. I just don't act like it."

I gave my brother a beaming smile. Braeden wasn't nearly as bad as he thought.

Drew's passion was and would always be cars. He'd been racing them as an amateur since he got his license. Our dad didn't think it was a lucrative enough career path, and my mother was naturally afraid he was going to kill himself.

I worried about that too, but I never said so. I couldn't. He always looked the most at peace when he was behind the wheel.

"He's good," Trent spoke up. "Smoked my Mustang."

"You two have been racing?" I asked, my eyes bulging. I had no idea Trent was so interested in cars. I always just saw him as a football player and a frat boy.

Trent shrugged. "Just messing around."

"Maryland has a team," Romeo said. "Ron Gamble owns it."

"Who's Ron Gamble?" Drew asked.

All the guys at the table groaned.

"He's the richest man in the entire state. He owns the Knights. He owns everything," I said.

"And y'all know him?"

"Rome's his golden boy," Braeden said.

Romeo didn't disagree; he just shook his head. Then he said, "I could find out if there's any spots open."

"Are you shitting me?" Drew said, completely abandoning his food.

I smiled and little butterflies took flight in my stomach. I never really thought about having Drew here in Maryland full-time. I loved the thought. Our family was growing.

"I'm not promising shit," Romeo warned. "I'm not as in with Ron as B thinks."

"Liar," Braeden said around a cough.

Romeo ignored him. "And you'd have to prove yourself, but I could maybe make a call."

At that moment, a couple girls came up to the table with papers in their hand. They stared at Romeo with stars in their eyes and a blush on their cheeks.

"Can we have your autograph?"

Romeo tossed down his fork and leaned back. He gave them a million-dollar smile and turned his blue eyes on them. "Sure."

I was pretty sure one of them swooned.

Rimmel barely even glanced up, like she was used to this. Like people approaching him was a regular occurrence.

After he signed the papers and posed for a quick selfie, the girls went back to their table.

I leaned across toward Rimmel. "Pretty soon you're gonna need a full-time stylist."

She groaned.

Romeo heard and draped an arm across her shoulder. "Hell no, she won't. She don't need to change 'cause people know who I am. I don't give a rat's ass what people think. My girl is hot."

Rimmel smiled at him but then glanced at me. I knew what that meant. It meant even though everyone at this table liked the way she looked, she still might have to start dressing it up a little. We might not like it, but as the #BuzzBoss regularly pointed out, status did mean something.

And I knew Rimmel. She'd never do anything to bring down Romeo's image.

"Maybe I could stick around," Drew said cautiously.

I clapped and leaned over to hug him.

"I can find a place, maybe get a job…"

"You already got a place," Braeden said. He glanced at Romeo, who nodded and said, "Rent's pretty cheap."

Drew glanced at Braeden sharply. "You'd want me to move in, even after I nailed you in the face?"

Braeden grunted. "I nailed you back."

Drew felt his jaw where there was still a large purple bruise. "I guess you aren't so bad after all. My sister could do worse."

"*Andrew*," I warned. That wasn't a compliment. Geez.

"It's cool, baby. Long as he accepts I ain't going nowhere."

Drew leaned in and whispered in my ear. "No hope for you and this one?" He motioned at Trent.

I glared at him.

He laughed. "I'm kidding. B's cool."

I still didn't stop glaring. "No more bonehead comments like that. *And* you gotta talk to Dad," I told him. "You can't use me as an excuse."

After a moment, he nodded. "I will."

"Good," Romeo said. "It's settled. We'll talk later."

Drew nodded.

Breakfast was light the rest of the morning. We hung at the table long after the plates were cleared away. I liked hanging out with these guys. I felt like this was where I belonged; these people were my family.

After a while, Romeo sighed. "Drive me to the airport, baby?"

Rimmel made a face but then nodded.

"You're leaving?" I asked.

"Back to the grind." He sighed. "But I got tickets for everyone for some upcoming home games, and I'll be back for Christmas."

Braeden stood. "You put yourself out to come here, bro. Thank you."

"It's not a hardship to be home."

"Still. You drove in yesterday and now have to fly back."

He grimaced. "Riding in that death machine—"

"Hey!" Rimmel objected.

Romeo winced and said, "I mean *nice* car. It wasn't too fun, but it's a quick flight back. I'm gonna drive the Hellcat back after Christmas. I miss my car."

"Want me to drive you to the airport?" Braeden asked.

"Nah, gives me some extra time with Rim. But hey, call my dad. He has something he wants to talk to you about."

"No shit?" Braeden said, excited.

Romeo smiled so wide I saw all his teeth. "It's not a contract, but it's definite talk. I think this spring it's gonna be on. Keep playing hard, *Hulk*."

"Wait, what?" I said, getting up. What did he mean?

Romeo turned to me. "Might have to share your boy here with the Knights next season."

My mouth dropped open and released a squeal. Half the diner looked at me. "Are you serious?"

Braeden turned to me, excitement on his face. "What do you think, Blondie? Think you can handle dating a pro football player?"

I threw myself at him. Like full-on body tackle. It didn't even knock the wind out of him. "I'm so happy for you," I whispered in his ear. "I'm so proud of you."

He chuckled. "It's just talk right now. We'll see."

I glanced at Romeo over B's shoulder, and he winked.

I knew it was going to happen.

Braeden and Romeo would be back together on the field.

It was perfect.

After I released Braeden, I went for Romeo and hugged him hard without hesitation. He and I had grown closer over the past year since he and Rimmel had started dating. Our relationship hadn't been the easy kind like B and Rimmel knew.

But it was no less real.

It seemed whatever wall was left between us came crumbling down last night when he was there to comfort me. Maybe I'd been intimidated all this time by his larger-than-life rep. By his alpha status. But Braeden was just as much an alpha as Romeo.

And like Romeo pointed out, he and I were a lot more similar than either of us realized.

"Thank you, Romeo," I whispered.

He kissed my forehead and then left with Rimmel.

When the three guys and me were out in the parking lot, Braeden turned to Trent. "Would you mind dropping them at the house? There's somewhere I gotta be."

It was the first I heard of this. "I'll go with you," I told him.

"It's just boring stuff, babe. Gonna go talk to Rome's dad. Don't you have to work soon?" he asked.

"It's just inventory," I muttered, sorry I said I'd go. The boutique closed early tonight because it was Sunday, which made it a perfect time to inventory and pick out new clothes for the next season. I usually didn't help with it, but since I'd called in sick so much lately, I offered to help so Monica wouldn't fire me.

"I'll try and make it home before you go in. If I don't, I'll be there tonight to walk you to your car."

Over my head, he glanced at Drew. An unspoken conversation seemed to happen in rapid time.

"I'll be there." Drew promised.

Ugh. They were arranging for me to not be at home alone. Like a babysitting crew. Even as my head rejected the idea, my gut whispered it was for the best. I wasn't ready to be alone yet. Not after last night.

Not after I was sure I saw Zach.

CHAPTER FIFTY

BRAEDEN

Going to see Anthony was just an excuse.

An excuse for where I was really going.

But I wasn't no liar. So I did swing by Rome's childhood home, and I did talk to his dad. The Knights really were interested. I guess seeing me throwing the ball around with Rome had piqued Ron Gamble's interest.

He looked up my stats. This season's were most impressive because I'd been playing with a chip on my shoulder and an axe to grind. When Gamble asked Romeo about career goals and if I might be interested in a spot on the team, he directed him toward Anthony, knowing his dad would want to handle all my contracts.

Rome got a good deal. Anthony really watched out for him. And even though I wasn't Anthony's son by blood, I knew I was like family to him and he'd take care of my career better than any agent could.

Right now he was just fielding interest, and from what I learned, Tony was also schmoozing Gamble pretty slickly. As in he was making sure the team stayed interested and kept the lines of communication open.

There was no offer on the table; it wasn't even the right time of year for that. Anthony seemed to think it was all in due time, so he had me sign some basic crap on the record stating he was within rights to help negotiate any kind of deal that might arise. And since he'd become familiar with the Knights and their entire club, he told me exactly what I needed to do in order to keep impressing them, starting with showing up at as many Knights games as I could and sitting with Rim. He wanted me to be seen with Romeo out in Knights territory. Basically, he wanted me to start a buzz.

It seemed the media was this family's best friend, and the more public support and popularity we gained, the more bargaining power Anthony would have. It was all so political and had nothing really to do with the game.

But I had to play it to get on the field.

And man, I really wanted to play with Romeo again.

Not only that, but this was my future we were talking about. The future that up until this point had been pretty unknown. I'd always believed Romeo would make it to the NFL, but I never thought I would. Not that I didn't want it. I did. I really fucking did. I just never wanted to let myself dream too big. The letdown would be too steep.

I wasn't ego-filled enough that I thought the only reason they were interested was solely based on my playing. I was a damn good player and I knew I'd be able to bring it on an NFL level, but the interest started with Romeo.

I wouldn't even be surprised if Romeo hadn't put a little pressure on Gamble once he asked about me.

I wasn't mad about it. Rome got my foot in the door; it was up to me to do the rest.

This was a dream job, and it would give me a chance to do what I loved and make a shit ton of money while I did it. I could buy my mom a new house. Some fancy place she never thought she'd have.

I could take care of Ivy, make sure she never had to worry about money ever again. I knew she didn't care about that, not really. After all, if she did, she never would have started dating me to begin with. But on a purely intrinsic level, knowing I could take care of her financially satisfied me.

Yeah, I was going for this. I was letting myself want it.

Turns out wanting stuff for yourself and having the balls to really reach for that shit made life a lot more exciting than just coasting along and "having fun."

After I left Rome's old place, I didn't go straight home.

Hells no.

It was a goddamned miracle Ivy forgave me. When I looked in her eyes this morning, I really saw the forgiveness too. I thanked every single star I ever saw in the midnight sky for that too. I knew things between her and me were going to be okay. I knew we'd come out on the other side even stronger and closer than before.

But.

(There's always a but, isn't there?)

Right next to the love and forgiveness in her beautiful eyes, I saw something else. Pain. Darkness. Fear.

And for that, I was still pissed.

Pissed that someone as beautiful and bright as her would be forced to endure such shit. That she would now have a permanent scar inside her from the atrocities Zach put her through.

And those panties. The red fucking panties that just happened to "show up" in our bedroom. Someone put those fuckers there. Someone came into our house, into her safe place, and totally jolted her existence by forcing her to remember.

I would never forgive the person who did that to her.

Never.

I knew who it was too.

Missy.

AKA #BuzzBoss.

AKA Bitch I wished I'd never met.

I drove straight to Cypress Hall from Romeo's neighborhood. I didn't know what room she was in, but I'd find out in two seconds flat.

I might not use it much anymore, but the charm that used to get panties dropping was still beneath my exterior. I parked the truck in the back of the lot and slowly strolled up to the sidewalk. Girls were all around, talking, texting, and laughing.

I smiled at all of them. Flirted with a few. I knew a lot of the faces and understood mine wasn't so unfamiliar either. When I got up to the door, a group of girls was coming out, and I put on my best roguish grin.

"Ladies," I called.

"Braeden," the one in the center of the group said. "Surprised to see you here."

"You know I love the ladies." *If Ivy heard me now, she'd totally kick my ass.*

"Thought you were taken?" she purred, coming a little closer. I tried to hold her stare while still making sure the door hadn't closed behind them. One of her minions was still in the doorway. "Or is all the speculation on the Buzzfeed true?" She made a pouty face. "Are you single again?"

Ah, yes. I'd seen the notifications. Missy was busy trying to make everyone think Ivy and me were a match made in hell.

I spread my arms and grinned. "You know me. Nothing but a mystery."

"That's not really an answer," one of the other girls replied.

"Tell ya what," I drawled, dropping my voice and stepping up to the girl who asked me the question. She was all right, with honey-brown hair and brown eyes.

She definitely wasn't Ivy.

"The second I'm back on the market, you'll be the one I look for."

Her glossy pink lips pulled up into a catlike smile. Girls were such bitches. Made me wonder how they hell any of them survived high school.

"I'd like that." She dragged a finger down the center of my chest.

I literally had to force myself not to step back.

My how times had changed.

"See ya later, thirteen," she said in a breathy stupid voice.

"Ladies." I watched them all start walking away before I lunged for the door as it was almost completely shut and pulled it open.

Inside the building, I saw a couple girls walking down the hall. With a quick smile and a single question, I knew where Missy was. I jogged up the stairs and knocked on her door.

Seconds later, her face appeared.

Her gray eyes widened when she saw it was me. She moved to slam the door directly in my face, but I was faster, slapping my palm on the wood and pressing back open.

"What do you want?" she glared.

"We need to talk."

CHAPTER FIFTY-ONE

#DumbBlonde
2 blondes drove to Disneyland. They saw a sign that read "Disneyland Left" so they started crying and drove back home.
#BuzzBoss

IVY

I love clothes.

I loathe counting them.

I mean, seriously, there can never be too many tops, jeans, skirts… whatever. But when you work in a boutique, doing inventory is a necessity. And since it was so close to Christmas and the New Year, that meant clearing out the old and getting ready for the new.

I, for one, was ready for a new year. I couldn't say this year had been a bad one, because it brought me Braeden. I hated the rape and wished fervently it never happened, but I didn't regret the things we'd been through as a couple because they made us stronger, so strong I was very confident we'd be able to get through anything else life threw our way.

But some distance from the unpleasant things would be nice.

I looked at the changing of the calendar year as sort of like shedding of old skin and welcoming new.

Ooh, maybe I should get a new wardrobe. And a haircut. Who cared if Missy got the lob first? I didn't have to let her dictate what I did and didn't do.

I did get a big discount in here and my father did keep asking me what I wanted for Christmas…

I was going to pay extra close attention to the catalogues when we got them out so I could pick some totally cute things I knew I would want to buy.

I changed before coming in to work this afternoon. I put on the long-sleeved shirt with the polka dot sleeves and back I got last week. I paired it up with a pair of destructed jeans and a pair of high-heeled cream boots.

It was freezing out; the air kinda smelled like snow. You know that fresh scent that permeated the air whenever it got super cold and the clouds hung low. It was dark; it got dark by like five thirty now. Every once in a while as we worked, I'd look out the big front window, expecting to see the white flakes falling against the black backdrop of night.

So far, it still wasn't snowing.

I wondered if Trent and Drew finally gave up on working on their engines in the driveway. When I left, they had spotlights out like even the lowering sun wasn't going to deter them. Drew seemed more relaxed now that it was settled he was going to stay. He'd been so tense before; it made me regret I hadn't talked to him sooner about the pressure he felt from Dad.

Maybe I'd talk to him when I went home for Christmas. Maybe if I did, he'd give Drew a break. Or maybe I'd bring B home with me. That would give Dad plenty to focus on and he wouldn't worry so much about what Drew was doing.

It was a devious little plan.

I liked it.

I smiled just thinking about Braeden. He was remarkable and so incredibly selfless. Sometimes when I looked at him, it amazed me that he was mine. I promised myself to find ways to show him just how much I loved him in every way I could. He deserved it.

After several hours of work, we had the floor of the boutique completely inventoried and the jewelry stock in the display drawers accounted for as well. One of the girls clocked out. She'd been there since noon and it was her time to go.

Monica was filling out paperwork, and I started marking pages in catalogues of stuff I thought would sell well with the college crowd. Not everything I marked would be ordered, as I didn't have final say. That was Monica's job, but I hoped she chose some of the things I chose. I felt like I had a pretty good eye.

Actually, these past few months working here taught me a lot about myself. About my passion and what I loved. I always knew I loved shopping, clothes, and makeup, but I never really thought about turning my hobby into a career until I started styling Rimmel.

I absolutely loved picking outfits, mixing and matching pieces, and helping people look awesome but still like themselves. I liked being in this boutique and surrounded by the stuff I enjoyed. When girls came in to shop, I adored talking trends with them and hearing what they thought about new styles.

It was something I could totally see myself doing for a long time.

Maybe I would open a boutique of my own. Or maybe I'd just become a personal stylist.

Hell, I could do both.

Find your style with Ivy, I mused.

I liked it. A new year. A new dream? Perhaps a new major?

I might take some time to think about it a little more, but I knew in my heart I was ready to dive in. I could take a few business and marketing classes, maybe a few design courses. If I added them to the ones I'd already completed, I could probably graduate next year with a Liberal Arts degree.

And then go into fashion.

Maybe I would start up a fashion channel on YouTube and talk style and show people how to dress their best.

Yes. Yes. Yes.

I could totally do that. And I would be happy.

Excited, I squealed beneath my breath and went into Monica's office in the back to ask her what she thought. I couldn't wait to talk to Braeden and Rimmel. I was already getting ideas and plans in my head.

"I was just coming to see you," Monica said when I stepped in.

"Yeah?"

"I just got a call. My son is sick and I need to go pick him up at the sitter's. We're gonna have to finish up for the night. We can go through orders this week sometime."

"Oh no! I hope the little guy feels better."

She grimaced. She was a beautiful woman, in her late twenties with long red hair. "It's a stomach bug. If I call in sick tomorrow, you'll know I caught it."

"Well, if you need me to pick up extra shifts, you have my schedule," I offered.

"Thanks." She picked up her purse and already had her keys in hand. "Would you mind locking up on your way out? I need to go. He was crying when the sitter called."

"Of course!"

She grabbed my hand on the way past. "I really appreciate this, Ivy. I'm sorry to make you do this on your first day back from being sick."

"It's no trouble," I said and walked her to the front door, unlocked it, and let her out, giving her a wave. I locked the door back up and went toward the counter.

I'd just stack up these catalogues and turn off all the lights. Then I'd get out of here. Hopefully, Braeden would be home when I got there and I could surprise him with getting off early. I was looking forward to another night spent in his arms.

I went into the back and shut off the light in Monica's office, pulling the door around as I went. The time clock was on the far wall next to a small fridge and coffee pot no one ever used. I located my timecard and pulled it out, slipping it into the machine and listening to it mechanically stamp down my quitting time.

As I was placing it back where it belonged, the overhead light flickered.

I paused and glanced up. The light came back on just as before. I finished putting the card away and then went to the rack near the backdoor to grab my purse and coat.

The lights flickered again.

And again.

The feeling I wasn't alone caused a cold sweat to break out over my forehead. I shuddered and took a deep breath.

Keep it together, Ivy. Now's not the time for a panic attack. It's just electricity. Everything's fine.

The lights stopped flickering and the knot in my stomach unclenched. Feeling proud I managed to keep an anxiety attack away, I started out front again, my heels clicking on the tile.

Before I made it, the lights gave one final flicker and everything in the boutique went completely dark.

So much for keeping it together.

My heart started to gallop in my chest and my breath came in short gasps. The counter was only a few steps away, so I headed in that direction, keeping my footing cautious because it was so dark.

When I got out into what I knew was the main room, with the counter right in front of me, I felt around the top, searching for my phone. I could light up the flashlight app to see enough to get the hell out of here.

I couldn't find my phone.

My hand started searching, frantic, my movements a lot more erratic.

Panic was coming fast now.

My phone had been right here just a minute ago. It was lying right beside me as I went through the magazines, in case Braeden called.

Wait a minute.

It was pitch black in here. So dark I couldn't even see my hand in front of my face. Why? There was a streetlight just outside, and it would have cast enough light to at least make it possible to see.

I looked up sharply in the direction of the window.

The streetlight was out too.

In fact, everything outside was just as dark as it was in here.

"Where is it?" I worried, returning to the search for my phone.

"Looking for this?"

The deep voice cut through the dark and was so incredibly close I screamed and jumped back.

"Who's there?" I asked, even though I was terribly afraid to find out.

"I'll give you three guesses," the man intoned.

I didn't need three guesses. I recognized his voice.

Deep down… Your body will remember…

His haunting words knocked around the inside of my brain, erasing all logical thought and replacing it with mind-numbing terror.

Then in the dark, a small light lit up just in front of me. It was my phone. The screen saver was of a picture of B and me after one of his football games. He was in uniform, dirty and sweaty, his handsome face grinning into the camera, while I was at his side, looking put together as always with a braid in my hair and an equally happy smile on my face.

Our lit-up, smiling faces provided illumination for another one tonight.

The glow from the phone screen cast an ominous, shady glow upward, much like a flashlight did on a night out in the woods.

I screamed.

Zach's eerily illuminated face broke out into a smile.

It was evil, sadistic even.

"Ivy," he spoke. Just hearing my name cross his lips made my skin crawl. "We meet again."

CHAPTER FIFTY-TWO

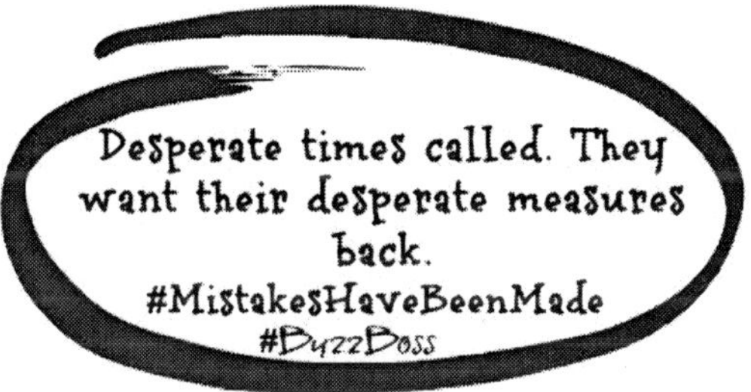

BRAEDEN

I invited myself in.

If I waited for her to do it, I'd likely grow old and die before she got around to it.

I brushed right by her and walked farther into the room. She sighed like my visit was such a great imposition, and I chuckled.

"Not happy to see me."

"Not bloody likely."

"Nice room ya got here," I said, glancing around at the basic dorm. It was basically the same shit she had last year, just in a different space. It made me kinda sick how familiar I was with her shit. Especially the gray-and-white bedding with yellow accents.

I seriously regretted ever getting involved with her.

"I feel kinda bad for your roommate though. Poor girl doesn't even know she sleeps next to Satan."

"If you came to insult me, you can just leave."

"I'll leave when I get good and fucking ready," I said, the conversational tone in my voice gone.

She sucked in a breath at my harsh words and just stood there like I made her nervous. Good. I trusted myself more now than I ever did before.

I would never hurt her physically. Even if I got the urge to ring her neck, I wouldn't. I knew now I wasn't built that way.

But I didn't mind that she wasn't sure.

"Why are you here?"

"Thought you might want to know your little stunt worked. Ivy remembered. She spent the last four days crying. But unlike what you hoped, she bounced back.

My girl is a lot stronger than you think she is. And so is our relationship."

As I spoke, I gauged her reaction. First her eyes widened, then they turned sad, and now they just burned with anger.

"I don't know what you're talking about."

"Cut the shit, Missy. I know it was you."

"What was me?"

"Why'd you do it, huh?" I demanded. "I thought you didn't want her to remember. I thought you wanted to keep your grimy little part in what happened to her a secret."

"I was *not* responsible for Zach raping her," she growled.

Ah, did I finally make a dent in her armor? Was me suggesting she was even at all associated with the vile crime committed against Ivy too much for her conscience?

"Maybe not." I allowed. "But you used it against her, which is just as bad."

"I'm sorry for that." Her shoulders slumped.

I almost believed she meant it. "Then why? Why couldn't you just leave well enough alone? Why did you have to come into our house and torture her? Was it one last thing you could do to rip her world apart?"

"For the last time," Missy said, "I don't know what the hell you're talking about."

I ticked off reasons I knew she was lying on my fingers as I spoke. "One, you know where we live. Two, you could have sweet-talked Drew into some kind of access to the house. Three, you had motive. Four, you were in and out of her dorm last semester, which gave you the perfect opportunity to take the panties. Five—"

"Panties?" She interrupted me. Her nose wrinkled and she genuinely looked confused. "Let's just say for argument's sake I really didn't do it. What the hell are you talking about?"

A little note of something climbed up the back of my neck. "Her red panties. The ones with a four-leaf clover on them."

"Her lucky panties?"

I nodded. "She was wearing them that night. She lost them. They turned up in our room, on our bed, the other day. Just like that. Brought everything back. Now she has to live with those images in her head. Forever."

Missy turned thoughtful, like she really was just hearing about this for the first time.

"Cut the shit, Missy," I snapped. "I know it was you. You left a note."

"What did it say?" she asked, spinning around to look at me.

Why was she playing this game?

What if she really didn't do it?

"It said 'Don't tell.'"

"Why would I do that?"

I gave her a look.

Missy shook her head. "Maybe you should ask yourself who else you pissed off. Who else might want to hurt Ivy?" she snapped and walked to the door like she was going to kick me out.

"No one else knew what happened to her. *No one.*"

"Except Zach," she whispered.

"He's locked up, remember? He's not due to get out 'til next summer."

"You need to leave," she said.

Why the hell was she acting so weird, all cagey and shit?

"Not until you admit what you did and tell me why."

"I didn't do it!" she yelled. She pressed her lips together and a weird look came across her face.

"What?" I said. "What is it?"

"Nothing."

"Missy," I growled.

She grabbed the door handle and flung the door open. "Get out right now or I'm gonna start screaming."

I stalked to the door, pissed off. When I got there, I noticed something hanging on the front of the door. It wasn't there when I first got here.

It was a black dress. Looked like there was a note pinned to the front.

I glanced at Missy. Her face had gone white.

"I agree. Black isn't your color." I moved out into the hallway. I heard the wrinkling of paper behind me as I started to walk away.

Her low gasp was audible. "Braeden?" she said, her voice low and scared.

"What?" I snapped. God, she was irritating.

"I've made a horrible mistake."

The look on her face. The sound of her voice. It put me on red alert. I went back to her side and ripped the note out of her hand.

Wear this tomorrow night.

When we celebrate the removal of our mutual problem.

—Z

The note folded in my hand when it tightened into a fist.

Ivy told me she'd seen him.

I told her it was just a dream.

What if it wasn't?

What if he was somehow here? What if he was lurking around waiting for the perfect moment to shut her up?

"What the fuck did you do?" I roared.

Missy started to cry. I didn't have time for tears. I grabbed her by the arm and pulled her back into the room, leaving the dress on the door.

"Tell me right now, Missy, or so help me God…"

A sob ripped from her throat.

She told me about going to see Zach. About their talk. About how she asked him for his help.

The entire time she talked, black spots literally swam before my eyes. My muscles just kept growing tighter and tighter, and my stomach grew heavy with ice.

"But he's still there, right?"

She just looked at me.

"Right!" I yelled.

"They let him come home for the holidays. So he could be with his dad."

"You fucking went there, got him all riled up, and then those bastards turned him loose?" I exclaimed. I was yelling so loud I knew the people in the rooms beside could hear me. Hell, the entire hall probably heard.

"I was upset and angry. I didn't want anyone to find out. I didn't want to get kicked out of school," she wailed. "I'm so, so sorry."

"Sorry!" I screamed. "You fucking visited a rapist, one that is fucking sick in the head, and you basically put him on her trail!"

"I think he might be obsessed with me," she said weakly.

I laughed. And then I laughed some more. "Wakeup call, bitch. Not everything is about you."

She shook her head. "That's not what I'm saying!"

I was going crazy. My muscles quaked while I paced the tiny room like a caged lion.

"Listen to me!" she pleaded.

"Say it fast," I growled.

"When I went there, he seemed lonely. I grabbed his hand. He acted like he hadn't been touched in years."

Oh my God. She is insane. She's no better than him.

"A couple weeks ago, I started getting anonymous gifts. A book of classic plays I love, original sheet music from a New York musical. Flowers, a single rose…"

"So?"

"I thought at first I had a secret admirer. Maybe a guy from my acting classes. But then the dress." She pointed to the door. "That dress came from the boutique. The one where Ivy works. She refused to sell it to me the other day."

"Get to the point, Missy," I snapped, still pacing.

"You saw the note. It's from Z. Zach. He's been watching me. He's been sending me gifts. He must have seen me at the boutique with her. He must have seen her refuse to sell me that dress."

"She would have told me if he came in there to buy a damn dress!"

"Maybe he stole it," she whispered. "Maybe he doesn't want anyone to know he's around."

"Except you." I pointed out.

"He said he was going to help me. He didn't want anyone to find out either, because then his padded cell would become a permanent home. He said he was going to help us both by making sure Ivy or you never told anyone."

My blood ran cold. I literally felt like there was ice water rushing through my veins.

Someone was ringing the bell on the door at the boutique.

She said she saw him.

The fear in her eyes was all too real.

Zach was after Ivy. He wanted to shut her up.

Permanently.

I lunged across the room and grabbed Missy by the shoulders. She gasped when I jerked her close. "If he hurts her, I promise you there will be nowhere on this entire planet you can hide."

I let go of her. She dropped to her knees and started sobbing. I dropped the crumpled note beside her and rushed out the door.

CHAPTER FIFTY-THREE

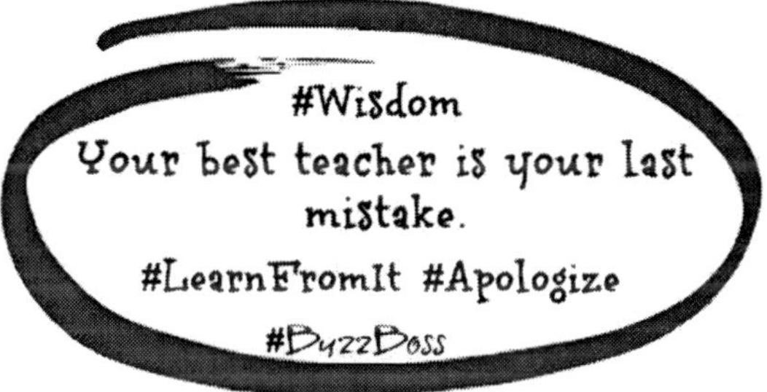

IVY

It was cold outside. The heat wasn't terribly high inside, yet I felt a rivulet of sweat slide down my back, between my shoulder blades and under my bra strap.

The ominous look to his usually boy-band appearance wasn't helping matters.

He looked like he belonged in some made-for-TV movie where a bunch of good-looking teenagers go on a killing spree.

Stop thinking about that! I almost laughed because that was so not going to happen. Zach was my walking horror film come to life. He was my worst nightmare (literally) and the one person that had the ability to reduce me into a helpless lamb.

When I said nothing and only stood there staring, he smiled. His teeth appeared rotted in the shadows of my phone's light. "Aren't you glad to see me, Ivy?"

Stop saying my name!

"I thought you were locked up," I managed to get out, my voice sounding hollow to my ears.

"Got some time out for good behavior," he replied.

"There's no way," I said, my brain finally switching into survival mode. *What in the hell took so long?*

Find a weapon. Escape behind a rack. Disappear in the dark. You know this place. He doesn't. Use it to your advantage.

I could barely hear my thoughts because my heart was pounding so loud. I took a deep breath and tried to relax its racing. I needed to calm down. I needed to get out of here.

"Oh yes, the doctors at the facility seem to think I'm doing much better. I must agree. I barely think about Romeo and Rimmel anymore."

I didn't say anything. I started moving ever so slightly toward the counter where there was a cup full of pencils, pens, and a pair of scissors.

"Do you know why I haven't been thinking about them anymore?" he asked.

"I don't really care."

"Yes!" he yelled. "You do!"

Oh my God, he was totally off his rocker. How in the hell could any doctor think he was stable enough to walk around in society without any kind of supervision?

"You're right," I said, changing gears. "I do. Tell me why."

The phone screen went dark, momentarily plunging us back into obscurity. I moved fast, lunging toward the counter, pleading with my heels to not make a sound. My hand collided with the cup of pencils and pens, and it fell over. I heard it all scatter and some if it fall to the floor.

I wanted to weep.

"What are you doing!" Zach yelled.

On impulse, I grabbed the stapler, because it was the only thing in reach, and held it behind my back.

"Nothing," I lied.

My phone screen lit up again, his face came into view.

"I think about you, Ivy. I think about you all the time."

Bile rose up the back of my throat.

"Do you ever think of me?"

Was he for real? I went to sleep at night and prayed to never think of him again. I was scared to close my eyes because I was afraid I would see his face. Of course I never *thought* about him. I hated him. "No."

"Liar!" He laughed.

"I think you think about me all the time. Every day." He stepped closer, and I gripped the stapler. "You remember that night, don't you?" he taunted. "The night I had you."

"Not much of it," I stuttered even as the memories of that night replayed in my head like a slideshow. My knees were starting to shake; my body felt like I'd been running and my limbs were just exhausted.

"That's too bad." He spoke like he really was sorry. "It was a beautiful night. A shame you can't remember it all."

"You drugged me," I said, anger replacing some of the fear. How dare he stand there and try to scare me with memories of the rape he committed?

"A means to an end."

"Did you cut off the power in here too?" As I spoke, I silently turned the stapler over in my hands and felt around for the round button on the bottom.

"The whole street," he said proudly. "Can't have anyone seeing me when I drag you out of here."

Everything inside me flat-lined for very long seconds. Then, as if I'd been brought back to life, I gasped, air making its way back into my lungs and my heart pounding again.

"I'm not going anywhere with you." My voice held more bravado than I felt.

"Oh, but you are."

I found the button and pressed it. The bottom on the stapler loosened and it became a long weapon in my hand. I flipped it around and gripped it so hard my fingers hurt.

"Braeden will be here any second. He always comes at night when I close."

"I know," Zach replied. "I've been watching you."

"How long?"

"A while."

"You were in the driveway last night," I said.

"And in the stairwell at the dorm. And here the night a *kid* was ringing the bell on the door. I even left you that memento, the red panties from our night together. I was hoping it would bring back some memories. I was so happy when I realized it did."

Tears burned the backs of my eyes. He was a stalker. He'd been following me around for weeks and I hadn't even realized it.

"But why?" I asked.

A car drove by on the street, and I looked up, praying I recognized the shape of the headlights. But it wasn't Braeden. It was just some random stranger, and they'd already passed.

"No more questions," Zach said. "We need to go."

"Go!" I panicked. "Go where?"

"You didn't think I would kill you here, did you? It would create such a mess. I prefer to have you disappear. People will think you just ran away."

Kill me?

Oh, hells no.

He let the screen go dark and pulled it down away from his face. I saw his shape move in the darkness. He stepped forward and reached out like he was going to grab me.

I made my move. I jolted forward with outspread arms and shoved him into the counter. He wasn't expecting me to charge him, so I caught him off guard and he fell into the half wall.

His arm came out and grabbed me. I cried out at the force with which his hand closed around my arm. He squeezed so hard I thought the bones might break.

I pushed the pain away and brought up the stapler. I wasn't exactly sure where I was aiming. I didn't care as long as it hurt him.

I brought the hammer against his body—I think it was his chest—and I pushed in, giving it all the weight I could.

He screamed as the staple shot into his chest.

I tore my arm free and ran, knocking over a rack of clothes as I rushed. I fell over but got back up and started screaming for help.

"Help!" I screamed. "Help me!"

"You little bitch!" he roared and raced after me.

I sprinted to the door, praying to God I could make it outside before he caught up to me. I heard him trip and knock into a few things. My body came into contact with glass. It was so cold from the outside air. I gave a relieved cry and reached for the handle to pull it open.

There wasn't one.

Shit! I'm too far over. I'm standing in front of the window, not the door!

I shoved off the glass and raced toward the door, tripping but recovering as I went. I threw myself at the entrance, my hand closing around the handle.

It swung out and cold air hit my skin. I screamed again.

A hand closed around the back of my shirt and pulled me back with such force I heard the seams tear.

I kicked out my foot, and he grabbed my ankle, slipping my shoe off in the process.

“Get off me!” I screamed, still hanging on to the door handle with everything I had.

I felt like a rope in a tug-of-war.

Unfortunately, it was a game I wasn’t very good at. He grabbed my other foot and pulled off the boot, then took hold of both my ankles and pulled me so swiftly I lost my grip and hit the floor. If I hadn’t caught myself on my hands, I would have busted my face.

Zach let go of me and leapt on top of me.

I had a flashback of the night he raped me, and my body froze up. Everything slowed down as I fought for control of my body and thoughts.

My eyes were adjusted enough in the dark now that I could see his face. It was twisted into a weird happy grimace, like being on top of me gave him sick pleasure.

“I was just going to kill you,” he said. “But now, having you under me, maybe I’ll have a little fun before I do. No one will know anyway. You won’t be around to tell.”

Like a bucket of ice water, clarity poured over me. I gasped and, feeling it near the tips of my fingers, gripped the stapler, pulling it back into my hand. Using the anger and fear inside me, I brought it around and smacked Zach in side of the head.

The metal stung in my hand when it slammed into him, and I let go at the same time he fell to the side. I scrambled up and pushed out the door, practically falling out onto the sidewalk.

"I-vy!" he roared from behind.

I started to run.

CHAPTER FIFTY-FOUR

BRAEDEN

I should have believed her.

I should have looked around outside that night a little harder.

I never thought in a million years that Zach would be let out for good behavior. Whoever the hell authorized that should be fired.

My tires squealed when I sped out of the lot behind Cypress Hill and pointed the truck in the direction of our house. I wasn't sure where to go. My head was spinning. I had to know if she was okay. I had to warn her he might actually be lurking around.

I whipped out my cell and hit her number.

"Shit!" I yelled when it just rang and rang.

When her voicemail picked up, my gut tightened at the sound of her melodic voice. I cut the connection and thought. Maybe I should call Zach's house, ask his father if Zach was even in town. Maybe Missy was lying.

Maybe this was all an elaborate ruse so I wouldn't blame her for the red thong stunt.

I dialed Ivy again.

She didn't answer again.

I glanced at the clock. She was still supposed to be at work. I dialed the landline for the boutique. An operator came on the line, saying the phone was disconnected.

I slammed on the brakes and made an illegal U-turn right there in the center of the street. My foot was laying on the gas, pushing my truck as fast as it would go toward the store. A weird sound came from under the hood and the truck began to slow despite my efforts otherwise.

It made a strange coughing sound and stalled out. Right there in the middle of the road.

"No!" I yelled and slammed my fist on the wheel. The horn blared under the force of my hit, and I cursed.

I tried three times to turn the engine over and get her started again. It wasn't happening.

What the fuck was wrong with this thing and why was it happening now? I kept all the maintenance up to date, did it all myself. I knew this truck was in great condition. It shouldn't be leaving me stranded.

Especially when Ivy needs me.

My legs jolted when I catapulted out of the cab and popped the hood. It was dark and I had to use my cell to see, but everything appeared fine. I didn't see any reason the truck shouldn't be running.

Unless someone tampered with it where you can't see.

Acting on pure instinct, I slammed the hood and walked around the body, looking for something, anything that might tell me what the hell was happening. My eyes zeroed in on the gas tank, and I leapt forward and opened the small door that led to the tank.

I flipped on my cell again and shined it at the gas cap.

There was a gritty white substance in the little well just behind the door.

What. The. Fuck?

I grabbed the cap and turned it. The sound of something scraping filled my ears. Once the cap was pulled free, more white granules spilled out.

"Son of a bitch," I whispered, wiping a finger in them.

I didn't need to call Zach's father anymore. I didn't need any other proof at all to know he was in town.

This was all the proof I needed.

The motherfucker put sugar in my gas tank. It probably cycled through the fuel line and was clogging everything up, making my truck stall.

I kicked the side of the bed. This truck was completely useless now. Completely un-drivable until I cleaned out all the damn lines.

He did this on purpose.

He wanted to make sure I wouldn't be able to get to her.

Putting truck was in neutral, I pushed it to the side of the road and left it there. My house was only a couple miles away. I could make it there faster on foot than it would take me to call someone and wait for them to come.

So I ran.

I pushed myself as hard as I could. My feet ate up the miles until our street came in to view. Once the house came into sight and I confirmed Ivy's car wasn't parked in the driveway, I ran even harder.

When I got there, Trent and Drew were in the driveway, pieces of their engines all over the place.

"You talk to Ivy?" I demanded, pounding up the drive. Sweat soaked my clothes and dripped off my chin.

Drew jerked around and cursed. "Where the hell did you come from, man?"

"I ran. Have you talked to Ivy?" I tried not to gasp the words as I sucked air into my lungs.

Sensing something was wrong, Trent stood up. "What's the matter?"

I looked at their cars, also completely un-drivable. Perfect speed machines sitting right there taunting me.

I looked at Rimmel's bubble and almost laughed.

I needed to get to Ivy, and I needed to get there fast.

The Hellcat.

"Rimmel inside?" I asked.

"Yes," Drew said.

"I need you to stay here, watch her. Don't freaking let her out of your sight."

"What the fuck is going on?" Trent asked.

"Zach's out."

He sucked in a breath.

"I need you to watch Rim. Don't leave her alone. Not even for a second."

He nodded, and I took off running toward the garage.

"What about Ivy?" Drew yelled after me.

"I'll take care of Ivy," I yelled back.

In the garage, I snatched the extra set of keys off a nearby rack and hit the button to open the door. The Hellcat roared to life the second I turned the key, and the smooth sound of the engine gave me hope.

I backed out of the parking spot and navigated around Drew's and Trent's car parts and then tore down the street. I had no idea if Rome would be pissed about me tearing up the road in his car.

I didn't have time to ask. I didn't really care.

I sped to the boutique and pulled up right in front of the building. There was a power truck right down the street. Large spotlights provided light for them to work on something. From the looks of the pitch-black street, I would guess they were trying to restore power.

A gnarly feeling worked its way down the back of my neck, and intuition told me the power hadn't just gone out because it was cold outside. When I got to the door of the boutique, I pushed and it opened.

It was so dark I couldn't see a thing, so I pulled up my flashlight app and shined it into the room.

"Ivy!" I yelled.

The place was a mess. Racks of clothes were overturned; a display of jewelry was on its side. There was a stapler lying beside the door and pencils all over the floor. I shined the light down on the floor as I walked, looking for anything, a clue… a sign.

The light glinted off something shiny, and terror ripped me open.

I picked up Ivy's necklace off the floor. The one she never took off.

This was the sign I was looking for. I knew she was in trouble. I knew he'd come here and somehow forced her out and was taking her somewhere with intentions I didn't even want to think about.

I realized I was jumping to the worst possible scenario. I knew I could be totally blowing things out of proportion.

I prayed I was wrong.

But if I was right…

As I ran to the car, I shoved her necklace in my pocket and dove behind the wheel. I gunned the engine, making the men down the street turn and stare. I sat there for a minute, not sure where to go or what to do.

Where would he take her?

A single idea formed in the back of my mind. It was the best and only idea I had. On impulse, I ripped down the street and turned in the direction I wanted to go.

I had no idea if what I was thinking was even close to the truth, but I didn't have the luxury of time. It was a gamble, a gamble that had really shitty odds.

A gamble I was going to take.

I had to.

I just prayed to God I held the winning hand.

CHAPTER FIFTY-FIVE

IVY

He caught me.

It was time to up my cardio. And I definitely needed to learn some self-defense.

I made it to the corner of the boutique, and just as I was about to disappear down the dark alleyway, he grabbed me from behind. He smelled like a combination of sweat and blood when he wrapped his arm around my waist and towed me backward.

His other hand slapped over my mouth, preventing me from screaming more.

Not that it mattered.

My screams went unheard.

My pleas for help unanswered.

No one was coming to help me tonight. It was just like the night he raped me.

Except tonight you aren't drugged.

Tonight you will fight.

I bit down on the fleshy part of his hand and recoiled when I tasted the metal flavor of blood. Zach yelled but didn't let go. Instead, the hand holding me around the waist grabbed my side and twisted.

My knees buckled and I cried out. It was a muffled sound, but my God did it hurt. Fresh tears fell down my cheeks and the spot stung even after he let go.

"Do it again and I'll just kill you right here," he growled right in my ear.

Why was he trying to kill me? Why did he suddenly want me dead? I couldn't understand. Hadn't he hurt me enough already? What did I ever do to him?

I didn't want to die, and that meant I had to stop fighting at least for a minute to buy myself some time. I needed to think. I needed a plan.

Somewhere very close by, my cell rang. It was the ringtone I used for Braeden. I knew it as well as I knew my own name. As Zach towed me backward quickly, he grunted and completely ignored my phone.

It must be in his pocket. If only I could reach it.

The ringing cut off.

I felt my body slump.

Zach giggled. "Ivy's not here right now, but leave a message after the tone. Beeep!"

We were in front of the door to the boutique now. I realized he was dragging me back inside. "My car's out back in the alley," he explained.

Great. I've been running in the direction of the car he planned to kidnap me with anyway. Good move, Ivy.

My phone started ringing again. Braeden. My heart leapt. He knew something was wrong. He knew and he was coming. I just needed to buy some time.

I had a very bad feeling I was running out of time.

The phone cut off again, and a sob tore from my throat. Zach laughed.

I began to struggle again, and in the midst of my attempts, I reached up and yanked the necklace B had given me right off my neck. It hurt to remove it. I didn't want to, but there was no other choice.

I let it fall from my fingers, leaving it there in the middle of the boutique. He would come here. He would see it and know I hadn't left of my own free will.

Because Zach was practically dragging me through the place, he wasn't able to hold my phone for light. The second we got in front of the counter, he stumbled and fell. I rolled quickly, catching the outline of my purse, which I'd dropped when he first showed up.

Anyone who ever said a girl's bag wasn't one of her greatest weapons was clearly not a girl.

I skittered away, but once again, he was faster.

He caught me by the ankle and yanked. I fell onto the floor and rolled, kicking out with my free foot.

It caught him right in the balls.

His face froze for one second and pain screwed up his features.

And then he screamed, pulled back his fist, and hit me right in the face.

I must have passed out, because when I opened my eyes, I was sitting in the passenger seat of what had to be his car. There was a BMW emblem on the steering wheel and the interior was black leather. It smelled stale in here, like it had been sitting in a garage for a long time.

Yeah, like the entire time he was locked away.

The side of my face hurt. It was on fire, and I fingered it gently, pulling in a breath when I touched the swollen flesh.

"I like you better when you're drugged." He sounded out of breath.

"I liked you better when you were locked up." I just sounded pissed. I wasn't even scared anymore. I was just angry and confused. I wasn't going to let him rape me again. He'd have to kill me first.

"Just like Romeo," he muttered. "Always thinking you're better than everyone else."

"What?"

"You know," he said, like he was thoroughly annoyed. "What is it with blonds? They think they can have whatever they want. Take whoever they want. They think the rules don't apply to them." His words were coming fast. He made no sense, and when I glanced down at the dashboard, I noted he was driving eighty miles an hour.

I reached for my seatbelt and clicked it into place. He didn't even notice. He was too busy going on and on about blonds and why he hated them so much.

Zach was completely off his rocker. Like there was something truly wrong in his brain. He was insane, and that made him even more dangerous. I didn't think I could reason with him, but I could at least try.

"Why are you doing this?"

"I just told you!" he yelled and slapped the steering wheel.

"Because I'm blond?"

"Because you're going to open your big fat mouth and tell everyone what I did to you. Then I'll be locked up for good. Do you know what they do to handsome guys like me in jail?"

I'm sorry. This was a very scary, serious situation. But I couldn't get over the fact Zach thought he was good-looking…

Ew.

"I won't tell anyone." I lied.

"That's what I told her."

"Told who?" I echoed.

"Missy." He looked at me with a smug smile. I wanted to scream for him to keep his eyes on the road. I wasn't sure where we were going, but I knew we were going there fast. "She came to visit me, you know. She brought me a basket full of stuff."

Missy went to visit him in the mental ward? Was she the one who put him up to this? Just when I thought she couldn't get any skankier, she goes and does something like this…

"Why would she do that?" I asked myself.

"Because she realizes how perfect we are for each other. She understands me. She knows what it's like to be a victim of a blond. Tossed aside for someone new."

I didn't speak crazy, so I decided saying as little as possible would probably be my best option here.

"I can't let you tell people what I did. It will ruin me. It will ruin her. I won't have you getting in my way."

"I'm not the only one who knows what you did," I said.

"Your boyfriend's next."

My blood ran cold. The little bit of calm I was gaining flew out the window. "No!"

"I thought about killing him first. But I want him to suffer when I tell him all about what I did to you. It will make his death that much more awful."

"Why?" I sobbed. "Why would you hurt him that way?"

"Because of what he did to Missy!" he yelled. "He betrayed her, just like my mother betrayed me!"

"What?" I asked, confused. *Did he just say his mother?* I thought we were talking about Braeden.

All of a sudden, a set of headlights blinded us from the rearview mirrors. They approached fast, so fast I barely had time to register they were there until I was squinting from the glare.

"No!" Zach screamed. "How did he find us?"

Blinking against the sudden light, I turned in my seat to stare out the back window. I could hear the smooth purr of an engine and then I saw a flash of neon green.

That was Romeo's car!

Zach pressed on the gas, and the car shot forward. My eyes stayed glued to the Hellcat, and I almost shouted amen at the top of my lungs when the car increased its speed easily to catch up.

"Damn him!" he yelled. "I thought he was out of town."

I glanced at him and shrugged. I wanted him to think it was Romeo. The guy was clearly Zach's trigger. Maybe if he thought Romeo was hunting us down, he would make a mistake.

Romeo was out of town. He'd gotten on an airplane this afternoon. That might be Romeo's car, but Romeo wasn't the one behind the wheel.

I knew exactly who that was.

He was coming for me.

CHAPTER FIFTY-SIX

You don't know what you are alive for, until you know what you would die for.
#AuthorUnknown
#BuzzBoss

BRAEDEN

"Yeah!" I hollered and hit the steering wheel the second the BMW's taillights came into view.

If I had been wrong about where he was going with her, it would likely have cost Ivy her life. But I wasn't wrong.

The stars were on our side tonight.

He was taking her out to the place I'd brought Ivy at the beginning of the semester. The place we'd spent the night in the bed of the truck.

It was one of the closest yet most isolated spots in town. Zach hadn't gone to high school with Romeo and me. He went to some uppity private school. Even so, all the kids knew about this place. Everyone hung there, so I knew he'd know about it too.

I knew he saw me when his BMW shot up the road. Fuck, he was already flying. It scared the shit out of me. I wondered if Ivy was okay. If she was even conscious. My hands gripped the wheel and I pressed on the gas.

The Hellcat shot forward with barely a sound. This car was a fucking machine. Romeo had opened it up a couple times on an open road, but nothing like this. I was going over a hundred miles an hour, in the dark, nearing a one-lane road.

This was dangerous as fuck.

But I didn't care.

All I cared about was getting to Ivy before Zach could hurt her worse.

I just had to wait him out, not lose his trail, and when he pulled over—which he had to do at some point—I'd get her back.

And then I'd kill him.

Killing wasn't something I thought I'd ever do.

But he wasn't walking away from this.

Oh, hells no.

Impatient and wanting just a glimpse of Ivy, I increased the speed even more and pulled up alongside his little sports car. I had to try and see her now, because in just a couple miles, this road would turn into a one-lane road and I'd be forced to hang back.

Zach looked at me from the driver's side window. I knew he couldn't see in because the windows in this thing were tinted.

I leaned forward, trying to see around his angry face. I caught the outline of someone sitting in the passenger seat, but I couldn't see if she was okay.

I rolled the passenger-side window down, hoping to get a better look.

Zach's face registered surprise when he saw it was me behind the wheel. He probably just assumed it was Romeo.

I saw his mouth moving, but I couldn't hear what he was yelling.

Suddenly, Ivy jerked forward and looked around him.

Our eyes locked together.

She was okay.

Well, maybe not okay, but she was alive.

She mouthed the words I love you, and I held up two fingers.

Times two.

Zach realized we were communicating, and he looked between us. Then he lifted his hand and smacked her. Her face turned away with the impact, and I let out a yell.

"You son of a bitch!" I roared.

He laughed.

I had the sudden urge to run him off the road, just ram the Cat into his car and take him out.

But I couldn't because Ivy was in that car.

I glanced back ahead and noted the road beginning to merge into one lane.

Zach saw too.

I tried to get another look at Ivy before I had to slow down. I leaned forward and Zach leaned down. *What the fuck was he doing?*

Ivy was leaning against the passenger seat, staring in my direction. I could see the sheen of tears on her cheeks.

Zach sat back up, cutting off my view.

His face filled my line of sight and he smirked, an ugly, smug look.

Then he held up a shiny object. The dash lights glinted off the metal.

It was a gun.

CHAPTER FIFTY-SEVEN

IVY

The second he pulled out the gun, I knew it was now or never.

This was it.

The only moment I would have to save my own life.

Braeden was here. He was trying to get to me, but B couldn't save me.

Only I could do that.

Zach laughed when the Hellcat dropped behind him and the lane narrowed. Trees lined the roads, and up ahead stretched spacious fields with apple trees dotting the distance.

"Sorry, bitch," he said and leveled the gun at me. "The arrival of your boyfriend means our time is cut short. It's good news for you. One bullet to the head and it will all be over. Not near as fun as what I had planned, but sometimes we must improvise."

Sick bastard.

"What are you going to do?" I asked.

"The second your dead body goes flying, lover boy will stop to save you. Then I'll stop, and as he's crying over your lifeless, bleeding body, I'll shoot him too. I'll be in Mexico before anyone even suspects it was me."

"It's a good plan," I told him, even though it sucked. "There's just one problem you didn't think of."

He frowned. "I thought of everything."

I shook my head. "You forgot about me."

On impulse, I grabbed the barrel of the gun and shoved it up in the air. He pulled the trigger, and the loud shot and the sound it made as it ripped through the roof made me scream.

We fought over the gun, the car swerving wildly on the road. But I didn't stop. I kept fighting. I knew I was going to die, but at least this way I could take Zach with me.

At least this way, Braeden would still be alive.

"No!" Zach roared and wrenched his hand free of mine. He brought the gun back down and pointed it at me once more.

I reached out and grabbed the steering wheel, giving it a yank and veering the car right off the road.

CHAPTER FIFTY-EIGHT

#BreakingNews
Reports of a well-known Hellcat speeding through town and a car exploding are sending shockwaves thru Alpha U.
#BuzzBoss

5 MINUTES LATER…

BRAEDEN

The time I felt the most helpless in my entire life was when I was sitting next to my mother's hospital bed, watching her fight to live through the injuries she sustained from my father's vicious temper.

Until now.

Nothing, and I mean *nothing* in this world, could compare to the sight of watching the car with my entire life in it swerving erratically all over the road, hearing a gunshot, and then watching the car turn sharply off to the side, hit a large stump, and flip over.

Three. Times.

My life flashed before me like I was the one dying, and every single image I saw was of her.

Ivy on top of me.

Ivy with desire in her eyes.

Ivy laughing.

Ivy dressing the damn dog in a pink tutu.

She was it. She was all I saw.

It seemed like it took forever for the car to stop rolling and finally lie still. Even after it landed, it still rocked back and forth a little, like the momentum it had gained from the speed at which Zach was driving would have catapulted farther.

That is if the tree it hit hadn't gotten in its way.

I hit the brakes and was out of the car in seconds flat. Running through the brush, across the field, and finally into some trees, I screamed her name.

Please, God, don't let her be dead.

Please. God.

If she is dead, just take me too.

When I got to the car, I skidded to a halt. The driver's side was facing me. I could see Zach inside, held in by the seatbelt. His face was covered in blood, and I couldn't tell if he was alive.

I didn't care.

I scrambled around the car to the passenger side. All the windows were blown out, glass and debris everywhere.

"Ivy," I cried. "Ivy, answer me!"

I dropped down on my stomach and dragged myself right up to the window, ignoring the stinging cuts of glass as I went.

She didn't answer. She didn't call out my name.

A sob ripped from my throat. "No!" I yelled and stuck my arm inside the window. I couldn't see her, but I knew she had to be inside.

"No!" I roared again, lifting my face and shouting up at the sky.

Millions of stars blinked back at me, lighting up the night sky.

Tears blurred my vision as I felt around and slid in closer.

Something found my hand and latched on.

"Ivy!" My voice broke. Her hand was so small, but when I said her name, she squeezed my fingers.

"I'm coming, baby. Hang on! Don't you die on me!"

The smell of gas reached my nose. It was pungent and unwelcome. The gas tank was punctured, and it was likely spewing gas out all over the field around this car.

I shoved my head inside and saw her.

The seatbelt kept her inside, but she was badly beat up and her face was covered in blood. Just seeing her like that scared the shit out of me. Her body was limp and twisted. I knew the second I unlatched the seatbelt, she'd crumple onto the roof.

I wouldn't fit through the window and inside the mangled car. I couldn't go in there and use my body as a shield for hers.

"Ivy can you hear me?" I asked.

She made a sound, and I laughed, but it was desperate. "Best sound I've ever heard," I told her. "Listen to me, baby. We gotta get you out of there. I'm gonna unlatch the seatbelt and you're going to fall a little. It's probably going to hurt, and I'm real sorry about that."

She made another sound. I wanted to believe it was her way of telling me to do it.

The scent of gas was getting stronger, and I was very afraid I was working on a limited clock. It took me a minute to reach the seatbelt latch, but the second I did, I pressed it. The entire car groaned when she fell. The sound of her body hitting made me sick.

I pressed forward, shimmying my entire torso inside the window and wrapping my arms around her hips. I couldn't reach any farther, and it forced me to half drag her out.

It was a painstaking process because she felt like dead weight and I had to go backward through a broken window with debris littering the grass. When I got far enough out, I let her lie there and jumped to my feet. I reached down and lifted her the rest of the way and hefted her into my arms.

"Ivy!" I said, trying not to sound like I was completely panicking. "You're out now. I got you. Everything's going to be fine."

She didn't make a sound and her eyelids didn't flutter.

I was very afraid the process of getting her out of the car had been too much.

I backed up from the wreck and, on my way, stepped in the growing puddle of gasoline. It was spraying everywhere, all over the ground and the car.

I ran away from the mess, cradling her as close as I could. She was so still. So bloody.

When I thought I was far enough away, I dropped to my knees and laid her on the ground. I pulled my shirt over my head and used it to press against a still-bleeding cut on her head. As I did, I looked for bullet wounds, afraid she'd been shot.

All I saw were injuries from the accident, no bullet holes.

"Brae…" She tried to say my name but couldn't.

My chest heaved just hearing her say anything at all. "I'm here, baby. Thank God you're alive. Everything's okay now. I'm calling an ambulance. Stay with me, okay."

"Always," she whispered.

I yanked my phone out and called 9-1-1. When the responder came on the line, I told her where I was exactly and begged them to hurry. She asked for details, and I started to give them to her when the sound of Zach's scream drew my attention.

Ivy whimpered. She must have heard it too.

"Shh, shh," I said, leaning over her and trying to hold her close without moving her so much.

"Please hurry," I said into the line. "We need an ambulance. And maybe a fire truck. The car's leaking gas. I'm afraid it's going to explode."

Zach screamed again. "Help!"

I laid the phone next to Ivy and kissed her on the forehead. "I'm gonna be right back, sweetheart."

"No," she whimpered. "Stay safe."

"I promise."

I ran back to the car where Zach was struggling to get free. His seatbelt must have been tangled or jammed. When he saw me, his eyes turned desperate. "Braeden, help me. I can't get out."

I just stood there and stared. I watched him struggle for a few minutes. That dark place I always wrestled with?

I let it consume me.

Zach stopped and looked at me. "You're not going to help me, are you?"

"No."

"That's murder."

"Murder. Karma. Righting a wrong." I shrugged. "Call it what you want. Whatever it is, it's exactly what you deserve."

He started struggling anew. Panic replacing all smugness on his face.

A small flame lit up from the rear of the car. I stared at it as it grew.

Zach peered out the window and started to beg. "Please help me. Please don't let me die."

"Hope you like hell, you son of a bitch."

I turned around and walked away. He continued to beg, but it fell on deaf ears. A few steps later, the small flame lit into a great fire with a single whoosh. I picked up my pace and ran to Ivy. Just as I dropped and covered her body with mine, the car exploded.

Heat from the flames blew in our direction. I heard debris hitting the ground and the groaning of metal.

In the distance, I heard several sirens. I knew they were coming for us.

I hit END on the phone and pulled back just enough to look down at Ivy's battered face.

Her eyes were open. "He's dead, isn't he?" she asked.

"Yes."

She nodded. "I'm glad."

"Me too."

She didn't ask if I had an opportunity to pull him out, though I was sure she probably knew. If she ever asked, I would tell her. I let him die.

Maybe that made me a murderer.

But I never said I wouldn't kill to protect what was mine.

The most dangerous man in the world is one who had nothing but found everything.

That was me.

And in the end, I didn't have to pose as anyone but myself. Because in the end, I was exactly who I was supposed to be.

An ambulance rolled to a stop at the side of the road. A police car and a fire truck followed right behind.

"You still with me, baby?" I said, pulling back to wave at the men.

She groaned.

I looked up at the stars and thanked them.

HAPPILY EVER AFTER (AKA EPILOGUE)

#ResultsRIn
They weren't just pretending.
Turns out their <3 is real.
#Braeden&Ivy
#SometimesLoveConquersAll
#BuzzBoss

IVY

I spent three days in the hospital.

One for every time the car flipped.

I had a severe concussion, a broken wrist, a split cheekbone, stitches in my head and my shoulder, a few broken ribs, and a black-and-blue body to match.

But none of it hurt.

Not much anyway.

Because I was still alive. Because Braeden pulled me out of the car. I knew I never would have been able to get out on my own. If he hadn't been there, I would have died the instant the car exploded.

He saved my life.

In more ways than one.

Not only did he ride in the ambulance with me to the hospital, but he literally never left my bedside. The nurses probably would have complained if he hadn't charmed them all into loving him too.

I was in and out of it the entire first day; the pain meds kept me groggy. But sometimes I would wake up to see everyone sitting around the bed, and sometimes it would be just Braeden.

I could have sworn at one point I heard Braeden telling Romeo he was sorry he left his car on the side of the road, and I wished I'd been able to stay awake long enough to hear what he had to say about that.

Braeden's mom even checked on me. Sometimes she was in her uniform, because she worked on another floor. My parents were here too. They were staying at a hotel just down the street.

At night, B would climb into the bed with me after I begged him to, and I would snuggle into his side (as best I could) until the nurses would come in and shoo him out and back into the chair.

I'd been fully ready to die that night. I hadn't wanted to, but I would have sacrificed myself to make sure B was safe.

I'd never tell him that, because I'd only get a lecture, but deep down, I think he knew why I forced that car off the road.

He never asked and I never told.

Just like when I heard him tell the police he didn't have enough time to get me out of the car and then go back for Zach before it blew up.

At the risk of sounding totally heinous, I wasn't sorry he was dead.

At least now, all of us could live our lives without wondering if he was out there, watching and waiting.

Missy came to the hospital. Braeden wouldn't let her in. She came back the next day, but he'd already notified the staff and they wouldn't let her come down the hallway.

I know she probably wanted to say she was sorry.

Sometimes sorry wasn't good enough.

Sometimes nothing was.

Missy was nothing to me now.

Just someone I used to know.

When the doctor finally signed my release papers and the wheelchair was wheeled in, I was so happy to go home I actually cried. It made me feel like the worst kind of Nancy, but no one seemed to think so but me.

I even caught B clearing his throat a few times.

Thankfully, it was just me and him on the way out. Everyone else was at our house waiting for us. I was looking forward to seeing them all, but I really just wanted time alone with my guy.

The nurse let Braeden push my wheelchair, and on the way down the hall, he slowed and almost stopped in front of a room. Inside was a man lying in a bed. I heard some kind of sports playing on TV.

Braeden stared for just a second and then started pushing me again. I reached around and covered his hand with mine. "I'll wait if you want to go say hi."

He leaned down and kissed me softly. "Nah. He's just somebody I used to know."

I knew it was his father. And I also knew he'd closed that door to his life. He no longer feared he was like that man; he was no longer scared he would turn out the same.

Braeden had his demons just like the rest of us, but unlike his father, deep down, Braeden was a good guy.

"You're my favorite person ever," I told him in the elevator.

"Well, that's a relief." He crouched down next to the chair so we were face to face. "I'd hate to think you were gonna spend the rest of your life with someone you didn't really like."

Behind us, the nurse chuckled.

He reached into his pocket and pulled out a very familiar silver necklace. "I've been holding on to this for you. Think you might want to put it back on?"

"You found it," I whispered, staring at it resting in his palm.

"The stars are ours, Blondie." Braeden stood and fastened it around my neck. Then he moved behind the chair to push me out into the lobby. "She's my girl," he told the nurse.

I resisted the urge to tell him she probably already knew that.

Instead, I smiled at her and nodded. "Yes, I'm his girl."

THE HASHTAG SERIES
CONTINUES
FALL 2015 *with*

LOVERS GONNA LOVE

Details Coming Soon

AUTHOR'S NOTE

Gray hair? ✓

Chewed nails? ✓

Messy hair, red eyes, a Romeo hoodie that needs a good washing? ✓✓✓

All these things and more went into writing this book.

Let me just cut to the chase and say this was not an easy book to write. Not at all. It was the hardest book in this series. I can't say it was the hardest book I've ever written, but it was damn close.

I say this for many reasons. None of which have anything to do with my underwear and shoes. Seriously. Did you just read that? WTH am I talking about underwear and shoes for?

Oh, that's right. Because I used up almost all my brain cells writing this book. Ha!

Anyway, if you'd like to know why this book was so hard for me, I will go on. If you don't want to know, then stop reading here.

…

So you stayed.

I like you.

This book took a little longer to complete than I originally planned. It's actually released a month later than I wanted. And even releasing then has been a huge stressor, not just on me, but on my editor and my formatter, etc.

As I was writing #Poser, I made a trip to Nashville to the large book convention UtopYA (now known as Utopia). Going to a convention is a lot of work, lol. But we won't talk about that. I was blown away by the amount of support and enthusiasm the *Hashtag Series* was shown. Like honestly.

It is 100% accurate to say the *Hashtag Series* (ahem, Romeo and Braeden) have taken over my life. Seriously. I'm even contemplating trading in my car for a lime-green Hellcat.

Not strange at all.

Especially since I will likely be like Rimmel and require a stack of books to see over the dash…

So suffice it to say, it seems normal for me to love this series and to be so invested. BUT I wasn't really prepared for how many other people love it as much as I do. The kindness and the outpouring of support and people coming up to me to talk about it was overwhelming. (In a good way.)

And then I won *three* awards. All three of them for the *Hashtag Series.*

If I hadn't realized before how much this series is loved by readers, then I did then.

Best Contemporary Cover (#Nerd), Best Contemporary Lead (Romeo!), and Best Contemporary Series.

Like, whoa.

I honestly didn't expect to walk away with awards. With so many great books, so many great authors… Why me?

Those three awards now proudly sit on my shelf in my office. I still smile when I think about that night. I'm still in awe of YOU, the reader. The fact that you have FULLY embraced a story and characters I love so much yet was afraid would get lost in the vast sea of books is so humbling yet so very incredible.

And this is where the hard part comes in.

Because now I know. Now I know how loved B and Romeo are. Now I have an award of Best Series to live up to.

#Poser needs to be worthy of all this love. #Poser needs to be on the same level the first four books have been. I gotta tell you, it's daunting. It's overwhelming because I so badly want to deliver a book that is fitting of its place in the series.

But not only that.

The subject matter of this particular book was intimidating to me. Rape. Abuse. Lost friendship. Betrayal. Mental illness.

I usually stay away from rape. Yes, in past books, I have alluded to rape or a character is almost raped (but the deed is stopped), but what happened to Ivy… it was something I never planned to write. I guess that's why it made a good story, because *I* didn't write it. The characters did.

Sometimes it twisted my stomach. Just the horror of what happened to her. The weight Braeden must have felt while carrying around that information—especially knowing what kind of past he lived through and how he felt about abuse toward women.

It actually took a lot for me to step into those worlds. And I don't mean just to write it. But when I write it, I also to some extent have to feel it. It was draining and exhausting.

That being said, I still am not one hundred percent sure I did the subjects justice. Ivy basically lived with rape without realizing it. Like a PTSD victim, but not knowing she was traumatized. She basically thought she was going crazy because she couldn't get past her one-night stand and the guilt she felt. Then with the sudden panic attacks, the freak-outs when someone touched her unexpectedly, and the nightmares…

I tried to show everything she was dealing with internally without going overboard.

And then there was Zach.

Oh, Zach. When I first decided to write an entire section in Zach's point of view, I wondered how it would work. I knew I wanted to do it and I had a lot of his backstory already in my head. I also knew many readers had asked for this, for a glimpse into his crazy.

But delving into the mind of a person who is highly mentally unstable isn't easy.

I'm not mentally unstable.

At least most days.

Ha-ha. Kidding.

Writing someone who is was hard because it's hard to write something I've never actually experienced. Some of the scenes with him made me feel sick and icky. But I wrote them. I figured if he made me feel that way, then I was probably on the right track. Even when things didn't make exact sense, I felt that was on point because *he* doesn't make sense.

And Braeden. Oh, Braeden.

His character growth in this book kind of took me by surprise. But in such a good way. I knew he would grow. But I didn't know how much. The way he was really there for Ivy even at his own expense really got me in *here* (I'm pointing to my heart right now). Again, I can't say if I handled the stuff between him and his father the way everyone thinks I should, but for Braeden, it felt right. It felt like he did enough, said enough, and came to terms with enough that he was able to put to rest a lot of the darkness inside him that he blamed on his father.

I'm not really sure that kind of abuse and childhood is something one ever really "gets over." I think it's more about learning to live with it as part of yourself while also understanding it doesn't define you.

Same with rape in a lot of ways.

So yeah, that was why this was such a challenging book to write. But even so, I enjoyed it. I love these characters so much, and when I sit down to write their stories, it's almost like watching a movie, because I don't always know what's going to happen.

I don't know what I'll do when I have to say goodbye to them. I'm not ready to do that yet.

You know what that means?

Yep. Another *Hashtag* book is coming your way.

Soon.

But until then, I hope you enjoyed this one. I hope you found it to be truthful, entertaining, and above all else, a justice to the rest of the series.

As always, I want to acknowledge my editor, Cassie McCown, who seriously had to strap on a cape and edit this book for me—and do so in less time than usual. It seemed mean to hand her a longer book and give her less time to edit. But she took the challenge and conquered it. And for that, I seriously appreciate you, Cassie.

Also, quick shout-out to my husband and two kids for putting up with me while I wrote this book. For not getting mad when I had to work while we were at the beach on vacation. For not getting upset when I forgot to cook dinner and rolled around in a smelly hoodie (because I can't write without Romeo). Thank you for putting up with my insane schedule and supporting me. And for being a *Hashtag* household. Because seriously, these books haven't just taken over my life, but my entire family's lives.

Thanks to ALL of my fan club girls, Cambria's Nerds. Melissa Stickney, who keeps the place running when I'm off in la-la land. To Adrienne Ambrose, who pimps my stuff like nobody's business, and to Sada Walker Maciel for always, always supporting me. I think you might be my biggest supporter, Sada.

Lastly, thanks to Cameo Renae and Amber Garza. These girls are my rocks, my writing besties, and cheerleaders. If they weren't there to tell me I could do it, then maybe I never would have.

So guys…

Keep reading. Keep being #nerdy. And THANK YOU. Times Two.

See you next book!

XOXO —**CAMBRIA**

Cambria Hebert is an award-winning, bestselling novelist of more than twenty books. She went to college for a bachelor's degree, couldn't pick a major, and ended up with a degree in cosmetology. So rest assured her characters will always have good hair.

Besides writing, Cambria loves a caramel latte, staying up late, sleeping in, and watching movies. She considers math human torture and has an irrational fear of chickens (yes, chickens). You can often find her running on the treadmill (she'd rather be eating a donut), painting her toenails (because she bites her fingernails), or walking her chorkie (the real boss of the house).

Cambria has written within the young adult and new adult genres, penning many paranormal and contemporary titles. Her favorite genre to read and write is romantic suspense. A few of her most recognized titles are: *The Hashtag Series, Text, Torch,* and *Tattoo.*

Cambria Hebert owns and operates Cambria Hebert Books, LLC.

You can find out more about Cambria and her titles by visiting her website: http://www.cambriahebert.com

Lightning Source UK Ltd.
Milton Keynes UK
UKOW02f0617021016

284268UK00004B/152/P

9 781938 857768